REMANDED TO THE NIGHT CAFE

M.E. SMITH

Remanded to The Night Café

Printed in the United States of America

ISBN
Print: 978-0-9993793-0-1
eBook: 978-0-9993793-2-5

Cover art by rafidofigitalart.com

www.DragonRealmPress.com

In memory of

Janet Kathryn Adsit

In the Court of the Noir King

2 PM December 22nd
The Night Café
1277 Reed Shore Drive

From the battered television above the bar, the blonde newscaster's urgent lead pitch sliced through the clatter of lunch plates. "Rescue Services are retrieving the body of Assistant District Attorney, Vincent Ritter, from Gulf Canal," she read. "Investigators believe he fell or jumped from Walker Street Bridge early this morning—"

The sole customer at the bar, a man in a long, dark, rumpled coat, slumped his shoulders and said to the young, heavy-set bartender, "Pour me another one, Joey."

Stretched out in the corner booth, Rex Brunet absorbed the news report; his cold eyes hid his interest in the story. "Funny, how these things happen," he commented aloud, "and a day after you walk, Saul."

"Glad he's gone," Saul Reeve said, perched on the edge of his seat, across from Rex, "after what that golden boy said about me during the trial—" The short man with silvered hair rant collapsed into angry silence.

"He ends up dead just after you get released," Rex reiterated and shifted his heavy frame towards Saul with a narrowed gaze.

"What? No, Rex! It's not like that—"

"Just checking. The acquittal wasn't cheap."

"Let's face it. After Cavanaugh trashed his case, he went from champ to chump."

"Sam's the best bent lawyer in the city," Rex said recalling the short, doughy lawyer with the oily smile. "He said he'd take care of the white knight and he delivered."

"Now, we've got an open playing field."

"Only if the rumors about The Syrian are not true."

"Horseshit!" Saul spat back. "The Syrian is just a boogeyman story."

"I've got Sam checking in to it. It's good to have you back, Saul."

Saul scanned the near-empty restaurant and said, "I've been eating Municipal lock up slop for three months. Why are we celebrating in this artsy-fartsy dump? There are plenty of good steakhouses."

"I like the service here; they know the customer is always right." Rex grinned, as the meek restaurant manager, Theo, approached the booth.

"Uh, Mr. Brunet, what can I get you?" asked the thin young man in service whites, clasping his pale hands in front of him.

"Yeah, get me a porterhouse, well-done," Saul cut in, "and make it quick."

"Absolutely, sir," Theo said. "On your tab, Mr. Brunet?"

"What do you think, asshat?"

"Just asking," Theo said. "Anything for you, Mr. Brunet?"

"Yeah, Theo," Rex said. "Tell me about the Euro-fag who painted that shitty picture, again." He pointed to the large print hanging on the far orange-reddish plastered wall.

"That's Van Gogh's Night Café," Theo said. "It's kind of the raison d'etre of the place. Joey came up with the idea." He nodded to the quiet, acne-scarred bartender.

Rex compared the garish painting to the cafe. The well-used pool tables sat on the left, faux brass gaslights hung low over the small tables. Overhead, the exposed ductwork painted bright yellow and booths to the right, all served up on a bleached oak floor. "So," Rex concluded, "you boys copied the whole painting. Damn, I thought you fuckers were supposed to be creative."

"Well, I mean—"

"Relax, Theo, I'm just fucking with you," Rex said. "Anyway, tell Saul the story of that painting." He turned to Saul and said, "You're gonna love this, Saul."

"Well," the twitchy manager with short brown hair began, "Van Gogh imagined a place where one can ruin oneself, go mad or commit a crime."

"That sounds like the Saturday night trifecta to me," Saul jibed.

"Maybe it's just an apt description of the world," a rough voice interjected from the bar.

Rex gaped at the interloper and demanded, "Who the fuck asked you?"

Smiling, the man at the bar trained his dark glasses on Rex and said, "Nobody."

"You got anything better to do than butt into other people's conversations?" Rex said. His scarred hands clenched into fists.

"Not really."

"Skip!" Saul said. "It's not worth the scene. I'll deal with it."

Saul swaggered over to the man and said, "Look, friend, you upset my associate. You might want to find someplace else . . ." He tapped the bulge under his warm-up jacket of green silk.

"Not a problem," the man said, dropping a couple of bills on the damp bar. He reached for his long white cane propped next to him, and shuffled to the double doors of green paint and tarnished brass. "Thanks, Joey," he said. "I'll be back after the first, when my check comes in."

"Who was that douche?" Saul asked the fat bartender and glared after the slump-shouldered blind man in the shabby long coat.

"That's Prof," Joey said, wiping a glass. "He lives over at the 'March." He nodded towards the decrepit hotel across the street.

"Figures, why do you let losers like that in here?"

"His money is as good as anyone else's."

Out on the street, Prof shuddered; the bright afternoon sun failed to warm the cold December air. He sighed and shook his head; mistakes compounded mistakes. His fellow patients at the hospital schooled him well: never call attention to yourself. Less than a week out and he let his mouth get him in trouble, again. He never expected his lapse in judgement broadcasted to the world on the twelve o'clock news.

He considered crossing busy Reed Shore Drive back to Hotel Mittelmarch, a crumbling brick glory from the Twenties, but the consequences of last night demanded contrition. Extending his long white cane, he turned left and followed the cracked sidewalk.

In most neighborhoods, the Christmas decorations fluttered and rustled against the streetlamps; they didn't here. Pedestrians passed him on his left: some jabbering on cellphones, more clipping along with purpose, and still others meandering where the sidewalk took them. All of them ignored Prof's reluctant pilgrimage.

Just a coincidence, he thought, avoiding the long thread of coincidences that brought him here. Seven weeks ago, he was someone else: a respected college professor, a friend and a husband. After five weeks in the hospital and an indifferent cab ride to the Mittelmarch, he no longer recognized himself.

"*It's amusing how the mind fumbles to make sense of things in the face of tragedy,*" the woman's voice whispered in his ear, "*creating connections where there are none and ignoring obvious ones.*"

"Shut up," Prof said aloud, not caring who heard him. In the hospital, the other patients advised him in whispers in the corner of the foul-smelling dayroom to never admit to the doctors or staff that he heard her, lest he never leave. Still, she spoke to him in the darkness when no one was around and the scent of saffron filled the air.

"*You can try to ignore me, Prof,*" she continued, "*but taking no action is still a choice of action.*"

"Enough," Prof said, trudging onwards. "I didn't ask for any of this."

"*But you did, dear heart,*" she said, "*you agreed, one year and a day.*"

Five street crossings and four thousand twenty-one steps later, he reached out and ran his hand along the top of the rough stone fence. His fingers brushed against the cold iron bars that sprouted atop the wall. When he counted forty-seven bars, he turned right, took four steps, and dusted the fresh snow off the slats of the bench. In front of him, the never-closed black iron portcullis of Our Lady of the Nativity Cemetery beckoned him. Last night, things changed, he thought, easing down upon the bench.

Prof wandered into the maze of memories that brought him to this splintered bench last night. He recalled the bells of the church tolling twelve times, heralding the beginning of the winter and the finer details of the memories gelled. Too tired to walk and too awake to sleep, he found this quiet bench to rest, oblivious to the light fall of snow upon his shoulders.

He heard welt-soled shoes pat the concrete from a distance. Good shoes, he's not a pedestrian, Prof noted. The footsteps ceased a few feet to his right.

"Mind if I sit down?" the newcomer asked in a polite, reserved tone.

"Why not?" Prof said. "It's the city's bench."

"Thanks."

Prof listened to the rustle of worsted wool as the worn slats of the bench shifted. "A professional, huh?"

"Yes, I'm a lawyer in the District Attorney's office. My name's Vince."

"Well, Vince, nice to meet you. My name's John. What are you doing out here?"

"Could ask the same of you, John,"

"Well met, counselor," Prof said. "I'm still getting used to being blind; it's thrown my sleep schedule off."

"I'm sorry, how long?"

"Long enough to get my meds straight and learn to get around."

"Is it . . . permanent?"

"Never got a straight answer on that one," Prof said, shaking his head. "They called it a conversion disorder brought on by traumatic stress, whatever that means. It could come back today, tomorrow or never."

"So, they just cut you loose?"

"Pretty much, it was a waste of time and facilities. They call it 'care in the community,' so I have a load of free time until I get better, all at taxpayer expense."

Prof caught the rustle of cellophane and the fresh sweet scent of crocuses. "Are you here to pay respects to someone?"

"Sort of."

"Crocuses are hardly the best choice," Prof said. "They're supposed to represent hope and, in some instances, hallucinations."

"They were the first thing I grabbed at the florist. She told me they were the last of the season." The silence of the empty street dominated the moment as Vince considered his reply. "I'm here to put things right," he said.

"Sounds pretty vague."

"Yes, but if you knew what I was planning," Vince replied, "you'd think I'm crazy."

"Look who you are talking to; I'm in no position to judge another's state of mind."

"I remember some story about a blind man waiting outside the gates of Hell."

"Abandon all hope, ye who enter here," Prof said, "surrounded by the souls of the undecided."

"Except," the young lawyer said, "I'm not undecided."

"How so?"

"I lost a case, today. I failed."

"Happens, we all lose something."

"But this one was important," Vince said. "The defendant was a piece of work, killed a family man in cold blood. An open and shut victory. At the last second, the key witness rescinds his testimony and the mountain of circumstantial evidence gets tossed out. If I'd gotten the conviction, we could've broken a major syndicate."

"Would've beens, should've beens and could've beens are all the same; you didn't," Prof said, "so, deal with it."

"That's not the point! That's not the way it is supposed to work."

"Vince," Prof said, "the way it looks on paper and the way it actually works are never the same thing, get used to it."

"Not this time. Sometimes, you got to repay blood for blood."

"I don't follow."

"You got that right, John" Vince said, "You can't follow where I'm going."

The young lawyer popped the cold brass latches of his calfskin briefcase. Atop the neat array of pens, briefs and notebooks, he regarded the blood collection bag. After four shots of bourbon, he'd cut the deal at the ignored free clinic. Even in the DA's office, the whispers of the gutter penetrated the sterile halls; the city's office of last hope resided there. He'd cleaned out his account and went to make his bid. In the airless back office of the shabby clinic, the middle-aged nurse practitioner listened to his toneless story. In the end, she took his offered cash and a vial of his blood. In return, she gave him this pint of blood from a dead toddler and exact instructions on what to do next and added, "Sometimes, to put things right, it requires a sacrifice."

Vince arose and like a petitioner, approached the wrought iron gates of the cemetery, flowers in his right hand, the offering of blood in his left. He disappeared beneath the massive stone archway of the black gate.

Sick with fascination, Prof listened to Vince's footsteps fade away. Indistinct murmurings crossed the distance. A faint hint of sulfur wafted on the icy breeze followed by a soft chuckle. As the wind gusted, he caught a man's sobbing, and then, silence.

Long moments passed as Prof strained to fathom the outcome. Bold footsteps echoed out of the gateway and paused at the entrance. Prof sensed its leer as it paused to regard him. Curiosity sated, the entity then strode to the heart of downtown.

Minutes later, a new set of footfalls issued from the cemetery, this one slogged in a broken gait. He passed Prof without word as he shambled towards Canal Street. Definitely welt-soled shoes, Prof thought.

The hum of the street light above broke Prof from his reverie. "I should have said something," he muttered, "yet, I doubt I could have changed anything." Finally, he added, "I didn't, so I have to deal with it."

He bowed his head in silent prayer for the young attorney and himself in hopes some higher power paid heed. He arose, took up his cane, and began his slow trek back to the Mittelmarch. He paused and smelled the warm familiar smell of saffron. "*The first steps of your trial,*" the sweet voice whispered in his ear, "*only three hundred sixty-four to go, my love.*"

The Last Fare

6 PM December 24th
Nighthawk's Dinner
123 Cedars St.

Prof downed the last swallow of coffee from the heavy porcelain cup and braced for the walk back to the Mittelmarch in the cold, drizzly rain. A year ago, he spent Christmas Eve with Lila and her family at her parents' house around the fireplace catching up on the last year's news. Now, he planned to flop on one of the shabby couches in the hotel lobby and listen to the radio. This year, at least, he got to avoid his ex-father-in-law's probing questions about his job at the English Department.

He liked Don, Lila's father. The tall, balding man with a cheerful smile offered advice when he thought Prof needed it. Prof's mother died three years earlier and his own father left when he was eleven. Don and Martha accepted Prof into their family circle until Don's last phone call that ended with, "John, you're a good man, but blood is thicker than water."

"Anything else, Prof?" Jane, the waitress, asked.

"No," Prof said, laying out his few bills for the tab, "I'm good. I just wanted to say thank you for letting me back in tonight, after the incident . . ."

"Forget it, Prof. Harry's an ass."

"Still, I shouldn't have been in here in that shape."

"You were having a bad day. Anyone could see that. Harry thinks this place is a bistro where businessmen take meetings, or that's what he tells himself."

"I didn't realize it had gotten that far out of hand."

"A lot of people talk to themselves," Jane said. "You might need to turn it down a notch, and stay out of here during the day. Harry may not own the place, but his brother-in-law does."

"I prefer it here at night. It's quieter and the company's more convivial."

"Well, thanks. I've tried to give this my best shot for what it's worth."

"Any word on your grant application?"

"It's still, uh, in the pipeline."

"*Does this sound familiar, Prof?*" the voice interrupted.

"I understand," Prof said, "listen, Jane. These things take time and sometimes they don't go through the first time. I can't count the number of times I got turned down."

"It really doesn't matter, anyway."

"It's Christmas Eve. Don't worry about something that can't be fixed tonight. You'll be off in a couple of hours. Go home and enjoy it with, Rich." He slid off his bar stool and grabbed his cane. "Life is short and brutal some days, but it does get better."

"Yes, Rich," she said, "Merry Christmas and goodbye, Prof. The Christmas tree is three feet behind you."

"*Prof,*" the voice whispered, "*I shouldn't intercede, but don't make the same mistake you made three days ago.*"

Pausing, Prof reflected upon his bodiless companion's words. "Merry Christmas, Jane," Prof replied, "and thank you. It may not seem like much to you, but you have made a world of difference for me." He stepped out into the cold street with a blast of warm air following him.

Jane watched the unsteady blind man totter down the sidewalk back to the flophouse he called home. With her last customer gone, she locked the door and killed the main lights in the front of the house. She set about to perform her half of the closing duties, while Burt, the short-order cook frantically scrubbed the kitchen, looking forward to getting home to his wife and son. In the half-light, she listlessly wiped the tables and reflected upon Prof's well-meant words. As she refilled the salt shakers, she felt she should be feeling a sense of relief, for this was the last time she'd close the diner and make her way to her half-empty apartment.

"That's fucked up," Nathan said, draining his bottle of cheap wine. "You lost your job because you didn't like the color of the faculty lounge?"

The fire from the rusted burning barrel crackled and illuminated the loading yard of the dilapidated warehouse.

"That was the cherry on top of this shit-sundae," Prof said, reclining on a stack of weathered loading pallets. "I wasn't the superstar and I wasn't kissing enough of the right ass, or left, depending on how you look at it." He toyed with his bottle, the second of the night.

"Merry frickin' Christmas!" Nathan yelled, hurling his empty bottle at a shadowy corner. The shattering impact sent rustlings in all directions. "And to all a good fuckin' night," he added.

"Got to love that old yuletide cheer," Prof said. "Ever notice that if someone is going to kill himself, it's always around Christmas?"

"Shit, isn't that the way it goes? Everyone around you is blissed out on joy to the world and you're drowning in crap. You lose your job, your wife is banging your best friend, or you get busted running a three-card Monte—"

"Just out of curiosity, Nate, how'd your day in court turn out?"

"Well, I got probation and a fine. Could've been worse. My guys booked before the heat got there, so that pretty much kept my ass out of Municipal."

"Good shills are hard to come by, eh?

"Hey, Prof, you didn't do too bad," Nathan said, "for a first-timer."

"I suppose I got away with it."

"Are you kidding me?" Nathan said, "You played it perfect. Keep the clerk occupied, fumble for the cash, and we walk away with eight bottles for the price of one. Textbook, sir." He raised his half-empty bottle in salute.

"To profitable endeavors," Prof said, lifting his bottle.

"And not getting caught. See? Didn't I tell you this would be better than hanging out in the lobby of the 'March?"

"All right, Mr. Gascon, your point is well-taken."

Prof had met this strutting little trouble-maker a couple of days earlier. Nathan lived on the same floor at the Hotel Mittelmarch. Whenever they passed in the hall, Nathan always acknowledged Prof with a, "How's it going?" Always on hustle somewhere, Prof suspected the young man favored sporting a swankier look than his current beat-up bomber jacket and ragged running shoes, but tough times hit everyone.

Tonight played different. Prof had been sitting in the cathedral-like lobby of the hotel amidst the frayed couches and threadbare carpets. He neither wanted to go back to his claustrophobic room, seven flights above, nor venture out into the wet streets. The drafts from the front doors were bad enough.

"Hey, Prof!" Nathan had said on the way to the ancient revolving door of tarnished brass. "Got plans for Christmas Eve?"

"No, Nathan."

"Not even going out and tie one on?"

"No," Prof said. "I can either go out and get drunk tonight or eat for the rest of the week."

"How much you got to spare?"

"Three, maybe four bucks," Prof said.

"That's enough, c'mon," Nathan said, grabbing Prof's coat sleeve. "I got an idea."

Three hours and two bottles apiece later, Prof and Nathan basked in the warmth of the fire, enjoying the fruits of their crime spree.

"'Scuse me," a raspy voice interrupted, "do either of you gentlemen have some spare change?" A man in a tattered anorak, soaked at the shoulders, scuffled into the firelight.

"No, can't say that we do," Nathan said, looking over at Prof.

Prof nodded and said, “It is Christmas after all.”

“Here you go, Merry Christmas,” Nathan said, offering the man one of their remaining bottles.

“Much obliged, Sirs,” the man replied as his thin knobby fingers grasped the neck of the bottle. A liquid cough surged up from deep in his lungs and he caught it on his coat sleeve. “Excuse me.”

“That sounds bad,” Prof said.

“You ought to get checked out,” Nathan said. “Your eyes are all yellow.”

“Yeah,” the man said, “I was planning to go over to the clinic on Ayrshire, but they close early.” He took a long swig from his bottle.

“There you have it, Prof,” Nathan said. “Just like I was saying earlier, I rest my case.”

“Nathan, no one’s obligated to give a shit about you, me or—” Prof said, gesturing to the newcomer.

“Bruno.”

“Okay, Bruno,” Prof said, “welcome to the club.”

“What club would that be?”

“The Neck Deep Club,” Nathan added.

“One of you fellas calls for a cab?” called a voice from the street beyond the snarled and warped chain-link fence.

Out of curiosity, Prof staggered through the half-hanging gate to the sidewalk. The taxi’s engine purred. “No, my friend,” he said, resting his hands on the cold door of the taxi to steady himself, “I’m afraid you’ve got the wrong bunch.”

“Shit!” The young cabby said. “So close to the end of my shift and it’s another no-show.”

“Sorry about that,” Prof said, turning away. “Merry Christmas.”

“You sure you don’t need a ride anywhere?” The cabby said, “I’d rather just run the clock down on the shift than go into overtime, seeing how it’s Christmas and all.”

Prof considered the offer. A ride around town in a heated cab had some appeal. After he and Nate finished the wine, what was he going to do?

Stumble back to his room and sleep it off, preferably through Christmas day.

"*Prof,* "the voice cautioned, "*don't do this.*" Her voice was faint and distant; his drinking aided this.

"Shut up," he muttered, taking another swig of sickly sweet wine.

"Uh," Bruno interrupted, shambling upon the scene, "you available, cabby?"

"Sure, Buddy," the cabby said, "you got a place in mind?"

"Naw," Bruno coughed, "I'd just like to get out of the cold."

"I was planning on cruising over to the far side of the river," the cabby said. "They got some nice places over there and I could use the company."

"Sounds like a good an idea as any," Bruno said. Prof heard the cab door open and Bruno slide into the back seat.

"How about you, Sir?" the cabby addressed Prof.

"I'm good."

"Hey, wait a minute," the cabby called back.

"What's that?"

"My last fare left this as tip," the cabby said, shoving a bottle wrapped in a paper bag into Prof's hand. "I can't drink anymore."

"Thanks, sir," Prof said, "but I can't accept this."

"Don't worry about it."

"Prof?" Nathan said, putting a hand of Prof's shoulder, "Why'd you wander out here and who were you talking to?"

Prof turned back to gesture to the cab behind him, but his hand waved through empty silent space. Bewildered, the Prof handed the bottle to Nathan.

"Twelve-year-old scotch?" Nathan said. "Holding out on us, Prof?"

"No, it's just—" Prof cut short, "Never mind."

Jane shivered in the chilly night air as the wet city street spread into the darkness. The drizzle of rain soaked through her royal blue slippers and the inside of her pink terrycloth bathrobe. Behind her, the renovated brownstone she and Rich leased loomed behind her with darkened windows like eye sockets. She waited but failed to remember for what or who. A predatory purr of a car engine heralded the blinding flash of the white sedan's headlights. A car door creaked open and dark figure approached Jane.

"Hey, you called for a cab?"

"I don't think so," Jane said, startled by the pale, young man in the hooded black sweatshirt. "I don't know what I'm doing out here."

The man adjusted his dark sunglasses and said, "It takes all kinds. Look, Mort, my dispatch, sent me out here. My shift's almost up. If I call in a no-show, he'll just run me to the other side of town. If you need a ride, it'll help me out." He looked down the empty street and added, "I don't think you want to hang around here too long." The wind moaned in concurrence.

"I guess you're right," Jane exhaled and watched her breath cloud. "But, I doubt I have any money." She rummaged through the pockets of her bathrobe.

"Hey, relax," the cabby said with dismissive wave. "Like I said, the ride is on the house, you know, gratis."

"Wait a minute, I think I found some," Jane said as the empty prescription bottle slipped out of her bathrobe pocket and clattered to the sidewalk.

"Come on, Jane," the cabby said, draping an arm over her shoulder, "there's nothing left for you here."

Jane relented to the cabby's lead. They approached the white sedan with the legend on the door:

Boatman's Cab Service
"The Last Name in Commuting!"

Inside, Jane warmed up from the blasting heaters. The cab pulled away smoothly from the curb.

"K. Ron Forder?" she read aloud from the hack license pinned to the cracked vinyl of the driver's seat.

"That's me," the cabby said, grinning, looking back. "Where to?"

"If I had a clue," Jane said, "I wouldn't be out wandering at two in the morning in my jammies."

"Works for me, Jane," Ron said, swerving the cab around the corner. "Don't worry about this." He flipped the switch to the meter. "Mort will have my ass if I don't register the miles," he added.

"How'd you know my name?" Her hazel eyes narrowed and the ticking of the meter grew louder.

"You look like a Jane," Ron said without taking his focus off the dark, empty street ahead. "You drive a cab as long as I have, you can tell a lot about your fares."

"So, does that comment usually impress most people?"

"No," Ron replied with a grin, "but it's a pretty good line of crap, isn't it?"

"Some would say it's pretty cliché."

"Oh, well, my poor customers suffer."

Through the fog, Jane glimpsed a sooty, brick monolith with gaping black holes for windows. "Where are we, anyway?"

"Chrysanthemum Street," Ron answered, "near the Hotel Mittelmarch. I pick up fares over there all the time. Transients, mostly, the 'March's full of lost souls. Any idea where you want to go?"

"Any place but here," Jane said with a shiver. The cab sped past a duo of men huddled around a steel barrel fire.

"I know, pretty depressing," Ron said as the cab rolled into the thick white fog.

Jane's vision frizzed around the edges and a roaring filled her ears. The cab swayed violently. She saw a blinding, white light in front of— no, over—her.

"Hey! You okay back there?"

"I got dizzy for a moment," Jane slurred.

"Look, if you are getting car sick, let me know, I can pull over. I don't want to have to clean puke out of the back seat at the end of my shift."

"No, I don't get sick easily. It's just . . . It's—"

"What?" Ron said, glancing at the rearview mirror.

"I don't know," Jane exhaled in frustration. "It's been a bad week. I remember the bathroom in my apartment . . ." She broke down in silence.

"Go on, Jane," Ron urged, never looking back.

"It was a bad week," Jane repeated, gazing at the clean floor of the cab. "Monday, caught my boyfriend, Rich, cheating on me with one of those bitches he works with. All makeup, tits and no brains. Then Dr. Aksoy called me into his office yesterday and told me the board denied my grant, so no job. And I got my thesis review—"

"How long were you seeing this guy?"

"Three years."

"Sounds like you were due for a change," Ron commented.

"Maybe."

"So, why was your grant denied?

"Dr. Aksoy said the board didn't think it went deep enough to represent the department. Looks like I'm stuck waitressing."

"Well, that sucks," Ron said. "If you feel like you need a break, there's this place across the river. It's nice. You interested?"

"Sure, whatever."

"No, you either want to go or you don't want to go. I'm not burning the gas for 'whatever.'"

"Hey, take it easy. I want to go."

"Okay," Ron said, "I'm sorry I blew up. It's just the traffic's a bitch. I don't want to waste my time with someone who doesn't know what they want."

Jane read the green overpass sign:

Stygian Memorial Tunnel
1 Mile

It flew past them into the dark oblivion. The ticking of the cab meter slowed. Above her, she saw the bright circle of light again. Was there mumbling in the background?

"You still with me, Jane?"

"Huh," Jane jumped, "yeah, I mean sure. Where are we going again?"

"I told you, a place across the river."

Fluorescent lights glared off the white tiles of the tunnel looming large in front of the cab. Above the mouth of the tunnel, two green signs read:

Sheol Industrial Park **Keep Left**	**Elysian Fields Resort** **Keep Right**

Jane's head pounded. The slow ticking of the meter transformed into a piercing drone. Somewhere, Jane heard someone whisper, "We're losing her." She squeezed her eyes shut. Through the doorway, she spied the brass bed covered with her grandmother's quilt. In front of her, she saw her own lined reflection in the bathroom mirror, the immaculate sink, the cold white tile, the open medicine cabinet and the pills.

"Stop!" she cried. "Stop the cab, Ron!"

"Jeez!" Ron said, spinning the wheel and slamming the brakes. The tires screeched in protest as the highway twisted and warped beneath them. The cab idled for a quiet moment at the mouth of the white tunnel.

"Well," Ron said, after a long moment of silence, "that's gonna be hell on the tires, brakes, suspension and frame."

Looking down the long pristine tunnel, Jane saw the serene lights of the other side beckon. "I want to get out of here."

"Fair enough," Ron said with a shrug as the engine started and the transmission dropped into gear. The cab hurled down the expressway, away from the tunnel and back into the bank of thick fog.

"You're not mad at me, are you?"

"No. Everybody goes across the river eventually; it takes real guts to stay on this side for as long as you can. I wish I'd done it your way. Life is short and brutal some days, but it does get better."

"What are you talking about?"

Ron pulled aside the collar his hoodie. A deep, red welt encircled his neck.

"I'm sorry."

"So am I," Ron said, slowing the cab.

Jane heard the familiar whoosh and whisk of a rain-soaked road. The night fog broke up; the air smelled cleaner. "Now what?" she said.

"My shift's up," Ron said, as he pulled up to the curb, "and this is where I drop you."

"Ron," Jane said, "thanks, is there anything I can do for you? I mean, at least, I owe you for the ride."

"Forget it," Ron said with a grin, "like I said—gratis. Merry Christmas."

Jane slipped out of the cab. The harsh white glow of the tile shone through the sliding glass doors with the word "Emergency" illuminated in red above them.

"A hospital?" Jane blurted in surprise. She turned back but the cab and driver had faded into the night.

Jane cracked her eyes; the blinding fluorescents bore down upon her and the thin vinyl mattress she lay. She wrinkled her nose at the astringent chemical stench. Her stomach muscles ached. She rubbed her face and her hand came away with streaks of black soot. The young, haggard doctor hovered over her and said, "Ms. Davis, we almost lost you last night. I have never seen anyone survive an overdose of that size. You're very lucky."

Fashion for All Occasions

9:30 AM January 2nd
Wrightsway Park Square

Prof sat at the small scarred table which passed for his desk and held the two-month-old letter that changed his life. He didn't need to read it; the words remained permanently imprinted on his memory:

Dear Professor John Clarke:

I would like to inform you that your position with the White University English Department will be terminated effective immediately.

Human Resources will provide you with a packet of information (attached) which includes details on a severance package, continuing employee benefits, and your final paycheck.

If I can be of any help during this transition, please let me know.
Sincerely,

Dr. Artemisia Shivmann, Department Chair and Professor of English and Woman's Studies

"I'll bet she liked informing me," Prof muttered, "and her idea of help during this transition would have been a push down a flight of stairs." He put the letter down.

No tenure, no publications and no alliances—that situation never ends well. Lila always pushed him to socialize more, but he never quite fit in with his colleagues or hers, the high priests of the accounting universe.

On the right side of the table, the nondescript stationery box of brown cardboard sat; he tried his best to ignore it.

"*Haven't you heard, darling?*" the familiar sweet voice chimed. Soft, feminine hands rested upon his shoulders. He imagined a shadowy presence behind him. "*Avoiding the obvious never solves the problem. It only festers and rots, much like you are doing, my love.*"

"Enough!" Prof said and grabbed his black wool jacket. He picked up a notepad and pen and clattered down the hallway.

Out in the cold street, he opted to follow the sidewalk down to the Canal. Finally, he paused at the apex of Walker Bridge. The swift, freezing waters rushed many feet below him and reminded him of the night in front of the cemetery. "No, that solves nothing, either," he thought. He crossed over the bridge to Wrightsway Park Square.

"Gentrified," Prof noted as his mood calmed. The shops and boutiques surrounded the small park of bare trees and bushes. Although early, many shoppers raced from store to store to get the last after-Christmas deal before they disappeared like the fluttering decorations on the fake gaslight streetlamps. The rich aroma of a coffee shop enticed his empty stomach, but he ignored it. The bank wouldn't release his funds until noon. Jane had been absent from the diner for three days after Christmas. He stopped by every night, but without Jane there, he wouldn't stay. Relying on overpriced convenience store fare, he burned through the last of his cash a day and a half ago.

He extended his cane to navigate the unexplored terrain. Prof spun sideways as his shoulder clipped another pedestrian.

"Excuse you, Sir," a strong baritone voice snapped.

"W-what?" Prof replied, regaining his balance.

"I said, excuse you," the voice said, drawing near. The rustle of a cashmere overcoat and the footsteps of leather soles followed. "You are not particularly skilled in the matters of etiquette, are you?"

"Look, I'm blind—"

"Your uniqueness," the other said, "does not make you necessarily useful to society."

"That was uncalled for—"

"Says the man who smells like he enjoyed a nice bowl of whiskey for breakfast. I find it disheartening that the vagrancy statutes have been so narrowly defined these days."

Prof's jaw clenched and his hand gripped the cane.

"By all means, young man," the other said, "do exactly what is in your nature."

"Good morning, Judge Adams," a heavy voice rumbled, "Prof."

"Sergeant Serrano," the judge addressed the new voice. "You are ten seconds too early."

"For what, Judge Adams?"

"A battery charge," Judge Adams continued. "This man was about to attack me."

"Really?" Serrano said. "Is that true, Prof?"

"No," Prof said. His head bowed and his grip on the cane slackened.

"All I see here is a misunderstanding," Serrano said. "No laws were broken, but you would know better than I do, your honor."

"Indeed, I do," the judge asserted, "and such persona non-grata must be kept in check. That, I believe, is your job, Sergeant Serrano. I bid you a good day." The judge stormed off.

"Too late for that," Serrano said. "Of all the SOBs you could have tangled with, Prof, you had to pick Judge Ray Adams."

"It was an accident—"

"Doesn't matter. The old bastard is already on the phone to Municipal. Prof, I'm in a bad spot here, just so you know. I can't charge you with anything, but if your name shows up on the docket, it's my ass as well as yours."

"I don't plan—"

"Shit," Serrano said, "I hear that all the time. Hell, I shouldn't have to tell you this. The places you go and the company you keep. You're two steps away from being a statistic."

"Professor!" A bright feminine voice interrupted, "I've been looking all over for you! You are late for your fitting appointment, no?" She slipped her smooth, manicured hand around his. "Sergeant Serrano," she gushed, "it is so wonderful that you take an interest in the less fortunate citizens."

"Well, just doing my job, Ms. Fox," Serrano said.

"And you do it so well! Why, I was telling Demetria just yesterday that I felt so much safer with you around. Come along, Professor; let's get you sorted out." She eased away from the befuddled law officer with Prof in tow.

"Thanks . . . Ms. Fox," Prof murmured once out of earshot of Serrano. "Most people would not have gotten involved."

"Don't mention it. I've always had a soft spot for underdogs, and my name is Reyna," she said and pushed open a glass door. The welcome chimes tinkled.

"Welcome to Fox Fashions," a female voice droned, "a bold choice for bold women—"

"It's just me, Demetria," Reyna said, as she regarded the young woman with long black hair and silver jewelry perusing the latest issue of *Cosmo*.

"Good morning, Reyna," Demetria said. Her heavily mascaraed eyes brightened. "No walk-ins or deliveries, yet. And your only appointment isn't 'til after lunch."

"How to Capture the Heart of the Man of Your Dreams in Seven Easy Steps," Reyna read aloud from the glossy magazine cover. "Any good?"

"I've gone through steps one through three. You know, taking inventory of who I am, what I can improve in myself and what I am looking for."

"So, step four is?"

"Find out where the type of man you want hangs out."

"Wonderful! I've always enjoyed hunting."

"Sure," Demetria said, "easy enough for you to say, but they don't hang out a sign for 'The Hot Guy Preserve' for the rest of us."

"Oh, Demetria, don't be so gloomy. It's never attractive."

"And this is?" Demetria inquired as she studied Prof.

"Oh, manners," Reyna said, "this is Prof. I've seen him around and invited him in for shelter for a moment. Prof, this is Demetria, my assistant manager and hopeless romantic."

"Kind of cute in a burned-out way," Demetria assessed, "but a little too old for my tastes."

"Demetria," Reyna sighed, "I did not bring him in here for you. The good professor needed rescuing from a rather awkward situation with Sergeant Serrano—"

"Nicky?" Demetria blurted as her eyes glinted with interest. "Is he still out there?"

"No," Reyna said, peering out the display window past the stylishly-dressed mannequins, "he's moved on."

"Aww, I was hoping to—"

"Yes, Demetria," Reyna returned, "I know what you were hoping to do." She turned back to Prof. "It would seem the danger has passed."

"Then I thank you kind ladies for your hospitality," he said with a mock bow, "and I graciously take my leave. May your day be prosperous."

Demetria tittered, "Reyna, you always find the most interesting guys."

"Don't be a stranger, Prof."

"Too late," Prof said with a smirk, "they don't come stranger than me." He stepped out into the frigid air of the bright street.

"*Only three hundred fifty-three days more, my love,*" the voice whispered to him.

Reyna removed her full-length coat of silvery white fur and hung it neatly behind the glass display counter. She surveyed the shop. Spiral steel hanging racks were baited with colorful outfits, and belts and hand bags lined the main floor. The shoes in the simple half-loft lay in wait for bargain-hunters. To the back, an alteration stage with immaculate three-paneled mirrors next to two changing booths stood ready to receive her clients. Over to the right was the cool storage wardrobe she built herself. Satisfied with her little domain, she readied herself for the surprises of the day's business.

"You know," Demetria said, "we could make more money if you put in a couple more wardrobes and rent space during the summer."

"True, Demetria," Reyna mused, admiring at the stark beauty of the bare brick walls, "but we just don't have enough space to pull that off yet."

"Or money," Demetria added.

"You have to think positive—"

"I know, I know, positive thinking yields positive results."

"Ah! You are learning your lessons well, young one."

"If you say so, Sensei," Demetria said, rolling her eyes.

"That I do," said Reyna. "Now, if you would be so kind as to inventory the new acquisitions in back," she said, handing Demetria a clipboard.

"Certainly, madame. I never thought the world of high fashion could be this exciting and dramatic."

Reyna looked on as Demetria walked back to the storeroom. She shook her head and thought, "Kids today.. ."

The chimes dully announced the first customer of the day.

"Jane!" Reyna greeted the slim brunette in the heavy wool overcoat of dove gray. "It's wonderful to see you after the holidays."

"Hi, Reyna," said Jane with a half-hearted smile. "Hope you did well for the season."

"Oh, better than expected, I suppose, but how are you doing?"

"I've been better," Jane said with downcast eyes, "but they say any day above ground is a good one, right?"

"Indeed they do, but then again, they say a lot of things. What's really going on?" Intrigued, she cocked her head and her nose twitched.

"Everything is fine, really- "

"Jane," Reyna observed, "you have dark circles under your eyes, and frankly, you seem a little worse for wear. You've been crying,"

The burden welled up from Jane's chest; she tried forcing it back down. Finally, "Everything's just fallen apart!" flooded out of her. A heavy sob followed.

"Easy, little cub," Reyna consoled. "Come sit down and tell me all about it." She coaxed Jane to the wrought iron café table and chairs between the alteration stages.

Quietly, Jane recounted her last month of failures: Rich's betrayal, the grant denial and her brutal interim review. Somehow, she managed to omit the three dark days in the hospital.

All the while, Reyna listened and absorbed every word.

"I've blown it," Jane concluded.

"Jane," Reyna said, giving Jane's hand a slight squeeze, "I have heard comparable stories before, but that doesn't make it any easier. After the chase you've just been through, I am impressed you stuck your head out of your warren."

"I guess I am at a loss of what to do now."

"Oh, that's obvious," Reyna said with a mischievous smirk. "Revenge."

"W-what?"

"Oh, I'm not talking about those foolish feuds or bloody vendettas; only men would dream up something that simple and messy." Her long red hair grew darker in the shifting light from the windows. "The woman's way, and I believe it to be superior," she continued, "is living with style, despite all obstacles."

"But, I'm broke and—"

"If it were all about money, everybody would do it. If you are going to live, live with style. All, it takes confidence and, of course, panache."

"I'm out of both of those, too."

"Hi, Jane!" Demetria said with her skull-festooned purse in hand. "I'm off to lunch." She flitted through the store and out the door.

"She's really taken the goth thing to a new level," Jane observed.

"We're working on that," Reyna sighed. "I hope it's only a phase. Fortune knows I can't keep anything black in stock." She pursed her ruby red lips and pressed a perfectly manicured fingertip to them. "However, I have just had a spark of inspiration," she said. "Jane, dear, are you up for a bit of retail therapy?"

"Is there any other kind?"

Reyna crooked her finger and Jane followed up the stairs to the shoe loft. In the far back corner, Reyna crouched and rummaged through a stack of black shoe boxes. "Aha!" she said and presented the box to Jane. "Take them," Reyna teased, "they don't bite."

Jane stared at the black sling backs of velvet suede. The silver threads of the embroidered scorpions danced across the vamps and the lustrous jet heels curved gracefully into the delicate backs. "They're beautiful," Jane murmured.

"I got them from an estate sale awhile back," Reyna reminisced. "The lady was supposed to be something else, at one time. I believe her name was Brabin or something like that."

"They're fantastic," Jane admitted, pushing the box back to Reyna, "but, I can't afford them."

"How much can you afford?"

"For those? You're talking Le Chateau des Chasseurs goods on a Shoe Stable budget."

"Okay, hypothetically, how much can you afford?"

"Forty," Jane said, wistfully gazing at the box cradled in Reyna's arms.

"Hmm, you know only the right kind of woman can pull off this look. She must be sharp, daring and a little bit dangerous. Are you that kind of woman?"

Jane bowed her head slightly and raised her eyes; her shy smile turned into a bold grin. She whispered, "Yes."

"Condition one met. Do you promise to keep these out of Demetria's hands, at all costs?"

"I'll fight to the death," Jane hissed, which ended in a giggle.

"Condition two met. I believe I can let these go for forty dollars, if you agree to the last term."

"And that is?"

"You have to wear them out of the shop."

The money and the shoes changed hands. As promised, Jane wore the shoes out of the shop. Standing straighter, Jane opened the door with resolve.

"One more thing, Jane!" Reyna called from the loft. "Lose the coat, honey. They might think you bought it here."

Jane laughed and promptly flipped Reyna the bird.

The quick calculation in her head balanced. "Down a thousand in the black and up a thousand in the white," she thought. "Not bad." The sunlight brightened the inside of the store.

After lunch at the Chinese place down the street, Reyna hurried back to the shop. Demetria's enthusiasm covered many of her shortcomings, but sometimes, customers needed the savvy that came with experience.

"You're incompetent! I demand to see Ms. Fox now!" sailed out the door along with the jangling of the door chimes. Inside, Demetria cowered behind the register as the woman in the pantsuit and severe make up glowered.

And I hoped for a slow afternoon, Reyna thought, gauging the situation. *I should be wearing a fire helmet, but red on red is so tacky.* Steeling herself, Reyna called out, "Why, Ms. Belford, what a pleasant surprise! I wasn't expecting you until, I believe, Monday."

"Ms. Fox, I've come in for my coat, but this young lady says that it's not here." She straightened the collar of her maroon designer suit with white piping and exchanged her disdainful scowl for an expression of professional politeness.

"Of course, Ms. Belford," Reyna concurred, "I do believe I did say that I expected the order to come in Monday. It was a long shot, at best, that it would come in today and we would call you—"

"I put three hundred dollars down on that coat, and I need it tonight."

"Your coat is not here—"

"You have an entire rack in your back room; I saw them there."

"What were you doing in my stock room?" Reyna said.

"Looking for your sales clerk," Ms. Belford snapped. "You didn't have anyone manning the front of the store. My time is important."

"Demetria," Reyna said, "you're makeup is running, dear. Why don't you go in back and clean yourself up?"

Demetria nodded and left the front of the store. Ms. Belford's glare followed her to the stock room door. "She wouldn't last five minutes as one of my employees," she snorted.

"No," said Reyna, "but she has a good heart and that counts for a lot in my book."

"Hearts don't get you far in my business, I should know. I have several in jars on my desk."

"Metaphorically, of course, Ms. Belford. Your shareholder meeting is tonight, no?"

"Yes, that is why I must have one of those coats."

"Of course, I understand. That's my business."

"You need a refresher course on customer service. Rule one: the customer is always right."

Reyna appraised the smug woman with the fake Rolex on her left wrist and the keys to the leased Mercedes dangling in her right hand. The corners of Reyna's mouth upturned slightly. "I just might have something that suits your needs," said Reyna, stepping to the fur locker. "It's part of my vintage collection." She ran her fingers lightly across the row of hanging furs and plucked one from the extensive line.

"Here we go," Reyna said, spreading the coat upon the glass counter for inspection. "Such a lovely piece."

Ms. Belford stroked her fingers through the satiny fineness. "This might seem . . . ostentatious."

"Hardly! This is the finest example of Alaskan Sable from the Gilded Age. In fact, the original owner was Henrietta Green."

"Who?" Ms. Belford said, looking up.

"I'm surprised you don't know her. She was the richest woman in America at one time. They used to refer to her as the 'Queen of Wall Street.' Imagine showing up in this for cocktails. The bragging rights!"

The sunlight through the store's display window waned.

Reyna watched the mixture of lust, pride and greed fill Ms. Belford green eyes, just as expected.

"How much?" Ms. Belford blurted.

The gold card slid through the reader and the coat went home with Ms. Belford.

"Four thousand in the black and a loss of three thousand in the white," Reyna calculated once more. "Not good, not good at all."

The inside of the store grew shadowy as dark clouds rolled across the sky.

"Come out, Demetria," Reyna called. "The big, bad businesswoman's gone."

"Are you sure?" Demetria said, now composed. "I was just checking in the shipment—"

"Don't worry about it. Next time, just lock the door when you're doing that alone. I should have thought of that before."

"Uh, Reyna," Demetria said from behind the register, "I think we got problems. The register and the card reader are offline."

Reyna winced; she had hoped for one more sale today.

"Oh," Demetria continued, "when I was back in the stock room, some of the pipes started knocking together and making scary sounds."

All for selling one skunk coat, Reyna thought. *I never get a break*. Still, it was afternoon and her karma tally would not be due until sunset. Her forearms itched as new cinnabar fur sprouted underneath her sleeves. One more sale could save her.

As the shadows of the late afternoon grew long, Reyna watched the door. The knocking pipes grew louder as she attempted to distract herself by filling out stock orders. Her ears twitched and she looked forward to grabbing a couple of pigeons for dinner. *Come on!* she thought, dropping her pen. *I really don't want to spend the night outdoors, again. Fur or not, it's cold out there.*

Quarter to five, the door chimes jingled happily one last time.

"Rachel!" Demetria squealed and bolted from behind the counter. "We haven't seen you in forever!"

"Hello, Demetria," Rachel said with a forced smile. "Sam and I have been really busy over the holidays.'

"Is he still working those long hours?" Reyna said. She noted Rachel's austere navy turtleneck without jewelry.

"Yes, he's still under a lot of stress. He works so hard."

"I know," Reyna said, "and you are just trying to keep him happy. It is so hard being married sometimes."

"It is, but he did give me some money to go treat myself."

"And you found yourself here," Reyna said.

"Rachel!" Demetria cut in. "We got a bunch of those silk dresses in that you like."

"Uh, thanks, Demetria, I really don't want to try anything on. In fact, it's good seeing you, but I need to go."

The knocking pipes got louder.

"Before you go," Reyna said, "would you care to look at some of my jewelry? I designed it myself. You really have good taste." Her eyes lit with hope.

"Okay," Rachel said.

Reyna eased the tray from the display case and clicked the halogen lamp. The dazzling array sprang to life.

Rachel's eyes focused as she bit her lower lip. Her hand hovered over a pair of bright gold earrings with fiery, luminous stones of red and gold. Cautiously, she picked the pair up. "I like these," Rachel said.

Reyna suppressed her grimace and said, "A wonderful choice. They're called tiger's eyes. Those are my latest creations."

The knocking of the pipes lessened yet Reyna still had to hide the faint whiskers on her upper lip with her fingers by faking a sneeze. It didn't count as white if she profited.

"How much?" Rachel asked.

"Tell you what, Rachel," Reyna obliged. "Let's call it a belated Christmas present, on the condition you wear them out of the store."

"Thank you, Reyna; you've always been such a good friend," Rachel said, putting the earrings on.

The knocking pipes were barely audible now.

Reyna sighed. "Here," she said, offering a scarlet envelope. "This is a gift certificate for Ms. Lee's across the park. Her manicures are the best. You know, every big cat has got to get her claws sharpened occasionally."

"Reyna, I shouldn't."

"Please, Rachel," Reyna implored.

"Oh, all right," Rachel said. "Reyna, you always have everyone's best interests at heart. I have to go now, bye."

The pipes went silent and still.

"Weird," Demetria said, "the register and the card reader just kicked back on."

Watching the early winter sunset darken the park, Reyna heaved a sigh. In the white fifty, in the black two hundred fifty, she assessed. And near broke, but at least she would spend the night at home and warm. No one told her being a probationary human would be easy.

As the streetlamps of the park kicked on, the interior of the store brightened slightly.

Epiphanies

6 AM January 6th
Fidelity Courier Services
4664 Corral Drive

Better you than me," Aaron said, watching the cold sleet pour down on the sidewalk outside. "It's nasty out there." The still-dark morning sky remained heavy with thick black clouds. He turned up the rattling space heater as an afterthought.

"Yeah," Gabe said, putting his coffee cup down, "it's gonna be rough out there dodging the cagers." He pulled the yellow Gore-Tex rain pants over his ragged oil-stained jeans. "What's in the pipeline, so far?"

"Still early," Aaron said, leafing through the service tickets. He scratched his thick black beard. "Most of the law offices don't start calling in until eight. I got a couple, but they're realtor contracts. Real flyweight stuff."

"The kids are still sipping their lattes," Gabe said with a mirthful twinkle in his bright blue eyes.

"Hey, hotshot," Aaron said, brushing the remains of his Danish pastry off his faded blue sweatshirt, "they get the job done and they don't scare the daylights out of the receptionists."

"Are you implying that I have an image problem?"

"No, but, I'd rather have a clean-cut kid in bicycle shorts and a helmet deliver purchase agreements to Augustus Investments Limited. Less trauma all the way around."

"Sound business strategy."

"It pays the bills, most of the time," said Aaron.

While Gabe pulled the rain jacket over his faded vest, Aaron noticed the dark spots on the denim from a series of absent patches. "Gabe," he inquired, "you and your bros aren't affiliated?"

"Nah, we went independent a while back. It's a politics thing."

"So how come you're not working in the shop with Mike and Uri?"

"The shop will bring in only so much money," Gabe said, slinging his black nylon bag over his shoulder. "Could be worse. I could be working third shift on the meat wagon like Ralph."

The ding of the battered computer broke the silence. "Well," he continued, "looks like you got your first run. 225 Joseph. Warehouse district."

"Sounds like one of mine."

"I don't know, Gabe. Scraping road kill off the streets or becoming road kill yourself."

"Hey," the large, blond-haired biker said, pulling his hood up, "someone's gotta deliver the message."

In the icy rain, Dorothy handed off the satchel filled with the casino's nightly take to the tall, young courier in the yellow rain suit, his piercing blue eyes filled with kindness. He climbed back on his tricked-out Harley and peeled out of the gravel parking lot into the pre-dawn drizzle. She looked back to the double doors of the warehouse and hoped she hadn't aroused anyone's suspicion, especially Tim, the manager.

With slumped shoulders, she slid into the driver's seat of her bronze Lexus. Exhaling, she closed the car door and the engine purred to life. One more time, she checked her rearview mirror to see if anyone saw her leave the casino. By sunrise, she would be far away from the city and this snake pit where she had worked for so many years. She could have walked away and no one would have cared, but like the courier told her, sometimes you must put things right before you're free.

Tim Courtland backed against the long bar of the warehouse casino. At eight in the morning, the casino stood silent. Even Sheppy, the old guy who cleaned up every morning, went home an hour ago. When the bank manager called to inquire why they did not receive this morning's deposit, his heart skipped a beat. He paused after hanging up; he dreaded the next call. Thirty minutes later, Saul Reeve and Mr. Brunet rolled onto the casino floor.

"So, let me get this straight," bleary-eyed Saul spat, "A courier you'd never seen before went into the cage with Dorothy? What the fuck are we paying you for?"

"It seemed legit. I mean, Dottie locks down the cage at close, does the cash count and the courier comes in and picks up the take. That's the way we've always done it."

In the background, Rex Brunet, Saul's boss, observed the exchange in his black leather coat. His expression remained stony as he listened.

"Except you'd never seen this courier before," Saul added.

"He was a big guy; long, blond hair with a beard, kind of youngish, wore a rain suit and rode a hog. Look, this is the kind of guy you want to move that kind of cash."

"Except he wasn't one of our guys, fucko!" Saul snapped, punctuating his remark with a hard slap to Tim's face.

"Easy, Saul," Rex interrupted, "it's happened. Let him speak. If he can't talk, we don't get the money back." He studied the cowed manager with neutral gray eyes and said, "Tim, is it? Come on and have a seat and we'll sort this mess out."

They took their seats at one of the small tables near the craps table. Saul brought over a bottle of vodka and a couple of shot glasses from behind the bar and went back to the cage.

"Go ahead, Tim, help yourself."

Tim poured himself a shot. His hands shook, as he downed it.

"Better?"

Tim nodded.

"Okay, Tim. Let's get to business," Rex said, leaning in. "So, Dorothy calls in this new courier this morning, right?"

"Yeah, she's been acting weird the last couple of weeks," Tim said, looking down at the empty shot glass. "Quiet, not smiling much. . ."

"Any ideas why?"

"I think the whole thing was getting to her. Sure, great money, but. . ."

"Women," Rex said, "and the kind of fucked up shit they pull."

"I know what you mean, Mr. Brunet."

"Of course, they're smart, too. Not like us."

"How do you mean?"

"Call me Rex, Tim. I've never met a woman who planned something like this who didn't have some sucker lined up to take the fall for her," Rex said. "You know what I mean?"

"I've seen some messed up shit, and yeah, there always seems to be a woman involved."

"I feel for the fucker who got taken by this bitch," Rex said, shaking his head. "One of your guys got a shot of leg and started feeling like a man. That's when she starts filling his head with the wrong ideas. Then she bolts and leaves the guy to face the music. We figure out who this guy is. Well, yeah, he's a moron, but no less than any of the rest us."

Tim bowed his head.

"It's a nice set up," Rex said, admiring his warehouse. "Air conditioning, heating. Someone always wants to place a bet, get a drink or play the tables after hours. I've always been proud of how well this place does. Takes work to keep something running like this. You know what the most important skill to do that is?"

"No, Rex, that's why you're the boss."

"It's knowing people, knowing what they did and what they're going to do next.

It doesn't matter how much money and clout if you can't see who's gonna fuck you over. You know what I mean?"

Tim nodded without looking up.

Rex urged, "Come on, Tim, you were banging her. I've heard this story way too many times. Own it; you got taken for a little pussy. You'll feel better." Rex glanced over Tim's shoulder.

"You're right, Mr. Brunet, I fucked up."

With two whispers, Tim slumped face down on the small table. Saul holstered the silenced automatic under his wrinkled warm up jacket.

"Got an address?"

"Yeah, Fidelity over on Corral. Found the card next to the computer, stupid bitch."

"Get someone over there."

"You think it was the Syrian?"

"Nah," Rex said, "Looks like she's scammed and ran."

"Yeah," Aaron said, "I got the details of the run here in the system." He mistyped the entry and the computer beeped in protest. "Just give me a second." His hands shook, as scarred stranger on the far side of the counter scowled.

"Get it!" Clancy said, rapping the plywood counter with the piece of rebar. "I ain't got all day."

"Just a second," Aaron said, as his uncertain fingers tapped the keyboard. "I think I got it."

The computer beeped again.

Clancy's eyes went dead as his rough face went slack. He brushed his dark, styled hair back from his pitted face. His black leather jacket rustled as he raised the piece of rebar over his head.

Aaron's brown eyes went wide. A rush of frigid air filled the office as the glass door burst open.

"Hi, Aaron, got another run for me?" Gabe said, brushing the sleet from his shoulders.

Clancy spun about to regard the newcomer blocking the doorway in his wet, yellow rain gear. The courier pulled his hood down revealing his long, sandy blond hair and a scruffy beard.

"Yeah, Gabe," Aaron said, "one just came in a few minutes ago."

"You pick up a delivery over on Joseph?" Clancy said. His thick fingers tightened around the piece of steel.

"I might have, but it's company policy not to talk about runs. Confidentiality." Gabe said.

"The people I work for don't care about company policy."

Gabe glanced over at Aaron, who gave a slight nod.

"Sure," Gabe said, "I had a run over there this morning. The lady turned over the parcel and I delivered it."

"You'd better come up with some details, asshole."

Details?" Gabe said, dropping his courier bag from his shoulder. "Sure no, problem. I picked up a load of cash and left. The lady got in her car and hauled ass. She's out of the state by now. Seemed like a big weight off her shoulders."

"So, where'd you drop the cash?"

"Hmm, let me think. . ." Gabe mused as he scratched his beard. "Oh, yeah, One Justice Plaza. Room Twelve A. Department of Human Services. They appreciated the donation to the Battered Women's Shelter."

Clancy's neck muscles tightened and he lifted the rebar.

"Consider your next move, Clarence Parsons," Gabe commanded as his voice dropped to an authoritative rumble. "What you do now will have repercussions for a very long time."

Clancy hesitated under the courier's cold, piercing gaze.

"When one inflicts violence upon his neighbors," Gabe said, "it is said that they will boil in the blood they spilt."

Clancy stared with a gaping mouth. Seconds passed; he slowly placed the jagged piece of steel on the counter and walked away, pale and shaken.

"Hey, Clancy," Gabe called after him, "that's just my take on things, but I'm just the messenger."

"Gabe," Aaron said, "I sure wish I could hire you on full-time."

Prof slumped on the stained couch in the lobby with his head tilted back, taking in the morning news from the tinny radio. J.J., the desk clerk in the sloppy flannel shirt, took mercy on Prof and switched the station from classic rock to the news channel. He planned to listen for half an hour or so, before the pundits and demagogues kicked in their daily two-cents. Right now, he needed news from the real world. The sleet, wind and rain compounded his mood, foul and bored.

The revolving door creaked out a turn. The thread-bare carpet muffled the tread of the workman boots.

"Yeah, sure," J.J. said, "he's over there."

The heavy steps stopped in front of Prof. He heard someone shift and rummage through a nylon bag. "John Clarke?" the man said.

"That's me," Prof said without changing position.

"Got a package for you, sign here."

Intrigued, Prof pulled himself from his sprawl and scribbled his signature. "I thought you fellas used those electronic things these days," he said and handed back the cold piece of aluminum.

"I reckon they do that at the fancier places," the courier said, placing a small box of embossed cardboard in Prof's hands.

Nestled in the velvet lining, Prof lifted out the fountain pen of metal and textured enamel. Weighing the solid heft of the pen in his palm, he asked, "Any idea who sent this?"

"Nah, I didn't get that, but there's a card in the box."

"Would you please?" Prof requested, passing the card back to the courier.

"Sure," the courier said. After clearing his throat, he recited, "'My Dearest Professor, some are called to bear the message and some are called to witness. Which one are you?'"

"Is there a name?"

"Nah, woman's handwriting, though," the courier said, handing the card to Prof.

"So, who—"

"Hey, I'm just the messenger," the courier cut him off and walked away.

Theo shuttled between the tables during the full-tilt lunch rush. His thin face bore the stress of success. Joey accommodated the diners at the bar, there not being much call for drinks at noon.

"Nice, Prof," Lou said and tore into his hamburger.

"Yes, it is," Prof said, holding the elegant pen. "I wanted to buy one like this for myself when I got my Masters, but money was kind of tight at the time."

"Prof," Joey said, "that's the kind of thing that you get as a gift, not buy for yourself."

"I suppose you're right, Theo," Prof said, tucking the pen back into his pocket.

"Any idea who sent it to you?" Lou asked, wiping his hand on his green work shirt.

"I got an idea, but it sounds crazy."

"Crazy?" Lou laughed. "Any man who drops twenty on the Knicks is crazy."

"It seemed like a promising idea, at the time."

"Kind of like hiring those two assclown brothers," Lou said. "I caught them trying to haul my plasma cutter out of the shop. Goddam meth heads."

"Never know what's going on in a man's head," Prof said, "until he acts on it."

"The game's on at eight," Lou said, hauling his girth from the barstool. "Are you in?"

"Already placed my bet."

"Let me guess—"

"Twenty. The Knicks," Prof admitted.

"Guess I know what's going on in your head," Lou said, heading for the door.

"You have no idea," Prof said.

On the other side of the café, Demetria picked at her salad niciose. Between the smart lunch and the run back to work, she hoped to burn a few calories. She liked The Night Café's ambience, but she didn't relish the dash through the cold, wet streets in her black vinyl jacket to the shop. Reyna's bright side philosophy just wasn't helping today.

"Mind if I share a table with you?" the man with the broad shoulders in the dark suit asked.

"Sure," Demetria said, "have a seat."

"Thanks," he replied as he eased into the seat. "Never liked eating at the bar."

"You're more than welcome," Demetria said. Professional haircut, polished wingtips and dark eyes all in one package, she noted and approved.

"So," he said, glancing her plate, "what are you having?"

"A salad."

"Rabbit food?" he said with a sour face. "You look like the kind of girl who'd enjoy a burger and fries, not that joyless compost."

"I would, but I got to keep the pounds off."

"Off where?" he asked wide-eyed, taking an exaggerated glance at her body. "You must have got a line of boys.. ."

"If it were only the case. I just never seem to get that second glance."

"If I was only ten years younger," he said, looking deep into her eyes, "I'd be lining up with the rest of the studs. If they don't give you the second look, sometimes you just got to grab them by the lapels and seize the night. You know carpe nocturnum."

Demetria blushed and looked away with a faint smile.

A blond-haired biker in faded riding denims swaggered through the door. Demetria's tablemate watched the man grab an empty stool at the bar. Glancing down at his gold wrist watch, he said, "As much as I'd like to stay, I got business downtown."

"But you just got here."

"Sorry to do this," he replied hurriedly, "but this is the least I can do." He snatched up Demetria's bill. "Save your money for that burger, sweetheart," he added with a grin and left.

On the table, a small crystal vial of gold liquid sat in front of Demetria. Picking it up, her first thought was to call him back to return it to her generous companion, but he disappeared out the door. It warmed her hands as she turned it over and watched the honey-like contents ooze from one end to the other. Looking deeper into the vial, flecks of light cascaded through the solution. Mesmerized, her pulse quickened. "Carpe Nocturnum," she whispered.

Jerome claimed his spot between the women's restroom and the row of battered vending machines in the grubby bus terminal. He watched the arrival boards and waited for his catch of the day. The icy, grime-covered bus ground to a halt, the doors opened with a hiss, and the exhausted passengers trundled off. He spotted her immediately.

The twelve-year-old in a baby blue ski jacket clung to the far wall as she clutched the straps of her pink backpack "Prime meat," he whispered to himself as he readied his smooth approach. He took a deep breath and eased forward to claim his prize. Then, "Shit…"

Out of the corner of his eye, he saw the heavy, black wool overcoat of Sergeant Serrano at the coffee stand. The Authority cops weren't shit, but Serrano—never mess with Serrano. Jerome stalled.

As if sensing Jerome's hesitation, a man in a yellow rain suit interceded and approached the bewildered girl. From his black nylon shoulder bag, the stranger handed a small box to her. She opened the box and stared. Her lip quivered and tears rolled down her face. The big man pulled back his hood, revealing his long blond hair. Dropping to one knee, he opened his arms and gave the girl a hug. Whispering in her ear, she pulled back and nodded in trust. Gently turning her around, he pointed out Serrano, drinking his coffee and perusing the sports page. She squared her shoulders, wiped her nose and shuffled over to the big cop.

The cop with friendly eyes put the paper down when he saw the little girl approach.

Looking down and shifting her feet, she spoke quietly. Serrano listened and nodded. In the end, he draped his large arm over the girl's shoulders and guided her out of the terminal.

With a faint smile, the courier watched the cop and the girl leave. The smile left his face when he stood and looked at Jerome.

"Jerome Merrick?" the courier addressed Jerome.

"Nobody calls me that, man," Jerome challenged.

"Sorry, my bad, I mean you're Slydog, right?"

"That's right."

"Great!" the courier said. "I got a message for you, if you'd please sign here." He handed Jerome a black box.

Jerome opened the box. Inside, a card rested atop the contents. The bright red, angry scrawl read:

Jerome, get out of town and find another line of work.

Love and Kisses,

The Original G

"What the fuck does this mean?" Jerome said, looking up from the gift box.

"Who knows, Slydog?" the courier said. "A man with your rep has probably pissed off a few people."

"You're fucking with me," Jerome accused, balling his fists.

"No Slydog, you got it all wrong. You're the apex of God's creations, but look what you did with it. Much as I would like to see your mouth filled with molten lead or walking in a ditch with the hide stripped from your back by rusty barbed wire, I'm just the messenger. Oh yeah, you didn't look at the rest of the package."

Jerome pulled the polished brass knuckles from the box.

"Neat!" the courier said. "I have one just like it."

Jerome caught the metallic flash across the courier's knuckles before everything went painfully black.

Theo inspected his dining room. The floors were mopped, the white linens were out for dinner service and the candles on the tables were lit. In the back, Joey checked in the liquor delivery. Lunch had been a full house. He'd been told countless times that opening a restaurant was the quickest route to bankruptcy by his parents, Joey's mom and the bankers, but the last couple of months of success provided him and Joey that spark of hope. It was too early for the dinner crowd and the pool players didn't hang around during the weekday. It would have a been a quiet afternoon, save for his only customers.

He glanced at the three men in booth in the far corner. Mr. Brunet and Mr. Reeve claimed the booth an hour ago. Grim-faced, they ran Theo ragged for beer and appetizers, all on tab, of course. Soon, a short, tubby man in silk suit and diamond cufflinks joined them. He sported a bandage on his face. This was one party Theo dared not upset.

The battered front door banged open and Prof shuffled in and grabbed a seat at the bar.

Theo winced and sighed. Saul Reeve was engrossed in the conversation and didn't notice the blind man's entrance. The peace was nice, but wouldn't last long.

Theo checked his watch again; he hoped his insurance policy would show up soon. Dad did tell him to protect his investment.

"What the fuck happened to your face, Sam?" Rex blurted as the chunky lawyer slid into the booth.

"This?" Sam said, pointing to the thick patch of gauze covering his right cheek. "This is what happens when you don't keep your wife in check."

"Rachel did that to you? I didn't think she had it in her."

"She almost took my eye with her nails."

"You did straighten her out, though?"

"No, she grabbed the kid and took off in the car."

"I can have some people look into it for you."

"I'd appreciate that, Rex. The good news just keeps getting better."

"All right, how about my money?"

"Without the lady who signed off on this," Sam said, "you're not going to get the money back anytime soon. Yeah, we can file, but it'll be at least nine months before we see any movement. On top of that, taking back money from a do-gooder organization never plays well. My advice is to write it off."

"Shit!"

"I made a couple of calls about this Syrian," Sam continued. "He's real and he's here."

"So, what can we expect?"

"He deals in stolen goods, fake branding and hijacking, and doesn't have any interests in the unions or gambling from what I can tell. I get the impression his crew is independent, no patronage."

"Easy enough. If he wants to set up shop, he's got to pay rent. No conflict of interest, from what you tell me. We all get paid."

"Worth a shot," Sam said, "however, don't push it on this one. He's got a bad rep."

"We've dealt with bad actors, before; they always back down with the right motivation."

"Rex, play it easy on this one. He likes fire and doesn't care who gets burned."

"I got plenty of firemen on the payroll. Arrange a meeting."

"And the last order of business," Sam said, looking directly at Saul, "the last act of a certain promising District Attorney is going to cause us some problems."

"I didn't have anything to do with Ritter," asserted Saul; his hand gripped his beer bottle.

"Never said you did, Saul, but it turns out he called for some outside help. Adams is pissed."

"So, what does this mean for us?" Rex demanded, focusing on Sam's jowly countenance.

Sullenly, Saul scanned the near-empty bar. Joey, the soft boy bartender, engaged in quiet conversation with that drunk fuck from a few weeks ago. Saul's blood boiled as he slid out of the booth, unnoticed by Rex and Sam, and sauntered over to the bar.

"No," Prof told the young bartender, "you don't get it. The Greeks believed that everyone had a destiny and if you avoided it, well…everything turns to shit."

"I read Plato and some Aristotle," Joey replied. "I really didn't pick that up."

"You see it more in the dramas," Prof explained. "Try Euripides or Sophocles."

"You boys having fun playing with yourselves?" Saul interjected cheerfully with a slap to Prof's back.

"Not really," the man in the faded blue oxford shirt said. "Just discussing the finer points of classical Greek philosophy. Not something that you'd be interested in."

"You know what I'm interested in?" Saul asked.

"Not really..."

"I'm gonna tell you, anyway. I'm interested in why a blind, alky freak that lost his job is still showing up here when I told him to get lost."

Prof turned to face Saul.

"Oh yeah," Saul elaborated, "I asked around about you. Heard you couldn't hack it, even spent time in the looney bin. So, why the fuck are you here?"

Prof smiled. "'Cause it's a free country."

Saul slammed his long neck bottle into Prof's temple. Prof crashed off his barstool and slid down the front of the black bar.

Strong hands grabbed the collar of Saul's jacket and the waistline of his pants. Almost weightless, Saul's feet barely touched the floor as he crashed through the front doors and into the street. Pivoting, Saul charged back through the doorway only to run head-long into the giant with crossed arms.

"Sorry," the man with long, blond hair stated, "the owners of this establishment find your behavior unacceptable. Please do not come back." He closed the door in Saul's face.

Rex rushed into the center of the uproar. The young man in the faded denim vest turned to regard him.

"That was my friend, you piece of shit!" Rex growled, his finger poking the solid muscle of the biker's chest. "Do you know who I am?"

"Yes," the biker spoke, "you are Rex Brunet. He is Sam Cavanaugh and that is Saul Reeve." He nodded to Saul, scowling outside.

"So, you know what you're doing is a mistake, right?"

"Depends on the way you are looking at it," Gabe replied.

"Just so you know how bad this is going to go—"

"Look, I am off-duty," Gabe sighed. "As much as I'd enjoy delivering the message, I got better things to do." Gabe opened the door for Rex and

Sam and said, "Gentleman, management reserves the right to refuse service."

Without protest, Rex and Sam joined Saul on the sidewalk.

Before closing the door, Gabe said, "And boys, I may not be here every night, but you'll never know which nights I am here." The door slammed shut.

"So, I take it you accept the offer," said Theo while wiping his hands.

"Looks that way," Gabe replied.

He crossed the foyer to the bar, where Joey held a bag of ice wrapped in dish towels to Prof's head. "You're determined to go looking for trouble, Prof," he observed.

Prof shrugged his shoulders and sighed.

Spotting the small corner stage in the back, Gabe called out, "Hey Theo, you have live music in here?"

"Only on Friday and Saturday nights," Theo replied. "Just a couple of college kids playing jazz."

"Do you know if they need a horn section?" Gabe asked.

Personal Business

10:30 PM February 14th
Nighthawk's Dinner
123 Cedars St.

Prof scraped the last of his apple pie à la mode from the plate. By middle of the month, he'd dropped small pleasures like dessert from his budget, but Jane treated him to dessert for a few moments of conversation. Tonight, few chose the grubby little diner as patrons sought more romantic dining options. He noted she paid a lot of attention to the only other diner. He wished the witty young grad student all the distractions she could handle. He listened to her story of Rich, the cheating boyfriend, but he only commiserated. His own romantic track record put him in no position to offer her advice. When she started talking about the grant refusal though, he perked up. Here, he could be some help.

"Failing is part of the game, Jane," Prof said. "The only way to learn is to screw up."

"But I put so much work into it and it got trashed."

"You've got the knowledge," Prof said, taking a drink of coffee. "Take down the structure, rearrange, redirect and build a new argument. Sometimes you have to tear down to build up."

"Thanks, Prof," the curly-haired brunette said. "Does it ever get any easier?"

"Not really, but if it is something you love, the fight is always worth it. Can I get a cup to go?"

"Sure," she said. "After all of the free advice, I ought to be paying for your dinner."

"You know, I really don't know what my advice is worth, considering my current situation."

"Any advice at this point is welcomed."

"Well, if I were to give you one piece of advice I could guarantee, I'd say take a chance."

"What?"

He nodded to the only other customer at the far end of the diner.

Jane blushed. "Prof, you're just trying to get me in trouble."

"A little trouble isn't such an undesirable thing from time to time. Happy Valentines' Day."

The harsh fluorescent light glared upon gold and green of vinyl booths. Save for the hiss of the grill and the clatter of plates, the diner was quiet. At the other end of the gleaming black Formica counter, the unkempt blind man adjusted his long, beige rain coat and seized his white cane. Pausing on his way to the door, he smirked at Vic. He tottered out into the wintry night, shaking his head as if enjoying some personal joke.

Vic checked his watch, again; he needed to leave soon, too. He picked up the paper with a rustle. The headline of the late edition read:

Fifth Body Found in Canal! Blood Killer Strikes, Again!

What was it with Americans? Such a strange folk. They devoured such carnage in the news and their entertainment, yet turned pale at the thought of staining their hands with real blood. The Russians and the Saudis were crude, but they never minced words. He smiled, recalling the farce which had passed for a negotiation earlier.

In the dim conference room of the firm's empty penthouse office, he'd met with the two young warlords in Brooks Brothers suits.

"This is highly irregular," the sweaty little man uttered. "I don't feel comfortable with this."

"What's the problem?" Vic said, gazing out the panoramic window. The fortresses of glass and steel glittered before him. "Great view, by the way," he added, enjoying a chance to show off. His English flowed out flat and perfect. All the time watching his movies paid dividends.

"You understand our corporation has certain foreign investments," the tall, blond-haired one said. "We need discretion. Our company has an image to uphold globally." His solemn gray eyes almost convinced Vic of his conviction.

Get on with it, Vic thought.

"Our stock price lives and dies by how the public perceives us."

"I see," Vic said and turned to regard the man in the polished wingtips. "You'd be surprised how similar your demands are to those of my typical clientele. Like you, they all desire discretion."

"Yes," the short one interjected while mopping his brow with a clean handkerchief, "but this is so unorthodox and carries substantial risk."

"Friends, you're risking your entire investment. If the situation sours, the opposing party conquers and your capital is plundered. The risk already crouches at your gate. A near, dear friend of mine once told me, 'Fortune favors the brave.'" Vic said and paused. He weighed the mettle of these warriors and asked, "Well, gentlemen, I ask you, do you have the nerve to seize the fortune for yourselves?"

The two executives pondered that for a mere second before both shook Vic's hand.

It was almost eleven and Vic was that much richer for an hour of work. With a couple of emails, an international wire transfer, and one phone call, he would prime the terrible engines once again. He sighed; this sort of thing used to be glamorous. The diner seemed a good place to wait out the next item on his agenda. He wasn't that hungry anyway.

"More coffee, Sir?" she asked with a smile.

A cigarette butt floated in the cup of brackish coffee; no way had she missed that.

"No, thanks," he said back and shot her a bright smile. "By the way, you can call me Vic...Vic Teppish." He winced. It was a lame alias, but the other three or four I.D.s in his battered, black flight bag had to last him.

"Well, Vic," she said and brushed a stray strand of hair from her face, "are you in town on business or pleasure?"

"Business," he said. His facade faltered slightly. "You know...road warrior."

"Ever been in town before?"

"A couple of times," he lied. “I actually spend more time abroad.”

“Really?” she said, leaning in. “Where’ve you been?”

“Most the time, I’m in Europe, but I have had to make a few side trips to Africa, Near East, Turkey—”

“Turkey! I’m writing my thesis on Mehmed the Second’s influence on modern Turkish culture.”

“Chucklehead,” Vic spat, “and pile of worthless poetry to boot.”

“Pardon?”

“Uh, nothing. I didn’t care for Turkey,” Vic said. “It was just an all-around unpleasant experience. Lousy food, filthy accommodations and rude hosts. Anyway, so what do you do when you’re not writing about old Turks?”

“You mean when I’m not here,” she said with a shy laugh, “serving aid and comfort to the fine citizenry of this great metropolis?”

“I figured you were out teaching the lame and healing at Sunday school,” Vic countered with a chuckle.

“Shows what you know about women, Mr. Teppish,” she said and smoothed her skirt. “Maybe I like to hit the after-hours jazz clubs or catch a midnight movie.”

“Smoke-filled dens of iniquity, populated by sinners with their vices. What’s a nice girl like you doing hanging out in places like that?”

Her voice lowered to a sultry whisper. “I’m just looking for the right kind of sinner.”

“And I don’t have your drink order, let alone your name.”

"Jane," she said, and pointed to her nametag. "Didn't your mother ever teach you it was good manners to know who your servers are?"

"Unfortunately, no, Jane," Vic said with a smirk. "I was raised by wolves."

"Poor dear," she cooed. "If you stick around, I might just teach you some manners."

Vic glanced down at his watch. "I'd love to, Jane," he said, "but I have to take a meeting. Do you know where Azell Street is?"

"Sure, it's near the college, but I wouldn't go there after dark."

"Yeah," Vic replied, assured this would put her off.

"Well, I get off in twenty minutes, I could show you the way."

"Great," Vic lied, as he pulled a twenty from his overstuffed wallet. "Would you get my check, please?"

"Sure thing," she said as she took the twenty and walked back to the register. He watched her lithe figure move her red and white checkered uniform like an evening gown. Wits, smile and charm—she had all three.

His smile turned wistful. He wanted to see her in that little black cocktail dress and those new shoes that she was thinking of. Resolved, he rose from his stool.

"Here you go, Mr. Tepp—" her words trailed off as their eyes locked. Gently, he slipped into her mind.

"Jane," he whispered as the back of his hand brushed her soft cheek, "forget about me."

"I forget you," she murmured as her hazel eyes stared vacantly into his.

"Good, good," Vic praised her and slid the one-hundred-dollar bill into her apron pocket. "Now, sleep." He brushed his fingers over her eyes.

In the cool night air, the blue sedan crouched in the humming yellow light of the street lamp. Four thousand dollars bought transportation—reliable, nondescript, and disposable. He picked up the hardtop last night from a car lot he'd never see again. True, a stolen car would save cash, but he hated thieves. The car protested as he keyed the ignition.

He shook his head and grinned; he realized he just pulled off a perfect Bogie moment back in the diner. He knew the large-headed actor with a lisp would have played the scene the same way with Lauren or Ingrid. The man with the troubled past gives the dame the brush-off to protect her because he didn't get personal with anyone anymore.

The sterile business district yielded to the expressway; the world transformed to a blaze of city lights. Vic always enjoyed driving this way—the speed, the wind, and the buzz of the engine. He almost wished he'd chosen that cheap convertible instead of the sedan; it felt closer to galloping a good horse. He guided the car down the off-ramp onto a road lined with buckled fences and trash cans. "Back to work," he thought as he eased the car to a deliberate crawl.

The thumping bass of a radio nearby rattled the doors and windows. The car knocked and sputtered as he killed the engine. As an afterthought, he grabbed the nylon flight bag. Sure, he could replace most of the stuff, but the electric shaver made his evenings less complicated. Brushing a bit of lint off his suit, Vic realized he'd overdressed, yet the local kids eyed the car and ignored him. The car would disappear long before any trouble started.

Under the few working streetlights, the dumpy row houses loomed large. A pistol shot echoed in the distance, more of a pop than a crack. Vic guessed it was .25 caliber, at best. At least the amateur chose the right neighborhood to do his business; places like this never have witnesses.

He found the house; he didn't know how. Over the years, Vic hypothesized theories of why's and how's, none of them rational or scientific. The cold rush just went up his spine. The closest to an explanation he got was from an ancient hunter in the German forests.

"A wolf knows another wolf's lair," the old man had said with a feral grin. His iron gray hair was tangled and full of burrs. Vic remembered him as if it were yesterday. For three nights, Vic stalked the man through the majestic forests. Just as soon as he thought he had cornered him, the old man slipped into the curtain of evergreens. On the fourth night, Vic finally caught up with the wiry thin man in worn hunting leathers sitting on a stump in an old clearing. The old man let out a belly laugh. He'd watched

Vic blunder through the thick undergrowth for an hour. Vic and the hunter spent that final evening around a fire trading stories.

"*Just another fading memory,*" Vic thought and wondered what happened to the wily old hunter. After the World Wars, he returned to the forests, now meticulously managed. He never sensed the old man, again. Now, Vic crossed the weedy postage-stamp lawn and climbed the crumbling brick steps. When the owner had bought the house, the neighborhood was the place to be. Now, only an experienced eye discerned that this locale had glory days, long ago. He knocked on the door.

"Can I help you?" asked a youth with flowing locks.

Vic peered into this boy's mind. His name was Etienne and he served his master. That single thought replayed as an endless loop in the youth's psyche.

Vic worked his will upon this man-child's crippled intellect and said, "I'm looking for him. Could I come in and wait? You are taking care of his house, correct?"

"Yes," the doe-eyed youth said, "yes, of course." He stepped back from the door to let Vic in. He looked as if he'd just received First Communion in his fresh, white poet's shirt, save for the black leather pants.

With the age-old protocols satisfied, Vic grabbed Etienne's delicate lower jaw and flexed his wrist. After the loud snap, the minion dropped to the floor. As he crossed the threshold unimpeded, Vic felt nothing; he detested these little jackals.

Vic closed the front door and cased the inside of the house. The walnut paneling, crown molding and impressionist paintings clashed with the dilapidated exterior. He considered the problem lying on the floor at his feet; unfortunately, minions didn't disintegrate like their masters. Down the hall, he spied an open door with stairs.

"I'm getting too old for this nonsense," Vic muttered and heaved Etienne over his shoulder.

As he expected, the rot always started in the bottom of the barrel. At the bottom of the rickety staircase, he flicked the light switch to gauge the damage. In the arid light of the incandescent bulb, Vic surveyed the charnel house that was the master's playroom.

They had hung her from the joists with barbwire. Naked, of course, the femoral arteries slit to drain her blood into the pan beneath her feet. Her nipples gnawed off and her eyes gouged. Angry, red welts crisscrossed her body, and her sex had been ripped out by God knows what. Pretty, at one time, now, she was dead, but not by much, and not slowly.

In the corner, an altar of black wood squatted in the dust, covered in the wax of many candles. Vic recognized the decaying grimoires and occult texts on the rough shelf behind the altar. A sweet, lilac smell pervaded his senses. The amateur kept souvenirs of his games, rotting behind the loose bricks in the wall. Yes, he'd ventured down this road, too, once upon a time, but it hadn't consumed him like this.

Back upstairs, Vic found the study plastered with royal blue velvet wallpaper hung with sinister tapestries and lined with shelves of leather bound books. "Just another peacock with delusions of grandeur," he appraised with a shrug.

Out of habit, he gazed over the titles of the books, most of them never opened. He didn't judge on that point, for in his youth, he considered reading foolish, too. He spotted a familiar yellowish volume, the only book that had been well-thumbed through. Of course, it was the first edition from Archibald Constable and Co.

Shaking his head, he remembered befriending the theater manager long ago. Smart and charming, the Irishman had explained all the modern wonders to Vic, like typewriters and phonographs. One night, Vic erred by revealing to his friend that his new science failed to explain many old realities. Places reversed, Vic understood why the young fellow betrayed him. Bram earned respect from likes of Wilde, Whistler and Irving, but Vic paid by cleaning up the consequences of that lapse in judgement ever since.

He helped himself to a glass of bourbon as he sank into the burgundy leather wingback chair in front of the granite hearth. He couldn't drink, but still enjoyed the complex layers of aroma from the crystal tumbler. At least this fool didn’t stock up on that nasty Tokay like the others. For once, he hoped for a Plan A situation.

Plan A consisted of trying to reason with the amateur. Vic always tried Plan A because if it ever came to this, he hoped someone would reason with him. It never worked that way; they always chose Plan B, but he still maintained hope.

"Etienne!" the master boomed. The sound of his boot steps stormed down the hall. "Where in God's name are you?"

"Sorry, Dumere, Etienne won't be joining us this evening," Vic said. “He had an accident." He put down the glass and pulled himself to his feet.

The pale, gaunt man with slick dark hair paused. His tailored black suit shone in the firelight; the dark fires raged in his eyes. "You've certainly got a fool's courage."

"Regardless," Vic said, peering at the tapestry inscribed with blood red Cabalistic icons, "I am here and we need to talk… By the way the symbol in corner is inverted and reversed.”

"Arrogant and irreverent! You have no idea who I am, nor what I am, let alone what I can do.”

"You’re Xavier Dumere," Vic said. They always wanted the ego stroke first.

Dumere cocked one of his pencil-thin black eyebrows.

"One of Her Majesty's Select Guard and one of her lovers, before the revolution and before you died. You've tried to impersonate aristocracy on several occasions and fell flat on your face each time," Vic concluded. "I know exactly what you are. As for what you can do, well, that remains to be seen."

"Very good," Dumere said. "It's tragic you will never be able to share your observations with another."

His dark eyes locked on Vic’s. He felt the icy force of Dumere’s mind bore into his. Vic allowed him access, for knowledge leads to wisdom sometimes.

Dumere's eyes jerked wide. "You're, you're—" he stammered and stepped back.

"That's right, Dumere, I am."

"I've looked so long," he fumbled. "I never thought—Why do seek me out now?"

"Because, Dumere, you're an amateur and what's more, you're sloppy, very sloppy."

"Who are you to judge me?" Dumere roared, slapping his chest. "I survive two centuries on my own, and you appear from nowhere to tell me I broke one of your damned rules!"

"No, there aren't any rules for our type, only survival. Your actions here threaten my survival."

"My sacrifices came from the lowest common stock. They will not be missed."

"Dumere, your plan is already headed south. You made a name for yourself in the local press. Let's face it; you've done a lousy job covering your tracks over the years. All it's going to take is one smart guy with a computer to play connect the dots."

"And if they do?" Dumere glowered. "We are creatures of the night and nigh unstoppable."

"You just don't get it, do you? This isn't the old days. They'll catch you, dissect you and study everything about you," Vic countered. "After that, well, they never needed much prodding to commit genocide."

"You lost your nerve, old one."

Plan B, Vic thought, and swept the sawed-off shotgun from beneath his trench coat. He blasted Dumere in the gut with two barrels of buckshot.

Dumere slammed into the wall and crumpled. Vic hoped he shattered Dumere's spinal column; otherwise, this would get complicated. Injuries regenerate, nerve tissue just takes longer. He had about twenty minutes before Dumere would be trouble again. Enough time for him to finish the job.

He dragged Dumere down to the basement and dropped him next to Etienne's corpse. If his mood were lighter, he would have paused for a moment and quipped, "all in a night's work." He didn't.

Squatting over Dumere, he popped the cuff button on his shirt and speared his hand into Dumere's midsection, just under the breast bone. Feeling around, he grabbed the meaty fist-sized ball and yanked. The heart blood rained down upon Dumere's black shirt as Vic squeezed it dry. Finished, he dropped the clump of crimson meat on Dumere's chest. The body collapsed into a heap of fine gray ash, leaving only Dumere's exquisite black suit.

"Sorry, Dumere," Vic whispered, "I really tried."

He considered burning the place down, but discarded the idea as too much trouble. With one last glance at the basement's carnage, he wondered if this would be the way it played out for him.

Pulling on his coat, he climbed the creaking stairs out of the basement. Sure, most of the monsters showed their colors the moment they changed. His niece, Erzsebet, amidst the corpses of all those young girls, covered in their blood, had lost control immediately. On the other hand, Dumere's slow burn lasted a century. He finally snapped in London, a decade before Vic caught wind of his exploits. He figured there weren't many older than him left, even the old German hunter disappeared. Time was the greatest predator of all.

Vic hesitated on the porch as the rosy fringes of dawn crept upon the horizon.

He remembered the last time he bought a laptop and the salesman explained the concept of managed obsolescence. Everything carries a shelf life and when he went out of date, it would be a problem. To light a smoke and let the sun take him sounded like a simple solution. Fumbling in his pocket, he pulled out the crumpled piece of paper, the bill from the diner, which read on the back:

666-555-1626

Call me!

Jane

He smiled. It was worth a shot, take the risk one more time and get personal. The horizon lightened even more. How long has it been since he raced the dawn home? "Too long!" he answered himself. His leathery wings swept towards the pinkening sky.

Successful Interview Techniques

7 AM March 15th
Courthouse Annex Bldg.
1 Justice Plaza

Jerry regarded the man in black glasses and rumpled jacket. He sat next to the only vacant, rigid plastic bus seat and his hand clutched Styrofoam cup filled with black, tepid coffee. *At least he's not a panhandler,* Jerry observed as he took his seat next to the man.

It was early; his stomach churned in anticipation. Jerry shifted his feet as the bus rumbled from stop to stop.

"Nervous?" the man said, looking straight ahead.

"Yeah," Jerry said, removing his gold-framed glasses and wiping the lenses with the small soft cloth. "Up for a promotion at work."

"That's always good," the man said. "At least, it shows they recognize your contributions."

"Certainly, hope so. Been busting hump since I graduated."

"How long?"

"About three years."

"Still early in the game for you," the man said. "Keep your head down, your mouth shut, and you'll go far."

"How about you?"

"I neither kept my head down, nor my mouth shut. Now I am going as far as the Social Services offices to talk with my caseworker."

The bus slowed to a quaking stop; the doors hissed open.

"My stop, pardon me," the man said, sliding past Jerry. "Good luck."

"Thanks," said Jerry, as he watched the man exit the bus.

In the men's room, the ventilator fan rattled away. Prof pulled the flask of rum from his coat pocket and unscrewed the plastic cap.

Are you sure this is what you want to do, Prof? the voice said. The scent of saffron overpowered the bland commercial air freshener.

He replaced the cap on the bottle and whispered, "Who are you, my conscience?"

"*No, Prof. You should know better than that by now.*"

Exiting the bathroom, he thought he was ready to face this quarterly review. The last three months on his own almost washed away the fear, loss and shame, but the weight dropped upon his shoulders the moment he crossed the threshold of the chattering waiting room. He knew the other clients by experience. The new ones huddled in the corners, arms and legs crossed and looking straight ahead. Others eyed the intake desk with their stacks of files in their laps, ready to impress the caseworker with their progress. Finally, the long-termers slumped and studied their shoes. Prof shuffled down the row of rigid plastic seats, adrift on a sea of institutionalized despair.

"Pardon," he said, maneuvering past one of the long-termers to take his seat.

"S'okay, man," the long-termer muttered. Prof's nose wrinkled from the man's sour, unwashed smell and envisioned an unshaven man in a worn army field jacket in need of a haircut.

The voice chided, "*Perhaps he's just a mirror.*"

"Hush!" Prof whispered. The quiet murmurs reminded Prof that he'd called attention to himself again.

After a few uncomfortable minutes, the receptionist called, "Mr. Clarke? Mr. John Clarke? Please proceed to room B to see Ms. Tate."

Mary Tate tucked the face sheet back into the client's file. She committed his details to memory: caucasian male, thirty-five years old, graduate education, unemployed, divorced, suffering from Conversion Order blindness precipitated by emotional trauma and hospitalized for five weeks. Sad, but typical; she wondered what made this patient so special.

The door opened and the man with slumped shoulders reached into her office.

"Good morning, Mr. Clarke," Mary said, rising from her office chair to lead him to the interview seat.

"Thank you, ma'am," he said, easing into the steel chair beside her desk.

"Okay, Mr. Clarke, this is your quarterly review. I need to assess your well-being, progress and capacity to care for yourself. Do you understand?"

The man nodded behind his dark glasses. He wore a wrinkled grey overcoat covered in lint, but at least he had shaved and attempted to comb his graying hair.

"You understand, Mr. Clarke, that your living stipend depends on two things: one, you are participating in your weekly treatment program, and two, you do so drug and alcohol free."

"Sure do, Ms. Tate," Prof said. "I do everything I'm told to do..."

"Any progress?"

"I'm not sure what qualifies as progress in this case. I mean, I go to the Counseling Center once a week and do the computer classes there. I listen to every book on tape that they loan me and I work with the advanced therapy equipment on my own time."

"Advanced therapy equipment?"

With a grin, he pulled back the left sleeve of his coat to reveal the large, red rubber band around his wrist and said, "I'm supposed to pop this when I start thinking a critical thought." He drew back the rubber band and continued, "For example, the third *Godfather* movie is so over-rated." He let the rubber band snap back against his wrist.

"Oh," she said with a laugh. "You do realize they meant self-critical thoughts, don't you?"

"Yes, I just want to make sure I get them all."

"That brings us to the question about drugs and alcohol."

"You give me a living stipend, right? I can eat for a month and have a roof over my head, or I can go party for a couple of days," he said with a shrug. "I prefer to stay out of the cold, so no, I don't do either."

"You know I can have you tested at any time, correct?" She waited for the break in his façade.

"Sure, you want me to pee in a cup or is this a blood collection?"

"We don't do that here," she said, satisfied with his response. "I'm required to inform you. State law."

"Okay, anything else?"

"No, Mr. Clarke," she said, "that will be all. We will need to meet again in three months. Just make an appointment with the receptionist on your way out."

"Well, Ms. Tate, I will take my leave. Thank you and have a wonderful day."

"You, too, Mr. Clarke," Mary said, penning her notes. *3/15 Client displays no apparent flagged behavior,* she scribbled, *however, he appears too well-adjusted for personal circumstances. Recommend further observation. M.T.* She slipped her note back into his tagged file. If this was all a front, he'd slip up; Mary knew all clients revealed their shortcomings in the end. She still puzzled over why this client warranted further scrutiny, but her promotion depended on watching the selected clients. Looking up at the hinged gold-framed pictures of Joe and Joe Junior on her desk, she smiled; the promotion promised to make their lives better.

In the hallway, the voice whispered in Prof's ear, "*I'm so proud of you! You handled that so well.*"

"Shhh! Not in here," Prof said under his breath on his way out the door.

Kenneth sat in the sterile conference room, scratching his pen on the yellow legal pad. He watched the closed door for the oncoming tempest. Judge Adams retired a year before Kenneth joined the DA's Office, but he'd heard all the stories. No longer a terror on the bench, Adams stormed the halls of the courthouse as a consultant. Soon, Kenneth learned to recognize the signs; the closing of doors, fervent typing and hushed tones. Now he understood the cold sweats and pale faces of his predecessors. Last year, he'd inherited the liaison duty to Adams. Within minutes, he expected to witness a clash of egos of monumental proportions.

"Good morning, O'Brien," the Judge said. He placed his tan overcoat on the tree along with his hat, and straightened the jacket of his dark blue three-piece suit. After checking his ancient, gold pocket watch, he continued. "Much to do I see." He strode to the head of the white table and set down his worn leather brief bag.

"Good morning, Judge Adams."

"No jacket, this morning?" Judge Adams said, glancing up from his neat stacks of paperwork.

"No, your Honor, I left it in my office. I didn't want it wrinkled."

"Fair enough, I can respect fastidiousness."

With a dry mouth, Kenneth waited as the bald little hawkish man reviewed his agenda notes. After the long, silent inspection, Judge Adams set the file down and said, "I see that young Ritter invited outside assistance."

"We found the request while cleaning out his files; he must have done this before the…accident."

"Of course, he did," the judge said, "and he did so through the required channels. I expected nothing less; he was an excellent young lawyer. This should have been brought to my attention earlier. I could have stopped this."

"I understand, but when something like this happens you expect some oversights."

"I do not," Adams said. "In fact, the very idea that you anticipate disorganization troubles me, O'Brien." His sharp, blue eyes focused on

Kenneth. "I am most disappointed in how this city has been run since I left office," the judge continued. "Thugs preying on honest citizens and now this…Syrian. Vagrants in the mercantile district. A city only survives when the laws are enforced. As far as I can see, this is not being done here."

Kenneth swallowed hard.

"Mr. O'Brien," Adams said, his features softening, "I do not hold you accountable. You are only a small cog in the machine. With your help, we can get it running correctly again."

"Certainly, your Honor," Kenneth said. He relaxed, only slightly.

"So, has Agent Jones been properly accommodated?"

"Yes," Kenneth said. He avoided giving the Judge extraneous information. Jones' low-key arrival a couple of days before Christmas seemed routine, but by the beginning of the new year, the purposeful agent had laid claim to an office bay on the third floor. Over the following weeks, the smooth, amiable man requested and secured interviews and files from the various city offices with ease. He answered only to his superiors in Washington.

"Now, this Special Agent Jones has been brought into assist us in bringing order to the city. He has brought some of his own…personnel, but he has requested more manpower for his task force, correct?"

"Yes," Kenneth said, "we posted the opening a couple of weeks ago. I advised my people not to go anywhere near it."

"A prudent decision, Mr. O'Brien. Your office will be busy enough with the consequences. I do not want you to sacrifice your people. So, has Jones made his choices?"

"Only one, some kid working in the Vault."

"Really?" Judge Adams said. "City Planning? I usually do not have much to worry about down there. It is a well-run department."

The three men in dark serious suits entered the conference room.

"Judge Adams," the one in the lead said, extending his hand, "I've heard so much about you." His chiseled features bore a shark-like grin.

"And I, you," Judge Adams said. His bony hand returned Jones' vise-like handshake with equal force. "Please be seated."

The newcomers took their seats; none carried notebooks or pens.

"For the record," Judge Adams said, "I find all of this highly irregular. I also find your methodologies distasteful."

"Yet," Jones said, "all of the protocols that summoned us here have been observed correctly. Do you agree?"

"Unfortunately, yes."

"Your ADA requested our aid. You have a problem and he requested our help. As distasteful as it may seem, we are the solution."

"Had I known earlier," Adams said, "you would not have been an option. However, process must be respected."

"Then please let me introduce my field team," Jones offered. "This is Agent Erskine and Agent Rhodes. They form the spearhead of this joint task force." He gestured to his identically dressed associates. The youthful Rhodes clasped his hands and peered around the table while experienced Erskine leaned back, rubbing his chin as if calculating the possible outcomes. Both reeked of the same air of superiority that surrounded their boss.

"From Washington, I assume," Judge Adams snapped while glaring at Jones, "like you?"

"Of course," Jones said with a chuckle, "from…Washington. I selected them personally for this investigation."

"So, with these experienced professionals," the judge said, "why would you need to pull personnel from our staff?"

"You know, the usual reasons, your Honor. I need the eyes and ears of a local, an insider. I only need one to be effective and efficient, so the drain on your resources will be minimal. It would be in everyone's best interests that we get the job done quickly."

"You have settled on this young man," the judge said with personnel file in hand. "I just spoke with his supervisor and she had several optimal candidates."

"I like this one. Women are excellent, but their priorities are different. This one is young and ambitious. I like them hungry."

"I see. You understand all standard operation parameters will be enforced? By that, I mean no innocent blood will be spilled."

"Of course, Your Honor, there will be no civilian endangerment. After all, we're here for the perpetrators."

"I will leave you to your candidate," said Judge Adams. He gathered his accoutrements and left the room with Kenneth.

"Funny thing is," Jones said after the door closed, "when you come right down to it, they're all perps in one way or another."

Erskine and Rhodes smiled in unison.

Jerry Sawney tapped the toe of his polished wingtip as he sat on the bench outside the conference room. Half an hour earlier, Janet, his supervisor had tapped him on the shoulder and told him they were ready for him upstairs. Leaving his cubicle of vendor invoices and spreadsheets, he followed her out of the basement office of City Planning.

"Just so you know, Jerry," she said at the breakroom doorway, "there are other candidates who really needed this opportunity." She rejoined Lisa and Monique, her other employees, in the breakroom.

Finally, Kenneth O'Brien, the paunchy ADA in a tie and shirtsleeves, left the conference room with Judge Adams, speaking in hushed tones. O'Brien gave a quick nod to Jerry and hurried down the hall to keep up with the judge.

Jerry readied himself and stepped into the doorway.

"C'mon in, Jerry!" the large man said.

"Thank you, sir," Jerry said with as much confidence as he could muster.

"No need to stand on formalities here. My name is Bill Jones. Just call me Bill." He offered his hand across the table.

"Thanks, Bill," said Jerry as he vigorously shook Jones' well-manicured hand.

"Have a seat and let's get started."

Jerry took his seat in front of the three clean-shaven men in sharp suits. Jones pored over Jerry's one-page resume while the two men flanking Jones formulated their own assessments with hard stares.

"Three years in City Planning, good annual reviews and a master's degree in accounting," Jones commented. "Nice! You look good on paper, Jerry. The question is: are you ready for the big show?"

"I am ready to do whatever it takes."

"I don't know," Rhodes said, "you got the credentials, but no law enforcement experience. This might be the deep end of the pool for you."

"Jim," Erskine said. "Granted, he hasn't gone to the Academy. But I think he's just what we need in this situation. He grew up here and he knows the city. Besides, you got to start somewhere. Hey, your recruitment wasn't much different than his."

"Point taken, Lew."

"Guys," Jones interceded, "let Jerry speak for himself."

"Look," Jerry shot back, "I don't have law enforcement experience, but you say you need someone who knows the city. I grew up here, I went to school here and I work here. I'm a quick learner. Hell, I straightened out five years of payables in three weeks. I got no problems working long hours. I just want the chance…" His voice trailed off.

A moment passed. Jones' stare broke into a grin. "Well, boys," he said, "I don't know about you, but I am willing to give Jerry the chance he wants."

"I guess some on-the-job training will get him up to snuff," Rhodes said.

"Now, this is where the work begins," Jones said. "You'll start out working the books for us, expenses, informant payments, and the usual. Eventually, we may have some field work for you. I won't kid you, Jerry. The city is screwed up. Bad cops, dopers, thugs, but the worst problem is this."

Jones reached into his breast pocket and placed a small glass vial filled with a honey-colored liquid on the table.

"What is it?" Jerry asked, examining the vial.

"A new synthetic," Jones continued, "worse than meth, coke or heroin put together. Easy to manufacture, taken orally and doesn't show up on drug screens. It brings out the worst in people."

"That bad, huh?"

"That it is," Jones said. "I am going to need a dedicated man to take care of this problem. Someone who is willing to make sacrifices."

"I'm your man."

"I thought as much," said Jones. "Look, take the rest of the day off and start fresh tomorrow."

"Thanks, Bill," Jerry said. He shook hands with all three and left the room.

Jones looked down at the conference room table and smirked.

The vial was no longer there.

A Taste of Corruption

7:45 AM March 16th
456 Bianchi St.

Silvery motes of dust danced in the sunlight above Mary's defiled body. Face down and naked, the supple curve of her back was now angry red tatters of flesh revealing her spine and rib cage. Beautiful last night, now she was a pile of steaming meat. Jerry sprawled on the stained mattress next to her. His wrinkled dress shirt chafed his skin and he inhaled the ammonia smell of urine. His empty stomach heaved in vain; the nausea was back. She was the second Mary he had met the night before.

Sitting up, his joints creaked in rebellion. From his vantage, the abandoned store, devoid of furniture and covered in gritty dust, appeared cavernous. Thin beams of weak sunlight poked through the boards covering the windows. The empty vial glittered against the green linoleum floor. He scrambled for it until he saw his hands and nails, purplish black and the skin greenish-gray with oozing sores. It brought the nightmare into clear, cold focus.

Jerry left the interview with Jones exhausted and elated. He mulled over going down to the Vault to move his personal stuff upstairs, but decided against it. The barrage of two-edged questions from Janet and the girls could wait until tomorrow. He took the main elevator down and sped through the cathedral-like atrium of the courthouse, pleased to avoid any unnecessary confrontations.

Out in the chilly noon street, he considered the possibilities. He considered returning to his studio apartment and doing the usual: zoning out in front of the television or playing video games. But then he remembered Bill's words about seizing an opportunity. Between doing the usual and working, Jerry realized he had done scarce else for the last three years. He smiled as he ambled off in a random direction from the courthouse.

Soon, the towers of glass and steel were replaced by old storefronts of crumbling red brick. The young professionals in immaculate suits hurrying to their next meeting yielded to the aimlessly-dressed folks wandering amidst the jungle of neon lights and jangling music. His pulse quickened as his memory of work and the sense of routine faded away.

He wandered past the pawnshops and their second-hand treasures, the small unique restaurants with their cloying aromas, and the dive bars with their clattering glassware. None of this intrigued him enough to stop. He held onto this sliver of free time like a miser held onto a silver dollar.

A door of cracked red vinyl swung open and loud music spilled into the street. Within the smoky darkness, he caught a glimpse of black lace and pale skin under a blue light. For a moment, Jerry considered going in, but it was still too early to drink and watch what he couldn't have.

He passed a sex shop on Corral Drive called "Come Play with Me." He grinned at the blatant double entendre. Still, Jerry walked on; cheap thrills without company depressed him.

As the sun set behind the buildings, hundreds of angry red eyes glared at him from the grimy, darkened windows. He quickened his pace. In places like this, you were either a predator or prey at night. He followed the woman in front of him. Entranced by the suggestive swing of her miniskirt-clad hips, he knew she was open for business. Under the street lamp, she turned and smiled slyly at him. He looked away in panic, not knowing the next steps of this intimate dance.

Mercifully, his rapport with her shattered when the bearded man in the filthy army jacket barreled out one of the nondescript storefronts and staggered into him.

"S'okay, man," the grizzled man mumbled as he patted Jerry without looking up and wandered off.

Instinctively, Jerry ran his hands over his suit after the encounter. His wallet, his keys and his phone were still there, yet he felt a slight bulge in his breast pocket.

He retrieved the object and stared. The same vial that Agent Jones displayed in the interview this morning now lay in his palm. Jerry had never touched the vial containing the thick amber liquid, yet it still found its way into his pocket. He could return it tomorrow morning, but how would that look? Bad. Fling it away like he never saw it? Good.

The vial warmed to his touch and its weight was substantial in his hand. He peered deeper into the thick, languid depths of the liquid and his fist closed around it. He couldn't bring himself to toss it. He worked too hard to get this far, but what had he really gained? A basement apartment, a dim little cubicle, no friends and the constant paranoia about his co-workers' agendas. The warmth from the vial crept up his arm. Was that much to lose? Much like the interview this morning, he saw an opportunity. He could take this one, too. Didn't Jones say it didn't show up on drug screens?

Anything for kicks, Jerry thought, as he broke the seal on the lead stopper. The musky, spicy aroma tickled his nose as he tipped the vial. A single drop oozed and hung on the lip. The sweet, burning taste landed on his tongue. The drop rolled to the back of his throat and dropped like a pebble into his stomach.

"That was fun," Jerry muttered as he returned the vial to his pocket. He took ten steps, before it hit him. The rippling started like a punch in the stomach that made him reach for the graffiti-covered wall. Gasping for breath, a shudder passed through his body. His knees buckled. Lightheaded, scorching air flooded his lungs, as cold sweat trickled down his face. He stalked down the dark streets, following an alien instinct. The city writhed beneath him, and he wanted more.

He felt the bass of the music pulse like his own heartbeat. A neon sign glared the words "The Night Cafe" in the window. The line of hopeful partiers snaked around the corner. Jerry yearned to be inside the palace of red, orange, dark wood, glass and brown leather. He raised his hand and watched an aura of bluish mist roll off his cold skin. His reflection in the window seemed fainter than those who waited behind the velvet rope. He passed the bouncer with the sharp eyes and broken nose and walked unimpeded into the foyer.

The flashing lights and mirrors from the small stage in the corner only added to the shadowy carnality of the club. The acrid cigarette smoke tore into Jerry's lungs as he hung close to the wall, safely enfolded in the shadows. People passed him without notice. The dance music boomed throughout the club. Over at the worn, lacquered bar, a group of women laughed and drank. He smelled their musky perfumes and listened to the rustle of their short dresses. One with lustrous brown eyes looked his way. She seemed to scan the shadows on the wall as if she knew he was there.

His stomach tightened and the cold raced up his fingertips. Numbly, he rushed to the restroom. The filthy gray tile seemed to absorb the light. Jerry clutched at the urinal. The rank odor of vomit and urine only made things worse. Someone had scrawled, "Party 'til U Puke" in the crevice between the tiles.

"Hey, man," an easy voice called from behind him, "you okay?" He felt someone lift him to his feet.

"Yeah," Jerry coughed, "I'm fine, thanks." He regarded his benefactor in the pale blue silk shirt.

"Nothin' but a thing," the young, blond man said. "Rough night?"

"Yeah, just a little run down, I guess."

"Got some coke, you want some? It'll get you straight."

Jerry felt the warmth of the vial in his shirt pocket. "Thanks, but I'm holding myself." He produced the vial and took a sip.

"Suit yourself, chief," the man said, cutting lines on a scratched mirror. "What do you have there, anyway?"

"Some serious shit," Jerry heard himself say. "This stuff rocks the house." Something oozed out of his pores.

"You mind parting with some later? Sounds killer."

"Why not now?" Jerry said and hazy blue smoke rolled from his hand to bridge the space between them. Through his ears, nose and mouth, the smoke entered the young man. Jerry felt the man's body heat creep through the smoke back into him. He considered the dealer's eyes, now dull and flat, and said with a wicked grin, "Party 'til you puke, dude."

Numbly, the man nodded, as he set the mirror up for another hit. Jerry left. The kid deserved his last moments alone.

The music bombarded his ears as the glaring strobe light framed the dancers bathed in electric sweat. Jerry glided through the crowd of people effortlessly. Lust, violence, hunger, greed—none of these sensations described the yearning he felt. Weaving and sidestepping, he followed his urges past the throng. He sensed each of their wounds or secrets. In the corner booth, he spied her.

Her unblemished skin glowed in the pale candlelight as her deep brown eyes gazed at the drink before her. She smiled and nodded at the comments made by her companion, a young man with a hungry smile and long red rock 'n roll curls.

"Hey!" Jerry said, sliding into the booth next to her. "How's-"

"Joe?" She completed the question for him. "He's out of town on business. I'm here with a few friends from work."

"That's great. If Joe keeps it up, he'll do fine." He glanced over at the redheaded man in the leather pants, who lost his grin. He added, as he offered his hand, "My name is Jerry."

"Carson," the man said as he squeezed Jerry's hand.

"Heard about the band, Carson," Jerry said, as Carson secrets flowed into him. "Tough break. How are you and Lorraine doing? I guess little Jimmy is, what? Four, now?"

Carson looked around and swaggered off to the dance floor.

"You know him?" she blurted.

"Nah, just know his type. Mess up his entrance, and he's down." The ease of the lie scared Jerry.

"Well, thanks, Jerry," she said and squeezed his hand. "I really appreciate your help."

"You're welcome..."

"Mary."

"Okay, Mary," he continued, "would you buy me a drink?"

"Why would I do that?" she said with a laugh.

"Because I just saved your virtue from Carson."

They drank, laughed and watched the other patrons. Jerry felt the coldness return to his limbs. The darkness slithered off his skin, writhing like black worms. All the while, Mary spoke in loving tones about how much she missed Joe, and the happy life they had together. The shadowy tendrils stretched across the table to caress her cheek. Her dark eyes shone in the candlelight. Panicked, Jerry willed his rebellious aura back to him.

"Look, Mary," Jerry said, "it was nice meeting you, but I got to go. Got some work to catch up on." He slid out of the booth quickly.

"Uh, Jerry," she said, reaching for her gold clutch, "I'd better leave, too. I mean, my friends seem busy, and I don't want to go to my car alone. Would you walk me to my car? It's over in the parking garage."

"Sure," Jerry heard himself say.

They walked into the cool night air, neither saying a word. On the fourth floor of the concrete garage, the fluorescent lights flickered noisily. Their pace slowed the closer they got to her car. Leading the way with keys in hand, she glanced back at him with a dazzling smile. He listened to her heels click and echo off the empty walls of the garage, and he could just make out the panty line under her beige dress.

His reason clouded as he pressed her back against the dingy concrete wall. Mary snaked her tongue into his mouth. Jerry squeezed her firm breasts as she moaned hungrily. His hands reached under her skirt and pulled her pantyhose down. Jerry's cock quivered in the breeze as he slid into her. Her legs locked around his waist as they pounded together like a well-oiled piston. The darkness poured off Jerry, probing and filling all of Mary's orifices. Her ears, nose, mouth, cunt and ass. *More*, he sensed her body beg as she feverishly clawed his back. The heat and the light burned behind his eyelids as they came together. Jerry imagined the darkness filling her up inside as she gasped, "God, god, god!" Her exclamations died into whimpers.

The storm passed as quickly as it arrived. She composed herself quietly. "I've never done this…" the thought died on her lips as she climbed into her silver Camry and drove off.

Weak with nausea, Jerry watched her car disappear down the ramp and completed her thought with a whisper, "But you'll do it again."

Out in the streets again, he drifted through the gloom. The sky was a starless black dome covering the city, while the wind whipped around the corners of the abandoned church and moaned through the boarded windows. Jerry trembled with cold knifing into him. Exhausted, he dropped onto the cracked concrete steps. The empty pain racked his body. As he caught himself reaching for the vial, his fists pounded the concrete to resist.

A shuddered cry escaped his lips as he glimpsed translucent skin of his hands in the harsh light from the streetlights. Black spots of decay had set to work just underneath his fingernails. The veins popped from the dead white skin in a purplish hue. He retrieved the vial, hanging heavily in his pocket. Upending the vial, the drop landed on his tongue. The liquid had turned the color of clotted blood and tasted sour. Warmth and strength returned to his limbs.

Sounds of a fight caught his attention across the street.

"Kick the shit bag again, Andre," a kid in an orange shirt and dreadlocks yelled, as his fists plowed into the bearded man's face. "This fucker ain't got any money."

Sickly fascinated by the spectacle, Jerry watched Andre, a muscular youth in a red and white hoodie, slam his foot into the man's stomach. On his knees, the man retched up foul, acrid blood. A smile crossed Jerry's face as he advanced.

"You want some, too?" Orange-shirt challenged, glaring at Jerry.

"Yeah, all of it," Jerry whispered as the tangible shadows rolled off his hands.

"Bring the pain, white boy," Orange-shirt dared. He lifted his fists and began his boxer dance.

"My pleasure, your pain," Jerry said as his fist shot out. His black aura focused into a shadowy lance and leaped off his fist and through Orange-shirt's left eye, deep into his skull.

Orange-shirt screamed in agony. His life force drained through the darkness and back into Jerry.

"That's the stuff," Jerry groaned as the rush hit him.

Stunned, Andre edged away from the stranger in the rumpled business suit.

"Andre, where you going? I got something for you, too," Jerry called after him. The black tentacle cleaved away from Orange-shirt's remains and severed Andre's neck with a clean sweep. The body collapsed and the head rolled into the gutter.

The victim squatted, doubled over in pain. Jerry stood and crept toward him; the bearded man never looked up, reeking of cheap wine and body odor.

"Hurts, doesn't it?" Jerry said, relishing the man's exquisite agony.

"S'okay, man," the man mumbled and rocked back and forth on his heels.

"That's because those boys were amateurs," Jerry said as the multitude of inky tentacles oozed from his body and enveloped the man. With no screams of fear or pain, the tendrils drilled into the man's skin; Jerry realized this one was too far gone, just an empty shell. Disappointed, he dropped the pulped wreckage on the sidewalk and staggered on.

The further he walked, the more Jerry's mind surfaced from the depths of the fugue. There was no way back now. He looked at the vial. The last drop of the liquor oozed like hot, black tar.

"Hey, baby," a sultry voice whispered from behind him, "you want a date?"

"What do you have in mind?" he said. He turned to regard the young woman in the white rabbit fur jacket and shimmery purple slip top. Her bleached blond bangs framed her green eyes with a brittle shine.

"It's a bit late for dinner and dancing," she said with a smirk. The streetlights played like stars in her dark hair. She cocked her head knowingly as her green eyes pierced Jerry's soul. "Do you have any ideas?"

"I might. Do you know someplace near we could go and talk about it?"

"Sure, baby, follow me." She took his hand.

The dark building stank. Jerry heard the scrabbling and skittering of rats. A threadbare mattress lay in a pool of light. None of it mattered; he wanted her. "So, what's your name?" he asked.

"Mary, what's yours?"

"Jerry."

"Well, Jerry, are you a cop?"

"No."

"Good," she said. "What do you want tonight, Jerry?"

Hypnotized by her long legs, Jerry mumbled, "I want something…special."

"That'll cost extra."

"I can pay," Jerry said, pulling a wad of bills from his pocket and offering it all to her with sweaty palms.

"What do you want, baby?" she asked with a wide-eyed, innocent expression.

"I want to play Doctor," Jerry said, edging closer.

"Oh, Dr. Jerry," she cooed, as she parted her legs and lifted her black leather miniskirt, "I feel soooo empty down here." Her hand eased down her stomach and rested on her shaven cunt.

"Turn over," Jerry commanded her tonelessly. "I need to give you a thorough examination." He rubbed his crotch through his dress slacks.

She obeyed by getting on her hands and knees and easing her miniskirt over her smooth white ass. "What are you going to do with that big medical instrument, Doctor?"

He knelt behind her, unzipped his pants and sank deep inside her sweetness.

"Ohm," she gasped, as she thrust back onto his cock, "that's wicked good."

Jerry felt the vial in his hand and brought it to his lips. The last black drop rolled into his mouth. He dropped the vial and thrust harder. Waves of darkness spilled out of him, covering her and cutting her screams short. He succumbed to the black void within himself.

Jerry hugged himself as he rocked back and forth. Sunlight crawled across the floor.

"A rough night, eh, Jerry?" Jones said behind him. "Overindulged a bit?"

"How'd you know where to find me?"

"Easy, just followed the trail of bodies."

"Look," Jerry coughed, "I don't know what happened."

"Hey, not to worry," Jones said. "We all go on a tear once in a while, don't we, boys?"

"See, Jim?" Erskine pointed out. "I told you the kid had potential."

"You were right, Lew. A little OJT goes a long way," Rhodes said.

"Congratulations, Jerry," Jones said, "welcome to the team."

"Uh, what?"

"You passed your final qualifications," Jones continued. "This was a bit of test. Not the best score I've seen, but solid performance." He looked at Erskine and Rhodes, and said, "You two got any critique on his performance?"

"A bit heavy-handed for my taste," Erskine opined. "Typical rookie mistakes, but he hasn't had time to form any negative habits."

"What Lew is trying to say, Jerry," Rhodes explained, "is your instincts are good, but you got to know when to throw the small fish back. Let them commit bigger crimes. The bigger the perp, the bigger the bust."

"And let's be fair," Erskine chimed in, "they're all perps at one time or another."

"Word to live by," Jones said with a laugh.

"So, what now?" Jerry inquired.

"I don't know," Jones said. "Get married, move to the suburbs, and raise 2.5 kids?"

Jerry stared.

"Hey, don't knock if you haven't tried it," Jones said. "In the short-term, get yourself cleaned up. Team briefing is at nine. Here, I almost forgot." He fished a vial out of his pants pocket and placed it on the floor in front of Jerry.

"This will get you straight," he added with a grin. The trio left the building.

The cracks of light in the window darkened; Jerry's hand crept toward the vial.

"God damn, Prof," J.J. said, looking up from his paper. "You look like hell this morning."

"I sure feel like it," Prof replied to the front desk clerk, rubbing his throbbing temples.

"You know management doesn't allow liquor on the premises."

"I wouldn't know anything about that, J.J."

"Of course not, like the time you and fucking Gascon came staggering in here on Christmas morning never happened."

"Right," Prof sighed. "I promise I will never let it happen, again. Anyway, anything in the news?"

"What you expect out of this city. Three murders, a missing woman and a Federal Taskforce to combat crime. Now, sports—"

"Forget it, "Prof said, "I'll go down to see Lou for that. At least, he has free coffee."

Out in the street, a car slowed as it turned the corner in front of Prof. Headed downtown, he guessed, a black sedan with four men in dark suits. He smelled the dampness on the breeze and realized a storm was on its way.

"*You know, Prof,*" the silvery voice tinkled, "*every so often, the hero gets a moment of reflection. It is up to him to act on it or not.*"

Prof reached into his coat pocket and retrieved the half-empty rum flask and dropped it into the nearby trash can.

A Risky Proposition

6 AM March 22nd
Room 701 The Hotel Mittelmarch
1275 Reed Shore Drive

The jangling ring of the pay phone awoke Prof from his slumber.

"Jeez," Prof grumbled and pulled himself to the edge of the bed. Living in the room nearest the stair landing, he took it upon himself to answer the phone for the floor. After pulling on his ragged blue robe and worn-out slippers, he tramped to the phone, an ancient relic, probably the last one in the city.

"Hello?" He said into the phone receiver that smelled of booze and cigarettes.

"*Good morning, Prof,*" the familiar feminine voice said. "*How come we never talk anymore?*"

"Are you kidding me? You haven't quit talking to me!"

"*But you only said one word to me in the last three days! All that drinking isn't good for you.*"

"It keeps you quiet!"

"Prof?" Nathan said, tapping him on the shoulder. "Are you going to be ready for this morning?"

"What? Oh," Prof said, dropping the phone receiver. "Let me get dressed." He shuffled back to his room and slammed the door.

As Nathan hung the receiver of the scratched payphone, all he heard was the dial tone.

Prof showered and dressed. As instructed, he avoided shaving and barely ran the comb through his light brown hair streaked with gray, probably grayer than he remembered. As Nate said, "Bit shabby and down on your luck sweetens the pot."

He passed the worn table with the cardboard box resting atop it and paused. Avoiding it did no good; eventually he would have to open it.

"*Hanging up on me, Prof? We had a deal!*"

"And you fucked me!"

"I see why Lila left you. If you treat all the women in your life like this, you will always be alone."

"Prof?" Nathan said, pounding on the door. "C'mon we gotta go!"

"*This isn't over, Prof. Not by a long shot.*"

Pulling on his wrinkled green windbreaker, he flung open the door. "Let's go, Nathan."

At 7:00 AM, the bus terminal seemed grubbier than usual. Just outside the main foyer of smudged glass and painted concrete, Nathan set up his handmade plywood table. "Okay," he said, looking at his two co-conspirators, "you guys ready for this?"

"Let's do it!" Phil said, trotting to the orange trashcan next to the double-door entrance.

"Okay, we got a lookout," Nathan said, watching the scruffy young man in the red flannel shirt and cargo pants. He turned to Prof and said, "You up for this, old man?"

"Desperate times call for desperate measures."

"Shit, Prof! Don't wave that flag. The marks smell that a mile off. Try to be like me. The game is my home and I own it."

"I'll give it a shot."

"No," Nathan said, "come to play or cash out." He glanced at the shambling travelers exiting the front doors and squinting in the bleak morning sun. He continued, "Anyway, here comes our first bunch of fish, off the all-nighter from wherever."

"All right, all right!" Nate called aloud. "Find the little lady, red will set you ahead black will set you back. Make your bet, Chief."

Prof placed a dollar on the plywood.

"The man makes his play!" Nathan said, ramping up his spiel. "We got two stone cold studs and a red hot *chica.*" He displayed the queen of hearts and the two black jacks and dropped them on the table. A few of the new arrivals edged closer to the table.

Nathan's toe scraped the rough concrete. As rehearsed, Prof stuck out his hand and hesitated before tapping the card on the left.

"We have a winner!" Nathan said. "You gonna walk, old man?"

"Double down."

"Oh, so you think you're a player?" Nathan challenged. "Well, now let's make this interesting." Again, he showed the cards and dropped them on the table. The cards danced in a line under Nathan's fast hands.

Change jingled in the worn pocket of Nathan's bomber jacket and Prof said, "Left."

The onlookers murmured, drawn in to the scene by the blind underdog's good fortune. Nathan scratched his sleeve and Prof said, "Cash me out."

"So, that's how it is?" Nathan said. "Take me for a few bucks and make me look bad? Go on!"

Prof walked away; his pulse quickened from his moment of crime. He heard the shuffle behind him as another seized "the mark's park" in front of Nate's table.

An hour later, sitting at counter of Nighthawks Diner, Prof finished his second cup of coffee when Nate and Phil claimed the stools on either side of him.

"Sixty from the bus terminal, first thing in the morning!" Nate said, punching Prof in the shoulder. "Must be a new record."

"Nate," Phil said, "I thought using a blind man to prime the pump sounded stupid, but hey, it was like we hung out a billboard that said, 'give us your money, chumps!'"

"You're learning, Phil," Nate said, checking his watch. "Anyway, you guys just made the cut. Are you ready for the big show?"

"Hell, yes!" Phil agreed.

"You still cover my expenses, Nate?" Prof said.

"Of course, Prof, you take your cut out of the next pay out and scoot. I'll cover your tab."

"Just don't stiff Jane. I'd like to come back here when all is said and done."

By mid-morning, the Saturday sky brightened over Wrightsway Park. Prof, Nate, and Phil set up the game on the corner of one of the dim side streets that led away from the small circular park. Ringed by tables and racks of the sidewalk merchants, Wrightsway buzzed with activity. The first fair weather of the year brought out the crafters, hucksters and hustlers like the new leaves on the oaks in the park.

"You think we could get a piece of that action?" Phil said, watching the cash moving and card swiping at the street vendor tables.

"If we can build our nut," Nathan said, popping the legs of the table into place. "I heard there's a guy we can score some knock-off merchandise from."

A silver tour bus lurched and hissed to the curb across the street from their corner.

The side of the bus read:

Whitestone Tours LTD

"Sweet!" Nathan said. "Tourists! Game on!"

The scheme rebooted once more. Phil hustled off to his lookout point. Prof took his place in front of the table and followed the script. Nate, fueled by avarice, dropped deep into his game as he said, "The blind wonder wins again!"

"Double or nothing," Prof said.

"Amazing!" Nate gasped, scanning the throng of onlookers who had ambled over from the bus.

"Again, same stakes."

"Good God, old man!" Nate bellowed, scratching the sleeve of his bomber jacket. "You're going to clean me out!"

The spectators waited for Prof's next move.

The script called for Prof to move on, yet he wanted to place another bet, regardless of the plan. His stomach quivered in warning; enough was enough. "No, need to press my luck," he said, reaching for his winnings.

A few deflated exhalations issued from the bystanders as Prof stepped away from the table. He yearned for a cup of coffee and a table in the sunshine, far away from this debacle.

"So, lad," a white whiskered gentleman in a green derby said, "what do you call this game of chance?" He gestured with the end of his long-stemmed pipe to Nate's table.

"So glad you asked, Sir!" Nate said. "This is the fine American tradition of Three Card Monte."

"Really?" The short man in the derby said with a twinkle in his eyes. "I believe I speak for my fellow travelers when I say I would like to see a demonstration. What good is traveling, if you don't savor the local experience?"

The others, two Asian boys in matching Braves caps with fancy digital cameras, a gangly Chinese man with aviator sunglasses and a bowl-haircut, a swarthy young man with a goatee and his delicate pale girlfriend clinging to him, shifted closer to Nate's table.

"Absolutely!" Nate said. "Come on and play the game that made America great!"

The old Irish fellow slipped in front of table while offering his hand.

"Cassidy," Nate said, shaking the little man's hand, "Sean Cassidy."

Meanwhile, Prof took his fifty bucks worth of winnings and treated himself to a latte on the patio of Java Buddies. From respected academic to street hustler, who would have guessed? One year brought so many changes. Last Wednesday marked what should have been his eleventh anniversary. Looking back, he regretted so much; he'd distanced himself from Lila in the final months to avoid the awful truths. The voice may be imaginary, but that didn't mean she wasn't right. He spent the last three days in his room with two bottles of cheap whiskey, even though he'd promised himself to stop only a day earlier. With her voice muffled, he toasted to the gods of cosmic indifference.

It was Nate who coaxed him out from three dark days of sequestration. A quick couple of raps on his door last night heralded Nate's proposition.

"C'mon, Prof," Nate said, "Fred's still in Muni. I need to cover my bills. From what I see, you're coming up short this month, too."

Granted, Prof was running low on cash, but the upbeat scam artist's infectious patter sold him on this sketchy endeavor. In the end, the scruffy con man swindled Prof back into the sunlight. Now, Nate's virulent spiel drifted across Wrightsway on the fresh spring breeze.

The thrill of chance followed Nate's words and settled upon the shoulders of the market square's visitors like spring pollen.

"Mr. Fortescue!" the young barista said. "I'll have your black coffee and plain bagel ready in a jiffy."

"Not today," Mr. Fortescue said. "I think I'll have the triple cappuccino with a vanilla shot and a chocolate chip cookie."

"Electric purple sparkle?" Mrs. Lee said. "But Mrs. Barrington, you always get clear coat!"

The fragile snowy-haired lady, sitting across from Ms. Lee at the manicure station merely smiled.

Reyna looked out the shop window and her nose twitched. Grabbing her bug-eyed sunglasses and floppy white hat, she said, "I'll be right back, Demetria." She swept out the door with the chimes jangling.

Demetria, focused upon the near-blank dating profile on her computer, typed the message, "Let's meet up, hot stuff."

Ricky Wonker scratched his pockmarked cheek. The Science Club meeting had let out early and he found himself in the park amongst the vendors. Across the way, he spotted her, Melissa Phillips, still in her gold cheerleading outfit. Taking a deep breath, he strode over to Melissa, who was examining a tableful of bracelets.

"Hi, Melissa," he said. "Would you like to go see *Rocky Horror* over at the Strand tonight?"

Melissa's surprised look softened and she said, "Sure, why not?"

"I'll say, Mr. Cassidy," the little Irish man said backing away from the table with an empty wallet, "'twas a fine game. I almost thought I had you until those last couple of bets."

"You were doing great, but Three Card Monte takes years to master," Nate said, surveying the gathering. "Any other takers?"

The long-limbed Chinese youth hugged a pale redhead in a tiger print sundress and white floppy hat. The young boys bounced up and down, waving their arms, gibbering for Nate's attention.

"Hey, kids," a dark man in the loud Hawaiian shirt said to the boys. "I hear they got a stand down there with a real American treat, cucumbers on a stick." He pointed to the park square.

The boys looked at each other with glee and cried, "Cucumbers?" They skittered down to the park.

"Was that really necessary?" the aloof Chinese youth said.

"They're kids and this is an adult game," the stout man said and hopped to the 'mark's park.' "Besides I'm next."

"You truly have the manners of a goat-herder."

"Hey, Monkey-boy!" the new mark snapped. "You wanna bet? I got twenty that says you can't jump the width of my palm." He stuck out his doughy hand.

The Chinese man glowered and adjusted the yellow pencil tucked behind his ear. Before he could reply, the lady in the floppy hat turned him around and shook her head.

"Now what?" the swarthy man said as his girlfriend popped up on tiptoe and whispered in his ear while pointing to Walker Bridge.

"Aww, Nye, baby, I told you that was just a canal, not a river. Besides, I'm up."

She wagged her finger at him with a pout and flounced off toward the bridge, her black hair trailing behind her.

Turning back to the table, he scratched his bristling goatee and said, "Guess I'm paying for that later."

"So, you in or out?" Nathan dared, shuffling the three cards in his hands.

"Oh yeah. Go for it, buddy."

Over the hour, Phil edged closer to the growing crowd surrounding Nate. Nate always carped about showing initiative. A few side bets would make a sweet day that much sweeter.

From his seat on the patio, Prof listened to the bustle of merchants and customers increase to a feverish pitch, yet he still heard Nate's muffled spiel on the other side of the park.

"*Prof?*" the voice asked with a note of reconciliation. "*I'm sorry what I said earlier.*"

"It's okay, it's true, at least some of it."

"*So, we're going to talk?*" the voice continued with hopeful excitement. "*You know they are going to think you're crazy.*"

"As if I was considered a bastion of mental health, before."

"*Just remember, all you have to do is make it through the next two hundred seventy-five days.*"

"Just no more six AM phone calls."

"Talking to yourself?" a voice boomed as the visitor claimed a seat at the small vinyl table. "Some folks would say you're going off the deep end."

"And you're?'

"Oh, sorry," he amended, "my name's Bill Jones, Mr. Clarke."

"How exactly do you know my name?"

"Judge Adams. He's got a file on you."

"But why?"

"Don't take it personally," Jones said. "He's got a file on everyone he thinks is undesirable. Spit on the sidewalk, show up drunk in public. That sort of thing."

"This doesn't sound constitutional."

"Let's get something straight: the anal-retentive old fart doesn't give two shits about your rights. He just wants order," Jones said. "As for folks that don't fit in society? Well, society has got places for them."

"So how do I stay out of trouble?"

"You can't, but I might have a solution."

"And that would be?"

"Come work for me. You'd be under my protection and you wouldn't have to hustle for a few bucks to make grocery money with those shitheads," Jones said. "You know they're using you."

"So, what do you want me to do?"

"Easy, easy work. You're educated and unobtrusive. All you got to do is make a phone call now and again."

"Let me think about it."

"Don't think too long. Here's my card; if you feel like getting legit work, give me a call. I guess you can get someone to read it to you." Jones tucked the card into Prof's shirt pocket. "See you in the funny papers…or the cemetery."

"Goddam Wonker the Wanker!" a young voice roared off to Prof's left. A hard, flat smack and a crash followed.

"Kyle!" a young girl pleaded. "He only bought me a latte."

"Time to go," Prof thought and he abandoned his seat.

Tillman's stride carried him past the storefronts. Sweat rolled down his face as he strained to keep his breathing short and even. The ten second warning beeped from his sports watch. So close; if he crossed the street to Java Buddies, he would break his old time. Doubling down, he burst into a full sprint. The NO WALK sign flared. *Dammit, not this time!* he thought, gritting his teeth and bounding off the curb.

Reba eased off the brakes of the bus as she watched the countdown on the pedestrian crossing sign. She nudged the accelerator to avoid downshift. A clear walkway, a sure bet.

She heard and felt the thud in the front of the bus and her heart sank to her stomach.

Four stories up from the square, Greg prepared to remove the last shutter on the Harris Building. The Saturday overtime pay came in handy, but he looked forward to watching the game and enjoying a cold beer. He reached for his portable drill and grabbed an empty loop. He spied the drill where he left it on the neighboring scaffold, one platform down. Two climbs for one shutter seemed stupid. Undoing his safety harness, he leapt the five-foot gap and the knobby tread of his safety boot rattled off the edge of the other scaffold.

Deep in concentration, Nate watched his hands blur across the cards as he gunned his hustle. The pile of cash to his left grew with the size of the crowd in front of him. The gasps and cheers from the crowd fueled his blowtorch confidence and he delved deeper into the game.

Finally, the exhausted, stocky man dropped his palms to the table and exhaled, "Enough!"

Nate raised his eyes and spotted Phil working the crowd. "Oh, fuck."

"That...Was...Awesome!" the mark bellowed joyfully at his loss with both doughy fists in the. The blaring sirens barely registered to the throng.

"Nate, how you are doing, buddy?" Sergeant Serrano said with a wide grin, clamping down on Nate's right wrist and shoulder. "Having a pretty good day?"

Like smoke in the wind, the crowd dispersed. Nate caught a flash of red flannel vaulting over a fence. *At least Prof and Phil jetted,* he thought, *and its pizza night at municipal.*

Off to his left, the man in the green derby gave Nate the briefest of winks.

"Ohhh, me heart!" the bewhiskered man cried, clutching his chest. He dropped to his knees and looked heavenward. "To never see my lovely Eire ever again and to die a stranger in a strange land." He collapsed upon the red brick sidewalk.

The big cop bolted to the fallen man's side and keyed his mike for the code blue.

Two twins in Braves caps ran up and rolled the man over. Looking at each other, one uttered, "CPR?"

The other nodded enthusiastically

The small, prone man seized up and spouted a fountain of vomit. "Sorry lads," he said wiping his mouth with his verdant jacket cuff, "that won't be necessary."

"Ewww!" the boys cried in unison and scampered back to bus.

"You okay?" Serrano inquired as his eyes watered.

"Oh, I will be fine, good constable," the man said, hauling himself to his feet. "It was that damnable breakfast of bacon, egg and cheese muffin and black coffee. Next time, I stick to honest porridge and good Irish tea." A large, pants-ripping fart punctuated his words.

The Chinese guy looked to his co-traveler. "You mean we have to ride back to the hotel with that?" he said.

"What can I say?" his fellow traveler said, stroking his goatee. "He's an original master." He pulled his cell phone from his pocket. "Hey, Daddy-o, how are things running?" He spoke as they meandered back to the bus. "Cool! I think I found a solution."

As the band of stragglers moved back down into the square, Serrano looked back at the rickety table. Of course, Nate and the money had vanished. Serrano sighed and flexed his muscles. As many times as he had busted the little twerp, he deserved a break…just this once.

Eight blocks later, Nathan's sprint sputtered to a halt. With his hands on his knees, he gasped for breath. It had been a good run, both. He opened his hand to count the snatch of bills. His grin dropped.

He grasped a fistful of dead leaves.

Coming Attractions

6:48 AM April 12th
Wrightsway Park

The birds chirped in the early morning rain as Prof ambled down the sidewalk of the small park. In an hour or so, the merchants might set up their tables, depending on the crap shoot of the spring weather. For the moment, Prof appreciated the cool quiet.

In the center of the park, he heard a rustle in the bushes. Stepping carefully across the cold, slick grass, Prof approached the disturbance.

"Please!" Reyna said. "Whoever you are, don't come closer."

"Ms. Fox?" Prof said. "It's me, John Clarke. Are you all right?"

"Prof? I'm okay, but I really need some help."

"Sure, what can I do to help?"

"Can I borrow your raincoat, Prof?"

"Sure," Prof said, as he slipped the beige coat from his shoulders. "I think that the sprinkles we had this morning are pretty much over."

"Thank you, Prof," she said, taking the coat. "I really don't want to get arrested for public indecency." The bushes swished as she emerged from the undergrowth.

"Public indecency," Prof reasoned, "that means that you're…"

"Lucky my rescuer is a blind man." She slipped her hand in his and led him away from the bushes.

"Aren't we heading to your shop?" Prof asked. "It's on the other side of the park."

"No," said Reyna, "I left a key with Mrs. Lee."

"So, this has happened before?"

"Not so much these days."

"Must have been a wild night."

"And a couple of bad days," Reyna sighed. "I've always heard that Experience is the best teacher, but her tuition is *très cher*."

"Learn anything of value?"

"Why is it that we're attracted to things we can't have?"

"Human nature," Prof said. "There's a dearth of literature on that theme. Romeo and Juliet, for example—"

"Why does it have to be so complicated, though? You see someone wonderful and they belong to someone else."

"Look, I'm the last guy you need go to for relationship advice. My marriage was a train wreck."

"You were married?" Reyna said. "How did you know she was the right one?"

"Well, obviously, she wasn't. At the time, it felt right. She and I met in college at a room party," he said, remembering the lithe brunette with the bright hazel eyes. "We were both young and going places."

"So, when did you know it wasn't going to work out?"

"I should have known," Prof said, "but I guess you only see what you want to see. I just remember the argument about me finishing grad school. She was so afraid of being pregnant, broke and me sitting at the computer saying, 'Wait, honey.' So, I manned up and got my Master's. It seems so clear, now."

"Hmm, attraction now does not guarantee satisfaction later. Do you have a coin?"

"I think so," Prof said, rummaging through his pants pocket. "Here you go."

"Thanks for being a gentleman, Prof," she said, rapping on the glass door of the manicure salon with the dime.

"I'm trying to do better. Do you need me to stick around?"

"I'm good. I'll get your coat back to you as soon as possible."

"I'll check back later at the shop," said Prof walking away.

"*Wow, what a cheap thrill!*" the voice laughed. "*And on a week day morning, too.*"

"Just helping a friend out," Prof muttered, picking up his pace.

"*I know what kind a friend you want to be to her,*" she insinuated. The light breeze carried the scent of saffron far.

"I did what I had to do."

"*She was NAKED!*" the voice teased. "*Too bad you're blind.*"

"I guess I have you to thank for shielding my virtue."

"*Prof,*" the voice backed down, "*there is a purpose. You'll see.*"

"According to you, not for some time."

Ms. Lee peeked out of the back office of the darkened nail salon. Recognizing Reyna with her bright hair and wearing a man's raincoat and nothing else, the tiny woman with graying dark hair hurried to the front door.

"It happened again, right?" Ms. Lee snapped.

"Yes, ma'am," Reyna said with downcast eyes as she stepped into the pristine salon.

"Wipe your feet," insisted Ms. Lee, "I just mopped the floor."

Reyna wiped her muddy feet across the coarse, black rubber mat and followed Ms. Lee to the back office.

"Drink tea," Ms. Lee commanded, setting the graceful porcelain cup in front of Reyna.

After one sip of the astringent concoction, Reyna grimaced. "At the very least," she said, putting the cup down, "it clears my palate of the essence of dead pigeon."

"Good blend, it keeps you healthy," Ms. Lee said, taking a seat behind the simple table that served as her desk. "Now, what did you do this time?"

"I know that I'm still on probation, but I never realized how hard it would be to keep my karma balanced."

"Drink the five poisons and you will spend a long time living in a hole in the ground and chasing chickens."

"I prefer the seven deadly sins. It is much less complicated."

Ms. Lee clicked her tongue and sighed. "Reyna, I do not understand your fascination with western things. It is a foolish and boorish culture."

"Because it's bright and exciting," Reyna said. "For example, The Strand aired a Femme Fatal Festival the day before yesterday. It was a triple bill of *Scarlet Street*, *Gilda* and *The Big Sleep*. I donned my finest little black dress to show the poseurs how it's supposed to be done."

"Reyna," Ms. Lee cautioned, "pride is the easiest trap to fall into."

"It wasn't like that. I just wanted to look good for Perry—"

"You mean, Mr. Sterling. You know he's married."

"I know, but he always looks so dashing in his tuxedo when greeting customers in the lobby. He reminds me of Cary Grant. Well, if Cary Grant was 30 pounds overweight and had a full beard. I wanted to help him out. A bit of window dressing goes a long way."

"I do not like where this is going," Ms. Lee said, pinching the bridge of her nose.

"He always comes into the shop looking for bargains—feather boas, high heeled boots, and fishnet stockings."

"He's one of those?"

"Oh no," Reyna said. "It's not like that. He looks for costumes for the kids who put on *The Rocky Horror Picture Show* on Saturday nights. He dreams of producing the grand spectacle."

"Was his wife with him?"

"No, Shannon's more involved with the business end of running the theater. Accounting, advertising, that sort of stuff. I always thought she was kind of boring."

"Boring?" Ms. Lee said, raising her eyebrows. "Mrs. Sterling works hard so her husband can play. She runs a business…like me."

"But, Perry works hard, too. He envisions bringing a little culture to the Square."

"He's a peacock. Anyway, you should not get between them."

"Why?" Reyna demanded. "She doesn't appreciate his *joie de vivre*. I brought a load of clearance inventory to the afternoon matinee. I got there early and you know what I found?"

"I am reluctant to ask. Was Mrs. Sterling there?"

"No, she had gone to the bank to see if they could finance an Office Planet franchise by mortgaging that beautiful old movie palace."

"Oh, Reyna," Mrs. Lee said, shaking her head.

"The lobby was filled with smoke, the sprinklers on and the popcorn machine smoldering. Perry just stood there in the middle of this with tears in his eyes. So I walked up to him, wrapped my arms around him—"

"Reyna…" Mrs. Lee said.

"And whispered in his ear that everything will be all right. I mean, he's no good without her, right?"

"His character lacks the serene mind in crisis," Mrs. Lee said, heaving a sigh of relief. "So, what happened next?"

"Well, he told me that Shannon had called and the bank turned down the loan application. Not surprising; it's an old building and the box office receipts were never great. He said she went to a lawyer to see if they could sell The Strand. She means everything to him; he was willing to give up his dream for her. How can I compete with that?"

"You can't and you shouldn't."

"I realized that so I went home."

"Yet," Mrs. Lee said, "you still have to explain this morning."

"I went back to my shop and the front awning was shredded."

"No wind for the last couple of days," Mrs. Lee observed.

"Something like this always happens when I overlook something important."

"That was either laziness or ignoring the suffering of others on your part, neither of which is good."

"I called Shannon that evening," Reyna said. "Can you believe it? The lawyer she was talking to was Sam Cavanaugh."

"Born of the rat," Mrs. Lee said. "Never trust a rat. He is greedy. I've known him and his brother, Jake, since they were small."

"I didn't know he had a brother."

"He left long before you came here. Sam chased him out so he could marry Rachel."

"I thought he was more of a pig," Reyna returned, "especially after Rachel's last Christmas party. Anyway, I paid a visit to Sam the next morning at his office."

"This cannot end well."

"I wore the red sheath dress, you know the one."

"You were planning to give him a heart attack?"

"No, you do remember what the honorable Sun Tzu wrote about deception?"

"Of course, I do," Mrs. Lee said. "It would seem being immersed in this western cesspool has not eroded your proper education."

"I went to his private office and offered my old farm outside of town."

"But you said your farm was worthless and contaminated."

"To me, yes, but to a brilliant lawyer with knowledge of EPA superfunds and lawsuits, it could be a gold mine. I swear I could see the adding machine above his head. He bought it immediately. Since I tied up his funds, he couldn't buy The Strand."

"So, you profited at the loss of the Sterling's?"

"No," Reyna said, "I bought into The Strand as a silent partner."

"So, this still does not explain last night. You hurt Sam?"

"Well, he did ask me where Rachel was. He offered me even more money to tell him where she and Bobby were staying, but I declined. Finally, he got ugly and called me a stupid bitch for siding with his cunt wife."

"Oh, Reyna," Mrs. Lee moaned, "never repay evil with evil."

"I didn't. I just smiled, told him that the scars made him look like a tough guy and left."

"So," Mrs. Lee puzzled, "why did you spend last night as a fox?"

"Well, after I cashed the check and gave the money to Perry and Shannon," Reyna began with downcast eyes, "I stopped at the Industrial Cheesecake Unit to celebrate. I thought I had earned a reward."

Mrs. Lee asked, "How many?"

Reyna pursed her lips and quietly said, "Five."

Mrs. Lee attempted to suppress a giggle.

"I really tried to do everything the right way. I just seem to always fight against my nature."

"Reyna," Mrs. Lee consoled, "we all strive against our nature. This is what it means to be human." She leaned over the table and kissed Reyna on the forehead.

Reyna's mood brightened. "Well, I need to open up the shop." She quickly rose to leave.

"You come back later for a manicure and a pedicure," Mrs. Lee directed. "Digging holes all night is not good. Oh, and Reyna?"

"Yes?"

"Your tail's showing."

"Thanks," she said and tucked her bushy brilliant red tail back underneath the vent of the gray raincoat.

By 5:00, a day of brisk business had calmed Reyna's nerves. Demetria begged to leave early and dashed off to meet a new date. The chimes greeted the plump little man with swarthy skin.

"Mr. El-Hashen!" Reyna said, cheered by the appearance of the man in the vivid green cardigan.

"Ah, Ms. Fox," the man said, "it is wonderful to see you this fine afternoon."

"What brings you to out from Cedars Street?"

"My niece, Cindy, will be visiting me next month to help close out the shop and I wish to purchase a present to commemorate her high school graduation."

"Certainly," Reyna said. "Wait, you're closing?

"I finally have found a way to retire feasibly…and I truly do not wish to compete with this," he said and handed Reyna the business section of the newspaper.

"Fashion World by Ursula Opening in Wrightsway Park," Reyna read the headline aloud.

"I find such monstrosities an affront to commerce," El-Hashen said. "They drain the vibrancy and mutability from the marketplace. These are the reasons I became a merchant in the first place."

"Well, it explains why Sam considered buying the Strand in the first place."

"That would be Attorney Cavanaugh, correct?"

"Yes," Reyna said. "Do you know Sam?"

"Not directly, but I have a small difference of opinion with his business associates."

"What do you think your niece would like?"

"I am unsure of her garment sizes; children today grow so fast."

"Okay," said Reyna, "do you know her color palette?"

"Ah, her skin is as fair as alabaster, her eyes reflect the azure sky, and her hair is the color of the sun," El-Hashen pronounced with a grand wave of his arm.

"Al?" Reyna asked cocking her eyebrow. "This is your niece?"

"Great grandniece thrice-removed, something like that. I was never much for genealogy."

"How about a piece of jewelry from my private collection?" Reyna said, pulling the tray from the display counter. "In fact, I think this would remind her of you." She placed the charm bracelet in his hand.

Al stroked his thick black beard, as he regarded the delicate strand of gold festooned with camels, herons, winged lions, and oil lamps. "Yes," he said, "this will do nicely."

"No haggling? Al, what's the world coming to?"

"Haggling, for me, at least, Ms. Fox, is a point of pride. When it comes to others you care for, sometimes one must put aside your own desires."

Reyna's eyes sparkled with a flash of inspiration.

The shop door clattered open, the chimes jangled and Prof stumbled into the shop. "Hi Reyna," he said, "I just came to pick up my coat."

"Prof," Reyna said, rolling her eyes, "your timing is terrible."

"Reyna," Al said, "do not be too harsh on the gentleman. Some cultures believe the unbalanced are blessed by the hand of God. Anyway, if you could send the bill, I'll be going." With a wave, he collected his purchase and ambled out the door.

"I'm sorry, Reyna," Prof said. "I just got to thinking about what you said this morning. I wanted Lila so much that I couldn't see that we were headed separate places. She compromised and I compromised. In the end, neither of us was happy. I just don't want you to make the same mistake."

"Thanks, I appreciate your concern. I feel I'm over the unrequited love," she said, handing him back the raincoat, cleaned and pressed. "And Prof?"

"Yes?"

"Please let your lady friend know I am no threat to her."

"*You know,*" the voice whispered to Prof, "*I may have been a bit harsh on my first assessment of her.*"

At eleven that night, Demetria sat at her computer with mascara running down her cheeks. She'd waited an hour for him but he never showed. She clicked through pages of profiles of pretty boys called Radu or Vlad wearing black velvet and lace. She saw no future with any of them, but her friend, Rhiannon, swore there was no future, anyway. Maybe Reyna was right; she wasn't really Goth material deep down. A glint on top of her pink vanity table caught her attention. Next to her teddy bear, Sunshine, the vial she found weeks earlier waited. Drawn to it, she glided over to the vanity and picked it up with both hands.

Her dark, tear-filled eyes glittered as she whispered, "Carpe Nocturnum."

The Cost of Domestic Bliss

10 PM April 30th
Room 701 The Hotel Mittelmarch
1275 Reed Shore Drive

Sitting at the table, Prof replaced the box lid and dropped the heavy pen atop it. Maybe Lila was right; he wasted the entire day on this. Cradling his head, he reviewed the last months of his marriage circling the drain. Determined to make partner in record time, Lila worked long hours. Meanwhile, he spent his time grading papers and keeping up with the household chores. They saw each other briefly in the morning over the coffee machine and late at night when the other would slide into bed after whatever project kept them up late. No more did they spend Fridays ordering in pizza, drinking cheap wine and laughing at bad movies with Stan, his former roommate. The heavy-set, half-shaved journalist aimed to become an assistant editor at the rock magazine he'd worshipped since his teens. Those days, ambition hung heavy in the air.

"*Prof?*" the voice said. "*You need to walk away from this.*"

"Isn't that what I've been doing?"

"*The isolation isn't good for you and you need to eat,*" she scolded.

Prof considered her words. He could go to the diner, but Jane was dating a new man. The Night Café would be loud and busy on this Saturday night. The party laughter and the throaty rumble of the muscle car from the far side of the street confirmed this. Nathan spent his time jabbering on the phone and running off on vague errands. Today, he dropped by Reyna's shop and experienced the frantic pace with which the red-headed shopkeeper handled her clients; Demetria had quit a day earlier. He considered swinging by Lou's machine shop, ordering a pizza and listening to the game. The old man never took a day off nor left the shop early, but Prof wanted to avoid that black void, right now. In the end, he picked up the pen and reopened the box. "Grace in the face of certain calamity," he said aloud.

"Yeah, sure, that should be no problem," Lou said as he scribbled figures on a yellow post-it note. "Let's see you need 1000 virgin rods and 100,000 bolts. Market price. As always, my responsibility ends at the pier. Good doin' business with you, Mr. Teppish."

He hung up the grubby white phone. The service clock on the wall read 10:25. The shop was silent as a tomb now, which suited Lou just fine. The off-the-books work paid well-enough, but God help him if they ever caught him.

He regarded the picture on the desk of the smiling woman with long blonde hair streaked with gray. "Ah, Rita," he addressed the picture, "if you were around, we'd be out fishing instead of getting caught up in these shenanigans."

He swiveled the gray office chair to the map tacked to the bulletin board behind his stained and scratched desk. Red pins dotted the map of the United States, places where he and Rita had planned to fish when they could call it quits on the machine shop. Not happening; Rita died of a stroke a week before her fifty seventh birthday. Lou found her behind this desk, face down on a pile of bills. That was five years ago.

He looked at the I-beams that crossed the ceiling and the forty years of dust and grit that accumulated on them. With a VA business loan and a dream, he'd married Rita, that cute little high school girl he left when he enlisted. They paid off this place together, hired some of the local kids from the neighborhood. It felt good; it felt right. Now, it was something else.

The problem started simple. A friend of a friend wanted an AR-15 full-auto; Lou scored some extra cash and kept it quiet. Sure, all it took was just a couple of hours in the shop after closing. Another friend wanted some practice grenade shells. No problem, he still had friends and, later, sons of friends, on active duty. A phone call and a few dollars sealed the deal. Over the years, he met more people on both sides of the business, buyers and sellers. He did his best to hide it from Rita, but she did the books. Had she known? Probably, but she never let on. After she passed, he spent more time on these after-hours deals

The pounding on the door next to the loading dock roused Lou from his dank memories. "*Probably, Prof,*" he thought. The failed teacher dropped by to get a cup of coffee and listen to the game. On a rainy night back in December, Lou watched Prof shuffle up and down the cold street for an hour. He decided to call the stooped sad sack in for a cup of coffee. Lou made no judgements about the blind man; everyone hit the skids, eventually. He didn't think the drenched scatterbrain would last a week on his own, but Prof proved his mettle. Now and again, the blind man dropped by in the evenings; Lou looked forward to his visits, even though the egghead couldn't place a winning bet to save his life. He cracked the door.

The door slammed open, knocking Lou to the floor.

"Hey, Fat Lou!" hollered a young man with scraggly blond sideburns. "You surprised to see us?"

"No, Johnny," Lou said, as he tried to pick himself off the floor, "I guess I shouldn't be."

"Stay down, fat man," Johnny said, gesturing with the blue steel Saturday night special. "You going to pay me an' Andy what you owe us." His blue eyes were pinpricks.

"Johnny, look, you're out of your head. I don't owe you squat—"

"Bullshit!" the twitchy man said. "I figure you owe us, at least two thousand for the last two weeks."

Andy, Johnny's younger brother, shuffled in dragging an aluminum softball bat and hand-in-hand with a young girl in a black lace dress and torn fishnet stockings. He scanned the shop with vacant eyes. The cold, damp night air followed them in.

"Close the door, Andy," Johnny said.

Andy dropped the bat while groping to close the door behind him.

"Dammit, Andy," John sputtered, "wake the fuck up.''

"Johnny, babe," the girl teased, tousling Andy's brown hair, "go easy on Andy. He's had a hard night."

"Hush, Dee," Johnny snapped back. "If we're gonna make it back home, he's still gotta hold up his end."

"Demetria, Johnny," the girl hissed.

"What?"

"My name is Demetria," she glared and caressed Andy's rough cheek. "Not Dee." Her dark, mascara-caked stare bored into Andy's vacuous blue eyes. She popped to the tips of her toes and whispered into Andy's ear.

"Uh, okay, Demetria," Andy slurred.

Johnny rubbed his face and said, "If you two shitheads are finished, we got stuff to do."

"Kids," Lou said, still sprawled on the floor, "I don't want any trouble, but I don't have that kind of money lying around here."

"You sack of shit!" Johnny said, kicking Lou's leg. "I saw you pull in plenty during the day around here. Cash, too."

"Uh, Johnny?" Andy interrupted. "He used to run to the bank about six every day."

"Fuck!" Johnny spurted.

"You guys really didn't think this out much, did you?" Lou said, rubbing his knee.

"You got an ATM card?" Andy said. "There's one around the corner."

"Yeah, but there's no way I could get that much cash out until after midnight."

"Screw that!" Johnny declared, cocking the pistol. "I say let's do him right now and take what we can."

Lou closed his eyes.

"Johnny," Andy said, "take what? Anything we grab outta here isn't going to fit in the back of the Charger, and where the hell would we sell it this time of night?"

"Oooh, the freakin' space cadet speaks," Johnny jeered. "I think this up, drive all the way over here from the club, and what are you doing the whole time? Getting a shot of leg in the back seat."

"At least I'm not tweaked out and fixin' to get us nailed."

"You fucking traitor," Johnny said, training the revolver on Andy. "You'd go against your own brother once you get your own piece of thang."

"His?" Demetria interjected. Her perfect eyebrow arched and a sweet, heavy smile crossed her face as she padded over to Johnny. "Johnny, babe, sweet baby, I don't belong to him. You remember the deal, don't you?" she continued as she slipped her arms over his shoulders. "I said I belong to both of you."

Demetria nuzzled Johnny's neck. Johnny's eyes fluttered and his arms lowered to his sides. Her delicate pale hands glided down his soiled white t shirt and past his shining belt buckle and rested upon the crotch of his worn jeans. With Johnny pacified, Demetria shot a beckoning look to Andy and glanced down to the revolver, hanging in Johnny's hand. Andy eased the gun from his brother's hand.

"Andy," she said, "if you would help Lou up, I believe Johnny needs a few minutes of TLC." She took Johnny by the hand and led him to the employee bathroom.

"C'mon," Andy said offering Lou his hand. "You still got coffee?"

"Yeah, in the office." Lou heaved himself to his feet.

"Sit." Andy directed with the pistol to the battered desk chair as he poured a Styrofoam cup of day-old coffee. He dumped ten packs of sugar in to the tarry concoction. "Pretty fucked up, ain't it?" he said and sank onto the orange office couch of cracked vinyl.

"I'll say… I just don't get what's going on here. I mean, are you boys pissed because I fired you? Hell, you two goddam meth heads were stealing me blind."

"It started out that way, yeah, but then that lawyer called us up and said that Uncle Wilt left his place to us back home."

"You mean Coker Creek?"

"Yeah, how'd you know?" Andy trailed off. His eyelids drooped.

"Shit, Andy," Lou said. "I hired you both because you were from Coker Creek. Rita and I were going to go fish there when I retired."

"Your old lady… Man, I'm sorry. That sucks."

"You weren't even around when Rita passed. What's it to you?"

"I guess I understand," Andy said, as his pistol hand shuddered. "I never had anyone to lose before. Other than Johnny."

"No big loss there."

"He's always been trouble. Hell, he wanted to run back home and turn Uncle Wilt's trailer into a cooker operation, but he'll straighten up."

"How's that?"

"We're gonna be daddies, both of us." Andy's head nodded and the pistol slipped from his fingers.

Lou pounced upon the pistol and edged back. He trembled at his choice of bad options. Run and let them steal him blind? Call the cops and hope they don't find his inventory? He checked the pistol—six rounds, if he needed them. He glanced over at Andy, lolling on the couch. Lou crept out of the office and toward the bathroom.

Light from the single bare bulb spilled out from under the bathroom door. Silence owned the shop floor, save for the vague whispers echoing off the close walls of the bathroom. Lou eased the flimsy wood veneer door open with his gun hand.

Demetria sat on the pot, the strap of her black dress pulled down. She cradled Johnny's head to her breast, stroking his bushy blond hair. His jeans and underwear were undone and pushed down to his knees His cock, half mast, glistened in the weak light.

"That's it, baby," she urged Johnny, "drink it all up." Eyes closed, Johnny suckled hard at her nipple.

"What the hell?" Lou breathed.

Her calm brown eyes met his. "I'm sorry, Lou. This wasn't the way this was supposed to go, but this one," she said, pulling Johnny's eager lips away from her breast. "This one got ahead of himself. I can't be mad at him. He just wanted to be the best daddy ever." She dabbed away the dark, tarry smear around Johnny's mouth with a scarlet lace handkerchief.

"So where does this put us now? Like I told you, I don't have that much money on me."

"How far is Coker Creek from here?"

"I'd guess a day and a half, a day if you drive hard."

"So," she said, "how much would it cost us to get there?"

"A hundred, maybe a hundred and a quarter," Lou said with a shrug.

"Do you have that much?" Her dark eyes harbored a glimmer of hope.

"Well," Lou said, rubbing his chin, "I don't want to call the law in."

"We'll be gone before you know it. And you'll never see us again."

"Promise?"

"I swear on the lives of my children," she declared.

"Sounds like the best deal, I've had all night," Lou said, pulling his wallet from his back pocket. He pulled a few bills and offered them to her.

"Johnny-babe," she whispered into his ear, "get up and pull up your britches. We're going home."

In a daze, Johnny groaned and complied with Demetria's wishes. She pulled herself off the grimy toilet and smoothed her dress down. "You know, Lou," she said, surveying the decrepit bathroom, "this place could use a woman's touch."

"It's not like I haven't heard that before."

"If you would be a dear and fetch Andy, Johnny and I will meet you out at the car." She slipped past Lou with Johnny lumbering in tow.

"Okay, cowboy," Lou grunted, throwing Andy's arm over his shoulder and heaved. "You're going home."

"Great," Andy burbled, "gonna start a whole new life." His body hung off Lou's shoulder, slack and heavy.

"Yeah, that woman of yours is something else. You'll be home in no time," Lou said and did a double-take.

A rivulet of black snot with iridescent bubbles like roe eggs oozed from Andy's nose.

Jesus, Mary and Joseph, just let me get this mook out the door, Lou thought.

Lou guided Andy's teetering steps through the shop and out the door. Finally, he got Andy sprawled across the trunk of the cherry-red Charger. Demetria opened the car door and helped Lou slide Andy into the back seat.

"Oh, Andy-wandy!" Demetria chided, as she wiped the black goo from Andy's face with her red handkerchief. "You're such a mess."

"You sure he's good to drive?" Lou said, nodding to Johnny who sat in the driver's seat with an empty stare.

"Oh sure, he'll be fine. I'll just keep him full of coffee with lots of sugar."

Andy's face pressed up against the backseat window with eyes closed, breathing through his mouth. Lou stared as a large black fly crawled out of Andy's gaping mouth and buzzed around the inside of the Charger.

"Uh, Demetria?"

"Yes?"

"Look," Lou said with a forced grin, "I know how hard it is for kids these days, just starting out. I just don't want to see Johnny and Andy have to come way back here to support their kids." He handed her the rest of the cash in his wallet.

"Oh, Lou!" she exclaimed. "That's sooo sweet! But there is no way I would ever let them come back here. This city is no place to raise a family." She popped into the passenger seat of the Charger.

Lou kept smiling; he hoped she would say something like that. The Charger rumbled to life and rolled away. Only when the muscle car turned the corner and was out of sight did he turn back to the safety of the shop. Inside, he stood in front of his fishing map. "Well, Rita," he said, plucking the pin out of the map, "that's one dump I'm never gonna fish at."

Dulce Duets

6:45 PM May 17th
The Sawney Residence
203 Sunflower Lane

Mmm, that was delicious, honey," said Jerry, dabbing his lips with a linen table napkin." I don't think I have ever had a chop as tender as that."

"Thank you, dear heart," Mary said. "I had been saving them in the freezer for a special occasion. I thought it would be a wonderful way to celebrate our two-month anniversary."

"Well, an anniversary is a year, but I'd say our two months is a pretty good start."

"Oh, Jerry, you always agonize over the details." She lifted the tray of good china and silverware from the small dining table covered with a light blue formal table cloth.

"What can I say? It's the curse of the accountant. The devil is always in the details."

Mary put the tray down, stepped behind Jerry and raked her nails up his chest. "And," she cooed in his ear, "what a horny little devil my accountant is."

He responded by reaching back underneath her flowered apron and caressing her warm soft breasts through her thin, silky dress.

"If you keep this up," she whispered, "we won't make it out of the house for date night."

Jerry gazed up into her loving eyes framed with a cascade of dark blond hair and said, "Priorities, right?"

"If we're going to make it an evening, I'm going to need help with the dishes."

After a mad dash of gathering the newlywed china and shuffling it to the kitchen, Mary set her wedding and engagement rings on the counter, determined to keep these symbols of commitment forever this time. Jerry, with a towel with a bright red rose print tucked into his slacks, dried the dishes as she washed. Within the glint of the gold ring, she caught an image of Jerry, beckoning at the end of another suburban house's driveway, illuminated by the bright yellow flickering light of a blazing fire.

"A moment of your time, sir?" the man said, taking the stool next to Prof at the bar of The Night Cafe.

"Sure," Prof said, putting his neat bourbon down. "English isn't your first language, is it?'

"No, is it that obvious?"

"I wouldn't say so. I've gotten pretty good at listening to voices. I'm guessing Eastern Europe?"

"Romania, actually; however, I have not been back in a long while. My name is Vic Teppish."

"The mystery man that Jane has been dating. Pleasure to make your acquaintance, Mr. Teppish. What can I do for you?"

"It's about Jane. I've been seeing her a few weeks, but she seems, well, guarded."

"Hmm… She has had a rough time of it. Her last boyfriend was a real piece of work from what I understand. He cheated on her."

"From where I come from, that would have been a ticket for a short ride on a very long pole."

"Pardon?"

"Sorry, I let my anger get the better of me sometimes."

"I can respect that," Prof said, "but she's been hurt. You know, if you don't let anyone in, you can't get hurt."

"You mean getting personal."

"Exactly," Prof said, dropping a couple of bills on the bar for Joey.

"Can I buy you another drink? I want to thank you for your insight."

"Thanks for the offer," Prof said as he thought about that brown box on his table across the street. "If you really want to thank me, just treat Jane gently." He picked up his white cane and headed to the front doors.

"*That was rich, a short ride on a long pole*," the sweet voice tittered. "*I bet you thought of doing the same to Lila and Stan.*"

"Don't go there," Prof whispered. "Maybe if it was just about them fucking around, but there was more to it than that."

"*I don't know*," the voice jabbed, "*that kind of betrayal is hard to justify. Anyway, if it hadn't happened, you wouldn't be here with me.*"

"And that should be a consolation?" Prof said, crossing Reed Shore Drive back to the Mittelmarch.

"*Only two hundred eighteen days to go, my love.*"

Jane paused to enter the green door with a brass handle. Prof recommended The Night Café as a safe place to meet, if you could count on a mumbling blind man's opinion. Vic offered to pick her up at her apartment, but she still couldn't bring herself to let him that close, even after six dates. Neutral ground was the best way to go.

The clattering from the pool table off to the left and the scent of grilled food calmed her. Prof, for all his quirks, had been right about this place. At the black bar, Vic sat in his dark blue suit with his gray fedora by his side. He turned and his anthracite eyes lit up at her approach.

"Been waiting long?" she said.

"For a lady?" he said with a wolfish grin, as he smoothed his short black hair. "Eternity is never too long to wait."

"I like the suit. It beats the black or gray ones you usually wear. I was beginning to feel like I belonged in a Bogart movie every time we went out."

"Hey, don't knock Bogie. He taught me everything I know about American English."

"Goddammit, Phil! You fucking call your shots on a money game!" shouted an all too familiar voice from the pool room in back. A chorus of beer-fueled cheers followed.

"Uh, Vic," Jane said as her face clouded, "I know this is last minute, but do you think we could go someplace else?"

"Sure," Vic said, noting her troubled expression. "Is there a problem?"

"No, there's just someone I'd prefer to avoid."

Vic peered back at the pool tables and said, "I understand. Let's go."

"I need to stop at the ladies' room first."

"Might be problematic. It's back past the pool tables."

"I'll risk it," Jane said and braved the noisy entourage of young professionals with loosened ties.

"Jane, baby!" called the young man with sandy blond hair and blue eyes. Stepping in front of her, he blocked her path.

"I'm fine, Rich."

Smelling of beer and cigars, he used the pool cue to steady his balance. "So, how've you been?" he slurred. "I've missed you so much."

"I'm here with somebody."

"Wow, that was quick!" Rich blurted. "No time to mourn would what could have been with us?" A series of "oohs" and "ahhs" issued from Rich's buddies.

"After I came home and found you humping that tramp, there were no us!"

"Hey, Janey-baby, don't be like that," Rich said, snatching her wrist.

"Let me go, you piece of shit!"

"Look," Rich rambled, "we get married and you don't have to work in that shitty diner or waste your time in school—"

"I said let go!"

"Problems?" Vic said, looming in the doorway of the pool room.

Rich turned to confront Vic and his eyes grew wide.

"Jane, why don't you go freshen up?" Vic said, as his smile darkened. "I'd like to have words with this fine gentleman."

Rich grip on her wrist slackened. Perplexed and concerned, she cocked her head and looked back to Vic.

"Not to worry, Jane." Vic dismissed, "it's just guy talk."

Although Vic's jovial smile seemed genuine for the moment, the cold shine in his eyes told a different story. "I'll be back in a minute," Jane replied, wanting no part of whatever came next.

"Hello, Rich," Vic addressed the young executive while extending his hand. "Those South American deals go your way?"

"Uh, yes," Rich said, taking Vic's hand.

"Good," Vic said. "What did I tell you? Fortune always favors the brave. How about, now?" He tightened his grasp on Rich's clammy hand.

One of Rich's associates barked, "Put him in his place, Rich. You the man!"

"You know, Rich, he has a point," Vic said, squeezing Rich's hand harder. "It's bad form for the alpha to show weakness in front of the pack. Are you going to show them who's the big dog?"

Rich considered the pool cue in his left hand as he eyed the pale, angular face of the smiling man holding his right hand. Moments of silence passed. Finally, he gave the order. "Guys let's blow this dump." Dropping the pool cue, he filed to the door with the rest of his friends.

Moments later, Jane emerged from the ladies' room, composed, but dreading why the bustle outside the door had become so still.

Vic leaned over the pool table and sank the eight ball.

"Where'd they go?" Jane asked.

"Who knows, who cares?" Vic said, replacing the cue on the rack. "Nice place, but can't say I'm impressed with the clientele. Seemed kind of low-rent. I'll get the car."

The green minivan still exuded the fresh car smell as Jerry eased it through the darkened streets. Between the note on the car and the mortgage on the house, Jerry discovered the gravity of commitment, yet when he looked over at Mary sitting in the passenger seat with her air of happiness, the weight lifted. "Hungry, honey?" he inquired.

"Mm, always," she said, peering out into the dark streets. "Not too many street vendors out tonight."

"Just keep an eye out, sweetheart. Oh, Bill asked if you wanted to come down to work at the courthouse instead of Human Services. It'd be great working together."

"That's great," she trailed off. A flash of chrome from a passing sedan evoked a vague memory of a silvery butcher's knife approaching a heavy-set man slumped on a sofa, covered in blood. His name was…Joe?

"You don't sound that enthusiastic about the idea."

"It's complicated," Mary said, biting her lip. "I'll explain later."

Glancing off to his right, Jerry said, "Hey look! I think we just found a place open for business."

A young woman in a black cocktail dress stood next to a black Lincoln Town car. Jerry slowed the van for approach. From the shadows, a man in a dark blue suit and a gray fedora stepped between the young woman and the minivan. Glowering, his dark eyes shone red in the minivan's headlights.

"Uh, take-out, Jerry?"

"Take-out," Jerry agreed and piloted the minivan towards Corral Street.

Vic and Jane stood in the dark foyer of natural stone. The clatter of plates issued from beyond the darkened arch. A lounge-act refrain of, "Try to set the night on fire," died amidst gentle applause.

"Damn," Vic said, "we missed Izzy's first show. The next one doesn't start for an hour."

"Are you sure about this?" Jane said. "This looks like the kind of place you need reservations."

"Oh, sure, Izzy's a friend from way back."

"Good evening," the hostess said, making her way from the dark arch to her station. "Welcome to The Crucible Club. Do you have reservations?"

"Rachel Cavanaugh?" Jane blurted in recognition of the hostess in the stunning white blouse and formal black skirt.

"Jane!" Rachel said. "You were one of the last people I'd ever expect to see here."

"Reyna and Demetria have been worried about you. It's like you disappeared off the face of the earth."

"It has to be this way until the divorce goes through," Rachel said. "Bobby and I are in subsidized housing, but that doesn't cover everything. Thankfully, Mr. Lanza hired me on. You know Jane; I think I understand what you have to go through."

"Rachel, the difference between this place and the diner is the difference between a BMW and a Chevy. I am glad to see you land on your feet in something like this."

"Do you have reservations?"

Jane looked at Vic, who said, "If you would call Iggy up and tell him the voivode from big T is here, he'll understand."

Puzzled, Rachel said, "Okay," and picked up the phone and punched the glowing red button. "Yes, Mr. Lanza? I have a gentleman, who said the voivode from big T is here… Yes, Sir, I'll seat them immediately."

"If you'll follow this way, please," Rachel beckoned and threaded them through the maze of small tables beyond the dark arch. Blue smoke hung heavily in the air. Finally, Rachel unhitched a red velvet rope and seated them at a massive booth upholstered in leather.

"They allow smoking in here?" Jane said.

"Iggy wouldn't have it any other way."

"My friend!" said a little man with wild, fiery hair skittering to the booth. "It has been so long."

"Iggy," Vic said. "How's the restaurant business?"

"Gangbusters, my friend!" Iggy exploded. "I couldn't be happier." The velvet of his midnight blue tuxedo with yellow stars swished as he seated himself next to the couple.

"This is my friend, Jane Davis. Jane, this is Mr. Iggy Lanza, the hottest restaurateur in the city, blazing entertainer and warm human being."

"I'll forgive the last insult due to the former accolades," Iggy said. "Ms. Davis, you are looking quite lovely." He proffered his limp, slender hand.

"Thank you, Mr. Lanza—"

"Iggy, Madam," he said. "How such a charming lady came to be in the company of voi—"

"Vic," Vic cut in.

"Vic, is beyond me. Can I get either of you an aperitif? We have a fine selection of ports, vermouths and liqueurs."

"The usual for me," said Vic.

"Yes, yes, I know," Iggy said, rolling his eyes and shaking his head. "You don't drink wine. How about you, Ms. Davis?"

"Whatever the host recommends, I defer to his expertise."

"Wisdom and diplomacy," Iggy sighed. "Why do all the good ones fall for the troublemakers?"

"Speaking of troublemakers," Vic said, "what's this I hear you're pitching for the Syrian?"

"Vic, you know that it's family; however, he could use you as a consultant."

"Iggy, you know the Syrian and you know what he is about. I don't want to have to save your tail like last time."

"They grow back."

"Aside from that," Vic said, "you know my policy. I don't get involved in turf wars."

"Thank you, Vic. You have always provided good advice, my friend."

"And one day, Iggy," Vic said, "you may actually take my advice."

"Thank you for coming, both of you," Iggy said. "I must take your leave to do my next show."

"What did he mean by they grow back?" Jane said.

"Trust me you don't want to know."

The drinks arrived, Benedictine for Jane and a pewter mug of a dark liquid for Vic.

"What are you drinking?"

"Personal blend," Vic said, taking a sip. "Iggy knows my tastes."

Soon, the silvery dinner cart arrived and helpings of tenderloin served on onyx black china with a gold leaf lizard motif around the edges. Jane sampled the fare.

"I would expect something like this uptown."

"Iggy knows his craft," Vic said, pushing morsels from one side of the plate to the other. "He's been doing this for a long time."

"You don't seem to be eating much," Jane said, savoring her meal.

A sad, sweet look crossed Vic's face and he said, "Food these days is an aside to a good dinner for me."

"What makes a dinner worthwhile for you, now?"

"A charming and vivacious dinner companion."

"So, how is this dinner shaping up?"

"One of the finest I've had in a very long time," he said as his dark eyes peered deeply into hers.

"Oh," she uttered with a blush.

The drum machine on the stage fired up a slow, easy beat as a cascade of applause arose from the tables.

"Do you dance?" Jane asked with an anticipatory smile.

"It's been awhile."

"You need a refresher course, c'mon!" Jane spouted as she hopped up, took Vic's hand and pulled him to the dance floor.

Vic encircled her warm, vibrant body and began to lead to the languorous rhythm of the music. The awkward stiffness of their dance melted away as Iggy crooned a sonorous tune about a love lost on the dunes of fiery Irem. Jane relented as she rested her head upon Vic's chest.

Vic closed his eyes and reflected on summer days and blue skies long forgotten. For them, the rest of the world faded away around them until Iggy's voice trailed off into the light ovation of the house patrons.

"Thank you," Jane whispered.

"Jane," he said, looking deep into her shining hazel eyes, "I should be thanking you."

"Shh," she said, placing a finger to his lips. A sweet, soft kiss followed.

Leaving the dance floor, arm in arm, Jane spotted the long table of dark-skinned men in silk suits. She held up her hand and looked away and said, "I really don't need this, now."

"Ms. Davis!" the little man with a long face at the head of the table commanded, "please come here." He stood and beckoned her.

"Is this going to be a regular occurrence with you, Jane?" Vic said.

"Please, stay close," she whispered, giving his hand a quick squeeze as they approached the table.

"Dr. Aksoy," she addressed the man with the big-toothed grin, "what a pleasant surprise."

"Ah, yes, it is," the Doctor said. "I did not expect to meet you here. I would have thought this establishment well-beyond your modest means."

"It is, normally," Jane said, "but Mr. Teppish decided to treat me to a most wonderful evening."

"Teppish?" Dr. Aksoy said with a raised eyebrow. "A most unusual name. May I inquire about your profession?"

"International logistics and security, sir," Vic said, "but no business tonight. I am here for pleasure with a lovely companion." Cocking his head, he continued, "You're Turkish, aren't you?"

"Why, yes," Dr. Aksoy beamed. "I am here entertaining the trade delegation from my homeland." He gestured to the four stylishly dressed men sitting to his right in the booth. "Tell me, Ms. Davis," he inquired, "have you given thought of my recommendations on restructuring your thesis?"

"Yes," Jane said, "but if I do that, my work will always be considered ancillary to yours and I worry that I will be regarded as a sycophant."

"Look at the good you could do for my country," Dr. Aksoy said, "and this will guarantee your grant. Do not worry about your professional reputation for you will be under my aegis. Besides, you will marry and leave the demanding work to men—"

"Typical Turk," Vic interjected.

"Pardon?"

"Thieving Turks stealing the hard work of others," Vic snapped. "A long-standing tradition that goes back to Mehmed the Second."

"I warn you that Mehmed the Second is an icon in my country akin to your Lincoln, Jefferson or Washington," Aksoy remarked. The color raced up to his face and concerned murmurs buzzed about the table.

"You mean Mehmed the Bedwetter?" Vic laughed. "He pissed in his own bed until he was nineteen. Hell, he couldn't go onto the field of battle without bringing two dry tunics. As for George Washington, I never heard George send for three fresh minutemen at Valley Forge to ease his carnal needs."

"You dare?" Doctor Aksoy sputtered and glared. The youngest of the delegates arose from his seat across the table with blood in his eyes.

"Stay seated, gentlemen," Vic said, as he shoved the heavy table with one hand, pinning Dr. Aksoy's guests to their seats. "What are you going to do, Doctor? Deny my grant? Reject my thesis? I'm not American, *arkadaş*, I'm Romanian."

Dr. Aksoy and the delegates gasped for air, trapped by the table.

"Son of the Dragon!" Iggy hollered, appearing with two bull-like men in ill-fitting suits in tow. "What is the meaning of this disturbance?"

"Sorry, I—" Vic stumbled, releasing his hold on the table.

"Please forgive me, Mr. Lanza," Jane stepped in. "This is my fault. Dr. Aksoy and I were having a professional difference of opinion and Vic believed he needed to defend my honor."

Iggy's features softened and a faint smile appeared on his lips. "Void—I mean, Vic—showing nobility after all these years? Sometimes, what appears terrible is a blessing in disguise."

"We should leave, "Jane replied quietly. "Iggy, I'm sorry for the scene."

"Oh pish-posh," Iggy dismissed her concerns. "This place needs a little drama now and then. The only entertainment here is an old windbag."

"Iggy," Jane added, "I really liked that fires of Iran song; it was really touching."

"It's called 'Longing for the Fires of Irem,'" Iggy corrected. "It is a personal piece I wrote long ago." His eyes took on a brief, faraway stare. "Vic," he directed, "you must bring her back here. Perhaps her sophistication, good manners and excellent taste in music will rub off on you…"

"Taken into consideration, Iggy. Good night." Jane and Vic left.

"Now, gentlemen," stated Iggy, placing his hands on the delegates' table, "I would like an explanation of why you felt the need to upset two of my very dear friends."

"Did…did you refer to him as Son of the Dragon?" Dr. Aksoy stammered, looking very pale.

The music from the last dancer's set ended in Subrosa's. Awash in cigarette smoke, Jerry and Mary listened to bleach-blond Tanya's story.

"I came here for school," said Tanya, toying with a lock of her hair, "but dancing is exciting and the money's great."

"Can we get you another drink?" Jerry said. He tried hard not to ogle Tanya in her leopard skin bikini.

"No, I'm good. You folks are really generous."

"Well, Tanya," Mary whispered, as she leaned in, "it is so easy when you meet someone as talented and gorgeous as you." She moved her hand to touch Tanya's knee and stroke up her firm thigh.

"Are you two…liberal?" Tanya asked with a blush.

"And if we are?" Mary replied sweetly.

"Well," Tanya said, "there is a dating fine of two hundred dollars."

Jerry and Mary exchanged a knowing glance. Jerry opened his wallet and handed Mary the bills. "I'll go get the car," he said and got up and left.

Alone with Tanya, Mary passed the money to Tanya under the table. Tanya's eyes grew wide when she saw the amount. "Let me go get changed and I'll be right back," she whispered and hustled back behind the bar, her hips swinging the entire way.

Mary's pulse quickened as she opened her purse and retrieve the fold of paper. After a quick look around, she poured the powder into Tanya's fruit juice.

Her eyes focused on one of the blue stage lights. The shade of blue was exactly the color of the night light. She smelled gasoline and crept towards the blood-stained bassinet with the gleaming butcher's knife.

"Ready to go?" Tanya asked, breaking Mary's spell.

"I just wanted to finish my drink," Mary said, sipping her Seven and Seven. "Besides, keeping him waiting for a minute will make this so much more fun."

"I like the way you think," Tanya tittered, draining her glass.

Jerry drove the minivan through downtown for a half an hour. Mary peeped into the back seat. Tanya was sprawled upon the bench seat; her denim miniskirt rode high revealing her black panties.

"Looks like the baby is asleep," Mary said in a whispery giggle.

"A good night for takeout, sweetheart," Jerry said, never taking his eyes off the road.

"One heck of a night," Vic said, as he looked across the Gulf Canal. The reflections of the city lights bounced upon the slow-moving dark surface.

"I'll say this, Mr. Teppish," Jane said, perched on the edge of the Lincoln, "you sure know how to show a girl an interesting time."

"Seems to me the interesting events were only half my doing."

"Well," she said, "I really try to avoid trouble."

"You know, sometimes the only way to deal with trouble is head on."

"I guess you proved that works," she said, "most of the time."

"What can I say?" Vic said. "I might have a few anger issues to work out."

"I guess we all have baggage to deal with. Which reminds me, 'Son of the Dragon'?" She peered deep into his dark eyes.

"It's a really long story."

"I've got the time, Vic."

"Not tonight, it's getting late."

"Vic-y," Jane chided in a mock-Cuban accent, "you got a lot of 'splaining' to do." She draped her arms around his neck and kissed him, hooking her legs behind his.

"Okay, wow," Vic said, breaking the kiss. "Where can I drop you off at?"

"How about," she began with a twinkle in her eye, "my apartment?"

"Open your goddam mouth, Bitch!" Jerry shouted, as he slapped Tanya across the face. She writhed in naked agony, strapped down to the plywood table. Sweat poured off Jerry's body, soaking his black leather jockstrap. He pounded the table; they'd played too long and the cocktail had worn off. Now, Tanya lacked the supple compliance of an hour ago.

"Let me try, sweetheart," Mary begged, her hair dampened from the evening's passion. She adjusted the collar that was connected to her black PVC cat suit with chrome chains as she caressed their collection of toys, neatly arranged upon the table. "You know," she teased, as she picked up a butt plug of black latex, "you can get lure more flies with honey than vinegar."

After lubing up the plug, Mary leaned over Tanya's glistening body. Reaching underneath Tanya's spread legs, Mary gently stroked and cooed in Tanya's ear, "Oh, baby, Mama's going to make it all better."

Tanya's hips rolled rhythmically to Mary's ministrations. Mary eased the plug into her and Tanya gasped. Mary stroked and teased Tanya's mons and whispered, "That's it, baby. Let it happen."

Tanya rocked and writhed upon the table. As her mouth opened wide to moan, Mary dribbled the contents of one of Bill's special vials into Tanya's mouth; the convulsions occurred immediately. "Easy, baby," Mary said as she cradled Tanya's head, "don't fight it." The convulsions subsided and Tanya lay still.

Satisfied with her work, Mary stepped back and wiped her brow. "We need to get her dressed and drop her off somewhere before she wakes up."

"You are a natural at this, sweetheart."

"Honey, focus," Mary said, caressing Jerry's sweaty cheek.

"Not a problem. I know a store on Bianchi Street."

"Longing for your bachelor days, sweetheart?"

"Oh no, honey, it's just convenient. After that, I don't understand why you don't want to work downtown with us."

"As much as I'd love to," she said, looking down, "I won't be able to fit in this in a few months." She fiddled with a chain of her costume.

"You're losing me."

"Because, silly," she said, looking up mischievously, "I'm pregnant."

"That's incredible!" Jerry said, as he hugged Mary. "How long?"

"About two months."

"On our wedding night, no less! I got to let Bill and the guys know about this."

"Well," Mary offered, "you could do it over Sunday brunch. It seems I have some tender veal cutlets I've been saving for the right occasion."

Ice Cream Socials

11:45 AM June 8th
The Crucible Lounge
1856 Bessemer Avenue

Gentlemen," Iggy said, his voice echoing off the walls of dark volcanic stone, "please, keep in mind that I neither work for The Syrian nor am I'm involved his business. In this case, I am merely a representative sent on his behalf to find an agreeable resolution to this dispute."

"Really?" Rex said. "You represent this guy and you don't have a dog in this fight?"

"No, Mr. Brunet, I'm a restaurateur and entertainer by trade and I am acting in this capacity as a favor to a dear friend."

"Funny," Saul said, glaring at the small, goggle-eyed man, "for a guy who runs an eatery, you use some heavy-duty muscle." He gestured toward the two hulking men posted on either side of the entry arch, arms crossed.

"Who? You mean Sheridan and Lamar? They've been with me for ages."

"Still," Saul said, "it kind makes me wonder what goes on here."

Rex shook his head; he regretted bringing Saul to the negotiation table. At least Saul dressed up in sports jacket and slacks for the sit down instead of one of his usual track suits. "Saul," Rex said, "let's not get off subject. Mr. Lanza, The Syrian is conducting business in my town. I do not foresee this as a problem and I think he would value the services that we bring to the table."

"And those would be?"

"We have people who can move his inventory, and, of course, there is the question of legal authorities."

"I'm sure he is content with his current customers, but he would be interested your relationship with the local law enforcement."

"It's not just the cops," Rex said. "It goes farther than that."

"Without a doubt, Mr. Brunet, the scope of your own business interests requires far more than a few policemen. How much will your licensing cost?"

"Forty percent."

"I will relay your offer," Iggy said, "but I am certain what his response will be."

"You tell him," Saul said, "that this is insurance. You know, God forbid something should happen."

Sheridan and Lamar reached under their scruffy gray suit jackets. Iggy lifted one bony manicured finger. "Mr. Reeve, Sheridan and Lamar are a bit protective. Tossing about threats is much akin to waving a red flag in front of bulls." The two bodyguards resumed their stance.

Rex glowered at the silver-haired man on his right.

"What?" Saul said. Rex's hard-eyed, silent rebuke made Saul add, "I got to go to the can." He navigated through the dining room's maze of tables to the archway.

"Pardon my associate, Mr. Lanza," Rex said.

"Dickheads," Saul muttered, as he passed between Sheridan and Lamar. He crossed the vaulted foyer to the men's room, grumbling. Muscle or not, Rex needed to put the snotty restaurant owner in his place. A door flush with the walnut paneling popped open and Rachel Cavanaugh emerged, dressed in a pink t-shirt and faded jeans. Her green eyes grew wide.

"Rachel!" Saul said. "How you doin'?"

"Hello Saul, I didn't expect to see you here."

"Me and Rex have got business with the little freak," he said, pointing back to the arch. "So, what are you doing here?"

“Working. I have to go check in the vendor deliveries.”

“Rachel, you need to talk to Sam. He’s been so worried about you and little Bobby. He really wants to work this out.”

“Really?” she said, appraising Saul’s forced grin. ‘That’s what divorce lawyers are for.” She marched away and slammed the kitchen door behind her.

With a quick glance around, Saul slipped through the door Rachel had exited from. On the gray office desk, covered in papers, a computer hummed. With a couple of taps on the keyboard, Saul smiled.

“I will pass your offer on to him,” said Iggy as he and Rex passed through the archway to the foyer, “but I don’t think he will be receptive.”

“Thank you for your time and attention,” Rex said. “I am disappointed. It took time and effort to arrange this meeting. Your friend is not an easy man to get a hold of.”

“He is a very private individual, and prefers to conduct new business through proxies. Good day, Mr. Brunet.”

Rex joined Saul in the foyer and left through the massive wood and wrought iron doors.

Out in the sunny street, Rex said, “Saul, how many times do I have to tell you? You don’t drop the hammer that early in a negotiation.”

“Relax, Skip, you knew he wouldn’t go for it anyways, right?”

“True.”

“It sounds like he’s going to need some incentive,” Saul said. “On top of that, guess who I ran into?”

“Who?”

“Sam’s wife, Rachel. She’s working for that freak show. We could throw him a bone, too.”

“Make the calls, Saul,” Rex said. “It’s gonna be a busy day.”

"Thank you for coming in on your day off, Rachel," Iggy said amidst the stacks of boxes on the loading dock. "I am simply no good at this. I could never quite get the hang of the abacus and tablets thing."

"I need to thank you, Mr. Lanza," she said, putting down the clipboard.

Iggy cocked a bushy red eyebrow.

"I mean, Iggy."

"Much better, Rachel. With your current difficulties and a young boy to raise, I thought you could do with some extra funds."

"Well," she said, looking around the stacks of cold boxes, "your vendor bills are sorted and paid and I reconciled the credit card statements. I'll get this stuff back in the freezer."

"No need, Rachel, I'll get Lamar and Sheridan to do the heavy lifting. Add a couple of hours to your time sheet."

"Iggy, I really appreciate your kindness and you're a great boss," she said," but I can't work here anymore."

"Why on earth, not? Things are running so efficiently with you here. Is it the hours or the staff?"

"No. It's those two men who were in here just now. They know my husband. I don't want him to know where I work."

"Ms. Cavanaugh," said Iggy, placing a finger to his cheek and closing his eyes, "I am sorry to place you and your son in harm's way. I had no idea—"

"It's not your fault, Iggy," This is my problem. I'll deal with it."

"Of course, you will, Rachel; however, it always helps to have friends. Let me talk to some people. In the meantime, where are you parked?"

"I've kept the car in the garage. I didn't want to give Sam a chance of finding me and Bobby. I've been taking the bus."

"Hmmm, I think from now on that I will have a driver bring you to work, though that isn't an immediate solution. Do you think you can get from here to the bus stop without being seen?"

"It's only five blocks—"

"Excellent!" Iggy said with a sweep of his arm. "Now fly away home, mother bird. Thine hatchling needs thee."

"Always the showman, Iggy," Rachel said.

"Indubitably, madam," Iggy said with a deep flourish as he watched the lovely lady in worn running shoes trot down the alley.

"I...go...with...her?" Lamar snorted and stomped his foot. "Like...Ms. Cavanaugh."

"Ah, Lamar," Iggy said as he turned to regard the burly man with a shaved head. "Your guardian instincts are as astute as ever. But no, my dear friend, you are easily identifiable. They have seen you already."

"But...she...needs...protecting," Lamar rumbled back.

"Calm yourself," Iggy said, "no, I think subtlety is necessary here. Is that chap from Phoenix available?"

"You mean Freddie? Not subtle...messy."

"True," Iggy said, "but we've no other options. Make the call, now, so we can reserve some of his time. After that dismal tete-a-tete, I have a feeling Freddie is going to be quite busy, today."

The hiss of the grill and the murmur of the lunch crowd in The Nighthawks Diner flowed around Prof and Sergeant Serrano seated at the busy counter.

"A chocolate shake?" Nick said, peering over at Prof and the large frosty stainless-steel cup before him.

"What can I say?" Prof said with a shrug. "I'm taking your advice and trying to do things a bit differently." He took another slurp.

"Good to hear," the big cop said, flexing his massive arms, happy to be back in his summer blues. "You're looking better, Prof," he continued. "Laying off the sauce is helping, but if you really want to get healthy, you oughtta try one of those whey-based mixes. I get them at the gym all the time. They help build the bulk."

"I'll try that, but baby steps first."

"At least you're not hanging around with Nate anymore."

"Haven't seen much of him, lately. Pass him in the hall occasionally. I think he's got something big going on."

"Was afraid of that. Nate is gonna find himself in way over his head one of these days."

"What is it between you and Nate? You seem to have it in for him."

"Nah, I've known the runt since high school at St. Marks. He's a couple of years younger than me. He still holds the record for demerits."

"For some reason, I'm not surprised,"

"It's messed up. One week he contributed three hundred bucks to the football uniform fund, granted he got the money from selling pot brownies. The next week, we beat the crap out of him in the back parking lot after finding out he'd paid off a couple of the line men to throw the game. He's not a bad guy, but one day, he's going to go too far," Nick said, "and I don't want to be the one who sends him off."

"More coffee, Nick?" Jane interrupted. "How about you, Prof?"

"I'm good," Prof said.

"Here you go, Jane," Nick said, offering a five-dollar bill. "Keep the change…"

"Nick," Jane said, "we don't charge cops for coffee."

"I said keep it."

"Meet the last honest cop," Prof stated aloud, "in a city gone bad."

Jane and Nick stared at Prof.

"Would make a heck of a movie trailer, wouldn't it?" Prof said.

"You should write that down, Prof," Jane said.

"I wanted to write at one time, but you know work, marriage, life…"

"What's stopping you, now?" Jane said.

"*She has a point, Prof,*" the voice whispered in his ear.

"So, how's it going with this new beau of yours?" Prof said.

"A lady never tells," she said with a quick wink.

Rachel quickened her pace as she left the dim alley filled with trash for the bright sidewalk of broken concrete. Iggy's offer of help failed to calm her, for Sam's connections spread everywhere. For a moment, she regretted that night back in January.

Sam had arrived home late, smelling of whiskey. "Where's my fucking dinner?" he said.

"In the oven," she said. "It was ready two hours ago. You should have called."

"I work late to pay for this shit," he said, the color rising in his thick cheeks. His thick arm swept about the neat living room. "Don't go busting my balls."

The traces of scarlet shone brightly against the pristine white of his shirt collar. "Yeah, right, working… What's her name?"

"Fucking bitch!" he said as his backhand smacked across her mouth. "I should have left you with that loser brother of mine."

Knocked to the floor, hot tears welled in Rachel's eyes.

"Mommy!" She heard Bobby cry. Bare feet padded over to her and small soft arms encircled her.

"Get away from her, you little fuck!" Sam said as he yanked his son away. A thud followed. Sam's black oxford slammed into Bobby, who was locked in a fetal position.

The new earrings, a gift from Reyna that day, burned in her ears. A hot, swampy forest flashed before her. "In the mangroves," the voice of a British woman spoke, as if narrating a nature documentary, "the mother tiger must defend her cub from the male." Rachel's lip curled back in a snarl; she pounced.

Gathering up Bobby, she fled the house, leaving Sam holding his blood-covered face, howling. From the first uncertain nights in the women's shelter, she ran the gamut of lawyers, councilors and bureaucrats and cleared the hurdles placed before her. She secured a subsidized apartment for her and Bobby. The shabby two-bedroom in a bad part of town was very different from their home in the Gates, but it was hers and Bobby's and safe. Answering a small wanted ad, she'd found herself in front of the ancient brick building on Bessemer Avenue. Intimidated, but determined, she interviewed with the strange little owner, Mr. Lanza. Although she had not waitressed in over ten years, Iggy listened to her story and offered her a job. They were small victories, but they were hers.

When she and Sam had married, she was twenty-six weeks pregnant; it read like those last-minute miracles in a romantic comedy. After losing the man the heroine pined for, the successful romantic lead appeared and they lived happily ever after. At twenty, she gave herself a pass for innocence, but she owned the years of denial that followed. It started simple—a sly grin from Sam and one of his put downs at a dinner party for his clients. He raised the stakes with a serious talk about how she wasted his money. Later, after muffled phone calls and a few shots of bourbon, he screamed at her to keep out of his business. Every time, he came back with soft apologetic words, flowers or candy. She took it in stride; he never hit her without cause. Part of her thought she deserved it, until that night Sam kicked Bobby. Now, Rachel saw what was coming.

All the while, she played legal hide and seek with Sam. The lawyers insisted on patience. Certainly, the court would grant the divorce, but none could see a way to grant a restraining order without a witness. Sam, the consummate chess player, sacrificed temporary child support and visitation rights for a long-term game. She watched Sam before; it was never pretty. She suspected Sam had run his brother, Jake, out of town with a bad business deal. If he would do that to his brother, what would he do to her?

In the meantime, Sam looked for his opportunity.

She paused at a boutique window where a small placard advertised:

Hope for the Hopeless!

Fox Fashions Proudly Sponsors
A Blood Drive at the Ayrshire Avenue Clinic
Donate and Receive a 40% Discount for Everything in the Store
Be Compassionate AND Stylish!

She smiled. It made sense in a Reyna kind of way. As much as she missed Reyna and the rest of her friends, she dared not give Sam an opening.

"Yo, Rachel!" a voice called.

Turning, an unshaven man in a green ski cap man sat in a blue utility van. "Thought it was you," he said. "There's someone who wants to me talk to you."

"No, I don't think I have the time," she said, backing away.

"Did I say it was a choice?" he said, scratching his stubbled chin. The side doors of the van opened and two rough men in plaid shirts and blue jeans jumped out.

The roar of an engine and the screech of tires heralded the arrival of the bright red Trans Am, which slammed into reverse and skidded in neatly behind the van. With tires billowing smoke, a rail-thin man hopped through the T-roof and landed on the sidewalk, the gold spurs on his boots jingling.

"Howdy, ma'am," the deeply-tanned old man said to Rachel with a tip of his scarlet cowboy hat. "Gents."

"Move it, old man," one of the toughs said. "This is none of your business."

"Well, sonny," the man drawled, "why don't you let me be the judge of that?" He extended his hand. "You fellas can call me Freddie." The sun glinted off his large, gold belt buckle.

"I don't give a fuck who you are," the tough said, pulling his black nine-millimeter from the front of his pants.

Freddie's aged blue eyes shifted to Rachel." Ma'am, I would reckon this would be an appropriate time to high-tail."

Rachel bolted.

“So, you wanna slap leather, hombre?” Freddie said, reaching for his chromed Colt .45 Peacemaker.

The two men in flannel shirts blasted away a full clip each. Freddie staggered under hail of bullets and his gun dropped from his hand with a clatter. Wiping his hand up the front of his brilliant white shirt, he looked at his blood-covered fingers and grinned. “Ya got me, pardners,” he sputtered and collapsed across the hood of the immaculate Trans Am. His vacant blue eyes stared at the sky, still grinning.

“Fuck, this is all we need, Ronnie,” the man in the van said. “Get in. She’s got a good head start on us.”

“Is there a bakery around here?” Ronnie said aloud, while sniffing the air.

“Hey,” one of the others said, observing the copious amounts of white smoke rolling off the dead cowboy. “Bodies aren’t supposed to do that, are they?”

The cowboy and his car erupted in a fireball, engulfing the van and the men.

Saul slid into the passenger seat of Rex’s glossy black Allente. “Okay,” he began, “the Syrian’s got a deal going down on the pier tonight.”

“Get some people on it. Show this turd the price of not doing business with us.” He pulled the car away from the curb.

“Already done,” Saul said and slipped on his gold-framed sunglasses. “Have some hard fuckers from down south on it.”

“Good.”

“I haven’t heard back from the boys, but I had a couple of guys nose around the bitch’s apartment complex earlier. I passed the details on to Sam.”

“Whatever keeps the shyster happy,” Rex said.

"Hissss!" Bobby cried, as he jumped around the corner with the hand-carved, segmented toy snake.

Rachel leapt back in mock surprise.

"Gotcha!" he chuckled, mirth sparking in his blue eyes.

"Got you!" Rachel said, reaching out and pulling the blond-haired rascal close.

"Are we going for ice cream?" Bobby asked.

"Uh…" Rachel hesitated, still rattled from this afternoon. She had never looked back after she ran. She heard gunfire and a dull roar. The sirens followed, but she waited for the bus and shuddered the entire way home.

"It's okay, mom," Bobby said, his eyes downcast. "I know we don't have much money."

"Aww, sweetie," Rachel said and hugged him tighter. She hated he knew the situation. Money had been tight, but Jake, Sam's brother, had sent a money order from points unknown. This month, he sent Bobby the toy snake, the only present he'd received for this birthday. "Oh," she said, "I think we have enough for a treat." She patted him on the back.

"Can I bring Snakie?" he asked.

"I don't see why not."

After a brisk, two-block jaunt, they found themselves seats in the Happy Family Creamery, where Bobby dug into his double-dutch chocolate sundae with extra sprinkles and Rachel enjoyed one scoop of vanilla.

"Is Uncle Jake ever going to visit us?" Bobby asked between spoonfuls.

"That's hard to say; his job keeps him moving."

"He's a carpenter, right?"

"He's one of the best," she said.

"I think it's neat, building stuff."

"You could be like your father, a lawyer," Rachel offered.

Bobby grimaced.

"An attorney is a hell of a profession, sport," Sam said, walking up behind Bobby with an armload of roses. "You get to meet all sorts of people who know a bunch of neat stuff." He plopped down in a seat next to Rachel. "Hi honey, did you miss me?"

"Not really," said Rachel, concentrating on her bowl. "The white suit makes you look like a pimp." She fought to control her breathing.

"It's after Memorial Day and it's cooler," he said, mopping his brow with a handkerchief.

"At least the sunglasses hide the scars for the most part."

"Look, let's put the past aside. I know I have a temper—"

"No," she cut in, "you have an inferiority complex."

"To whom?" he said. He spotted Bobby's toy snake on the table. Picking up the toy, he announced, "I believe I have seen this kind of handiwork, before." The brittle toy snapped in two between Sam's fat fingers.

"You bitch!" Sam thundered. "You've been seeing him behind my back all these years."

"No! He's just helping me out."

"Helping you drive me into the poorhouse," he said, rising from his seat. The slap sent Rachel sprawling to the white tile.

"Leave her alone!" Bobby yelled, grabbing the cuff of Sam's jacket.

As Sam looked at the small, chocolate-covered hands that smeared his new suit, his vision grew red. A quick shove sent Bobby flying back into the wall.

"That's enough, mister!" a strong voice commanded and Sam's face slammed upon the gray marble tabletop. One wrist and then the other snapped into steel cuffs. "You are being charged with assault and battery," the officer continued.

"You're making a big mistake, officer," Sam said.

"That's Sergeant Serrano."

"Think about your next move, Sergeant. I got friends downtown."

"Are you two okay?" Nick said to Rachel who was tending to Bobby's bloody nose.

"A few bruises and a bloody nose," Rachel replied. "We've had worse..."

"Okay," Nick said. "I'll get you down to the station for charges. I'm sure this warrants a restraining order. I'd better call for a paramedic."

"Why? It's only a bloody nose."

Nick smiled as he lifted Sam's head and smashed it into the cold, marble tabletop.

"Check this shit out!" Lem whispered, as he poked through the heavily-laden tractor trailer with his flashlight. "Big screen TVs, this will be easy to move. Are you sure Saul said we don't have to kick something upstairs?"

"No," Blake whispered back. "He just said leave the bodies strung up. This is all about sending a message."

A set of headlights flared at the back end of the trailer.

"Goddam," Blake muttered, pulling his shotgun up and easing back towards the doors. "I knew this was too easy." Lem followed his heavy-set partner.

A man stood silhouetted in the yellow beams of the Trans Am. He lit his cheroot with a match, briefly illuminating his flat, maroon cowboy hat with gold conchos. He took a long drag off his cheroot and said in a low tone, "How you boys doin', tonight?"

"You picked the wrong place for a smoke break," Blake growled, gripping his shotgun tighter.

The man said, "Well, I reckon we all make mistakes from time to time." He flipped his dark red duster open to reveal the twin Colts strapped to his hips.

Blake and Lem responded with blasts from their shotguns. The stranger skidded across the firebird-emblazoned hood into the sleek windshield.

"Dipshit," Lem said, scratching his scraggly beard.

"Why the fuck do I smell cinnamon?" said Blake, looking around and wrinkling his nose.

The fiery blast of golds and reds was the last thing either of them saw.

Prof tapped out the number on the pad of the payphone. He listened closely for any activity on the quiet seven floor hallway. As the voicemail beeped, he spoke quickly. "Jones, this is John Clarke. We met a few weeks ago, in Wrightsway Park. I got some information you were looking for, if you're interested." He quickly hung up his phone.

"*Was that necessary?*" she challenged. "*He's a criminal, but he is your friend.*"

"Look," Prof muttered, as walked to his room, "it's like Serrano said. He is going to get himself in over his head. If he's stopped now, he might just have a chance."

"*I've always heard man is a rational creature*," the voice shot back, "*and can rationalize any atrocity. I'm disappointed in you, Prof; I thought you knew what betrayal was all about!*"

"It's not the same!" Prof said and slammed the door to his room.

Rennie watched the door and yawned. The major players had left the casino a couple of hours ago. On the job five months, and he still failed to adjust to the night shift. Mr. Brunet, impressed with his track record on collections, offered him the job after Tim quit. Rex's only major concern was to get the night's take deposited first thing in the morning. Other than the lack of sleep, the job ran itself. The cameras took care of the cheaters. Phil and Craig, who stalked the steel catwalks above with high powered rifles, kept the trouble to a minimum. All Rennie needed to worry about was an occasional drunk or a pissed-off loser

He heard the rumble of a tricked-out engine and the slush of gravel out in the parking lot. With a few steps, the steel door banged open. A young man in a bright red derby and a crimson shirt strutted in. He beamed a smile as bright as the gold bolo tie around his neck.

"Are you old enough to be in here, kid?" Rennie said.

"Old enough to drink, chase women, place a bet or take a life," the youngster spouted.

"You got proof of ID?"

"Why sure do, sir!" the young man said and produced a wrinkled piece of paper, yellowed with age.

"Freddie the Kid?" Rennie read aloud and looked up with a sneer. "Is this some sort of joke?"

"No, sir, this is what we refer to as a stick up," Freddie said with a laugh. He hoisted his .45 Peacemaker in the air and let off a shot.

Looking to the catwalks, Rennie placed a finger to his temple.

"All right, all you ladies and fine gentlemen," Freddie announced," please drop all of your valuables in front of me in a neat and orderly fashion—" The cracks of Craig's and Phil's rifles cut Freddie's speech short. Freddie dropped to the floor, still smiling, his vacant blue eyes staring at the corrugated steel ceiling.

Standing over the youth's body, Rennie asked, "Hey, did one of you guys leave a coffee cake in the microwave?"

The Earth Mother Blues

6:30 AM June 17th
Ayrshire Avenue Free Clinic
2050 Ayrshire Avenue

Vivian paused to smell the light pink rose, covered in dew. The dark sweetness of the scent reminded her of myrrh. She sighed as she looked at the myriad of petals littering the grimy concrete courtyard of the clinic. Long ago, rose bushes like this one had lined the street and given the road its name, Ayrshire. Now, a sad mix of crumbling brick apartments and row houses of worn clapboard replaced those bushes. Every morning, on her way into the clinic, Vivian paid her respects to this last rosebush; it was a battered survivor, like everything in the city.

"Good morning, Terry," she said to the muscular young man in green scrubs behind the admitting desk.

"Morning, Viv, ready for another day at the butcher's?"

"I really wish you wouldn't call it that."

"I've done triage under fire when I was in the service and working here makes that look like a walk in the park."

"You're exaggerating."

"Not by much," Terry said, tossing his pen on the stack of files, "and I never had to patch up kids."

"Terry," she said, "you graduated six months ago, and you just passed your boards less than a month ago. It's not easy, but it gets easier to deal with in time. It's about—"

"I know, compromise and survival," he said. He ran his hand through his cropped black hair. "Anyway, that guy picked up his package last night. I left the envelope in the bottom drawer of your filing cabinet."

"You need to learn the safe combination. We don't need to have this much cash lying around."

"Forget it," Terry said, getting up from his chair, "I'm already deeper in this than I want to be."

Six months, tops, she thought as she watched Terry pace away to the breakroom to get his usual black coffee. Like previous RNs, City Municipal or, better yet, Sapienta Northwest, would snap him up and his stint at the clinic would be a bad dream. As she had done many times before, she would write a glowing letter of reference for his application packet. Unlike the others before him, she would actually miss Terry.

She passed the rows of waiting room seats of molded chipped yellow plastic. When they opened at nine, the surge of patients raced through the front doors to check in and jockeyed for these seats. They waited, chattered, and grumbled as Terry or one of the other RNs called out their numbers. In the meantime, their children fought over the scant broken toys on the worn patch of carpet in the far corner. One RN, a plump little brunette with a dark sense of humor, used to refer to it as "God's Little Waiting Room." Vivian forgot her name; she had moved on, too.

Opening the door which read, "Vivian Greene, Nurse Practitioner, Director of Medical Services," Vivian retrieved the manila envelope from the bottom drawer of the filing cabinet. Her count of the fresh bills came to two thousand dollars, as expected. Four pints of clean blood every Monday and no questions stretched the supply budget just a bit further.

"*Lo! The ruin which his treachery led,*" the voice chanted in a rhythmic low moan," *for Prof is a total doo-doo head.*"

Prof sighed and put down his pen. "You know better than I do, that an elegiac couplet is completely inappropriate for a parode by a Greek chorus," he criticized aloud, closing the cardboard box. "Besides, to do it right, you'd need seven of your sisters."

"*There's nothing right about this, Prof,*" the voice accused, "*Nathan should've made bail and been back days ago.*"

Prof sat in silence. In this same chair nine days earlier, he'd heard the officious knock on Nathan's door, the muffled conversation and the sound of footsteps down the stairs.

He expected Nate to make bail and slide back into the Mittelmarch lobby that afternoon. J.J., down at the front desk, shrugged and said, "If he's not back by the 5th, I just go up there and put his stuff in storage. It's not like he's got a lot of shit. I've done it more times than I care to think about."

"*An English professor at a complete loss for words. You know I'm right; you threw Nathan under the bus and you're doing the same things that were done to you.*"

"Former professor," Prof said as his fists beat lightly on either side of his head and he rocked back and forth in his chair.

"*Pardon?*"

"I said, former professor," Prof exploded. "I'm broke, unemployed, divorced and blind! How the fuck do you think you're right? In what fucking dimension?"

"*The first three are of your own making,*" the voice said. "*As for the last, you agreed to our deal.*"

"A year and a day," Prof reasoned in a fuming black heat. "You know, that's the minimum sentence for a convicted felon. What the fuck am I convicted of?"

"*I can't answer that, Prof.*"

"Shut up!" Prof roared. He swept the cardboard box off the rickety table.

A solid knocking at the door followed the crash of the box. "Prof?" J.J. asked. "Is everything okay? There's a cab waiting to take you downtown."

Entrenched in her office, Vivian tallied the results of the weekend blood drive. "Guys, we need Reyna to do this again," she said to her office plants, her "immortals." The fiddle leaf in one corner, the butterfly palm in the other, the aloe plant on her desk and the hunter's ivy hanging above her never answered back, but thrived on neglect in the windowless office.

With a quick rap, Terry stuck his head in the office and said, "Vivian? The Jorgensens are here."

"Dr. Cohen needs to see them," Vivian said, looking up from her computer.

"He called in an hour ago."

"At least he called in this time. Dr. Willis?"

"Won't be in until after lunch, golf meeting," Terry said. "Vivian, it's bad. He's insisting on seeing you."

"This doesn't need to be dropped in the laps of the interns," she said and locked her computer. "Send them in."

A stooped, balding man in stained khakis shuffled in, leading a disheveled woman in a green sundress and a blank stare. Vivian waited while the man eased the woman into the office chair and he dropped into the other.

"Ms. Greene," he said, "she's gone. This morning…"

"Mr. Jorgensen, I'm sorry, but this day was coming." With effort, her green eyes remained dry.

"I know, I know," he said with a wave of his shaking hand. "If the Human Services people see Elsie like this—"

"We went over your options months ago."

"Options? You call that an option?" he barked, "You've seen that place. That's not an option; it's her dying in her own shit and piss!"

"Calm down, Mr. Jorgensen," Vivian said. "The Skymore Home is the only licensed place nearby. It's the best place for her."

"But they won't take me, too, right?" he asked. His lower lip quivered.

"No, they only handle late-stage Alzheimer patients."

"We've been together forty years..."

"Have you discussed this with your son?"

"Todd? Yeah, I asked him a couple of months ago. He said they've got no room since Lisa moved back in with the new grandbaby." He pinched the bridge of his nose and said, "Ms. Greene, I want the option that you gave Frank and Cathy Delanski last year."

"You know about that?"

"Yeah, I used to drink with Frank at the VFW before they passed away. He told me all about it."

"Then you know how it works?"

"Frank told me not to spread it around and I haven't. How long do you think it'll give us?"

Vivian rested her chin upon her hands and studied the skinny, wrinkled man and his wife, with her blank stare and half-open mouth. Finally, she concluded aloud, "Four days."

"That's it?" he said. "Frank and Cathy got a month."

"Different circumstances. Take it or leave it."

He regarded Elsie while rubbing his face. "Sure," he said, "let's do it."

He watched Vivian stand up and smooth her crisp, white uniform skirt. She locked the office door. In a daze, he watched the curvy nurse, her graying blond hair pulled neatly into a tight bun, bend over and retrieve a vial of blood from the small refrigerator next to her desk. Even with Elsie right next to him, he felt stirrings he thought had long since passed. Entranced, he asked, "Ms. Greene, you're not married, are you?"

"No," she replied sweetly, looking up from the vial with a knowing look. "It's complicated." She fitted the vial of blood, which she had drawn from a kindergarten boy who overdosed on Ritalin yesterday, into a syringe and placed it on a surgical tray on her desk. "Now, Mr. Jorgensen—" she said.

"Please, call me Cubby," he said with a slight blush.

"Okay, Cubby, you sound like your lungs are in pretty decent shape, am I right?" she said, fitting an empty collection vial into another syringe.

"Yup, worked forty-six years on the docks and never smoked."

"Perfect," she said, tying the rubber tourniquet around his arm.

"Why do you have to do this? Elsie's the one with problem."

"Sorry, Cubby," she said, sliding the sliver of steel into his vein, "in this world, there's no such thing as a free lunch. Make a fist." The dark red blood flowed into the vial. When it was full, she bandaged his arm. Taking the other vial, she lifted Elsie's limp arm and injected the boy's blood.

Elsie blinked and shook her head. As if waking from a nap, she looked over at her husband and said, "Cubby?"

"Elsie!" he said, his eyes watering.

"How, why…?" she puzzled.

"I don't have a lot of time to explain; hell, we don't have a lot of time," Cubby said, rising from his chair and taking her arm. "We need to go."

"I look a mess, Cubby," Elsie accused, patting her wild hair down. "How could you let me leave the house looking like this?"

"We'll get that fixed," Cubby said, leading her to the door. "I'll explain on the way."

"I don't understand. Where are we going?"

"We'll stop by the house first, and then we're going to the lawyer's. Thanks, Ms. Greene, for everything."

His first set of racking coughs echoed in the hallway.

"*It should have been thirty pieces of silver*," the voice nagged.

"Hey," Prof said, "that guy, Jerry, said he didn't find a record of Nathan being arrested." The bus rumbled away from the courthouse. The young man, whose voice had seemed familiar, greeted Prof in the atrium of the courthouse filled with a thousand busy echoes, and led him to the taskforce office bay which he referred to the as the Pit with a chuckle.

"So, where's Jones?" Prof said, taking a seat.

"He's a busy man," Jerry said, popping the latches to the cashbox. "He doesn't have time for stuff like this. Anyway, sign the receipt." He slid the clipboard across the desk to Prof.

"What about Nate? I don't want to testify against him."

"Look, your work is done. Just sign it and take your two hundred bucks."

"What about my friend?"

"Kind of late in the game to be worried about him," Jerry said, "seeing how you rolled over on him."

"Still, he hasn't made bail. I just want to know if he's okay."

"All right," Jerry said, "if this will get you out of my cubicle. What's his name?"

"Nathan Gascon."

Jerry tapped the keyboard of his computer. "I've got no arrest record for a Nathan Gascon. Sorry," said Jerry.

"So, what does that mean?"

"I don't know, I don't care, and neither should you," Jerry snapped. "Sign, get your money and have a lovely day."

Prof signed and took the cash. "Do you think you can call me a cab?"

"Do it yourself," Jerry said, swiveling his chair away. "You got money and I got real work to do. You can find your own way out."

Prof plodded out of the office bay with the money in hand and his head down. With his right hand on the wall, he traced his way to the elevators, out of the courthouse and caught the bus.

"*I guess you learn from what's been done to you,*" the voice said. "*After what happened with Stan and Lila—*"

"Enough!" Prof said, stuffing the money into his slim billfold. "I did what I had to do."

The bus lurched to a stop and Prof pulled himself up to exit. Once off the crowded bus, he decided to cut through the alley behind the

Mittelmarch where he and Nathan had practiced their signals one night many months ago. Avoiding the many pedestrians on this warm late morning, he would end up right in front of the Night Café in time for a quiet, early lunch.

Weaving through the steeplechase of overflowing garbage cans, Prof's neck prickled in the shady coolness of the alley. Was that breathing behind him? He paused at the metallic thump and roll of one of the garbage cans.

"Look, I—" he said. His words were cut short by a quick stinging stab between his ribs.

Falling to his knees, his breath rushed out of his side in mass of bubbling warm wetness. Desperate hands scrabbled inside his jacket and snatched his wallet. Before the blackness, he heard a scramble of footsteps trail away.

Sirens blaring, Pat braced as her partner, Ralph, snaked the rattling ambulance for all its worth through the busy streets. Jumping curbs and careening through yellow lights, the burly biker swung the wheel, his eyes locked on the young police officer waving his hands before them. Pat felt safe riding with Ralph until they got a call like this.

"What do you have?" Ralph said, trotting up to the young officer.

"Stabbing," the officer said, "just inside the alley. Looks like a mugging."

After a hard dash, Ralph and Pat crouched over the man. Pat spotted the bloody gash in the victim's light blue dress shirt and sliced the clothes away with her blade. The inch-wide wound sputtered red foam with each of the man's ragged gasps. "Jesus," she whispered.

"Get me a clear bandage, two by two, waterproof," Ralph demanded. On the far side of the street, he spied the bone-white taxi.

"Here," said Pat, dropping the peeled bandage in Ralph's massive palm.

"Man," Ralph urged the pale victim, "you gotta let your breath go. It sounds fucked up, but if you want to make it, let it go, now!"

The man shuddered and exhaled. As the last of the air trailed off, Ralph slapped the bandage over the wound and said, "Suck it in, guy."

The man dragged air deep into his lungs. Ralph's solemn brown eyes met the stare of the cabby. Ralph shook his head once and the cabby nodded. The white cab eased away from the curb.

Pat regulated the oxygen flow and pulled her mike to make the transport call. Ralph reached for her hand and said, "No."

"But we need to get him to Sapienta—"

"They'll only shuffle him to Central and he'll either asphyxiate or bleed out on the shuttle," Ralph said, scratching his thick black beard.

"So, we take him to Central."

"Too far. Let me talk to the cop," Ralph said.

"I need your help, Officer," Ralph said.

"Sure," the clean-cut policeman said, "what do you need?"

"Well, it's something that's not covered at the Academy."

"So how can I help?"

"Look, Pennington," Ralph said, looking down at the earnest young cop's name tag, "I need you to call in that the vic walked away from the scene. It's that or he dies in transit."

"But procedure—"

"Procedure will kill him, but we can save him," Ralph rumbled. "Jason Pennington, will your sacred oath allow this?"

Stunned, Pennington keyed his mike and said, "Central, Officer 1257. Victim's injuries minor. Refused medical treatment."

"Good man. A bit of advice—follow Serrano's lead. He's a good man, too."

"That's going to be hard," Pennington said. "They put Serrano on administrative leave this morning."

"What happened?"

"Hard to say," Pennington said. "No one's talking. It can't be good." The young cop moved on to continue his beat.

Returning to Pat, Ralph said, “Okay, now call this in as a no-show and we’re taking lunch.”

“I don’t follow.”

“Here’s the deal, little one. We’re loading him up and taking him around the corner to call in a favor.”

“You mean to Ayrshire.”

“You pick up quick, Pat,” Ralph said. “We’ll make a Senior EMT out of you, yet.”

“Found his wallet,” Pat said, flipping the brown billfold to Ralph. “Empty, of course, but his driver’s license says he’s John Clarke.”

Vivian left the break room, amazed how little trifles were transformed into acts of high drama by a group of tittering twenty-something girls. Breakroom lunch soap operas or a dreary burger fast-food joints, it was a tough choice. Big Ralph waited for her at the admissions desk, grinning from ear to ear.

“Hi, Viv,” he said. “You remember those ampules of gamma globin from last month?”

“Sure, they helped out a lot of people. It was very kind of you.”

“I got something I need your help with in Exam Room Four,” he whispered.

“Of course, Ralph; I suppose it’s one of those situations.”

“Aren’t they all?” he said and opened the door for her.

“Ralph, when are you going to realize you can’t save all of them?”

“Never and proud of it. Anyway, do what you can for him. Sucking chest wound with a potential collapsed lung.”

“You just love dropping this sort of thing in my lap,” she said, looking at the man resting on the table.

“Personally,” said Ralph, “I’d rather be out on a run.”

“How are the boys?”

"Hardly ever get to see them," Ralph said. "Gabe is either working or down at that bar on Reed Shore. Mike spends most of his time running the shop and Uri, well, he's Uri."

"He's the most interesting of the bunch of you."

"I suppose that's one way to describe him," Ralph said, exiting the room.

Prof's consciousness erupted to the tang of antiseptics and industrial cleaners. The steady beep of the EKG unlocked memories of that cold November night.

Lila's scream pulled him from their bed. He followed the sobbing to the bathroom where Lila sat on the pink bathmat wearing one of his old dress shirts. Blood covered the toilet seat and seeped into the bathmat where Lila sat, rocking. He bundled Lila into his old flannel bathrobe and tore through the chilly night streets in his ten-year-old Corolla.

"Call Stan," she ordered quietly, looking straight ahead.

"Sure," he said, "as soon as we get to the hospital."

"Promise?" she pleaded. Her face glistened in the street lights from the tear streaks.

Later, he watched through the safety glass window of the treatment room as the tired staff administered to Lila. Lila asked him to leave the room.

"John?" Stan said, trundling up with dark circles under his eyes.

"Hey, Stan," he said to his friend with the fashionable goatee, "she's been asking for you."

Averting his gaze, Stan entered the treatment room and approached Lila on the table. He only saw only the back of Stan's suede blazer but listened to Lila's sobbing words. Their exchange ended in a long, deep embrace.

"Mr. Clarke?" the charge nurse with drawn features said, "I'm sorry. Your wife has had an early stage miscarriage."

His eyes closed as his forehead rested upon the cold glass window.

"Mr. Clarke?" an unfamiliar woman's voice addressed him, "you're hurt bad, but I might be able to fix it."

"Yes," he gasped, "fix it."

"Do you have someone to call?"

"Billfold," he wheezed.

"If something goes in," she cautioned, "something's got to come out. It's not a sure thing, either way you pay."

"Do it."

The needle jabbed into his forearm. "*Prof? They are taking meeee!*" she screamed and the scent of saffron dissipated in the darkness.

"You're Mr. Stahlmann?" Vivian said, appraising the chunky man in the gray sports shirt.

"That's me," Lou replied with a crooked grin.

"Are you related to Mr. Clarke?"

"Nah, Prof just drops by the shop to drink coffee and listen to the ballgame some nights."

"Nights?"

"Ahhh," Lou said. "Since my wife passed away, I spend more time at the shop. Just seems easier."

"Sounds like you need a distraction," she teased. "Your shop, you're good with your hands?"

"The finest hands in the city. Anyway, does Prof need anything special?"

"The next three days are going to be touch and go," Vivian said, reverting to a professional tone. "He may make it; he may not. It would be best if someone watched over him."

"Shouldn't he be in the hospital, then?"

"He ended up here," Vivian said; she swept her arm around the full waiting room.

"Point taken. I guess I can put him up for a couple of days."

A man in a torn sweatshirt flung the glass front doors open. Head down, he thundered up to Vivian. "You're Ms. Greene, right?" he snarled.

"That's right," Vivian said. "What can I do for you, Mr.…?"

"Jorgensen," he snapped, "Todd Jorgensen."

"Your parents were in here this morning."

"I know that!" Jorgensen said. "You got your hooks deep into them, didn't you?"

"What are you talking about?"

"The goddam house is mine," he said, poking a finger at Vivian. "That's my inheritance. Dad called me up today all happy about how he and Mom are donating it to this shithole."

"I suggest you take that up with your father, Mr. Jorgensen. I had nothing to do with their decision. In the future, may I suggest you pay more attention to your loved ones' needs?"

"You don't tell me jack shit, fat bitch."

"Hey," Lou said, stepping between Vivian and Jorgensen. "You have the God-given right to make an ass out of yourself in public, but that's no way to talk to a lady."

"You her boyfriend?" Jorgensen shot back. "I just might enjoy beating the living fuck outta you in front of her."

"I don't know," Lou said, looking around the waiting room, "you might want to rethink that strategy.

Jorgensen's eyes followed Lou's. Several men stood amidst the growing murmurs.

"This isn't over, bitch," Jorgensen said as he stomped out the door.

"You okay?" he asked Vivian, who had grown pale.

"I'm fine, Mr. Stahlmann."

"Lou, call me, Lou."

"Could you give me a lift?" she asked. "I don't drive and my home isn't far."

"Sure, I'm local. I'd prefer to drop Prof off at the house."

"Thanks, let me get my things first," she said, hurrying off to the front desk.

Lou watched her walk away, wondering if he just saw her pear-shaped bottom sheathed in white wiggle just a little.

"Terry," Vivian whispered. "There's a marked vial in my refrigerator. Call those people downtown."

He looked up from his charts. "Those people are even creepier than the guy who comes in here every week. Why don't you do it?

"Please? Just this once?" she asked, looking back at Lou. "I'm leaving early."

"In that case, ma'am, carry on."

Between the two of them, Lou and Vivian managed to drop the semi-conscious Prof into the king-sized bed in the upstairs of Lou's row house. Flustered and exhausted, Lou cleared the newspapers off the couch so they both could sit and catch their breath.

"Thanks, Vivian," Lou said. "If it wasn't for you, Prof would be sleeping on this old thing tonight."

"I'm sure a big guy like you could have handled him," she said. "You did say you had skillful hands?" She popped the top button of her dress.

"The best in the city," he whispered, reaching out.

Later, surrounded by an empty large pizza box and several empty beer bottles, Vivian slung her white-stockinged thigh over Lou's as they lay on the lumpy couch. "Didn't I tell you that you needed a distraction?" she said, running a finger down his hairy chest.

"You're right. I guess I should listen to my healthcare providers," he said caressing her cheek. "How do you feel about fishing?"

Upstairs, Prof clawed at the flowered bedspread. Beads of sweat broke upon his forehead as he repeated the whisper, "She's gone…"

The Long Day

6:27 AM June 21st
Lou Stahlmann Residence
759 Casca Street

For three days, Prof thrashed upon the bed, only rising to use the bathroom or take a sip of water from the sink. These sparse moments, filled with regret, offered little relief from the endless loop of dreams that awaited him upon crawling back into the bed.

He graded the final paper of the towering stack. The yellow glow of the brass desk lamp burned his tired eyes. His students' words ran together into one mindless drone in his head. With his final duties discharged, he poured himself another glass from the half-empty fifth of bourbon beside him.

He'd spent three hours pacing through the half-empty cottage, remembering the furniture and mementos that once occupied the clean blank spaces. Lila and Stan had arrived with a rental trailer this gray Saturday afternoon. Listlessly, he helped them load up half of his life. As the possessions left the house, like the earthenware vase they bought in Greece on their honeymoon, Lila asked, as her hazel eyes shined in anticipation of his reaction, "John, do you want to keep this?"

Each time, his response remained consistent—a shrug of the shoulders and a quiet, "No."

"I'll…I'll just leave it on your desk," she'd said, carrying the vase to the den.

Avoiding the farewell, Lila climbed in Stan's tricked-out SUV with the signed papers, all neatly prepared, tabbed and highlighted, which reduced their thirteen-year marriage to the coda of two words, "irreconcilable differences."

Back on the porch, Stan offered his hand with a sincere expression. "John," he said, "I appreciate you being the bigger man about this."

Looking away, John said, "Whatever."

He exhaled in relief as the SUV strained to pull the overburdened trailer; he'd evaded mentioning the meeting with Artemisia on Friday.

"John," the lady with long, iron-gray hair and a smug smile said, "you understand the department is going through some cost-cutting procedures and we must eliminate redundant positions."

"I'll bet using those corporate buzzwords makes you feel like a real professional."

"I'd be careful, Johnny-boy," Dr. Artesmisia Shivmann said. "The separation package is more than generous. Let's face it. You are not a good fit here and frankly, your work quality has fallen off. Then, again, not everyone is talented enough to teach at this level."

John considered the words of the woman in the purple cardigan and crude hand-made jewelry. Since Artie's ruthless campaign for the department chair two years earlier, the department got younger and more feminine. In the end, John signed the separation notice.

Setting his drink aside, he turned his attention to the screen of his computer with Van Gogh's *Night Café* serving as the background. He clicked on the desktop folder listed as "Stories." Perusing each of the half-finished documents, he closed out the files, one after another, remembering the flashes of insight he'd scribbled down and later typed up. He swore to revisit each one someday.

He reminisced about his hellion days in school: the drunken, late-night writing mash-up which left him, and later the next day his Composition teacher, laughing; the beer and bull sessions with Stan, where he tossed ideas out like Mardi Gras beads; and his first publication in the student paper, which extolled the Swiftian virtues of The Christian Students' Union as a troop of syphilitic baboons. Soon, he learned that the good times never last. Late in his junior year, his string of triumphs and misadventures ended. After going on academic probation the second time, he still cringed at the memory of his mother's disappointed eyes and the scourging talk about "putting away childish things."

Manning up, he redoubled his efforts. Through grad school, marriage and career, the files still waited for him to fulfill his vow. Now, he stared for hours at a computer screen and contemplated how the lawn needed de-thatching. In the shuffle of compromises, he had traded away the magic which drew him to writing.

His eyes drifted to the vase Lila had left next to the computer. The black silhouettes of seven women danced around the circumference of the vase with a glimmering sea of sapphire blue behind them. He remembered the clear skies of the market that day and the promise of the bright future his life with Lila held as they haggled over the price. Of all the bare spots in the cottage to choose from, she'd placed it here. Stony-eyed, he stood and caressed the glazed surface one last time. Lifting the vase above his head with both hands, he dashed it to the wood floor with a satisfying shatter.

"If you got those things back, Professor," a whispery-sweet voice said from across the empty living room, "what would it be worth to you?"

"What?" John replied, looking up from the array of shards.

She stood in front of the open window, a woman with long, dark hair with wicked eyes. The shadows played across her form like a Grecian gown.

"Your balls," she said, padding across the living room. "You lost them a while back."

"I'm not sure what you mean." He averted his gaze from her supple alabaster form, but his eyes betrayed him.

"Shhh, darling," she said, bringing a dark-nailed finger up to his lips, "don't think about it; do it." Her finger traced down his lips, his chin, his chest, and her cool arm slipped around his waist.

"You smell wonderful."

"Saffron, dear, from home. I love the effect it has on my men."

"But, who?" he said. His hand reached out to cup her breast.

"Dear, dear, Professor," she said, opening his shirt. "You always held so much promise. I hoped you would have come to me willingly, but one must seize the opportunities as they come."

"A hallucination," he said, "brought on by stress and alcohol." An icy cold washed over him, as she undid his belt and slacks.

"A hallucination. Hmm…an interesting hypothesis." She traced his hard member through his clean, white undershorts, and said, "I bet my sisters never got this kind of response from their chaste little kisses."

"It's the only rational explanation."

Kneeling, her dark eyes sparkled with mischief. "So, tell me, Professor, can a hallucination do this?" She took him into her mouth.

"Ohh—I don't—"

She cut his words short with a stroke to his thigh.

"Oh, Prof," she said, "you do and you always will, won't you?" She grasped his burgeoning manhood and led him to the flowery couch that Lila had picked out. Now, a tinge of warm, pink life coursed through her body

His eyes drank in her naked, reclining form. Her black, silken hair, sweet breasts, and her damp, dark mystery beckoned him. His blood roared through his temples, yet he wanted to run away.

"Prof," she said, crooking a finger," you know what you want, lover. You've always known."

"Yes," he said, as he sank to his knees. Lost in a fugue of licking, sucking and biting between her legs, he was swept into a cold, lonely place. Her animalistic growls of pleasure filled his ears as he slithered up her hot, sweaty frame and thrust into her.

"Render unto me what is mine!" she said, flipping him to the floor with unexpected strength. She pumped furiously; he doubted how much longer his rigid, aching body would hold back the flooding release.

Her dark eyes opened, revealing voids of blackness. She smiled and said, "Do you want to come with me?"

"Yes."

"The price for this ride is expensive. Will you pay?"

"Yessss!"

A dark symphony emerged from their tandem screams as they bucked to the pulse of the universe. Agonizing pain and orgasmic pleasure twined together to feed off each other. Eons later, the throes subsided as the cold night wind swept across his spent body.

Still straddling him, she reached down and cupped his slackened face. "This makes the next part so much easier," she said, driving her long dark thumbnails deep into his eye sockets.

Prof screamed, pawing his face. Although the explosion of pain was all too real, no blood poured from his eyes. In the smothering darkness, he cried, "You fucking bitch!"

"Oh, Prof," she said, playing with his hair, "very few receive a gift like this. Show some gratitude."

"For what? Blinding me?" John countered, lashing out with his fist and connecting with nothing.

She grabbed his wrists and pinned him to the carpet. Leaning down close to his face, she said, "You want to rot rehashing grammar to brain-dead children? You need to change, but first, you need to relinquish your old identity."

"Why?"

"To create something new," she continued, "you have to destroy something old. It's the way it works."

"Whom the gods would destroy, they first make mad," he said.

"Leave it to an English professor to dredge up that nasty, old Longfellow quote," she said, "Actually, it's quite simple. Make it from one winter morn to the next, three hundred sixty-six days, and you get your sight back, if you survive."

"A year and a day…a trial."

“Look at it as more of a challenge or a journey. Either way, you agreed to the deal,” she whispered, “and, I’ll be with you always, my love.” Her long hair caressed his face as her kiss sealed their pact.

A gust of cold November wind rustled the sheer drapes and she vanished, leaving a faint scent of saffron.

In the morning, the cops found John on the floor of the sunny living room floor, curled in a fetal position, shivering, naked and blind. The dream continued with a string of impressions in the blackness: strong arms carrying him to the back of an ambulance, the cries and shuffling of the hospital, the sting of the injections and cups of pills forced on him to swallow.

As the haze of his thoughts lifted in the unfolding dream, he recalled the calm voices asking questions, his smiling, evasive responses to those inquiries, his grasp of the long, white cane as he learned how to maneuver down the hallways, and the shuffling and signing of endless papers. Finally, the dream ended with an indifferent cab ride, which deposited him on Reed Shore Drive. With a housing voucher in hand, he grasped his way up the crumbling steps of the hotel which became his home.

In a cold sweat, Prof awoke and pulled himself from the bed. Shirtless and shoeless, he groped his way out of the bedroom and down the stairs, following the aroma of fresh coffee.

“So, you’re back among the living,” Lou said. The rustle of newspaper followed. “I was just about to go check on you. You had us all worried.”

“Everyone?”

“Yeah, that little girl from the diner, Jane, dropped by yesterday and this morning. Hell, she brought a bag of groceries. Joe and Theo from the café dropped off some flowers. Even a couple of those bikers who run the shop across from mine were asking about you.”

“Bikers?”

"The blond one who works as the courier and the shaggy one who brought you over to Vivian's clinic. Are you planning on patching over?"

"Cute," Prof said. "Wait a minute, who's Vivian?"

"The lady who runs the Ayrshire Clinic. She spent the last couple of nights looking after you. She's, uh, really nice."

"You know, Lou, losing your sight means that your other senses become more enhanced. For example, I detected the change in your heartbeat, just now."

"From over there in the chair?" Lou said. "Look, she had a traumatic day and, well, I was worried about you…"

Prof smiled and said, "Gotcha!"

"Asshole!" Lou said, throwing a couch pillow at Prof. "Anyway, you didn't tell me about Reyna. Wow! Where the hell did you find her?"

"Reyna? She's just a friend. She's got a shop down on the square."

"I'd shop her. She dropped off a shirt since they had to cut yours off. Hope you like paisley," Lou said, tossing the silky rayon shirt in Prof's lap. "Anyway, she couldn't stay because of some big pet adoption thing she was running."

"Thanks, Lou, few people would have gone to the lengths you did."

"Hey, I'd miss your stupid bets. Yankees versus the Braves, tonight. You in?"

"Yeah, the Braves," Prof said, donning his wrinkled black jacket over the new shirt.

"See? You're a glutton for punishment. Are you sure you're good to go? An extra day here—"

"Thanks for the offer, Lou," Prof said at the front door, "but Ben Franklin said fish and visitors smell in three days. Besides, I got a lot to do and I got a feeling it's going to be a long day."

"Happy first day of summer, Prof."

“Joey! Why didn’t you tell me it was Judge Adams, who reserved the restaurant for today?” Theo said.

“Didn’t seem that important,” Joey said with a shrug, tying the straps to his apron. “He reserved the billiards room for an event and didn’t ask for any catering. Easy money.”

“Haven’t you heard the stories? If the Judge doesn’t like the service, you get a visit from the Health Department the next day.”

“So? We’re the best. If the Judge likes us, it can’t be anything but good.”

“Joey, if he doesn’t like us, he closes us down. We lose the café and the condo; we’ll have to move in back with my parents. I don’t want to go back working for someone else.”

Joey placed his hands on Theo’s shoulders and looked him in the eye with an easy smile. “Hey, easy amigo,” the heavy bartender said. “Like I said, we’re the best.”

“May I speak with Mr. Bartlett?” an elderly man said, removing his navy homburg.

“That would be me,” Joey said.

“Ah,” the man said, “you’re the gentleman I spoke to on the telephone. I am Ray Adams.”

“Yes, Your Honor,” Joey said. “If you’ll come this way.” He led the way to the back of the billiard room and removed the cover to the expansive snooker table.

The judge assessed the polished table’s green Strachan cloth and the supple leather pockets. “Hmm, this will do quite nicely,” he said, removing a cue from the rack and rolling it atop the table. “Your equipment is in excellent condition.”

“The table sees very little use. Most people prefer the billiard tables.”

“A game for louts,” Judge Adams said, scanning the orange-red walls with the hanging brass lamps. “Then, again, your décor reminds me of the low-houses of Paris. It is quite impressive, even if it does celebrate man’s baser instincts.”

"Thank you, Your Honor. The Café's design concept was my idea. May I take your hat?"

"Thank you, Mr. Bartlett," the judge said, slipping out of his navy suit jacket. "And if you will hang this up, too."

"Absolutely, Your Honor. Can I bring you anything?"

"A neat scotch, single malt, if you have it," said Judge Adams, pacing around the table. He lifted the two trays of balls from the shelf and placed them upon the table; the red, green and yellow ball along the "D" of the baulk line, the lonely blue ball in the center of the table, the pink ball perched atop the pyramid of fifteen reds, and the black, hiding behind the reds, deep in the baize. Stepping back, he critiqued his handiwork—perfect, as expected.

"Ah, my friend!" said a short, brown-skinned man in an exquisite tweed jacket of purple and orange plaid. "I see you have arrived early to prepare for our annual game, as I suspected." Three men filed into the bar behind him.

"I see you have arrived late, as I expected. You are going by..."

"Ali El-Hashen. Please, call me Al," the man with the neatly-trimmed beard said.

"Thank heavens; I was afraid I was going to have to spend the afternoon referring to you by that ridiculous sobriquet that is almost as colorful as your coat."

"Do you like it?" Al said. "I had it custom-made by a vendor of mine in Caracas. I felt since we are playing this game, that I should dress appropriately. I can get you one, too, at a modest discount."

"You're very kind, but no, thank you, Al." Judge Adams watched the three gentlemen, take seats at one of the oaken pub tables: a pale, red-haired man in an orange suit and black shirt, a young, clear-eyed Mediterranean youth in a yellow track suit, absorbed with checking his pulse and a grinning Native American elder with long, white hair, decked out in faded denims.

Judge Adams frowned and said, "A cheering section, Al, really?"

"They insisted," Al explained with a shrug. "They wanted to witness our last game."

"Last game? I don't follow."

"I have found a way to retire. It's time for me to go home."

"Well, that's something unexpected," the judge said.

"You haven't considered it, my friend?"

"I'm needed here."

"The city will survive without you, trust me, my friend," Al said. "I arrived at that conclusion long ago. Anyway, you set the rules this year."

"One frame. You must call all your shots and we'll ignore a point tally because sinking the black ball determines winner. Pick your home pocket."

"This one," Al said, tapping the right baize corner pocket.

"By default, my home pocket is the opposite."

"I'd prefer poker," Al said, placing the cue ball in the half-circle. "This game is almost as bad as chess."

"Says the man who draws five aces regularly. This game relies on skill instead of chance."

"Try as you may, Your Honor," Al said as the cue ball's impact drove the triangle of red balls careening in all directions, "you'll never quite remove randomness from any situation." The lone blue ball caromed off the side rail and knocked the black ball away from the chaos upon the table.

"No pots, Al. My turn."

Under the noonday sun, Prof wished to shed his black sports jacket, but he preferred to hide the loaned silk shirt with pearl buttons and ruffles. Her sweet voice remained absent from his thoughts, yet the quiet brought him no solace. Was the dream true? Did he cast her away?

As he trudged toward the Gulf Canal Bridge, he prayed Reyna's insight would offer a solution.

"Look out!" a man's voice yelled, knocking Prof off his feet. A roar of a car's engine and the grating crash of metal followed.

"You okay?" the man said, pulling Prof to his feet.

"Yeah, just what the hell happened?"

"I never saw anything like that before," the man said. "A white Taurus just plowed into the Honda dealership lot. Took out a row of red Civics, like some action movie."

"Thanks. You sound familiar."

"Perry Sterling," the man said. "I run the Strand down on the square, at least for the time being."

"Oh yes, Reyna mentioned you. I used to watch a lot of old movies when I could see. What do you mean, for the time being?"

"Once Ursula's Fashion World opens," Perry said, "that'll be the end of us."

"I don't follow."

"It's going to have an IMAX Theater attached, first run movies."

"But," Prof said, "you're not in direct competition."

"Doesn't matter," Perry said, "the square's going to change. They're even trying to get rid of the street vendors."

"I was hoping to go see Reyna."

"Good luck with that," Perry said. "One week, it's wigs for chemotherapy patients; the next, she's organizing a food drive. She keeps telling me to have faith and bank up on the good karma."

Distant sirens grew louder as the crowd grew to view the wreckage.

"Either way," Perry said, "it looks like we aren't crossing the canal here. Want to share a cab?"

"Uh, thanks, but I can do this some other time," Prof said.

"Joey, what the hell is mead?" Theo said, rushing up to the bar.

"It's a wine made from honey, dark ages stuff."

"We got any in stock?"

"Of course, not; nobody makes that anymore, at least not commercially."

"Shit, shit, shit," Joey said, grabbing a bottle from the wine rack and slamming through the swinging kitchen door. "Marc! You got any honey back here?"

"No, Theo," the young chef said, not looking up from his cutting board.

Theo opened the bottle of cheap merlot and sloshed it into a balloon glass. Looking around, he grabbed a handful of artificial sweetener packets and dumped their contents into the wine with a quick stir of his finger. After recomposing himself, he placed the wiped-down glass upon his tray and returned to their guests.

"There you go," Theo said, placing the glass in front of the red-headed man. "This is from…our personal stock." Beads of sweat rose on his forehead. "Can I get you gentlemen anything else?"

"Nothing for me, thanks," the youth in the running suit said, entering the data from his last run on his phone.

"Do you have salmon?" the elder said with a feral smile.

The other two groaned in unison.

"Poached or baked?"

"I prefer roasted," the man said. "Oh, if you could serve it up on a bed of sunflower stems and leaves."

"I'll see what I can do," Theo said, scuttling away.

"Was that really necessary?" the youth said, immersed in his performance charts.

"Once you've had a taste of fire-roasted salmon, you never forget it."

"Neither do the folks around Shasta," the red-haired man said, taking a long swig of his drink. His face turned sour and spewed the noxious, dark red liquid down the front of his orange suit. Shaking his head, he said, "Private stock, my ass."

At the snooker table, Al fired off his shot. The pink ball kissed the black ball, moving it away from the judge's corner pocket.

"Foul!" Judge Adams said. "Al, a family member, really?"

"Excuse me, sir?" the young lady said, leaning out from the window of her car. "Do you know where 12 Cedars Street is?"

"Sure." Prof caught the whiff of jellybeans and honeysuckle perfume from the sunbaked car. "You just go down this street three blocks and turn onto Corral Street and, no, wait. I believe that's a one-way street..."

"If you could show me the way," she said, "I'll be glad to drop you wherever you want."

"You know, that's the best offer all day." Tracing around the car with his hand, he found the passenger side door.

The little car lurched forward as the gears grated. "Sorry," she said.

"Not a problem. I think if we go four blocks and take a left on Ayrshire."

"Okay dokey," she said. "I really appreciate the help, sir.

"John Clarke. Most people call me Prof, these days.

"I'm Cindy."

"You sound a bit young to be driving around the city by yourself."

"I'm seventeen," she said. "I graduated high school. I can take care of myself."

"I'm sure you can. I was seventeen, once, many eons ago."

"You're not that old," she said. "So, what's Prof short for?"

"Professor, or at least I used to be."

"I start college in the fall," she said while waiting at the light. "Mom wants me to go Pre-Med and Dad thinks I'll make a better lawyer."

"Sometimes, you have to wander a bit to figure out where you're going. That's what freshman year is for." The little car swerved around the corner. "Is the clinic over on the left open?"

"Doesn't look like it. It's Sunday."

"Oh, I forgot."

"You're not sick, are you?"

"No, just hoping to get in touch with a lady who works there. Anyway, 12 Cedars should be along this block here," Prof said. "If you could drop me here, I can walk."

"Are you sure?" she said, tapping the brakes a bit too hard. "I mean, you've been a big help and all."

"The walk will do me good. Thanks, Cindy," he said, opening the door, "take care of yourself."

"Thanks, Prof, "she said, leaning over and giving him a quick peck on the cheek. "Nice shirt."

"Mmm, delicious," the man said, wolfing down the piping hot salmon.

"Glad you like it," Theo said. "Our chef, Marco, prepared the greens in the, uh, classic French wilted style." He avoided mentioning the sunflower had been sitting in a wine bottle on his desk in the back for three weeks. "Anything else, gentlemen?"

"No," the youth said, looking at his compatriots. "If you'd get the check, please."

"Absolutely, sir!" Theo replied, hurrying away.

Choking down the mouthful, the man in denim looked up and growled. "You assholes actually made me go through with that."

"You wanted salmon," the man in the orange suit said, dabbing the wine stains from his jacket with ice water.

"He's okay, that one," the old man said, watching the skinny waiter tally up the bill at the bar, "for an amateur." His grin revealed long canines.

The black ball teetered on the edge of Al's called hole. "Looks like I win," Al said.

"That is your problem, Al. You think order is a prison. Once you discern the underlying structure of the universe," the Judge said, lifting the cue into a high masse shot, "everything is possible and the music of the spheres rings out." With a quick snap, the cue ball spun crazily toward the pocket, rode the edge and snapped around, knocking the black ball into the judge's called pocket in the opposite corner with a satisfying rattle.

"You can't go in, Prof," J.J. said, sitting on the brick steps of the Mittelmarch. "At least not for a couple of hours. They're fumigating."

"On a Sunday?"

"The roach problem got to be too bad. Management didn't want the hotel shutdown for health code violations."

"As if the last couple of days could get any weirder," Prof said.

"On the bright side, looks like Nate didn't get busted after all."

"Really?"

"Yeah, came in this morning and got his stuff. They got him in some kind of internship program. They're even putting him up in a nice apartment."

"That's a bit of good news. I guess I'll go over to the café and wait the infestation out."

"Hey Prof," J.J said, picking up his newspaper, "nice shirt."

Prof walked into the cool refuge of the Night Café just as several men filed out.

One paused and said, "What a lovely shirt! Tell me, sir, who is your tailor?"

"Uh, Reyna?"

"Ah yes, Ms. Fox. You seem familiar. You are the gentleman with voices, yes?

"Used to be, Mr. El—" Prof said.

"Please call me, Al," the man said. "Should you find yourself down on Cedars Street, please come visit my store. Don't tarry too long though; my niece is helping me to close shop."

"Her name wouldn't be Cindy, would it?"

"As a matter fact, it is. Good day, Professor."

"He's back and on his feet!" Joey said as Prof approached the bar. He did a double-take at the sight of the blind man's shirt. It was a shimmery pink and white paisley with ruffled lace and pearl buttons. "Wow, disco is not dead, merely sleeping."

"Can I get a water?"

"Prof! You're okay!" Theo said.

"Thanks for the flowers, guys," said Prof. "It's great to realize you got friends. How come it's so quiet in here?"

"Private event," Joey said. "You should have seen Captain Stalwart over there."

"Hey, once I got the hang of it, it was no biggie. We're the best," Joey said. "Those guys over at the table tipped me two hundred…and a whoopee cushion."

"Really? I set this up and 'His Honor' went on about how great this place is and the splendid job we did, blah, blah. He shakes my hand and what do I get?" Joey said, pulling a coin from his pocket and tossing it on the bar. "A lousy silver dollar."

The silver coin rang and spun to a stop. A blindfolded woman with an eagle stood above the inscription that read, ".9995 Platinum."

A Sense of Stone Cold Justice

3:15 PM July 6th
Nick Serrano's Apartment
1887 Hughes Street

Nick watched the bright square of sunlight creep across the dingy brown carpet of his basement apartment and took another pull from the bottle of beer, his third this afternoon. Aching from his noon workout in the YMCA weight room, he shifted his six-foot-four frame on the musty orange couch. The two hours of free weights had taken the fight out of him.

This morning, his six weeks of administrative leave ended in that conference room. Captain Harris, Judge Adams and Internal Affairs Attorney, Aaron Schechter, sat at the broad polished table with Nick standing before them.

"Sergeant Serrano's ten years on the force has been a credit," Harris said, "up to this incident. Reduction in rank and eight weeks' suspension without pay."

"Normally, I'd agree," Schechter said, shuffling the reports in front of him. "However; Mr. Cavanaugh agrees to drop the punitive damages in exchange for Sergeant Serrano's voluntary resignation."

The beefy police chief with the walrus mustache avoided looking at the young cop while the lawyer peered at the judge from behind his steel-framed glasses, anticipating the old man's response.

"I agree with you, Chief Harris," the judge pronounced. "However, my first concern is the order and welfare of this city." His cold blue eyes locked onto Nick, as he said, "Sergeant Serrano, you have proven yourself a capable officer of the law, but your lapse in judgement will place an unnecessary burden on the city you have sworn to protect. I cannot force your choice either way."

"What?" Schechter said. "You can't leave this in his hands—"

"The agreement hinges on Sergeant Serrano's voluntary resignation."

After Judge Adams and Schechter left, Nick handed over his badge, service revolver and his letter of resignation to Chief Harris.

"Nick, take the administrative punishment and tough it out."

"Cap, if I stick around, Schechter makes sure I'd never leave Traffic. "

"Schechter is a brown-nosing, rule-quoting prick," Harris snapped. "He'd turn out his mother for hanging her laundry out her apartment window if it meant saving face for the administration."

"Still, I let my temper get the better of me. Judge Adams is right; I blew it."

"Wish you could have known him back when the judge was District Attorney. Adams cleaned up the streets and didn't care about standard operating procedures or law suits."

"Yesterday isn't today, Cap."

After his work out, he stopped by the diner for lunch and ate his Salisbury steak in silence and mulled over his string of failures.

The pounding at the door stirred Nick to the present,

"Fragging great, this is all I need."

"Look," Nick said, flinging the door open, "I really don't want to talk to anybody right now." He faced the tip of a yellow, conical wide-brimmed hat.

"Sergeant Serrano," the little old man said, looking up from underneath the hat, "you really want to talk to me now. It's about your future in law enforcement."

"Look, Fath—I mean, Rabbi Loewmann, maybe you haven't heard. I don't have a future, so the name's just Nick now."

"Precisely, Sergeant Serrano. I heard about your tribulations and I believe we can help each other. May I come in?"

"Sure Rabbi, pardon the mess. I've been kind of busy lately."

“Oh, it’s quite all right.” Rabbi Loewmann hobbled into Nick’s apartment.

“Well, Rabbi,” Nick fumbled, “what’s with the hat? Don’t you usually wear one of those yarmulke things?”

"Why? Is there something wrong with it?” the holy man said, removing the hat and examining it.

“No,” said Nick, glancing down at Rabbi’s severe black suit. “It doesn’t really go with the rest of the outfit.”

“It’s wool like the suit,” Rabbi Loewmann muttered. “Oh! You meant the style and color. I don’t pull it out often these days. You young people would call this Old School.” He replaced the hat on his head.

“What can I do for you, Rabbi?”

“My grandnephew, Hiram, a really fine boy, is special counsel to the Mayor. I'm sure a good word from him and the support of a local religious leader will put you back in the good graces of the police force, and with a clean record…is this not a good deal?”

“Sure, Rabbi, what's the catch?”

“What do you know about band of hoodlums called the Sons of Wotan?”

“Street gang, if you can call them that. Meth-heads cranked up on white power. They’re kind of a joke. Why? They been spray painting swastikas on your chur—I mean synagogue?”

“I wish it were that harmless. My people are the chosen of God, but with that blessing comes a great burden. If I were younger man, I would do this myself.”

“You need the cops, not me.”

“A badge and a gun do not make a lawman. The Sons of Wotan do things, evil things, on a higher level. I need a true lawman to needed set things right.”

“Rabbi, come on! What? You think these punks saved Hitler's brain? For Christ’s sake, they're loser Nazi-wannabes,” Nick said and dropped on his sofa. “I got more important things to worry about.”

“Like what, Sergeant Serrano? Wallowing in self-pity? You have no idea what they're planning.”

A roll of thunder rattled the windows.

“Nick," he said, "they took my grandniece.”

“Go to the cops, Rabbi. They can do something about this.”

“Between the warrants and protocols, it will be too late for her. One man, however, one good man, might be able to save her,” the Rabbi said. “Nick, you are that man. I can feel it. Do you know what a Golem is?”

“No, got anything to do with football or police work?”

“Neither,” the Rabbi said, opening his briefcase. “Do you recognize this?” He offered a tattered, yellow news clipping to Nick.

“Yeah, it’s the sports article on St. Mark’s for my senior year. Where'd you find it?”

“I've have my sources,” the Rabbi said. “Your team was city-wide champion that year, very impressive. They called you 'Nick the Brick', didn't they?”

Nick grinned. “Yeah, they sure did. But what's this got to do with your niece?”

“Everything, Nick,” the Rabbi said. “Back in the old times, when my people were in danger, they called for a defender, a Golem.”

“Kind of like one of those crusaders back in the Dark Ages?”

“Not quite. The Golem was a clay statue brought to life by an amulet that held the True Name of God. I don't have the time to make a statue, but I think a 'brick wall of a man' will suffice. Anyway, this is where the Science begins to look like art.”

“Kidnappings, skinheads, football and art? What the hell are you trying to say? I'm no rocket scientist, but— “

“It’s all right, you don't have to understand. You get your job back if you save my niece.” He pulled a delicate chain with a small Star of David amulet from his jacket pocket.

“But—”

“Enough with the 'buts',” the Rabbi commanded as he slipped the silver chain over Nick's neck. After clearing his throat, the Rabbi intoned, “As the law is carved into stone, the man who wields it must emerge from stone."

Pure white fire coursed through his veins. Nick felt the amulet weigh upon his chest like his badge did on graduation day. "All right, Rabbi, I'll see what I can do," he said. "You are coming?"

"This is a young man's job. I'll let myself out."

"Suit yourself, Rabbi," Nick said with a shrug.

The sky darkened from the coming storm and gusts of wind skittered stray litter across the sidewalk. With each step, Nick's anger grew. He'd collared the Sons for assaults, vandalism and petty thefts; all of them were under twenty and directionless. In short, punks. Father O'Brien would've straightened their asses out in a couple of football practices.

A heavy drop of rain splattered on his shoulder as he waited at the crosswalk. A bone-white taxi zipped through under the yellow light. The hooded figure in the driver's seat gave him a grin and a thumbs-up. As the light turned red, Nick lifted and heaved each step as if his legs had turned to lead. Halfway through the crosswalk, the light turned green.

Maybe the moron in the red minivan wasn't paying attention as he hurtled at Nick. Their wide eyes locked at the last second. The panicked driver slammed his brakes and the tires squealed into a skid. Nick stood rooted to the spot, thinking, *what a fucking way to go*.

Until the crunch of buckling metal and smashing of glass rattled Nick's ears.

Someone batted Nick's chest with a pillow. He opened his eyes and found himself imbedded chest-deep in the grill of the minivan. The driver clawed his way from behind the deflating airbag. *I don't need this,* Nick thought, wrenching himself free of the hissing wreckage.

"Look at my fucking car!" the idiot in lime green golf pants screeched, clambering out of the totaled van.

“Call Triple A,” Nick said, walking off.

“Hey, shithead!” the driver yelled. "Anybody tell you got an attitude problem?"

“Yeah, on a regular basis,” said Nick without looking back.

Unbloodied, Nick lumbered on. A bolt of lightning ripped across the black sky. Nick smiled; he didn't need Father O'Brien to straighten out the Sons of Wotan now.

Their leader, Jack Gunderson, was another story. Every time they shoved him in the back of a cruiser for distribution or procuring, the shaved head bastard spewed his master race rhetoric. Down at the precinct, “busting baldy” became part of a rookie’s initiation. Now, Gunderson fed the white supremacist line of crap to a whole new generation of losers. Asshole or not, Gunderson played the game well. Since doing his time in the pen, Gunderson hadn't been busted for so much as jaywalking; he let the kids take the heat.

No one was on the street; the sputtering rain saw to that. Cutting through the back alleys, Nick trudged to the Warehouse district beyond Bianchi. He passed the nondescript cinderblock facilities with gravel loading yards. Without the burned-out husk from the fire in May as a landmark, Nick would have lost his way.

Finally, he found the warehouse, that the Sons of Wotan called their 'Hall.' Walking through the half-opened chain-link gate, he saw two bald punks in black fatigues guarding the steel door with the swastika painted on it.

Crossing the gray broken asphalt, he called out to the youths, “Hey kids, it's about to rain. Don't you think you should run home to your mommies?”

“Get the hell out of here,” the youth said.

“Aw, come on,” Nick said, grabbing the youth's wrist, “no need to get ugly.” The sound of crushing bones peppered the air.

The whelp screamed. The other boy ran.

“Now, sir,” Nick said, as he released the boy's wrist, “I would like to have words with Mr. Gunderson.”

“Can't,” the kid said, nursing his arm, “he's inside and the door's locked.”

“You got the keys, don't you?”

“No,” the youth said. “The other guy, Whitey, was Sergeant at Arms for the ceremony. He's got the keys. There’s no way in.”

“Okay,” Nick said. “City General is five blocks over. They got a good ER. Go get your arm checked out and don't come back, ever.”

The kid backed down the stairs and broke into a staggering sprint across the lot.

Two hundred and fifty pounds of Pittsburgh steel crumpled from one solid kick of Nick’s running shoe.

Inside, forty shaved heads whipped about in surprise. The youths, seated at the semi-circle makeshift tables rose in response to the invader. Half-assed mock shields adorned the walls. A gust of wind knocked over the empty malt liquor cans and buckets of take-out chicken.

“Gentlemen,” Nick said. “Sorry to bust up your party, but I believe there's a young lady who needs a ride home.”

In unison, many of the young men brought small pipes to their lips and huffed. Their twitching grew into shakes and several dropped to the floor in full seizures. All of them foamed at the mouth and bellowed in rage as they tore at their clothes.

"Shield Brothers!" one gurgled, leaping in front of Nick. “I claim right of *einvigi!*” His muscles rippled on his thin frame as thick brown hair sprouted on his cheeks.

“Claim this, creep,” Nick said, driving his fist into the kid’s face.

Nick stepped over to the boy and proclaimed, “Next?”

Tables overturned as the throng of raving youths rushed forward in a skirmish line.

Smiling, Nick dropped into a three-point stance, remembering his glory days at St. Mark’s. As the thunder roared outside, Nick charged into the mass of limbs and bodies. Wading through the carnage, Nick swung his massive fists. Bodies flew in all directions. A two-by-four shattered across his back. Bones cracked and blood spurted, none of it Nick's. A knife ripped through his jacket, but no further. He hammered a blow to the top of the wielder's head. He stuck out his arms and clotheslined two of them and winced. Father O'Brien would have made him run laps for that one.

Above the yells and scuffling, the cracks of automatic weapon fire sputtered. Mosquitoes bounced off Nick's face and body.

Broken, bleeding, and scared, the punks ran, staggered or crawled to the door in panic. In the center of the floor, he saw her lying atop two weather-beaten crates in her rumpled Donna Whatshername business suit. Cute, if you liked the business-type.

"You're too late, Pork-boy," a grizzled voice said. "I got what I needed. Game over."

"Gunderson," Nick said, as he reached the girl's side. "I've been waiting for this for a long time."

"Well, Serrano," Gunderson said, "I guess you're just going to have to wait forever." He dropped an empty glass vial. The candlelight glinted off his sweaty forehead. Naked to the waist, the pot-bellied freak had covered his torso in tattoos since Nick had last busted him.

"Kidnapping, attempted murder… Gunderson, this is over the edge, even for you. You've been sampling your own product again."

"I didn't hurt the Jew bitch yet. I just wanted a couple of drops of her blood for this." Gunderson held the glinting steel mallet aloft. Cold blue fires danced in his eyes as the squat, troll-like man advanced.

"What?" Nick said. "Was fucking Sears closed?"

"You should be one of us; the Old Gods would welcome a warrior spirit such as yours." Lightning flashed through the skylight. "Once we offer up her heart, we can start Ragnarok and bring in a new age."

"No thanks," Nick said as he met Gunderson halfway at the central support pillar. "I like things the way they are."

"I pledge his death to you, Lord Thor!" Gunderson bellowed as he pounced and slammed the hammer down on Nick.

Steel on stone rang throughout the warehouse as Nick blocked the blows with his forearms. Outside, thunder cheered the battle. Nick countered with a hard jab to Gunderson's stomach. Nick peered into the Gunderson's cold blue eyes which showed no pain, only Gunderson's fury. The mallet fell on Nick's shoulder and showered him with blue sparks.

"So long as I hold this hammer," Gunderson roared, "I am invincible!" Blue arcs of electricity cloaked his hammer.

Nick grabbed Gunderson's arms above his head and grinned. His stony grasp guided Gunderson's blow into the steel post. The world exploded into white light as the ground rumbled.

Nick fell backwards. The seams of the warehouse creaked. Twenty feet away, Gunderson sprawled prone, wide-eyed without his hammer. Nick threw himself over the supine form of the unconscious woman as the roof crashed down.

Underneath the wreckage, Nick hoisted his frame upright, clearing away the crumpled steel sheeting. Across the way, Gunderson lay, empty-handed.

"Oops," Nick said, standing over Gunderson.

He hauled Gunderson, wrapped in several bands of steel rebar, and the unconscious girl to the remains of the loading deck. Looking at the receding storm clouds in the pink sky, he considered finding a phone.

"Personally, I'd leave him here," a red-haired man in dark shades said. "Niflheim is nice this time of year. Frozen rivers, black sun, dire wolves." He lit a cigarette.

"He needs to be put away."

"If you want justice, just leave him," the man in the orange suit said. "His sponsor will take care of him. He doesn't like backing losers. Anyway, I don't usually help members of the opposition, and but—" He tossed a vial of cut glass to Nick.

"What?" Nick said, looking up.

The stranger had slipped away.

He gathered up the woman in his arms and began the slow trek to the hospital. The rumbling of large cart wheels filled his ears. Behind him, Gunderson cried, “No! The goats-- ”

Nick never looked back.

“You can put me down, now,” she said as her green eyes opened.

“Uh, oh yeah, I'm sorry,” Nick said. He saw the resemblance to Rabbi Loewmann around the eyes, but only around the eyes.

“Thanks,” she said. “Do you have a name? I like to know the names of the men who save my life.” She brushed dust from her dark hair.

“Nick.”

“Nick, huh?” She said, looking at his chest. “Funny, you don't look Jewish.”

“Wha-yeow?!” Nick sputtered as the amulet around his neck burst into flame. With a flick of his wrist, Nick ripped the flaming piece of metal from his neck and slapped it to the ground. A silvery pool of molten slag was all that remained.

“Nick,” Prof said, “now, I understand why your eyes are brown.”

“Pretty good story, though,” Nick said, taking another swig from his mug.

“Sure, if you’re nine years old and an avid reader of comics.”

“Well,” Nick admitted, “it sounds cooler than the actual truth. Rabbi Loewmann got all the members of his synagogue to sign a petition to reinstate me because of how I handled that vandalism incident last year.”

“Let’s face it, Nick. You were born to do what you do.”

“Tomorrow, I’m back on the beat,” Nick said, draining his mug. “Tonight, I got a hot date and I got to get out of these sweats. There’s a rib shack down on 5th I want to take her to.” He hustled out the door.

Prof shook his head as he waited for Theo to bring the check. He slid around the booth seat to leave and bumped into Nick’s forgotten gym bag.

“Damn muscle head,” Prof muttered, straining to move the obstacle from the seat. “Does he carry his weight set with him?”

Undoing the bag’s half-snagged zipper, Prof reached in.

The musty bag contained only two items: an empty vial of cut glass and a short-handled mallet of cold steel.

The Devil in the Details

9:10 AM July 31st
Room 701 The Hotel Mittelmarch
1275 Reed Shore Drive

The last good cop in a city gone bad," Prof spoke aloud and clicked off the microcassette recorder. No, it sounded too dramatic.

"The stylish shopkeeper," he said, "admired by all, balanced her virtuous deeds against her greed, lest she lose her human form." Wincing, he stopped the recorder again. Another false start added to the pile.

"The scruffy street hustler looked to find that big score," he spoke again, "for he realized he wasn't getting any younger." Prof jammed the stop button and put the recorder down. Three attempts and three failures; it wasn't working. For the last three weeks, he'd sat at the rickety table for several hours and tried to compose a journal of his experiences. He started this project as a lark, just a way to make sense of his problems. At first, he tried freehand speaking into the microcassette recorder, but his dialogue degenerated into a series of "umms" and "ahhhs." Later, he wrote out his thoughts before speaking, but his perfect opening statements led to unfocused blurbs and the blurbs trailed off into frustrated scribbles. Finally, each sheet of the yellow legal pad became another crumpled wad in the overflowing wastepaper basket.

Even with the ratty curtains open, his room remained stuffy in the still morning air. Other than the faint morning traffic seven stories below, a hush reigned over the room. At first, he relished the silence; now, the quiet void gnawed at him. He missed her silvery, bell-like running commentary.

She may have been a delusion created by his emotional trauma, but she was his delusion, and no amount of writing alleviated his emptiness.

He attempted to see Ms. Green at her clinic the Monday after the three dark days at Lou's house but had made it no farther than the busy admitting desk. The harried male nurse called Terry dismissed him with, "Ms. Green is busy; I can put you down for an appointment in two weeks."

He shuffled out of the clinic and into the hot, busy noonday streets. He followed the course of his actions; the fear of Jones' veiled threats, the justification of his betrayal of Nate which he used to shroud his own self-interest and the betrayal itself. She'd called him out every step of the way and he had ignored her each time. The July sun beat down upon his shoulders like God's spotlight, illuminating his contemptibility to the world.

Over the weeks, bright spots appeared. Vindicated, Nick walked his beat with a renewed swagger, although his new love interest went south. He refused to talk about the details. Jane, between work, her thesis and her relationship with Vic, lacked time to brood over her own bundle of troubles. Between Lou's new social life and Prof's need to avoid an uncomfortable confrontation with Vivian, their radio sessions dwindled away. He evaded visiting Reyna. The cheerful, red-headed lady immersed herself in her karma crusades and he knew she would know he no longer had his companion. An explanation would lead to a confession of his sins.

Finally, Tuesday, three days ago, he'd steeled himself and assailed the clinic on Ayrshire one last time. Most struggle to silence voices in their head; he desired his back.

"I'm sorry, Mr. Clarke," Vivian said without looking up from her computer. "Once a transfusion is done, it's final."

"So, what I lost, I can't get back."

"Nothing's free. You're alive, deal with it."

He drifted out of Vivian's office like a ship without a compass. For two hundred dollars, he'd sold out his friend and lost the only guidance he had. He brooded at this table for the last three days. He dreaded his meeting with Mary Sawney, his case worker. He imagined she would ask her probing questions and scratch away on her clipboard while he fidgeted for the right answer, wondering if this would be the reply that sealed his fate.

"Grace in the face of certain doom," he said to himself, reopening the cardboard box.

"Let's make this quick," Sam Cavanaugh said through his wired jaws. "I got another meeting at ten."

"I need to free up some cash to rebuild the casino after the fire," Rex said. "I need out of that scheme."

Sam leaned over his antique desk and noted Rex's creased expression. The stress of the last couple months had taken their toll. "Sure," Sam said, "we can liquidate your position, but if you get out early, you are going to lose some serious gains."

"Doesn't matter. After what that fuck did to my casino, I'm hemorrhaging money."

"It's the price of doing business, Rex. I warned you that the Syrian was no one to mess with."

"He picked the wrong guy to mess with," Rex growled. "I got word that he's planning something big. I'm going to—"

"Rex, slow down. Think before you act. You got to use your head before you make your move, and you have to think five moves ahead."

Rex looked around the lawyer's office. The walnut and brass game clock on the partners' desk, the chess table in the corner. "It's all a game to you, isn't it?"

"No," Sam said, "the game trains you how to win at life. Learn the game and life falls into place the way you planned it."

"Any proof of that?"

"You ought to ask my brother some time."

“You got the money order,” the gravelly voice asked Rachel over her cellphone. “Did Bobby like the gift? I know it wasn’t much.”

“Yes,” Rachel answered, “he loved it. Jake, I wish you were here.”

“Rach, we’ve been over this. I can’t come back. You have a restraining order on Sam that ought to keep him off your back until the divorce goes through. Then you and Bobby will be free—”

“Jake, he wants unsupervised visitation.”

“Don’t do it,” Jake advised. “Never give—”

“Sam an opening, I know,” Rachel said, “but he’s agreed to make interim support payments.”

“Rachel, it’s a sacrifice move. The money isn’t worth it.”

“Don’t even think about moving your money into off-shore investments, Sam,” Rich said with his feet propped up on his desk of glass and steel.

“That South American deal you worked a couple of months ago was sweet,” Sam said as he eyed the privileged golden boy.

“It’s not about the pay out, Sam. The courts will find the money in a heartbeat and you know the ramifications of that.”

“Okay, I can move most of my assets into a trust fund for Bobby. That’ll keep Rachel’s paws out of my wallet.”

“If she has custody,” Rich said, “she’ll still have more leverage than you. Chances are good that custody will go to her. It’s almost a sure bet.”

“I’m working on that part. Anyway, my associate wants out—”

“Sam, don’t even mention that on the premises. Augustus can’t be associated with that enterprise.”

“Still, he needs his money as soon as possible.” The heavy lawyer grabbed his white fedora and left Rich’s sleek office.

Rich’s desk phone beeped.

"Mr. Allen?" Lois, his secretary asked. "It's Special Agent Jones on line one."

"Jones," Rich greeted. "What can I do for you?"

"Just checking in on my investment," Jones said. "How's the kid doing?"

"Great," Rich said, "just checked with his supervisor. He's passed the series 7 in record time. Got him cold calling during the day and training on presentations at night."

"I don't need a stock broker," Jones said. "I need someone who can close a deal in record time."

"It's part of the agreement," Rich said. "We train him off-site and you get a top-notch representative. In the meantime, we get to tap the talent to defray some of our expenses."

"Just make sure that it goes to plan."

Nate yawned as he surveyed the rows of cheap desks, manned by sales representatives with loosened ties and rolled-up shirtsleeves. Each of the young men jabbered the pitch to a customer and either passed the customer on to a waiting broker or moved to the next number in the endless call list. Urgency filled the air; they all wanted the same thing, to make the magic eighty sales. The cars, the houses and the cash was theirs if they earned that promotion to broker.

The last ten weeks had been grueling. That first afternoon when Erskine and Rhodes, in dark suits and sunglasses, dragged him from his room at the 'March changed everything. Instead of a ride down to J Plaza for booking at Muni, they swung the black Crown Victoria up Venture Way to Augustus Investments Limited, home of the corporate fat cats. In Rich Allen's office of glass, leather and chrome, Special Agent Jones made his pitch.

"So, you like these nickel and dime scams, Nate?" the lawman asked, pacing around the spacious office.

"I don't know what you're talking about."

"Come off it, Nate. I've seen your record. Street hustles, check forgery, pickpocketing. High risk, low return. You strike me as being smarter than that, someone who wants to make the big score."

"Doesn't everybody?"

"Yeah," Jones said, "but not everybody gets a chance like this. You go after white-collar criminal types for me and you can write your ticket anywhere."

"What if I refuse?"

Clean-cut Rhodes and Erskine exchanged grins and glances.

"Let's not dwell on the negatives, here, Nate. How long do you think you're going to last pulling these half-assed cons? You're two steps away from a long sentence in the state pen," Jones continued. "The last part I can guarantee."

The outcome decided, Nate took Jones's offer. Upon leaving, Jones turned him over to Rich Allen, the smiling investment banker, for training. After completing the necessary paperwork, they handed over the keys to the corporate condo and Rich drove Nate over to the Warehouse District.

"This, is it?" Nate said, gawking at the pale blue steel warehouse.

"You didn't think you'd start out in the corner office?" Rich said, pulling on his sunglasses and sliding back into his Mercedes convertible. "Go on in. They're expecting you."

Rich fired up the ignition and spun the sports car out of the parking lot.

"New guy, huh?" said the bald manager in a short-sleeved shirt, looking at Nate's paperwork. "Have a seat."

Nate looked out over the rows of workstations through the bay window of the office.

"Impressive, isn't it?" the manager said. "I'm Bernie."

"Nice to meet you, I'm Nate."

"Okay, let's get the ground rules, straight. You're here to learn. This is boot camp. If you can't cut it, you're out. You will be at your desk at eight and you work to nine thirty at night, so you can hit the west coast. From nine thirty to eleven, we have mandatory training. Once you pass your Series 7, you're eligible to start earning commissions. Hit eighty sales and you become a broker with your own crew," Bernie said. "Most of the guys don't last a month."

For the first time in his life, Nate applied himself to honest work. He hit his desk at eight, spun his spiel about the penny stock, Croco Conglomerate, at least one hundred fifty times a day, sat through the late-night study sessions for the license test and staggered into the one-bedroom corporate condo at one in the morning. Soon, Nate realized if he took the test early, he could be home by ten.

Bernie stared open-mouthed when Nate told him he wanted to take the test at the end of the second week. After he passed, Bernie patted him on the back because he'd never seen a perfect test score. With his strut back, the other trainees hit Nate up for tips. He told them to hit the books and study hard. He avoided mentioning that his test strategy consisted of coin-flips and picking the longest answer.

That night at nine thirty, Nate grabbed his laptop bag and headed for the door, looking forward to his hot date with a cold six-pack.

"And where the hell do you think you're going?" Bernie said, blocking the door.

"Home, I passed the test. No more classes for me."

"I'm afraid not, Boy Wonder," Bernie said, turning Nathan around. "You see conference room number two? Great! You have Strategies in Presentation from nine to midnight. Congratulations, Trainee Level Two Gascon."

The weeks dragged on from there. Nate sold shares of Croco Conglomerate in his sleep. It was the greatest investment in the world; he believed it. Now, he hung up his headset and yelped; he'd just made his eightieth commission. He strutted back to Bernie's office, high-fiving and fist bumping the cheering trainees along the way.

"Bernie! How's it hanging?" he said, leaning in the doorway. "You know what just happened?"

"I can guess, Nate. Come on in and close the door."

"So, what do I got to do to get my own crew?"

"Sorry, Nate," Bernie said, "you're a convicted felon. The Securities Exchange Commission isn't going to issue you a license."

"So, now what?"

"I can keep you on as a sales rep. You'll make pretty good money, once you clear your debt."

"What debt?"

"The usual. Training fees, testing fees, phone expense, office space and living expenses, but don't worry; we don't hit you up for that at once. Usually, we deduct it from your commission checks over three years."

"But, I'm not going to be here in three years…"

"I know Rich wants you to finish out Presentations. You're a special case," Bernie replied smugly. "You're out of here in ten weeks, so I'd just consider your commissions a donation to the rest of us who have to work for a living."

Stunned, Nathan wandered back to his desk. The impossible had happened; a shell game had taken him. Classic all the way, they'd gotten him to double down, over and over, and emptied his wallet in the process. With a wicked smile, he donned his headset and his fingers flew across the keyboard to pull up the call list. Tapping his microphone, he said, "All right, all right! Find the little lady, red will set you ahead, black will set you back. Make your bet, chief."

Roger hung up the phone and placed the credit card back in his wallet. That nice Mr. Gascon fellow seemed to know his business. He thought the boys down at the Mason Lodge would appreciate a bit of insider knowledge, too. Luckily, his daughter, Lucy, wouldn't see the credit card statement until the middle of next month.

"Agnes! You must hear about this!" Ella said to her sewing circle sister. "This charming young man promised me a five-hundred percent return on one thousand dollars."

"I'll look it up as soon as I get home," Agnes promised.

"He said it was an exclusive offer through his office," Ella said. She recited the phone number.

The ten other ladies in the parlor pulled notepads from their overstuffed purses.

"Jesus!" Chuck, the reedy floor supervisor, said, dropping down the chair in front of Bernie. "I've never seen it like this. The phone system is blowing up. We got sales coming out of our ears."

"When it rains, it pours. Looks like month-end bonuses are going to be hefty," Bernie said and peered out to the buzzing sales floor. Desk 27 was empty. "Where's Gascon?"

"He stayed real busy for a couple of hours and took a late lunch. He was pretty hot, even with sad news."

Bernie's cellphone rang.

"What are you idiots doing over there?" Rich Allen screamed.

"Selling Croco, Rich. We're having a killer run."

"Haven't you been watching the news? Croco spiked at two hundred per share. They've suspended trading pending investigation."

The wail of sirens barely registered with Bernie.

Madeline Nelson walked among the desks with their upturned phones and monitors knocked askew. In her professional opinion, this crew was either incredibly brilliant or awesomely stupid. She shook her head and pursed her lips. The equipment and setup screamed high-end backing with a seasoned crew, but the run this bunch had pulled today defied comprehension; the sales spikes, let alone the standard deviations, had set off the exchange's algorithms like fire alarms. Glancing at the sullen, handcuffed men lining the wall of the warehouse, the raid had netted only the small fish; the genius behind this cesspool had scrubbed away any connection. By chance and a hunch, she stopped at desk 27, the center of this mess.

"Who sits here?" she asked the bald manager.

"Nate Gascon," he mumbled and shifted his cuffed wrists.

Madeline examined the immaculate desktop. The drawers were completely empty, save for a welcome packet for new employees of Augustus Investments Limited. Opening the glossy folder, Madeline saw a defaced picture of the Chief Operations Officer, Richard Allen. Someone had drawn a moustache and horns on the smiling man's face and written above it, "Richie smokes pole when not ripping off little old ladies."

"Gentlemen," Madeline said aloud, "do any of you know what The Racketeering Influenced and Corrupt Organization Act of 1970 is?"

Bernie blanched.

"Not to worry," Madeline said. "I'm sure your lawyers will know what it is."

"What do you mean I can't get my money?" Rex said, glowering at Sam from across the desk.

"You'll be able to get your money back after the investigation," Sam said. "At least some of it."

"I need that money."

"Look," Sam said, "if it makes you feel any better, I'm in the same boat as you. We're second tier investors, unlike Rich—"

"And unlike Allen, you're still in one piece."

Rich sat on the concrete bench in the holding cell with his head bowed. Amidst the glare of bright lights and the chattering of the reporters, the solemn FBI agents had led him into the Municipal Annex for booking, while Larry, legal counsel for Augustus, had dodged and bounced beside him.

"Don't worry. Don't say anything and keep a low profile," Larry said. "We'll have bond posted in a couple of hours."

Staying in the corner closest to the door, he realized his Versace suit drew attention from a couple of young toughs on the far side of the crowded room of green-painted cinderblock.

The slam of the door heralded the entry of a newcomer, a man with a broken nose in a black leather jacket; he scanned the faces of the occupants. Spotting Rich, he sauntered over.

"A bitch, isn't it?" he said to Rich. "Not being able to smoke down here."

"It's city ordinance," Rich said. "Besides, it's a health hazard."

"You know what else a health hazard is?" the man said, grabbing Rich by the lapels. "Losing Mr. Brunet's money."

"I was just down in Holding," Jerry said. "They just carted Allen out in a stretcher. Apparently, he got into a fight with one of the other perps."

"Great, this complicates things, "Jones said. "I needed that greedy SOB. Did they bring in Gascon?"

"He wasn't in the boiler room when they made the bust."

"One asset out of commission and the other off the reservation," Jones surmised. "Hell of a day, Jerry."

"Uh, Bill?" Jerry said. "If you don't need me, I'd like to get home. It's date night."

Jones cracked a smile. "Sure, Kid," he said. "Give Mary a hug for me. What did I tell you about married life?"

"What can I say, Bill? When you're right, you're right." Jerry grabbed his coat and hat off the tree and left the Pit.

Watching his protégé walk out of the quiet office bay, Jones swelled with pride. Jerry and Mary had come a long way; they were two of his most productive assets. He opened the center drawer of his desk and retrieved a blood collection vial labeled, "J. Clarke." It smelled of saffron.

He picked up his office phone and dialed. "Mary, baby," he said, "that special project I asked you to watch. Yeah, if you could... No, Jerry doesn't need to know."

In the summer twilight of Wrightsway Park, Prof waited on the bench with the large portable stereo next to him. Exhausted from lugging the damn thing from Rondo's Pawn Emporium on Corral, he wiped his sweaty brow and puffed. No one ever said penance was easy.

Earlier this afternoon, he left his room to escape the heat and his failures. Without her, he expected a bleak walk in the cool afternoon shadows of the towering buildings. Passing the alleyway behind the 'March, he felt a twinge of pain between his ribs and the memory of the near-fatal mugging a month earlier.

"Psst, Prof!" Nathan called from the alley.

"Nathan!" Prof said. "I hoped you were okay. I asked about you downt—"

"Never mind that, Prof. I'm okay. I need you to do something for me." He pressed a ticket and a few bills in Prof's hand. "Get my boom box out of hock at Rondo's and meet me down at Wrightsway after dark."

As Nate hustled down the alley, Prof paused; Nate was trouble, but Prof set the hounds upon him in the first place. Due to his betrayal of Nate, Prof believed his mugging and the loss of her were karmic justice. Common sense told him to walk away, but his gut instincts sensed he needed to make things right for both of them. After making his way to the pawn shop, he staggered and stumbled to Wrightsway Park under the baking sun, apologizing to all he jostled with the large clumsy radio swinging by his side. He dropped onto the park bench and waited for Nate.

A quick shuffle across the grass heralded Nate's arrival minutes later.

"Thanks, Prof," Nate said. "I got a screwdriver in the back of the van."

"A van?" Prof said, grabbing on to Nate's shoulder and tagging along. "Since when do you have a van?"

"Since, they gave me a corporate credit card."

"Who?" Prof said. "I understand they got you in an internship program of some sort."

"Yeah," Nate said, jimmying the back of one of the speakers of the stereo. "It didn't work out…"

"So, what's your plan now?"

"Well, I figure I'm gonna have to stay out of the limelight for a while," he said, popping the back of the speaker off and retrieving a driver's license and a Social Security Card. "Anyway, thanks for retrieving my insurance policy."

"Insurance policy? Nate, what are you talking about?"

"Sorry, Prof, Nathan Gascon blew town; however, if you wish to leave a message for him, I'm Neil Grazer, a close friend of Mr. Gascon."

"Pleasure to make your acquaintance, Mr. Grazer," Prof said, shaking his head. "Nate, I'm the one who dropped the dime on you."

"I figured that, Prof. You're a smart guy, but sometimes, you're still a chump. Anyway, I asked you for help because I knew you'd follow through. If I didn't know my shills, I'd be out of business."

"Thanks, Mr. Grazer, that makes me feel a bit better. So, what's with the van?"

"Mr. Gascon had a yard sale at the corporate condo. Had some great deals, I made out like a bandit."

"What do you call that?"

"In the corporate world," Nate said, climbing into the van, "we call this a severance package."

Fools, Drunks and Children

9:30 AM August 14th
Ali's House of Wonders
12 Cedars Street

Cindy bounced down the stairs from her room into the store where Uncle Al labeled cardboard boxes with a permanent marker.

"Good morning, Uncle Al," she sang.

"Ah, good morning, Cindy," Uncle Al said, putting down the marker. "I have a fresh pot of mint tea with bread and yogurt."

"Uh, no thank you," she said, as her nose wrinkled. "I was planning on grabbing something over at the diner."

"Cindy, such fare is not healthy for you, or anyone else, for that matter."

"Uncle Al, you're beginning to sound like Mom."

"I gave your mother my word that you will be absolutely safe while visiting me."

"I'm a big girl," Cindy said. "I'm eighteen. I can take care of myself."

"Of course you are, little one, I forget myself. I just remember the blonde little girl on the pink bicycle with skinned knees."

"That was a long time ago."

"So, where are you going to explore today?"

"Just out and about, you know," Cindy said with a shrug. "Just trying to see a bit of the world before I start school, unless you need help around here."

"No, the esteemed Mr. Magnus picked up his apparatus yesterday, and Mr. Alhazred will drop by for his books this afternoon."

"You are really closing down? What about the carpets?"

"I expect that I will entire sell the inventory within weeks. This internet is a wondrous tool."

"Could you save one for me, Uncle Al? I'd like to buy one for my dorm room."

"No, little one," Al said, "I will gladly give you one as a gift. You worked very hard to get accepted to the university. I and your parents are most proud of you."

"Thank you, Uncle Al," Cindy said, hugging the stout little man.

"You are more than welcome, little one. You have always been my favorite niece. Now go and enjoy the day." He stood on tiptoe to kiss her forehead.

Cindy scampered around the boxes and out the entrance to the store with its soaped-up windows. She held a firm grasp on her pocketbook, just like Uncle Al admonished her to do repeatedly. Uncle Al's visits felt like the return of the great explorer with his exotic tales of the city. She'd jumped at the chance when he invited her to spend the summer with him to see the city for herself.

A couple of blocks up Cedars Street, she popped into the corner diner. The shabby booths of orange and red vinyl screamed, "Authenticity!" unlike the neat, orderly franchise places back in Cherry Brook. She picked up one of the laminated menus.

"Hi Cindy," the waitress in the candy cane striped dress greeted her. "What can I get you today?"

"I'd like to get the special, Jane," she said, "and a pot of coffee."

"Sure, I'll put that order in for you, right away," Jane said. "So, what's with the coffee? You usually get a large milk."

"Late night; I was up chatting with the nicest guy until early this morning."

"Really?" Jane said. "You get a summer in the city for free and romance to boot? I'm envious."

"And you want to know the best part?" Cindy whispered, glancing around the diner. "Don't tell Uncle Al, but I'm meeting him for coffee this afternoon."

"Okay," Jane said. Her face clouded, as she hurried off.

Cindy worked her way through the order of sunny-side eggs, bacon and toast, mindful of her schedule. As soon as she finished the last bit of toast, Jane appeared and said, "Anything else, I can get you?"

"Check, please," Cindy said, "and a to-go cup of coffee."

"You don't drink that much—"

"It's not for me," Cindy cut in, "it's for..." She nodded towards the door.

"Oh, that's so nice. Harry doesn't want him in here during the day," Jane said. "He thinks Prof puts the lunch traffic off."

"I don't see how; he keeps to himself," Cindy said, handing the cash to Jane.

"I'll get your change—"

"Keep it," Cindy said.

"Thanks, Cindy," Jane called after her. "Uh, Cindy, I don't want to get in your business, but meeting guys online can be really, well, dangerous..."

Cindy stopped and said, "He's a youth minister at a Methodist church, what could possibly go wrong?" She slipped out the door.

Jane shook her head as the smudged glass door eased shut.

Up Cedars Street again, Cindy saw the man in the rumpled black jacket, his dark sunglasses framed by his salt and pepper hair in need of cutting. He sat on the wrought iron bench in front of the multilevel concrete garage.

"Hi, Prof, I brought you a coffee."

"Good morning, Cindy," he said. "Bless you, kiddo. Out for another day of exploring?"

"Yup, thanks for letting me know about the Hopper Exhibit at the museum. The paintings reminded me of old movies."

"Yes, Old Ed really had a great eye on how America looked and worked." He took a long sip from the Styrofoam cup. "So, are you still planning to go see *Our Town*?"

"I'll give it a try, but to tell you the truth, it sounds way too much like Cherry Brook."

"So young and so jaded," Prof sighed. "I suppose I could send you down to The Strand to watch a Truffaut film, but I've always been a firm believer of understanding where you come from before looking elsewhere. Some would argue otherwise."

"Still assigning homework, Prof?"

"Old habits die hard. Anyway, have you heard back from that job interview?

"It wasn't so much of a job interview," Cindy said. "I mean, Mr. Johnson said I might be able to make good money as a model and it might lead to some film work."

"And you met this Mr. Johnson, where?" Prof said, cocking an eyebrow over the rims of his dark glasses.

"In front of his office on Corral Drive, only I don't think anything is going to come of it."

"Cindy, I think—"

"I don't understand, though," Cindy continued. "We talked for over two hours and he even took a few head shots. It really sounded promising. I haven't gotten a call back, yet."

"Well," Prof said, "these things happen for a reason. Wait a minute, did you say Corral Drive?"

"Yes, why?"

"It's probably nothing. Anyway, hope you have a wonderful day, just stay safe."

"Thanks, Prof, I will," Cindy said.

As Cindy scampered into the parking garage, Prof pondered his daily ramble down Corral Drive past a string of pawn shops, check cashing joints and day labor staffing offices. Like a line of molars, the office spaces stood ready to grind up the luckless, clueless or broken like so much meat. Yesterday, he'd detected an abscess in the row of storefronts by the rustle of strung-up cordon tape and a faint aroma of scorched sheet rock and melted plastic clinging to the doorway of a particularly nondescript office. After a moment's pause, he shook his head and concluded, "Probably nothing."

Cindy hopped into the small white Volvo station wagon, a graduation present from her parents. The car purred to a start, but she ground the gears to get out of the parking space. She did well in Driver's Ed last year with Coach Wilks, but that was driving an automatic. Dad said he wanted her to learn how to handle a manual transmission because you'd never know when it would come in handy. "Sure not now, Daddy," Cindy said under her breath as she popped the clutch and stalled again. Finally, she eased through the twilit maze of cars and into the early afternoon sunlight. "Freedom!" she thought, pleased with her success.

The little car zipped over Walker Bridge and the steel and glass buildings yielded to smaller, older brick buildings. At the light, she glanced around. It was still early. If she could find a parking spot, she looked forward to browsing the street vendors' wares before meeting Jerry.

As the light turned green, she dropped the clutch and the engine died. Her car lurched forward with a loud crunch. Stunned, she popped her seat belt loose and slid out of the car. A man in a bright orange tracksuit surveyed the crumpled front end of his blue Lincoln Continental. White steam poured from underneath the sedan's broad, wrinkled hood.

"Are you okay, sir?" Cindy said to paunchy man with styled gray hair.

"Shit, would you look at this?"

"Oh, God! I'm so sorry!"

"Damn," he said. "I got a meeting to make..." He turned to regard Cindy and the unblemished Volvo. His eyes lit up. "Ah, I don't see why you need to wait around for the cops," he said. "Why don't we just exchange insurance information and you go ahead, young lady? I'll tell them what happened."

"Thank you, sir."

"You're not from around here, are you, miss?"

"No," Cindy said, "I'm visiting my uncle for the summer." She looked down at the slip of paper he provided her. "Thank you for being so understanding, Mr. Smith." She pulled out her license and registration and offered it to the man.

"Not at all, Ms. Blaze," Mr. Smith said. "I should have known. You come across as a very honest and respectful young lady. Unlike a lot of the troublemakers around here."

Cindy climbed back into the Volvo and sped off.

Mr. Smith's grin turned predatory as the little white station wagon turned the corner.

"Well, if it isn't my good friend, Saul Reeve!" the large, tanned beat cop said as he strode up to the man in the orange track suit. His summer blues pitted with sweat stains in the noon sun.

"Serrano! It's a good thing that you showed up. Some little bitch just wrecked my ride and drove off."

"Absolutely," Nick said, "anything for an upstanding citizen like you. In fact, I'm so concerned that I was just about to call in a warrant check."

"Go ahead, check, Serrano," Saul said with a shrug. "I'm in the clear."

"Of course, you are," the muscular cop said, pulling out his notebook. "License and registration, please."

"There you go; I also got the license plate off the car. She backed into me and took off."

Nick looked up from the notepad, studied the buckled front end of Saul's car and looked back at Saul. "You expect me to believe that crap?"

"It was a hit and run, damn tourist kids."

"Is it drivable?" Nick said. He pulled his cap off and ran his fingers through his damp black hair. "It's not quite rush hour, but if we have to get you towed…"

"Let me check, I know a guy who owns a tow truck."

Nick sauntered to the rear of the sky-blue Lincoln to verify the license number. The tail lights flared to life as Saul inserted the key. One crank and the Lincoln purred. The car rolled one a foot forward, sputtered, and died.

The trunk popped open.

Nick grinned at the contents of the trunk and strode up to the Lincoln's driver door.

"Saul," he said, leaning into the window, "you having one of those days? I sure am."

Saul's mouth hung wide open.

Meanwhile, Cindy found a spot alongside the small, circular pocket park. She slipped the little station wagon into the large gap. On the far side of the park, she spotted the small sign which read, "Java Buddies." Checking her pink plastic watch, she knew she had plenty of time to work her way through the maze of tables and racks that lined the red brick sidewalk. Past the glittering jewelry, the new electronics and the paintings, she ambled, none really catching her interest.

"Hey, little lady!" said a young man with shaggy brown hair as he jumped directly in front of her. "You look like you could use a new purse!"

Cindy looked down at her pocketbook. Granted, it wasn't one of her good ones, but the little brown purse, stressed and stained, had seen better days.

"Look, let me show you some of what we got here," he said, taking Cindy's elbow and guiding her to the chrome tree of hanging purses. "Take this for example," he said, offering a bright red leather purse with elegant gold stitching. "This is a Contessa Soiree, top of the line."

"It's very nice, "Cindy said, "but designer stuff like this is way out of my price range—"

"You'd be surprised. You got to remember most of this stuff comes from two or three factories over in the Philippines. What you're paying for is an eight-hundred-dollar label. I can let this go for say…fifty?"

Cindy's eyes narrowed and her nose crinkled. "Twenty-five," she countered.

"Oh, I got a player on the hook," he declared with a toothy grin while rubbing his stubbly chin. "For you, I can go to forty."

She paused for a moment. Uncle Al would have accused him of thievery with substandard merchandise, but she wasn't Uncle Al. "Thirty," she offered.

"Are you kidding? I got kids to feed!"

"Okay, let's split the difference."

"Sounds good to me."

Cindy rummaged through her purse and popped some wrinkled bills from her wallet. "There you go," she said.

"That's great," he said, fumbling the money. "Here's your change and I'll get you the box."

"No need," Cindy said dumping her makeup, wallet, pens and address book into the new purse. "I'll just take it and go. Would you get rid of this old one for me?"

"Sure! You just made one heck of a purchase."

"I got to scoot now," she said. "I can't keep a man waiting."

Phil chucked the old purse into the nearby trash bin. *Two points!* he thought. He made the sale and short-changed her ten bucks.

"Here's your coffee, shitbrick," Nate said, offering the steaming cup to Phil. "Any business?"

"Hell yeah, Nate! I told you we'd be raking in the mad cash."

"For once, Phil, I guess you're right. Had to burn my nut to get the goods, but we'll make that up in no time."

"And you thought you were just paying rent on couch surfing at my crib. I just sold a bag to a teenybopper and scammed her. Double dip supreme."

"Nice! Just show 'em the bait and they'll bite, they always bite." Nate looked at the purse rack and paused. "Uh, Phil, which one did you sell?"

"The red leather one, you know? The one with—"

"The gold thread," Nate said, pinching the bridge of his nose. "You didn't..."

"Yeah, it was—"

"Fuck, Phil that was the bait. Where was she headed?"

"She said she was meeting someone."

Simultaneously, they said, "Java Buddies."

"Wait here and let's see if I can pull our nuts out of the fire," Nate said. He trotted back through the park. Over his shoulder, he heard a woman address Phil.

"Officer James, Bunco. Do you have a permit to sell these purses?" He picked up his pace and walked out of the park and past Java Buddies and never looked back.

Cindy entered the sun-lit establishment called Java Buddies. The aroma of fresh coffee and pastries hung in the air as a team of baristas filled orders behind the bleached oak counter. A girl in army fatigues and work boots strummed a guitar and hummed aimlessly on a stool in the corner. Cindy spotted him.

He put down his newspaper and stood; his warm smile flooded the room and he ran his hand through his well-groomed short hair. "Cindy?" he said.

"Yes, Jerry?"

"That's, right," he said and gestured for her to sit at the small black table. "Have any trouble finding the place?"

"Not at all," she said, admiring the simple artistic shop. "I've been past this place a lot of times, but I felt kind of funny going in by myself."

"It's a pretty friendly place. The coffee's great and the scones are pretty good, too."

"You know, I have never had a scone before," she said, leaning in, "but I'm not really a fan of coffee…and it's way too hot for it."

"How about a smoothie, then? The mango ones are the best."

"Okay, I'll give it a try."

"Be right back in a jiffy," he said and hopped out of his chair.

She watched him amble over to the counter in his bright yellow oxford shirt. *Cute,* she thought, *and a nice butt, too.* She admired the various pieces of folk art hanging on the white walls, all with conspicuous price tags. Cherry Brook would never have a place like this to hang out.

"Here you go," Jerry said, placing a scone and a tall glass in front of her, "just as the lady ordered."

She took a large bite of the pastry. "This is pretty good."

"Try it with a little cream and berries."

"Oh," she blushed, "like I said, I have never had a scone before."

"I give you an 'A' for enthusiasm, Cindy. Try the smoothie; you don't have to doctor that up with condiments."

She took a sip of the thick, cold smoothie. "You're right, it's good."

"So, you're studying to be a teacher?"

"Uh-huh, I decided to take the summer off before going back for my senior year."

"It's admirable that you are willing to be a teacher," he said. "It's such a noble profession." He took a long sip of his drink.

Cindy took a long sip of her drink, too. "Why, thank you, Jerry, but that is nowhere as important as a youth minister."

"Ah," Jerry shrugged, "what can I say? I am just doing my part. I mean, it's a well-to-do church, but that doesn't mean that the kids don't have problems."

"Well," she said, "for what it's worth, I think it is a good thing you're doing." She emphasized her words with a light touch to his hand.

"Thanks."

"So, what does a youth minister do for fun?" she asked.

"Assistant youth minister," he said. He glanced down at his watch and looked towards the door and the darkening skyline beyond. "Well, I like to walk around and look at old buildings. That's why I like this area so much."

"Really? That's one of the reasons I'm here in the city."

"If you're up for an adventure, we can go up a couple of blocks to Bianchi Avenue. Ever been there?"

"No, I sure haven't. What's up there?"

"Ah, just a bunch of storefronts from the twenties or thirties, but the masonry is really neat. If we leave right now, we could get there before its dark."

"Sounds like a plan!" she said and drained the rest of her glass.

"All right, let's head on out."

Just outside the coffee shop, Cindy gently tugged Jerry's sleeve and said, "Sorry to do this, but I need to stop at the ladies' room before we go."

"Sure, I'll just wait here."

"Thanks, it will just be a second." She slipped back through the door.

Jerry watched her tight little ass turn the corner. Beads of perspiration formed at his hairline and his pulse quickened. He'd stashed the rope, duct tape and knives in the store after taking the afternoon off for a doctor's appointment. Breathing deeply, he tried to calm down. No such luck. He felt himself tenting in his chinos. This one would be so sweet. Mary's special powder should kick in quick.

His mouth dried up and his vision blurred at the edges. As world began to sway, he leaned against the wall to steady himself. The rough brick raked his back as he sank lower. His vision transformed into a long, darkening tunnel and he attempted to puzzle out what was happening.

The tire jumping the curb barely registered. Straining, he saw the green minivan. Familiar, yet, Jerry could not place it.

"Oh, Jerry!" a female cried over him. She seemed familiar, too, but he could only make out her brunette bobbed hair and bright red turtleneck. Hoisted upward by thin, determined arms, Jerry tumbled into the passenger seat of the van, which smelled of peppermints and animal crackers. One door slammed, then the other. Something finally clicked in

Jerry's head. "Mary, I love you so much," he whispered just before his head lolled.

"I know, dear," Mary said, dry-eyed and focused as she eased the van off the curb with a bump and sped down the busy street.

Minutes later, Cindy washed her hands and gave her blond hair a quick fluff. She practiced her smile in the mirror. She rushed out of the bathroom and stopped at the front door. Jerry was gone.

She drove back from the park in silence, not even the tunes of her favorite boy band could cheer her up. She used the worn key to the green door at 12 Cedars Street.

"Good evening to you, dear niece," Uncle Al said, walking in from his back office. "Did you have a good day?"

"Sort of, I had an okay time, but sometimes things just don't work out the way you want, you know?"

"Trust me, Cindy; I am much more aware of that proclivity of fate than you are." He spread his arms wide, directing Cindy's attention to the racks and racks of men's silk suits that lined the walls.

"Uncle Al, how did—?"

"Unfortunately, I forgot to notify my supplier in Bangkok of my retirement. No sooner had Mr. Alhazred left then the truck pulled up to the loading dock. Cash on demand, of course."

"You could have refused. How are you going to get rid of them?"

"Just another obstacle to overcome," Uncle Al said with a wave of his hand. "It is much like that movie you showed me. The one with the burning city and the soldiers in blue and gray."

"You mean *Gone with the Wind*?"

"Yes, that's the one. What was it that lovely lady said?"

"Tomorrow is another day?"

"So, it is, dear one," Uncle Al concluded. "I'm about to make a pot of coffee and enjoy some dainties, can I interest you?"

"Thanks, Uncle Al, but I think I just need to go to bed." Cindy turned and climbed the rickety stairs.

Uncle Al watched her reach the top of the steps and shook his head. They were always so difficult at that age, not wanting to talk, especially to their elders. Twin wisps of smoke issued from his ears and dissipated into the air. *At least*, he brooded, *she could have bragged about her most excellent barter*.

Jerry cracked his sleep-caked eyes. The bare pine rafters seemed familiar, but not at this angle. He glanced to the right and saw the small basement window covered by Mylar and the stained corkboard on the walls; they were his home improvements.

"Jerry?" Mary called to him softly from out of view. "You're awake. That's good"

He realized she had bound him to the plywood table with thick leather straps, another one of his projects. She'd also sliced away his clothing with a box cutter.

"Dear heart," Mary chided, "I can understand violating the holy covenant of our marriage and I can even forgive that."

"Mary," he pleaded

"Shhhh," she said, touching her finger to his cracked lips. "But hunting alone? Do you want your son growing up without a father?" She stepped into his line of sight and he saw she was wearing her favorite playsuit, a shiny black PVC cat suit. She opened the antique Damascus steel straight razor with a pearl handle and looked at him.

"Oh, don't worry, my love, you are a man. You are, by nature, weak. Women have the most import job of all in society," she continued, running the cold, sharp blade across his chest and over his pale stomach. "Civilizing you…"

The razor crept lower.

The Art of Couture War

8:00 AM Sept 7th
Wrightsway Park

L*abor Day and I'm working again,* Beth thought. *No surprise there.*

"Keep up, Libby!" Ursula snapped. "We have much to do." The clipping of Ursula's white high heels upon the brick sidewalk set the pace for the entourage of photographers, lawyers and junior executives, all hustling to keep up with the fur-clad fashion magnate.

History repeats itself again, Beth thought. At every grand opening of a new Fashion Plaza, Ursula raced from store to store to meet and greet the local business community; Beth referred to these strolls as Ursula's victory laps, though not to Ursula's face, of course.

"Okay," Ursula said without breaking stride as they passed under the worn mezzanine of The Strand Theater, "and someone better be taking this down. The IMAX theater will run *Rocky Horror* once a year on Halloween. We can afford to let the kids have their little fun once a year. October is a good month to let a first-run feature slide."

"Got it, Ursula!" said one of the young women in a gray school girl outfit, scribbling a note in her leather portfolio.

"The street vendors," Ursula said, glancing over at the small park in the center of the square, "they're gone and not coming back, right?"

"The city council suspended permits for the opening ceremony," William, the eager boyish lawyer said, trotting alongside Ursula.

"What about a permanent ban?"

"I thought a temporary suspension would be enough—"

"Billy," Ursula said, "I didn't get to be Miss Congeniality in the Texas Belle Pageant with 'good enough.'"

Cowed and chastened, Billy dropped from the pack to make a call on his cell phone. "Lucinda!" Ursula said, sweeping into the small pet shop with open arms. "I just wanted to thank you for your help! My public relations team tells me that these are the healthiest doves they've ever seen."

Beth watched with dreaded admiration; Ursula reapplied her smile even harder to mask her dislike of the shop's smells and noises.

"Thank you, Mrs. Fontaine," the worn, gray-headed woman in stained coveralls said. "It wasn't easy finding five hundred white doves in twenty-four hours."

"Please call me Ursula. Since Jesus called my beloved Cecil home to manage his great oil field in the sky, I just don't have the heart to use his last name," she said and air-kissed Lucinda. She pushed a gold foil envelope into the pet store owner's hands and continued, "Please, drop by later. I am sure we can find something flattering for you."

With a practiced turn, Ursula swished out of the pet shop in a whirlwind of dark fur and vibrant summer silks.

"Lee-Lee," Ursula addressed her purchasing agent as they lingered outside the store, "only blue Persians and pedigree miniatures, no mutts or strays."

At their final stop, a quaint storefront with a lattice window door and white-fringed scarlet awning, two women stood. The tall one wore a crimson sweat suit and dark sunglasses, and a bright red ponytail stuck out of her matching ball cap. She worked the front door lock while her friend, a shorter, rounder woman in pink sweats covered in sequined flowers, waited impatiently.

"*Pardonez-moi*," Ursula said, "would either of you be Miss Fox?"

"That would be me," the tall woman said with a bright, genuine smile.

"Please, call me Ursula. I've been following all the wonderful things you've been doing for the community. Charity satisfies the soul so much more than actual monetary success."

"Why, thank you, Ursula. I've learned that the more light you bring, the more light you're given."

"Such a refreshingly youthful worldview," Ursula mused. "I wished more people thought like you do."

"Money is nice, but loving what you do makes all the difference."

"Here," Ursula said, offering each of the women a gold envelope, "these are certificates for complete makeovers. Our cosmetologists can work wonders for women your age, I mean, any age."

"You are most generous," Reyna said.

Accepting her envelope, Vivian feigned appreciation with half-hearted results.

Ursula and her staff hurried on with their rounds. Out of earshot of the two women, Ursula took Beth aside and said, "You've come a long way, Libby. It's time to show your colors. I want you to go back and make friends with that Fox woman. I don't see her as competition—"

"Vendor lists?" Beth cut in.

"Such a bright little girl. You're learning. In the meantime, I believe I will go get my morning tea," Ursula said as a troubled look crossed her face, "with lots of honey…"

"Reyna, why didn't you shred her? 'Women of our age!'" Vivian fumed.

"It's quite simple, Vivian; as the grand mistress wrote, let your plans be as dark and impenetrable as a little black cocktail dress, and when you move, be as striking as a stunning scarlet evening gown."

Vivian cocked an eyebrow. "The grand mistress said that?"

"Well, I paraphrased it. Anyway, let's synchronize watches."

"Reyna, your Tiffany watch doesn't have a second hand."

"I've heard that in the movies so many times, I just wanted to say it."

Vivian sighed, looking across the immense stage set up before the historical five-story Thomas Building. Once a stately icon of the square, the brick building was now festooned with flashing neon lights and an ultra-modern tunnel of mirrors at the entrance. “Reyna, I hope you know what you’re doing. Are you sure this is the right time to do this?”

“Absolutely, I have the perfect strategy, but unless I implement it, even the finest lingerie run through a washing machine will eventually pucker.”

“Your grand mistress again?”

“Of course. You know your part?”

“Yes, Reyna,” Vivian said with a blush. “I know I owe you for the blood drive, but—”

“I believe you are the one who said there ain’t no such thing as a free lunch.”

“Point taken,” Vivian said, sauntering across the street to the green park.

I wonder, Reyna thought, watching Vivian’s graceful rolling hips, *if I helped her with another blood drive, she would teach me to walk like that.*

“Ms. Fox?” a young lady in a formless gray business suit and pageboy haircut inquired.

“You’re Libby, right?” Reyna said.

“Well, I prefer Beth, but Ursula doesn’t think that’s perky enough.”

“I’m surprised she hasn’t said anything about your wardrobe, in that case.”

Beth glanced down and said, “It never pays to upstage Ursula.”

“I see,” Reyna said. “We’re so much alike.”

“How so?”

“It’s a survival strategy. Appear to be a knockoff when you are a designer label and a designer label when you are a knockoff.”

Beth looked to the stage and stifled a giggle with her hand. “Are you saying Ursula is a—”

“Let’s just say, if the tired old homily fits, wear it,” Reyna said and untied the red silk scarf from around her neck and placed it around Beth’s. “I can’t fix the major damage right now, but this ought to brighten you up a bit. I've always liked red silk. It's soft and strong, and red is a lucky color and gives you a sense of yourself. Besides, it really compliments your eyes."

"Ms. Fox, you know why I'm here."

"I know I'd do the same thing in her place. Most of my inventory is consignment, but I'm sure the new merchandise is nothing she isn't getting cheaper. You need to catch up with the rest of the flock, Beth. Just remember, act like a knockoff."

Beth gave a shy smile and walked back to the stage.

Inside her shop, Reyna dared not remove her sunglasses for the brilliant white summer sun flooded every inch of the shop. So many good things summoned so much light. She stepped to the wardrobe and felt her way to the back. She spaced the black garment bag just so to keep its precious contents from wrinkling. Inside the dressing booth, she unzipped it with the utmost reverence, whispering to herself, "Hail St. Gabrielle of Paris, patroness of all things fashionable."

She stripped off the sweat suit top and bottom and hung the baseball cap on the hook. From a new package, she rolled on the silk seamed stockings and clipped them to the waiting garter clips. Once dressed, she fitted and smoothed the opera-length gloves on her hands and forearms.

In front of the three-way mirror, she stepped into her black patent leather pumps. Bowing her head, she donned the midnight blue wide-brimmed hat with the perfect white band. Finally, she held her breath and looked up to survey her battle tunic in the mirrors; the dark navy skirt suit cut the classic silhouette that would echo in eternity. Raising her arms in the air, she said aloud, "Cry fabulous, and let slip the togs of war!"

Manning her command station behind the register, she opened the black leather case and retrieved the theatre-length ebony cigarette holder. She tapped the holder three times on the glass display case. The small CD player on the shelf behind her clicked on and the first ominous bars of Holst's *Mars, Bringer of War* filled the room.

Treading through the mirror tunnel to join her waiting staff on the stage, Ursula admired her handiwork; she'd designed the store entrance. On the entry side, the mirror panes bowed convex and coated half-silvered. Entering the store, the shoppers caught a glimpse of themselves shorter, wider and paler. On the exit side, mirror panes flexed concave and gilded with a touch of bronze. Upon leaving, the shoppers saw themselves as slimmer, taller and tanned. Looking down on the square, her pioneering spirit soared; the lush, green park would showcase a great commerce district, once cleared of undesirable natives.

Beth slipped through the growing crowd of early comers and climbed up the stage stairs.

"Well, Libby," Ursula said, "did you get what I sent you for?"

"Ms. Fox's inventory is mostly consignment with some common accessory merchandise."

"Did you get her specific vendors?"

"No, it just didn't seem plausible."

The identically dressed women, Lee-Lee, Brittany and Cherie, smirked in anticipation of Ursula's next words.

"Oh well," Ursula said, "perhaps that task was beyond you. Why don't you fetch us some lattes from across the way?"

"Yes, Ursula," Beth said, understanding what being the designated "coffee girl" meant.

"Oh, and Libby?" Ursula added. "I'd rethink that scarf. It's a bit trailer-park." She shifted her weight; her form-shaping girdle hugged her tighter than usual.

At the counter, Reyna's red and white whiskers sprang from her upper lip and receded. She checked her watch. "Three minutes to nine," she said to herself. She hoped to delay this sin, the first of many today. Biological weapons were a definite no-no under all arms treaties.

Vivian reclined upon the park bench and gazed at the bright sunlight filtering through the dense canopy of leaves. The tabloid dropped to her lap as her eyes closed and she dreamt of things of long ago. Birds chirped and squirrels scampered. She remembered the brook filled with fresh cool water that once flowed past this place.

A serenity crossed her face, picturing the carpet of wildflowers covering the meadow, each pistil and stamen filled with the promises of a color-filled future. Finally, she relived Lou's warm embrace and his strong hands kneading her hot flesh. Her hand slipped underneath the newspaper in her lap and a faint moan escaped her lips.

As her moan spread across the park, the ragweed and the grasses succumbed with a shudder, releasing their pollen in the air. The cones of the pine trees opened and released their spores under her ministrations. Finally, the stodgy oaks relented. The faint greenish-yellow cloud wafted across the park and settled upon the throng surrounding the stage.

Ursula cleared her throat and hoarsely addressed the adoring audience. "Today begins a new era for this grand old mercantile district—" Her statement was interrupted by a powerful sneeze. Through her watery, mascara-filled eyes, she watched the crowd sniffle and cough.

"Dammit, Cherie," Ursula said, her hand covering the microphone, "you were supposed to check the weather report, this morning."

"I did, Ursula. I didn't think that the pollen count would be that important."

"I see a great future for you," Ursula said, looming over the wide-eyed event coordinator, "in discount retail." She stopped as her pantyhose snagged; she'd gotten waxed yesterday.

"Reyna?" Vivian said, walking into the bright store. She held the tabloid paper to her waist. "Do you have anything I can wear home?"

With her cigarette holder, Reyna tapped a pair of pink Capri pants on the counter and a fresh pair of white cotton panties folded on top of them.

"They're my size," Vivian said, grabbing the bundle. "How'd you know?"

"Trade secret. Classified on a need to know basis."

Vivian did a double take. Reyna's black, wet nose twitched. "Reyna, your nose—"

"I love the smell of Chanel Number Five in the morning," Reyna said, inhaling deeply. "It smells like…victory."

"Yeah, whatever. Just so you know, you owe me two blood drives." Vivian hurried into the nearest changing room.

The glow of the shop lessened and Reyna removed her sunglasses. She picked up the phone and said, "Lucinda, is air support gassed up and ready for deployment? Excellent."

The CD player behind her clicked on once again. The urgent strains of Wagner's *Die Walkure Act III* floated in the air.

"With this act," Ursula said, holding the oversized silver scissors, "I declare this newest addition to my corporate family open for business!"

With a decisive snip, the large red ribbon fluttered away and as planned, the stage crew tore the lids off the ten wicker baskets around the foot of the stage. A flurry of five hundred snow white doves ascended to the blue sky above. Gorged on a diet of salty feed the night before, each one of the doves delivered the loose payload of their bowels.

The cries of shock and disgust leapt from the crowd as the spattering rain of dove excrement hit them.

"Give me that umbrella, you stupid bitch!" Ursula said to Brittany, her soon to be unemployed Public Relations Manager. "Ladies and gentlemen, if you will follow me into the store, we can finish the ceremony," she spoke to the crowd, clutching the umbrella. "I am also sure we have an ample supply of pre-moistened towelettes."

Across the park at Java Buddies, Beth sat on the patio and watched the ceremonial debacle with the tray of cooling lattes next to her. When Ursula told one of her staff "to get the coffee," it meant one thing; you were out. For three years, she'd witnessed at least a dozen other staff members demoted to coffee girl. To avoid hearing that dreaded command, Beth jumped on every demeaning task Ursula dumped in her lap, including hand washing Ursula's silk thongs. She pursed her lips; this wasn't what she went to school for. Stroking the red scarf around her neck, Beth opened her company-owned laptop one last time.

Reyna readied her frontal assault in the darkening store. By phone, Al assured her the special shipment delivery had succeeded. The call from Ms. Lee informed her that the manicurist's nieces were in position. During the conversation, Reyna's tongue thickened.

"Reyna, my nieces are good girls. Do not get them in trouble."

"I promise no harm will come…to them," Reyna panted.

"Reyna? It's happening, you go too far!"

"Valor…is the price…of victory," she managed and hung up. Seconds later, her tongue deflated and the store brightened.

Joe, Reyna's heating and air-conditioning guy, walked through the front door.

"You sure look pretty today, Ms. Fox."

"Thank you, Joe. You ready for your mission?"

"Ma'am, I know those Fashion World folks will cancel my contract as soon as they have their own maintenance crew up and running, but this is a might extreme."

"Joe, you're just the first. If we don't stop her, she'll take down all of us here on the square. We must make a stand, here and now."

"Since you put it like that," Joe said, "what do you need me to do after I deploy this?" He picked up the steel cage covered with a blue tarp.

"Just exit the fire zone; Princess has been briefed."

Remembering his Navy days from many years ago, Joe grinned and saluted. He executed a sharp about-face and left.

The store grew still darker as Reyna's tail sprouted beneath her skirt. She prayed she could hold out just a little longer, while she thanked fate that she chose to wear a thong this morning.

Finally, her last unit arrived.

Prof stood at attention as he waited for Reyna to finish her inspection. One evening last week, he'd returned to Reyna's shop after weeks of avoidance. With one glance, Reyna said, "She's gone."

Prof nodded and confessed his series of transgressions to the elegant shopkeeper, who listened to Prof's private agony. In the end, Reyna said, "There's no way you could see the consequences of this."

"Maybe," Prof said, "but I lost her just the same."

"With what I know of Vivian, which is a lot," Reyna said, "there is no way she can retrieve her, but that doesn't mean she's gone forever. She's still got to be out there somewhere."

"How? She's just a disembodied voice. Most people would say I'm crazy."

"I'm not most people, Prof."

"True, but I have no way of finding her. It's meaningless."

"Is she worth fighting for?"

A quiet moment passed before Prof whispered, "Yes."

"Then find meaning in your search for her," Reyna said with a sly smirk. "In the meantime, you can help me with a project."

Now, Reyna finished her assessment. "You'll pass muster, soldier," she said. "Just muss up your hair a bit."

Prof ran his fingers through his hair; he'd only resumed using mousse a month ago. His blue oxford shirt hung wrinkled and his brown dress slacks were covered in lint. He'd fished these out of his laundry bag this morning, all on Reyna's instructions. "Are you sure about the raincoat? It's kind of hot," he said.

"This is a commando operation, Prof," she said, surveying his battered and frayed trench coat. "Behind enemy lines, you need camouflage. Are you ready to do your duty?"

"Reyna, if this was anybody else…"

"But it's me asking," she said, "and getting out of that stuffy little room will do wonders for you."

"I don't see how this helps either of our situations."

"For me, you'll save a place; for you, a bereft lover seeks solace in glory upon the field of battle," she said. "This is one of the classic literary themes, but I don't need to tell you that."

"Okay, Reyna, as dumb as this seems, once more unto the changing stalls, dear friends."

Reyna's expression soured as her long, fuzzy red ears popped up past the brim of her hat. "You're not allowed to make laconic allusions; that's my job."

High on the second-floor balcony, Ursula watched the wanderings of the little people across the gleaming marble atrium. She picked at the salmon soufflé and snorted. She had cancelled the caterer's contract because she refused to serve her a raw salmon steak. The press lunch only fueled her temper; she needed the journalists to draw in those little people below her, but why was she obligated to feed them?

A woman's shriek pierced the air and a young woman in bra and panties bolted out of one of the changing stalls below. A man in dark sunglasses and a raincoat staggered out of the booth behind her. Two security guards rushed to grab the man. Ursula grinned; she had given the shift commander specific instruction on handling vagrants.

"I'm blind for God's sake!" the man pleaded. "I was only trying to find the men's room. They don't have braille signage here."

The glare of lights from one of the roving news crews focused on the man. The blonde news reporter extended her hand and escorted the man with a white cane, her microphone recording his every word. The security officers looked to Ursula and gave a shrug.

"Uh, Ursula?" the timid inventory manager said. "We have problems with the new shipment from Thailand."

"That's our fall line," Ursula said without looking up. "You walked it through customs?"

"Yes, but—"

"So, what's the problem? I see the display in the center of the floor."

"The entire lot was infested with fleas and lice. I just sent four stock boys home on sick pay."

Looking down at the half-empty racks of the fall display, Ursula snarled. "Get that off my floor and get to Human Resources for your final check."

Another turmoil erupted below as a disheveled teenage girl in a ragged t-shirt and shorts cried, "They took our passports and said we couldn't leave basement!" She clung to the other hysterical girl. The cameras of three other television crews panned to capture the moment on the opposite end of the atrium.

"Yeah, and they only give us water and crackers," the other added and shivered into sobs.

With one glare to her floor manager, Ursula's will was done. Four of the assistant sales associates dressed in identical gray skirt suits converged upon the news crews and blocked their view. Amidst the disturbance, Ursula realized the girls vanished. Fighting her rage, she looked down at her thickening nails, scoring deep ruts into the table surface.

Over the perfume counter, the brass ventilation duct grill clattered to the floor. From inside the vent, a pair of small beady eyes registered fear. Ursula saw the flash of a pink bow tied about its neck as it spun about and raised its white-striped tail to spray. The panicked cries arose and the throng of shoppers stampeded, only to be bottlenecked by the narrow tunnel exit.

"Get the car, Lee-Lee," Ursula growled over the cacophony below.

"Sure, Ursula," Lee-Lee said, punching the number on her phone. "Don't you want me to take your stole? It's still awfully warm out there."

Ursula gaped at the rich brown fur sprouting from her shoulders.

Min slowed her run down to a trot three blocks away from the store. She looked over at her panting sister and grinned. "God, Lei, they only give us water and crackers? Really?" she spouted in disbelief. "You wonder why you haven't got on the cast of *Rocky Horror,* yet."

"It worked, didn't it? C'mon, let's get home. I want to get out of these funky-ass clothes."

Red fur creeped up Reyna's arms; soon she would lose use of her hands. Customers streamed out of the front entrance of the once-dignified Thomas Building and poured into the square. Sirens wailed in the background. A pink stretch limo pulled up in front of the Strand in the setting sun. She spotted Ursula and her troops rushing to the limo with a pack of reporters nipping at her heels. Her last hope resided with Perry's coup de grace.

The CD player clicked on. Tchaikovsky's *1812 Overture Finale*, all bells and cannons, rattled the windows of the store.

All but one of the flash pots flared and boomed under the mezzanine, stopping Ursula and her fleeing team.

A bearded man in a powder blue leisure suit strutted out of the smoke with his arm wrapped around a woman in a sheer slip of a purple dress. Electric organ chords oozed out of the theater's exterior speakers. "Hey, welcome to the Strand Vintage Theater. Tonight, we're celebrating the Golden Age of Porn," he announced to all.

The reporters closed in to hear more.

"We have a triple-bill of classics with the greatest erotic stars of the era—"

"Stud muffin?" Shannon interrupted, her luminous eyes locked on her man. "Aren't you forgetting something?"

"Oh, baby cakes, how could I forget?" He beamed with a mischievous twinkle. "We've got a rare, hard-to-find bonus feature that our good friend Ms. Fox found for us." Perry looked directly at Ursula and continued, "Tonight, only at the Strand, the 1976 classic, *Farmer's Daughter Ursula Plows the Field*."

"You said there were no more copies of that!" Ursula screamed, throttling William, the lawyer. Her girdle snaps popped loudly.

Reyna bowed her head. Perry's surprise attack failed to win the war. She picked up the can of red spray paint, the final option. Resolved, she slow-marched to the latticed front door. One last charge to push the enemy over the edge, mutually assured destruction; neither of them would walk away from this unchanged. It was the way of war.

The CD player clicked on for the final time. Barber's somber *Adagio for Strings* wafted through the dark shop.

She looked around her little store, filled with shadows. She remembered the first time she saw the city lights reflected off the clouds at the farm. Later, she slipped through the busy night streets, dazzled by the light, color and scents. She knew that Mrs. Lee, Perry, Shannon, Joe, and Lucinda counted on her. She lost her place in the city; her friends kept theirs. In her head, she balanced the accounts one last time, so much black and so little white. It was the right thing to do; door chimes tinkled in agreement.

At the threshold, the overhead lights flickered to life.

"You are Mrs. Ursula Fontaine, CEO of Fashion World by Ursula Incorporated, correct?" the man in the suit asked.

"Yes! I am Ursula Fontaine," she glowered, dropping the young lawyer.

"Here you go, ma'am," the man said, handing her the document.

"What is this?"

"You are hereby served by the Department of Labor."

Looking past the man, Ursula spied the young woman in the gray school-girl suit with a red silk scarf tied about her neck. The woman clasped her face in mock terror.

"Libby! You bit—" Ursula screamed, lurching forward. Her white spike heel caught the unexploded flash pot and the front of the Strand lit up in blinding white light. The baying of a large brown bear rumbled through the square.

"That was one hell of a promotion stunt," the camera man said to the editor. "Fashion czarina transforms into a bear…"

"Ehh, those guys in Vegas could have done it ten times better, you know, the tall loud one and the little guy who doesn't say anything. Anyway, I figured they replaced the ticket window with a two-way mirror like they do at Disney World," the editor said. "Let's get back to the station. That Ursula chick is going to have bunch of lawsuits for reckless endangerment."

Prof chuckled as the van puttered off. Reyna was right; it had been good to get out of the room and see the world.

Back in the shadowy center of the park, Tanya watched the news crew pull away. He still sat on the bench, grasping his white cane. Mary had pointed him out earlier when she handed her the small, crystal perfume bottle.

The Sawneys, Jerry and Mary, had hired her as a live-in housekeeper, Mary's idea. Eventually, she would go to work for the taskforce downtown when she was ready. Jerry wanted her to go to work right away, but Mary convinced him that she needed some polishing before going to work, so she helped around the house during the day and aided the Sawneys in the basement on their projects at night. Unlike the other girls, Mary spent her time teaching Tanya what to wear and how to speak; she'd even convinced Tanya to let her hair go back to its natural chestnut brown.

This morning, Mary decided to forego finishing painting the nursery and treated herself and Tanya to an afternoon of shopping down at the square. In matching cotton sundresses, they strolled about the bustle of Wrightsway Park. Tanya worried about Mary, for Mary kept walking even though the heat and her pregnancy wore upon her.

"There he is," Mary said, pointing to the man in dark sunglasses talking to the news crew.

"Who?" Tanya said.

"That's the special bounty that Bill has been looking for."

"He doesn't look like much," Tanya said. "Are you going to call Jerry and let him know?"

"No, I don't think he's got the finesse to handle this."

"So, what're we supposed to do? Call Jim and Lew?"

"I think it's time we show a little bit of initiative, Tanya," Mary said, reaching into her heavy "mommy" purse. "I think you're the right woman for this." She handed Tanya the small sample bottle of perfume.

"What's this?"

"Something he can't resist."

Clutching the bottle, Tanya watched and followed the blind man from a distance as he tottered across Walker Bridge. She'd take her time and make her move soon.

The next morning, Reyna and Mrs. Lee sat sipping tea at the bamboo desk in the back of the manicure salon.

"You risked way too much, this time, Reyna," Mrs. Lee scolded.

"It was the only way I could stop her," Reyna said, wincing at the first taste of Mrs. Lee's horrid brew. "The object of war is not to give up your humanity for your friends but to make the other poor darling give up hers."

Mrs. Lee slapped palm to her face. "At least you are not mangling the wisdom of the venerable Sun Tzu."

"I've got a new one. To know your customer—"

"Enough!"

"Anyway," Reyna said, rising from Ms. Lee's bamboo table, "I've got to get the store opened this morning. I think I'm going to treat myself to a cheesecake."

"Reyna!"

"Kidding!" Reyna shot back.

The Desperation Run

1 PM September 15th
The Regal Building
987 Bianchi Street

Exhausted and hungry, Prof sat in the cool darkness of the dilapidated building. Amid the cooing and fluttering pigeons, he retraced how he'd ended up here. Every day for the last two weeks, he slipped from his room just before dawn and spent the day alone in the second story office of this boarded-up store. In the isolating, quiet gloom, he examined, valued and placed each fact of his situation; he knew the pattern was there.

At night, he fearfully crept the streets and alleys, stalking desperate portents; snatches of random conversations, blasts from nearby televisions, a dropped key he chanced upon or a rustling of newspaper in the corner. Like a tuning fork, he resonated with ominous intuitions that he would process into pieces of this dark puzzle the next day. Speaking to no one, he trudged back to his room and collapsed in bed in a dreamless sleep. He rose again at dawn to continue the harsh ritual without food.

He remembered the words of Dr. Hunter S. Thompson: "There is no such thing as paranoia. Your worst fears can come true at any moment." At this moment, the gonzo guru's words never ran truer. His loss of her never weighed heavier on his shoulders; he would have traded his soul for a trace of saffron and her jibes. He halted the yearning immediately. If the Greeks were right, everyone carries a fatal flaw; she was his. Someone else knew it and used it against him. Now, he dedicated himself to identifying his enemy as if his life depended on it.

According to one of the most unlikely soothsayers, his life did depend on it.

The Tuesday after the Labor Day fiasco at Wrightsway, he finished up his last luxury lunch at the café and ambled back to his room in the 'March. That prospect troubled him less these days; he could eat cheap at the diner and visit with Jane until the first of the month. He anticipated spending another fruitless afternoon at his table with his notepads and microcassettes.

The car screeched to a halt in front of him and a door swung open. "Professor John Clarke?"

"That's me."

"Jones wants to have a word with you downtown."

"Forget it, kid," Prof said, "I'm out."

"You think this is a request," the young man said, grabbing the sleeve of Prof's coat, "but I have orders to bring you in."

"I don't think so," Prof said. "I am through with Jones and all of his crap."

"Hey! Junior Five-0!" a loud raspy voice blurted. "You got a warrant for his arrest?"

"No, and it's none of your concern."

"When you drag a man off the street without probable cause, it's my concern, buddy. This is America!" the newcomer bellowed for all on the street to hear.

"You got no idea what you're dealing with, biker."

"I got a pretty clear idea," the newcomer said. "How come Jones sent out the junior varsity for this one?"

"I'm warning you."

"Or what?" the biker said. "You gonna take me downtown? Go ahead."

While the argument ensued, Prof eased away from the biker and Jones' errand boy. He placed the voice of Jones' lackey, the snotty kid named Jerry. Prof remembered him from the ill-fated trip to Justice Plaza back in June. The argument faded as he melded into the stream of pedestrians.

Under the cloudy sky, he crossed Walker Bridge and decided to start his daily ritual early. Since Labor Day, Prof took Reyna's words of encouragement to heart and searched for her. Every day at twilight, he wandered the streets, seeking her trail. Rarely, he caught a whiff of saffron or a silvery tinkle just like her laugh and rushed to investigate, only to be disappointed by a gourmet shop or a set of door chimes.

As he hunted, he imagined the conversation he would have with her when he found her. His apology, her acceptance, and the continuation of her nagging. He held onto these hopes like a man clinging to a capsized life boat. It wasn't enough to comfort him, but enough to keep seeking her, no matter the odds.

Tanya watched the man in dark sunglasses take a seat on a park bench in the grove of gold and red oaks in the center of Wrightsway Park after his long ramble. She had shadowed this man, John Clarke, every day for the last two weeks, and had acquainted herself with him. When Mary first pointed him out on Labor Day, Tanya failed to see what Agent Jones wanted with this bounty; all the others she and Mary tagged-teamed enjoyed money, power or both, but this blind man possessed none of these.

"Consider him a diamond in the rough," Mary said.

"I don't know, Mary. He sounds like more trouble than he's worth."

"All men are more trouble than they're worth," Mary said. "Even Jerry needed some polishing."

Tanya remembered the night back in August when she heard the rumble of the garage door at Mary's house. Without thinking, she put down the laundry she had been folding and went to her bedroom to get dressed for the night's project, another prize from one of Jerry and Mary's date nights. Mary met her in front of the door to the garage basement, her short dark hair tousled and her red sweater rumpled and sweat-stained.

"Not tonight, Tanya," Mary said. "This is a private matter between me and Jerry. Go to bed."

Tanya obeyed Mary and crawled into bed without question.

The next morning at breakfast, Mary buzzed about the kitchen table cheerfully while Jerry ate his oatmeal in downcast silence. Once finished, he grabbed his jacket and left for work without a word.

Watching the front door close behind her husband, Mary said, "A little bit of training goes a long way..."

That evening, Jerry trudged in from work, removed his jacket and donned an apron and fixed dinner for Mary and Tanya. He washed the dishes and, empty-eyed, kissed Mary on the cheek, before slogging off to bed.

"With a little work and patience," Mary whispered to Tanya, her eyes glittering with mischief, "you could have one of these, too."

This John Clarke was older than she liked, but as Mary said, "Older means stable and stable means predictable."

Like clockwork, he spent most of the day in his room in the dumpy hotel and ventured out in the evenings to either the bar and grill across Reed Shore or up to that greasy spoon on Cedars Street. After his daily late-afternoon meal, he wandered the streets randomly without fail for a couple hours. On these afternoon rambles, he would pause as if something caught his attention, but each time, he gave a shrug and tottered on. His route always changed, but his reactions were predictable. As Mary always said, "Predictable means manageable."

Now, just after the dull sunset, he settled into the park bench at Wrightsway. Dressed in slacks, a button-down shirt and his light black sports coat, he defied Mary's dismal opinion. With a little direction, he might be a catch.

Earlier, she watched Jerry try to bring the man in only to be foiled by a short, bald biker. The professor sidled off during the commotion. A good sign. As Mary always said, "A good provider knows to avoid risks." Tanya suppressed the urge to phone Mary to describe Jerry's failure. Tanya knew she could bring this perp in for Mary. Under Mary's advice, she got a spray-on tan and changed into a light flowery dress. Now, warm, scrubbed and ready, she dabbed the perfume behind her ears and in the hollow of her throat to make her approach.

"Hi!" she said. "Is this seat taken?"

"Not at all," Prof said, deep in thought.

"Thanks," she said sliding down next to him. "You're an educated man, aren't you?"

"I suppose that's one way to describe me. Some probably would say over-educated." He turned to his new companion and said, "How did you know that?"

"It's in the hands," she said, taking hold of his. "Yours are smooth, not like someone who works the trades."

"That was a pretty good observation." He heard the whisper of her dress, as she shifted closer to him.

"I could tell you more about yourself," she said and her touch coaxed his fingers to uncurl. She ran her manicured nail from his wrist up to the base of his palm. Leaning in, she whispered, "You've been abandoned by someone you love."

"Yes," he said, lost in the warm reassuring scent of saffron.

"I could replace her," she said, looking up to his becalmed face. She smirked; the perfume worked better than Mary expected. A chilly breeze sighed through the trees in the dying sunlight. She brought her lips closer to his and whispered, "You deserve so much better."

The empty beer bottle whistled past Tanya and Prof and exploded on the trunk of a nearby tree.

"You deserve so much better? Wow!" The biker laughed. "Hey, baby! Why don't you come over here and show me?"

Tanya leapt from the bench and faced the short, portly biker. She hissed, and her skin turned greenish-gray and her yellowed incisors sprouted from her mouth. "He's mine!" she spat with her blackened, forked tongue.

"Not this time, Skankola!" said the biker, pulling another bottle from the six packs. "Get lost. Or do you want another cold one?"

Backing away, Tanya screeched, "You'll pay for this!" and merged into the shadows cast by the wrought iron street lamps.

"Yeah, tell it to your next divorce lawyer," the biker said, plopping on the bench next to Prof. The biker looked at the puzzled blind man and said, "Hey, buddy! looks like you're popular, today. Beer?"

"Thanks," Prof said. "I guess I ought to thank you three times." He took the offered bottle.

"Not a problem," the biker said. "I promised a couple of my bros to keep an eye out for you."

"Your bros?"

"Yeah, Gabe and Ralph… You know the courier who plays the horn and the big, wooly guy who runs the meat wagon."

"And you're?"

"Uri," the biker said and took another swig of his beer. "For an educated man, you're a moron."

"Insult everyone you meet?"

"Nah, just the jackasses. You're stuck in your own little world; you just don't get the bigger picture."

"Had a lot my plate," Prof said, "with the blindness, poverty and the stabbing. What did you expect?"

"And you're still making the same dumb mistakes. I've seen it too many times. Shit, sometimes, I wonder why I bother…"

"With what?"

"Telling folks there are consequences to their actions," Uri said. "You tell a city to straighten up and fly right or they'll get wild beasts, plagues or a big-ass flood headed their way. You'd think they'd pause to think through their options, but do they?"

"Well," Prof said, "reason would say—"

"Reason! I try to drive the point home with everything short of a puppet show and they still pick the dumbass option," Uri huffed. "Come to think of it, I tried a puppet show in Pompeii. Reason never enters in their pointy little heads. Freewill was a dumb idea."

"So, what's this got to do with me?"

"Hey, dildo!" Uri said and popped the back of Prof's head with a smack of his beefy palm. "Smell the fresh, Columbian brew and wake up! From what I just saw, you're going to choose the dumbass option, like the last ten thousand shitheads I've tried to educate. You're at a major crossroads and you're just drifting. A bad idea. The number of your enemies are legion and they know about your lady friend—"

"You know about her?" Prof interjected. "Do you know where I can—"

"Not in my job description," Uri said. "Personally, if I were you, I'd stay off the streets and collect your thoughts. I used to tell folks to withdraw to a mountaintop, but that's totally old school."

"So, that's your advice, then? Lay low and think?"

"Look," Uri said, "I only pass on the suggestions, but it's up to you to follow through." With that, Uri hopped off the bench and traipsed into the shadows of the park.

Prof left the park that night shaken and avoided his usual haunts in the days after. He found an old store on Bianchi Street with an unlocked fire door. Up the rickety stairs, in the cool dusty silence of the second story office, he took refuge in his thoughts. Over the course of several days, he collected, sorted and assembled the facts he had at hand. Every night, he slipped out of the building and took a circuitous route back to Hotel Mittelmarch. In the end, his conclusions circled back upon themselves. To solve this puzzle, he needed more information.

Nathan barreled down the damp, brick alleyway, clutching the brown paper parcel. His blood pounded. They were closing in. A wild careen around the corner almost landed him on his ass. He wanted to drop the package, but one didn't walk away from one of Rondo's jobs. He gripped the package even tighter

He slammed into the rough brick dead-end. He looked back. No one…yet. He grabbed the fire escape's lowest rung and heaved. With a rusty squawk, the ladder dropped.

The climb through the derelict store bought him time. Not much, but just enough to figure out how this job went to hell. With any luck, he could pull this mess, not to mention his ass, out of the fire.

He wrinkled his nose as he crawled through the half-boarded window. The smell of piss permeated the dim room's shattered plaster walls. At least it was empty of crack heads, drunks and psychos; they'd gut you for a few bucks.

Creeping down the debris-ridden hallway, he listened; only pigeons cooed in the damp semi-darkness. Getting down to the ground floor and doubling back seem to be his best shot.

"Nathan?" a voice croaked from the shadowy doorway to his right. "Nathan Gascon?"

"Yeah," Nathan said. "What the hell are you doing here, Prof?"

"I come here to be left alone, though not today it would seem." The disheveled figure appeared in the doorway, dusting his worn gray trench coat. He adjusted the jet-black glasses on his eyes and picked up his white cane.

"Uh, yeah, Prof. You might want to clear out. There's trouble following me."

"Let me guess, Nate. You took the job from Rondo."

"How'd you—?"

"No one pays attention to a crazy, blind man. His crew was asking about you for two or three days. After all, it was your last known residence."

"You mean—?"

"Think about it, Nate. Why didn't he give such an easy job to one of his own crew? For a hotshot grifter, you sure missed the mark this time."

"Ex-grifter," Nathan said.

"Pardon?"

"I said, ex-grifter," Nathan said. "I am out of the game. If Jones catches me running a scam, he'll send me off."

"Yet here you are, neck deep in someone else's game."

"Ran out of favors, had to come up with some cash, fast. The only legit work out there is day labor and that won't put a roof over my head, not even at the 'March. Crossing Jones was the worst mistake I ever made. I heard he's even made Nick's life hell."

"Seems like Jones has got his fingers in a lot of pies these days," Prof said.

"You don't know the half of it, Prof. Jones' flunkies, Erskine and Rhodes, they aren't what they seem."

"Why not try laying low for a while?"

"It's harder to hit a moving target," Nate said and bolted down the stairs.

As Nate slammed through the fire door, he replayed the deal with the pawnbroker an hour earlier.

"Just deliver the package and the man will pay you," Rondo grinned, his gold tooth glittering in the dark storeroom. "Easy money."

"How come you don't get one of your crew to make this run?"

"My crew are hitters, not delivery boys. Badasses ain't discreet. This thing needs to go down quietly."

Rondo flipped the "Out to Lunch" sign in the storefront of the pawnshop. Between the two of them, the package, wrapped in brown paper, sat on the table. Nathan reached for it.

"Just remember, Nate. You take that package, and it doesn't leave your hands 'til you put it in the hands of the Syrian. You don't want to be the man who fucked up one of my deals."

He grabbed the parcel, barely larger than his fist.

"Good! The word was right about you, Nate. You're a stone-cold player. Just get the package to 12 Cedars Street. That's where the Syrian does his business. You go now and you can avoid rush hour and be back to your crib in no time."

"You got any protection you can loan me?" Nathan said, weighing the package in his hand. It felt solid and had a good heft.

"Hell no! If I wanted a gunfighter, I'd would have given this to one of my boys. I want a runner. Gunfighters go down and I lose the package. A runner avoids the fools and moves from point A to point B. That's all I want."

Nathan slid from the chair. "All right, looks like I got the job." He dropped the package down the front of the worn bomber jacket. It didn't bulge much.

"Just one more thing," Rondo said. "You go out the front door. Folks saw you come in here. It's bad for business if they think something isn't right about this place. If you can't trust your pawn broker, who can you trust?"

"Sure, as fuck not Rondo," Nathan muttered now. He quickened his pace and shivered; the cooling air cut into his sweaty body. He felt the late afternoon shadows gaining on him. He darted across the quiet intersection; not much traffic in this part of town. No black sedan, thank God.

He'd spotted the car as he stepped out of Rondo's. Just a black four-door, not tricked out, not old, not new, could have been a Ford or a Chevy, but it was bad juju all the way. He walked the other way. The car crept forward. *Shit!* He was made. Rounding the corner, he broke into a sprint.

He tore through the back alleys and clambered over rattling chain link fences. Out of breath, he emerged on the nondescript street, two blocks away. The black sedan crouched, waiting for him. Slipping back into the alley, he backtracked and twisted his route. He weaved and darted from one empty building to another, shimmied through cellar windows and dodged trashcans. When he emerged from this new alley, again, the black sedan squatted patiently.

"Shit, shit, shit!" Nathan gasped as he clung to the rough red brick for support. Sweat stung his eyes as the blurry sedan, a three-dimensional shadow, eased to a stop and emerged into cold-edged focus. The driver and passenger doors opened and two familiar men in dark gray pinstripe suits emerged.

"Say Lew?" the passenger said to his associate. "Did Jones say we have to bring this one back intact?"

"Not as I recall, Jim," Lew said, reaching under his jacket. "Jones just said to retrieve the package."

"Great!" Jim said, as his mirrored sunglasses reflected upon Nathan. "You know, we did miss lunch." He flashed a grin with fangs.

"Fuck!" Nathan said as he sped back down the alley. His vision pulsed in time with his heart. The pursuers' strides broke into a full sprint behind him.

"Way to go, kiddo!" Jim bellowed. "Get that old heart pumping! I like my meat bloody as hell."

Nathan shot around the corner, out the other side of the alley and across the street to another alley to lose them. He slalomed through the obstacle course of crates, garbage cans and dumpsters like a champion; fangs or not, Jones' boys didn't live here. It was only three; rush hour didn't start for another half hour. Damn, he would have to keep moving until then. At the corner of Hollow and Irving, he grabbed the chance to raise a distraction. Dashing across the intersection to the opposite corner, brakes squealed, tires skidded, steel crumpled, horns honked and someone yelled, "Asshole!"

"Shit," Nathan coughed, jumping the curb. Nick must be taking a doughnut break. Any other time, Serrano would have busted him on jaywalking, just on principle.

He trotted up the broken sidewalk of Hollow Street past the empty, weeded lot. With luck, he bought some time.

A bright green Land Rover screeched up beside him and its side doors exploded open. Two young, muscular men in fashionable tennis whites leapt out and tossed Nathan to the floor of the spacious backseat. The doors slammed and the Land Rover sped off.

"Sorry about that, old boy," a voice with a cultured British accent said over the hum of the Land Rover's engine. "We would have preferred to accomplish this a bit more gently; however, the short schedule called for stronger methods."

"It's all right, "Nathan said, catching his breath. He pulled himself up to the luxurious leather seating. "At this point, I'll accept a ride from anyone that doesn't have fangs."

"Fangs?" A thin, bewhiskered man in pince-nez glasses said, "Dear me, this does complicate things."

"Bloody Yanks!" spat the young man in the front passenger seat spat. "Always cutting corners and getting in bed with the wrong bunch."

"Now, now, Rory, the Americans can be impetuous, but their hearts are in the right place."

"But for Christ's mercy, sir!" Rory said. "Summoning those from the nether—"

"Enough, Lieutenant! We have a civilian aboard."

"Sorry, sir," Rory said, donning a headset and focused on the laptop.

The buildings zipped past the windows. Nathan checked his watch. "Uhh, pardon, sir," he said to the tweeded gentleman next to him. "I am not quite sure what this is all about, but—"

"We are members of a world-wide intelligence agency. We intercepted communiqués that a highly valuable, albeit dangerous artifact was to exchange hands this afternoon. For the safety of mankind, we deemed it necessary to intercede in this matter."

"Oh," Nathan said, looking down at the package still clutched in his hand. "Look, I had no idea what this was. I was just asked to run this over to some guy a few blocks over."

"Who were the particulars of this transaction?"

"Excuse me?"

"To clarify, who gave you this package and who is supposed to receive it?"

"Don't have a clue, sir," Nathan said. "I met the guy across the way and he asked me to deliver this to some other fellow in Wrightsway Park next to the fountain."

"Hmmm," Sir thought aloud as he stroked his gray beard, "I suppose we must bring the receiver into custody for interrogation."

"Bollocks!" Rory spouted as he swung about to confront Nathan. "You're feeding us shite!"

"That's the truth as I know it," Nathan said, "sure as my name is Neil Grazer."

"Mr. Grazer," Sir interrupted, "you should relinquish custody of the package."

"Sure," Nathan said. "You are looking to get that guy at the park, aren't you?"

"Well, of course."

"I'd recommend taking a right here," Nathan said, "or else you 're gonna be swamped in rush hour traffic. The guy could be long gone by then."

"The nav system says this is the ideal route," Rory cut in.

"Suit yourself, Rory," Nathan said with a shrug. "I lived in this 'berg all my life. That way is no good this time of day. It's your call."

"Chas," Sir said to the driver, "please follow Mr. Grazer's directions."

"Yes, Sir."

"Sure, go straight through the next two lights and make a left, Chas," Nate advised

"Now, Mr. Grazer," Sir continued, "the package, please."

"Oh, sure. Okay, Chas, next three lights have got long yellows, so floor it now to get through them." Nate offered the package to Sir.

Chas gunned the engine and zipped through the first yellow light.

One, Nate counted to himself.

"Mr. Grazer, please release your grip on the package," Sir said. Nathan's shoulder wrenched as Sir attempted to yank the package from his palm. "Hmm, the parcel seems to be grafted to your hand. Most curious," Sir concluded.

Two, Nate thought. The Land Rover hurtled through the second intersection.

"Pass his fool hand up here, Sir!" Rory demanded and pulled a wicked black steel blade from the armrest storage. He grabbed Nate's forearm, yanking Nate out of the seat, and said, "I'll get the damn thing away from him."

"Now, Rory," Sir said, "attempt to remove the paper before doing bodily harm to Mr. Grazer."

"This calls for expedience," Rory said, jabbing the razor point underneath the package, "not damn surgery—"

Three.

The world crashed and spun around on its axis. The inevitable crunch and shattering of glass followed a split second later. Heat and yellowy brightness surged from Nathan's hand as the door of the Land Rover gave way, throwing him clear of the wreckage. Then blackness.

He awoke to heat washing across his face. He opened his eyes to the smoggy city sky and the silhouettes of four or five people hovering over him.

"You okay?"

"Jesus! Did you see the size of that fireball?"

"Hey, buddy, my cousin's a lawyer."

"Quickly, Benjamin and Samuel!" demanded a female with a foreign accent as strong arms hoisted Nate upright. "We must get him to the van and seek medical attention." The world swayed as they dragged Nate to the back of a grimy white service van with the logo:

Pardes Plumbing

24 Hour Emergency Services

The van roared off as Nate skidded to one side, banging his head against the wheel well.

"Make no sudden moves, Mr. Gascon," the woman said, cocking her automatic pistol. "You are in our custody…for your safety, of course."

"Lemme guess, you're members of a top-secret organization who want to intercept this." He pointed to the package still clutched in his left hand.

"Correct, Mr. Gascon, that's quite astute of you."

"I catch on quick like that," he said. He pulled himself to a sitting position and faced the slim, dark-eyed young woman in brown coveralls. "Take it. I'll face Rondo and his crew; it can't be any worse than what I've been going through."

"You will be pleased to know, Mr. Gascon," she said, "that the proprietor of Rondo's Pawn Emporium suffered a massive heart attack about an hour ago. I am sure he will trouble you no more. The Tree of Life has many branches."

"Lady, I got no quarrel with you. The package is yours. Just drop me off at the nearest corner and I won't breathe a word of this to nobody."

"I am afraid it is no longer that simple, Mr. Gascon. You are now part of this or it's a part of you. Either way, it doesn't matter."

The van made a hard swerve and an abrupt halt. The rattle and thump of a steel garage door followed. Benjamin and Samuel leapt out of the van and flung open the side doors.

"Out!" she said, motioning with her small, silver automatic.

Benjamin and Samuel drug Nate from the van and over to the clean work table inked with a six-pointed star encompassed within a circle.

"Wait a minute," Nathan blurted. "You guys are…Jewish?"

"Exactly," she said. "We are here to ensure the survival of our people."

"Hey! That's great!" Nathan said, as Benjamin and Samuel strapped his forearm to the table. "I have friends who are Jewish. Nice folks."

"We need that package, Mr. Gascon," she continued. "You have no idea what will happen if this falls into the wrong hands. Fortunately, we are knowledgeable on what needs to be done to harness this."

"Like I said, great!" Nathan cut in. "I wish you the best. Let's just do what needs to be done and I will be on my way, really."

“Thank you for your cooperation, Mr. Gascon. Your sacrifice will be remembered for all times,” she said. “Samuel, is the equipment ready?”

“Certainly, Judith,” the serious young man in a plumber’s uniform said. “Rabbi Loewmann brought the supplies around this morning when he inscribed the seal.” He handed Judith a small black leather case. “The equipment was already here.” He gestured to the cutting torch kit in the dingy corner.

“Excellent,” Judith said, unzipping the syringe case. “We’re not barbarians. You will feel no pain and the torch will cauterize the wound. When your hand drops in the seal, it will have no choice but to serve us.”

Samuel rolled the industrial-grade torch to the table as Benjamin braced Nathan with his arm across his neck.

“W-wait,” Nathan sputtered, “can’t we talk about this?”

“Patience, Mr. Gascon,” she said, tapping the syringe. “It will be over before you know it.”

Samuel lit the torch with a whoosh and popped the goggles over his eyes. He lowered the white jet of flame over Nathan’s wrist.

“I’d look the other way, if I were you,” Benjamin advised, looking down upon him.

Steel doors slammed open from all sides.

“We’ve been breached!” Judith yelled, as a staccato of gunfire rang out across the cluttered garage. Benjamin sprang off him and Samuel dropped the torch.

“For *Dar al-Islam*!” a voice cried. “We take what is rightfully ours!”

“Fuck me, fuck me, fuck me!” Nathan whimpered, working the straps off his arm and plopping to the ground. On his belly, he skittered across the floor. Bullets whizzed and thunked in the hazy air above him. Light streamed through a doorway just ahead. He scampered through the door, across the cracked sidewalk, and down the crumbling pavement. He wondered if Samuel had doused the torch before—

The thundering roll of force rumbled through the street.

The blast of heat rushed past him. He sprinted hard; he knew better than to look back. Cedar Street was only two blocks over. His hand still clutched the brown paper parcel, soaked with his sweat.

Finally out of breath, his pace slowed to a shaking trot. In the dying sunlight, he looked to his left and shuddered.

Hung on the rusted chain-link fence, a faded blue sign read:

St. Joan of Arc High School for Girls

Back in the day, he and every other young player cruised the sidewalks around the dilapidated school, but only the foolish dared hop that fence. As choice as the Saint Joan's honeys were, the Sisters guarded their turf like pit bulls. He heard the stories from the few white-faced boys who jumped that fence for glory and game. Sure, the poachers exaggerated the nuns' reprisals, but the stern-faced Sisters sheparded their innocent wards and suffered no young bucks in their domain. If he crossed the well-worn athletic field, he was on Cedar Street. School let out hours ago; still, he wrestled the old dread. At the very least, it meant yet another month in Muni on a trespass charge.

"Oh, shit," he breathed, sighting the black sedan turning the corner. Grabbing the loose, jangling fence, he heaved himself over it. None of it mattered; he feared neither Municipal Lockup, Rondo's boys, nor vengeful nuns. He sped across the field until he hit the ground, tackled from behind.

"You have fun, Fucko?" Jim snarled, twisting Nate's arm behind him, "A bent fender, two traffic citations and a shitload of paperwork."

"Just take the package," Nathan said, face down in the grass, "just take it."

"Now, now, Jim," Lew said, "it's all in a day's work. The mook is being perfectly reasonable. We get the package—"

"Listen to him, Jim!" Nathan pleaded. "He's a smart guy."

"Look at this, you piece of shit!" Jim said, pointing at his rumpled, grass-stained suit. "Fucking ruined. Fuck reasonable." Black talons sprouted from the agent's fingers.

"Shit, Jimmy!" Lew said, grabbing Jim's wrist. "Have some sense of decorum. Out here in public, what are you trying to do? Let me finish—"

"Gentlemen," a calm, stern female voice pierced the evening.

"I say we take the package," Lew continued with his fanged grin, "and take him out for dinner."

"Gentlemen, you are trespassing on school property," the female voice declared. Nathan flinched; he recognized the voice from his teenage years.

Nathan looked past Jim and Lew. Twelve nuns in black habits and crimson wimples surrounded the three of them. Each carried two black canes.

"Official business, ma'am," Lew said with a charming smile to their frail leader. "Just apprehending a dangerous fugitive."

"Really?" she said, narrowing her eyes. "Which official would that be?"

"That would be none of your business, sister."

"Oh, I daresay it is," she said as her facial wrinkles tightened, "and it's Reverend Mother, Hell-spawn," She lifted her canes and connected the ends. The other nuns followed suit.

"Look, ladies," Lew said with a chuckle. "You're in way over your heads."

"Fortunately, we know how to swim," the Reverend Mother said. One end of her staff sported a long blade which glimmered in the fading sun. "Mr. Gascon, if you would, please come here."

Nathan approached her, wide-eyed.

"Don't look surprised, Mr. Gascon," the withered Reverend Mother admonished. "I remember all the young troublemakers, even the ones I never caught. This next part is not for you. I know that this is an exercise in futility, but go and try not to sin anymore." She stepped aside to allow Nathan to exit from the circle.

"Don't look back, don't look back," Nathan chanted, crossing the field to the gate on Cedars Street. Only five hundred yards and it was all over.

He stuck his hands in his pockets, hunched down and finished the final leg of the trek.

In the distance, he heard the Reverend Mother command, "Sister Disciples of the Cruor Lancea, advance!" There was a good reason he never jumped that fence way back when.

Exhausted, he stood before the storefront of 12 Cedars Street. The shop windows soaped over and the faded red awning rustled in the evening breeze. His left fist thudded against the chipped green door.

A sign in the window read:

"Everything must go!"

"Yes?" a short, stout man with a pair of black reading glasses perched low on his nose answered the door. He sported a tufted and stained yellow cardigan and streaks of gray shone on his thick black beard.

"Are you…the Syrian?"

"Why, yes, my young friend," the man said with a bold grin, "please come in. Please call me, Al." He swept his arms in a grand flourish to bid Nate entrance.

Nathan shuffled into the store with half-flickering fluorescent bulbs. Racks of suits lined the walls and the floor felt gritty beneath his dragging feet. He smelled a faint exotic aroma.

"Tough times, huh?" he said.

"Oh no," the Syrian replied, "I have been clearing out inventory in preparation of my homecoming. The carpets, as always, are easy to get rid of. The suits, however nice, are counterfeit and problematic to liquidate. You are Mr. Gascon, yes?"

"Yes, I am."

"I am most impressed with your work," he said. "I have been following it with great interest. You came most highly recommended."

Nathan blanched.

"Oh, come now, Mr. Gascon," Al said. "The local ruling classes are running circles with all of the calamities of this afternoon. I am sure they find you of no consequence. Personally, I find unmaking the made refreshing. It reminds me of my youth."

"I guess we all do crazy things when we are young."

"Ah, indeed we do. However, Mr. Gascon, before we complete this transaction, I must say, and please, forgive me…you look like camel dung."

Nathan regarded his stained and tattered cargo pants, the shredded leather jacket and the worn-out work boots on his feet. "What can I say? It's been a rough day."

"No, no, no, Mr. Gascon, condition is changeable and left to fate. A man of your caliber should have some flair."

"Let's just say the local haberdashery doesn't cater to folks like me."

"One moment," Al said and scurried away to an office in back. After several minutes of scuffling and muttering, he appeared in front of Nathan with a small valise and a garment bag over his shoulder. "This is for you, my young friend. If you would do an elder a favor, please get back in the game."

The sirens grew louder in the distance.

"Now, Mr. Gascon, unless you have the wish to explain yourself to the local caliphate, I suggest we conclude our business now. Please open the package."

Nathan tore the brown paper away from the parcel. Underneath, a crimson glass bottle engraved with a gold, six-pointed star glittered under the lights. A small bronze stopper rested in the neck of the spherical bottle. Gaping, Nate said, "I went through all of that shit for this?"

"Yes," Al said, proffering the envelope, "one upstart prince gets a bit of wisdom and I get stranded here."

Nathan took the envelope as the Syrian removed the bottle from his hand.

"It could be worse," Al continued, tossing the bottle from hand to hand. "I understand one of my less intelligent cousins had to pay seven boons to get his back. For me, it only cost five thousand dollars and a couple of suits."

"So, you're a—"

"Hardworking Syrian-American, who is composed of the essence of fire. If I were you, Mr. Gascon, I would take the back door and not look back."

Nathan raced out the back through the alley. The sirens grew louder and the fire trucks raced by. In the periphery of his vision, he sensed the night sky reddening from a fire behind him.

At Walker Bridge, which would lead him back to The Mittelmarch, he finally stopped. Leaning on the bridge guardrail, he caught his breath. On the far side of Gulf Canal, flames leapt high on Cedars Street.

"Evening, Nate," a big cop said, sidling up.

"Evening, Serrano."

"Saw your name on a file in the Task force office. Yours and Prof's"

"Yeah," Nate said, watching the fire, "they wanted me to go into business. Set me up with an internship and all that."

"Nate, getting involved with Jones…it's trouble. I'm not sure how, yet…"

"Not to worry, Nick, I've had a taste of an honest day's work."

"And?"

"It should only be attempted by professionals. Amateurs like me have no business fooling around with it."

"You know, Nate," Nick said, "you did jaywalk to get over here."

Nate looked aghast at the grinning cop.

"I'll let you off with a warning," Nick said, "this time."

In the cool evening shadows, Prof emerged from the crumbling store onto the streetlight-lit sidewalk. Standing taller than he had in many months, he walked back into the open streets with purpose. His time for hiding was over; Nate, in his haste, had provided the key piece of information. As for the puzzle of his current situation, Prof lacked one important piece: Jones' motives. It was time to plunge into the heart of this mystery.

The Prisoners' Dilemmas

9 AM September 30th
Nighthawk's Dinner
123 Cedars St.

A typical Wednesday morning, the patrons of the busy diner clattered at their forks and plates while wolfing down their breakfasts. Jane hustled between the customers for refills, checks and tips. The register rang as often as the door opened and closed. Brushing a stray hair from her forehead, she approached Prof's corner booth to refresh his coffee.

"John Clarke," Prof grumbled to himself, "P.I. or just a blind private dick?" He took another swallow of black coffee. His contact was due any moment.

"Prof," she said, "you're talking to yourself again."

"Harry isn't working this morning," Prof said. "Not to worry, sweetheart. I'm just working on my interior monologue."

"What?"

"Every dime-store detective novel uses it to advance the plot line. I figure it couldn't hurt my chances."

"What is this? The Case of The Disappearing Professor?" Jane said. "You've been ghosting for the last two weeks. Are you in trouble?"

"Not as far as I know, but I don't have all the facts, sweetheart. I'm just beginning to flip over the rocks and find out what's crawling underneath."

"Are you sure you're not hanging out with Vic on the side?" Jane said and cocked her head to the side. "You're beginning to sound like him."

"How are things going between you two?"

"Fine," she said, "I like being around him, but…"

"Go on, Jane."

"It's complicated. In seven months, I haven't been to his place and I can't get hold of him during the day. He could be married for all I know."

"Look him up on the internet."

"Tried it. He doesn't come up."

"Sounds like the only option is to ask him about it," Prof said.

"I'm afraid so. I'm just afraid of what I'll find out."

"I can sympathize. Trust me, it's better to know what you're dealing with."

"I need to get back to work," Jane said. "I have a meeting at school this afternoon."

"Didn't mean to take up your time. Take care, Jane." Prof fingered the page of linen stationery tucked into his shirt pocket.

Minutes later, Nick slid into the booth opposite Prof and placed his black cap on the table. Prof said, "Thanks for coming, Nick."

"Okay, Prof," Nick said, "normally, I'd say you've gone off your rocker, but…"

"Things aren't normal, are they?"

"No," Nick said. "I haven't seen Nate in two weeks."

"Same here. Last time I saw him, he was in trouble. He mentioned those agents of Jones."

"I saw him on the night of the big fire up the street," Nick said. "He seemed okay. I got the impression he was laying low for a while. Either way, I keep an eye on the morgue, just in case."

"Well, that's a small relief. I just don't get what Jones wants with me."

"He's got a file on you and Nate. I wouldn't be surprised if he had one on me, too."

"Why?" Prof said. "I thought the judge kept files on everyone of interest?"

"Adams is a stubborn old prick, but he doesn't keep files. He just complains to the Department when someone pisses him off, like you did. Files are Jones' game."

“So why did Jones send his errand boy around to collect me? I’m staying out of trouble.”

“Sawney? I understand his two big dogs, Erskine and Rhodes, got summoned back to Washington. Sawney’s a lightweight; I wouldn’t trust him to fetch the morning paper,” Nick said. “Jones offered both Nate and I jobs. How about you?”

“Back in the spring, I did some work for Jones.”

“Go on.”

“After talking to you about Nate, I got an offer to keep an eye on things. I called Jones on Nate. I thought it would keep him out of real trouble. I only did it once.”

“I guess Jones still thinks you are useful for something.”

“So why exactly is Jones here?”

“Organized Crime Task Force,” Nick said. “This all started last December. That ADA, uh, Ritter, the one who offed himself, wrote up the request to the Feds, first.”

“Ritter? Vincent Ritter?”

“Yeah, did you know him?

“No, I just remember hearing the name.”

“Anyway,” Nick said, sliding out of the booth, “you hear anything more, let me know. If I find something, I’ll let you know.”

“Take care, Nick”

“You do the same.”

In the small conference chamber of old wood and leather, Sam Cavanaugh sat in the ancient, hard-backed chair. Behind the long, polished table, Chapman and Schechter pondered the review papers. At the right end of the table, Judge Adams’ fierce blue eyes studied the proceedings. Sam kept his smile faint for the foregone conclusion.

"It's time for the bench to get new blood," Hiram Chapman said. "Mr. Cavanaugh has been in practice over ten years and has met all of the qualifications for a Municipal Court Judge."

"Seconded," said Aaron Schechter. "He also comes with high recommendations."

"Gentlemen, if I may opine," Judge Ray Adams said, rising from his chai., "You, Judge Schechter and you, Mr. Chapman, are new to your offices. I ask that you not be too hasty on making this appointment. Mr. Cavanaugh has the met the minimum requirements of the bench, but he lacks prosecutorial experience."

"Thank you, Judge Adams," Schechter said, looking over his steel-rimmed glasses. "As a member emeritus of the bench, your advice is always welcomed; however, the final consideration is left to me and Mr. Chapman, the Special Counsel to the Mayor."

Judge Adams shook his head and said, "Procedure has been observed, but I must protest your choice on this matter."

"Noted," Chapman said with a smug smirk, "Your Honor."

"I see," Judge Adams said. "As am I no longer needed, I take my leave." He snatched up his worn leather brief bag.

As the stout oak door slammed to a close, Sam sighed and said, "Well, that was easier than expected."

"Lucky for you this happened this year instead of last year," Schechter said.

"How's that?"

"If we had tried this last year," Chapman said, "the old bastard would have submitted his name just to block you, Sam, but since he turned seventy, he's no longer eligible to sit on the bench."

"Well," Sam said, "I guess it's time to pay respects to our benefactor."

"Give him our regards," Schechter said.

Sam swaggered from the conference chamber and down the back stairs to the busy office bay called the Pit. Past the young men and women answering phones and shuffling files, he pushed through the nondescript office door.

"Bill," Sawney said with a hangdog expression, "that asset over at Mittelmarch is off the radar. No one has seen him for two weeks."

"Don't worry about it, Jerry," Jones said, dismissing him without looking up. "Sending you to collect Clarke was a long shot, anyway. I've got other options on the table."

"Thanks, Bill," Jerry said, turning away. Sam noted the young man's face clouded with concern, as he left the small office.

"Kid looks like he's been put through the wringer, Bill," Sam commented aloud.

"Sam!" Jones said standing up. "Have a seat. How'd it go downstairs?"

"Smooth as silk, Bill, just like you said. However…"

"However, what?"

"I would've preferred a Civil Court appointment. There's more money there."

"Baby steps, Sam. I need you on the Municipal bench, for now."

"Okay, Bill," Sam said, leaning in. "I get the quid pro quo. What's a Fed like you want with Rex Brunet?"

"I was called in to clear up the organized crime in the city. I'm a smart guy, like you. You know as well as I know that isn't going to happen. The best you can hope for is to control it."

"Some might say you're overstepping your authority."

"I see potential here, Sam. With the right kind of leadership, who knows where this could lead? First, we got to separate the wheat from the chaff."

"Like Adams."

The black desk phone rang. "I got to take this, Sam," Jones said. "Your family problem will be resolved this afternoon."

Nick clambered up the service stairs to the police annex's polished busy main hallway. Jerry Sawney, Jones' brownnoser, loitered outside the Pit. He grinned at Nick and said, "Officer Serrano, how's things on Traffic?"

"Could be worse; it's still police work."

"The way I hear, it may not even be that for you; the things are changing."

"How so?"

"He means that the administration is undergoing some personnel changes," Aaron Schechter, now Judge Schechter, interrupted with peering eyes. "You know, a fresh approach to police work."

"I understand you got a promotion, Your Honor. Congratulations."

"Mr. Sawney," Schechter said with a nod. "I believe I met your wife, Mary and her friend, Tanya. She's truly a remarkable woman."

"Where did you meet her?" Jerry said.

"At a Youth in Crisis Seminar a while back," Schechter said, adjusting the blue silk pocket square in his jacket pocket. "She's really dedicated to her social work. A rising star."

Hearing enough, Nick walked away from the pair of suits and continued to his original destination, the watch desk.

"Serrano," Jerry called after him, "Jones wants to see you in his office, now."

"I don't work for Jones," Nick said without looking back.

"It might do you some good hear what he has to say," Jerry said, snaking alongside to the big police officer. "You don't want to work Traffic forever, do you?"

"All right," Nick said, following the young agent to the Jones' office behind the Pit.

Nick recognized Sam Cavanaugh leaving Jones' office. As they passed, the short lawyer scowled at Nick; Nick admired the lumpy jaw he'd given the jowly creep a few months earlier.

"Sit down, Serrano," Jones commanded with his feet propped up on the paper-covered desk. "Jerry, close the door."

After they all settled, Jones said, "Well, Serrano, it looks like you are running out of friends in high places. You give any thought to joining my task force?"

"A bit. I'd like to know what I'd be doing first."

"Looking before you leap; you're a smart guy. I like working with smart guys," Jones said. He opened his desk drawer and placed a vial of cut glass filled with an amber liquid on the desktop.

Nick noted Jerry's sharp intake of breath and watched the young agent fixate on the vial.

"Right now, I see this as the biggest problem in the city," Jones said.

"Okay," Nick said. "What is it? Crack, Meth, X?"

Glancing up at Jerry, Jones said, "Jerry, go tell Schechter and Mr. Cavanaugh I'll be out in a moment. I have to finish this up before lunch."

After Jerry closed the door behind him, Jones lowered his voice said, "It's the worst stuff imaginable. The boys in the lab still haven't figured out the composition or what the source is, but they nicknamed it, 'Lotus.'"

"Kind of dramatic, isn't it?"

"For a bunch of techs, yeah," Jones said," but once you see the users, you see why. They'll do anything for the next fix, but that's only the deluded, weak-minded fucks…not like you."

"I'll think about it," Nick said. He rose from the chair and left the room.

"Don't take too long, Nick, last chance. You don't want to be stuck on a Traffic beat for the rest of your career, do you? On the other hand, the mall is always looking for security guards."

The black phone rang one more time.

"Yeah, baby, nice work getting Schechter on board," Jones spoke lowly into the receiver. "No, I'm not mad. Your score is one and one, unlike Jerry's."

Out of the Pit and in the hallway, Nick sped past the smirking trio of Sawney, Cavanaugh and Schechter. He labored to keep his expression blank until he was halfway down the hall. His heartbeat pounded in his ears as he shuttled down the service stairwell and burst into the near-empty back lot. In his left shirt pocket, something jingled, a glass vial filled with an amber liquid. Enraged, he hurled the vial to the ground, shattering it in a wet star on the asphalt. Blue sparks flew off his massive fists as they slammed into the steel dumpster.

"Officer Serrano," Judge Adams commanded, "walk with me."

Nick turned to face the hawkish little man in the navy three-piece suit. "Why?" he raged.

"Walk with me," the Judge reiterated. "You are needed, but not here."

Nick's fists unclenched. "What makes you so sure of that, Your Honor?"

"Officer Serrano," the Adams pronounced, "I am no longer Judge Adams, just Ray Adams. A man who has outlived his utility."

"In that case, Mr. Adams," Nick said hustling to keep up with the old man's purposeful stride, "you may as well call me Nick."

"Very well, Nicholas. Explain to me why you are working a Traffic beat instead of working for Special Agent Jones."

"Jones," Nick said, choking down his temper, "the whole lot of them: Schechter, Cavanaugh, Sawney, they're rotten. This is my city; I won't let them trash it—"

"Not on my watch," Adams interrupted without breaking stride. "I believe you were going to say, correct?"

"Well, yes."

"Tell me, how do you plan to do this as a Traffic cop?

"I…" Nick paused as he fumbled for words.

"Let us suppose for a moment," Adams offered, as they rounded the corner to Justice Plaza, "that there was a way to rebalance the scales, to set things right. Would you, Nicholas?"

"Yes!" Nick declared.

"What if it meant you would no longer be on the police force?"

"I don't know," Nick replied, "I never thought about being anything but a cop."

They paused in front of the grand fountain in front of the Municipal Courthouse. Atop the splashing pool, the weather-beaten bronze statue of Lady Justice stood, sword and scales in hand.

For the first time ever, Nick watched the dour old judge's smile shine as he gazed at the blindfolded lady. After a moment of silence, he turned to Nick and said, "She still stands after all these years. That's one tough lady."

"She sure is," Nick agreed and cracked a grin.

"You know, Nicholas, I was here the day they set her to watch this city. It was the proudest day of my life."

"She's wearing a blindfold. She can't be too good at her job."

"It's been said that what defines a man's character is his actions when he thinks no one is watching," Adams said. "Trust me, she sees more than you think."

"How's that?"

"She's weighed you in the balance and have found you not wanting," Adams replied. "Your time is coming, Nicholas."

Prof nursed his coffee in the buzzing campus cafeteria and reviewed the interview in the spacious office by the Dean of Humanities, Dr. Serkan Aksoy.

"Mr. Clarke," Dr. Aksoy said, "we wish to offer to you a position as Adjunct Professor of English. It would reflect well on the Department to have a member such as you."

"As me?"

"Your…handicap," the goaty little man said, "would show our dedication to those less fortunate. Forgive me for my bluntness, I do not like the way you Americans mince words."

"So, this has nothing to do with my skills as a scholar."

"You have a reputation of competence," Aksoy said with a shrug. "I believe this is mutually beneficial for all parties involved. Good day, Mr. Clarke."

"An indifferent offer out of the blue," Prof mulled, "and made just before lunch. Not very auspicious." He stirred his coffee and reviewed the events that led him here. Monday morning, J.J. had called him over to the desk and handed him the linen-stock envelope.

The clerk obliged to read the request letter to him and said, "Hell, Prof, looks like your luck is finally changing!" He slapped Prof on the back.

Promptly, Prof had climbed the stairs to the pay phone on the landing and confirmed the interview with Dr. Aksoy's graduate assistant. After hanging up, he awarded himself with a small fist pump; now, he puzzled over the unknowns of this job offer.

"Prof?" Jane said. "What are you doing here?"

"Hi Jane, I got a job offer and had an interview this morning."

"Why didn't you tell me?" she said. "This is great!"

"If it didn't work out, I wanted to keep the failure to myself."

"Funny," Jane said, "I remember some blind guy telling me that failing was part of the game awhile back."

"Point taken."

"And," Jane said, touching Prof's hand, "to take a chance."

"Sounds like a smart guy."

"He is. Who did you interview with?"

"Dr. Aksoy, the Dean."

"Really?" Jane said. "He was just promoted to Dean a few weeks back. I don't understand why he's interviewing you for an English Department position. He'd consider it beneath him."

"You could say that. He implied I was to be the English Department's token gimp."

"Look," Jane said, "Aksoy is obnoxious and self-centered, but an offer is an offer. This is your chance to get your life back on track."

"Perhaps, you're right. Still, it feels like they're tossing me a crust of bread," Prof said, rising from his seat. "Anyway, I got to catch the bus back. Will I see you tonight at the diner?"

"No, I'm seeing Vic."

"Give Mr. Teppish my regards," Prof said.

Jane watched the tall man in the black jacket navigate the crowded floor of the cafeteria with his cane and practiced skill. She remembered the wreck of a man who had shuffled into the diner so many months ago. Now, she barely recognized him; he no longer drifted. *There's hope for all of us, I guess,* she thought. Taking up her nylon pad folio, she readied herself for the meeting she wished to avoid.

She crossed the breezy quad under the bright fall sky to the steps of the gleaming white Federal-style Administration Building. She paused before the rich walnut double-doors before entering, impressed by office upgrade that Dr. Aksoy's promotion granted.

"Ms. Davis, please sit down," the doctor said, pointing to the leather wingback chair from behind his massive desk.

"Good afternoon, Dr. Aksoy," Jane said, taking her seat. "Congratulations on your promotion."

"Thank you, Ms. Davis," the doctor in the tailored suit said. "I know we have differences of opinion on many matters, but have you reconsidered my recommendations about the focus of your research?"

"No, my decision is the same, as I stated that night at the Crucible Club. I feel it will compromise my professional integrity."

"I see," Dr. Aksoy said, lowering his eyes. "That gentleman you were accompanying, that unfortunate night, Mr.—"

"Teppish."

"Yes, Mr. Teppish. I have thought long about that incident. I realize now that I was in the wrong. Is there a way I can convey my apology?"

"I have his phone number, but you will probably get his voicemail."

"That would seem most insincere. Do you know where I could reach him by mail or personally?"

"I would have to ask him before giving that information."

"Most prudent, Ms. Davis," Dr. Aksoy said. "Thank you for your time. I respect your choices; however, I hope their consequences do not confine you in the future."

"You're welcome, Dr. Aksoy," Jane said. "I understand you interviewed John Clarke today?"

"You know this gentleman?" Doctor Aksoy said with a cocked eyebrow.

"He comes into the diner from time to time."

"Yes," Dr. Aksoy said, "I am offering him a position as an adjunct professor. I feel it is beneficial for him and the offer poses no risk to the department."

"How did you find him?"

"A friend recommended him. Good day, Ms. Davis."

Upon Jane's exit, Serkan picked up his cell phone and fulfilled his end of the agreement. "Yes, I offered Mr. Clarke the position," he spoke. "Of the other matter, she is still in contact with him and no, and she did not give an address. I am sorry, my friend." He ended the call.

"They are given the trappings of luxury, but in their hearts are blazing furnaces which do not give them rest at any time," his father warned him the night he departed for America. Now, many years later, he understood the weight of his father's grave words as he considered the half-empty vial resting upon his rosewood desk. Through his lovely proxies, his ally had proposed this enticing pact. As promised, he secured the Dean's chair, but Serkan still fretted about this deal he'd bound himself to. Employment for Clarke appeared innocuous enough; a blind man of no consequence could do no harm. His ally's interest in Ms. Davis' acquaintance troubled him more, if it was true what he suspected. One did not prod a lion with impunity.

Serkan needed to protect his own interests. As much as he disliked the labyrinthine organization of the Christians, he dialed another number given to him long ago by one of their representatives. Christian or not, ally or not, this was a point of patriotism and self-preservation.

"The Dragon was sighted," he stated and hung up.

For the first Wednesday afternoon in a long time, the shop floor of Stahlmann's Mechanics was silent and clean. Back in the office, among the stacks of boxes, Prof and Lou sat eating the lunch Prof brought from the Night Café.

"So, this is it, Lou," Prof said. "You're going to retire?"

"Yeah, I started cleaning up yesterday. I got prospective buyers coming in tomorrow."

"I was wondering why you weren't at the Café for lunch today. This seems sudden. You didn't say anything about it Monday night."

"I just got to thinking about the way things have been since Rita died," Lou said, regarding the map above his desk. "I came in yesterday and realized I'd been stuck in this cinderblock box, caught up in the choices I'd made over the years."

"Sounds like Vivian has been a good influence on you."

"She's a no-nonsense kind of woman. She told me everything had a price and asked me what this was costing me. It was got me thinking."

"Guess it's time to check out some of those fishing holes you've had tagged."

"Yeah, I'm going to buy an RV when I sell this place. I've already bought Vivian an open face reel."

"You know," Prof said, "most women prefer jewelry to show your undying commitment."

"Already got that covered. I brazed a couple of copper strands into a bangle bracelet. It was one of the first tricks I learned back in shop class," Lou said. "I gave one to Rita, my wife, before the Prom."

"A man who creates jewelry will never be at a loss for female companionship."

"Says you, Prof. I'm coming off a five-year dry-spell," Lou said. "Oh yeah, I just remembered. I got your winnings." He reached into his pocket and placed a wad of bills and a silver cigar tube in Prof's hand. "Your winnings from Monday night."

"What's this?" Prof said, fumbling with the tube.

"I bought that for myself, right out of Basic Training. It's been my good luck charm. I figure it's time to pass it on to someone else. I even left a Cuban in it."

"You know these things will kill you," Prof said.

"So, will betting on the Braves…or at least, break your heart and bank."

"Kind of like a woman," Prof chuckled.

"But what a way to go. Prof, could you do me a favor?"

"Sure, what do you need?"

"I'm going to mail you something, just to pass on to a mutual friend."

"Okay, what friend?"

"Vic Teppish."

"The guy Jane's been seeing? How do you know him?"

"It's complicated," Lou dismissed, "I've been doing business with him for a while. I'm holding on to some of his stuff in storage. If you'd just hold onto the key for him 'til he comes for it, I'd be grateful."

"Not a problem, Lou, what are friends for?"

"Nice place, Rex," Jones said. "Seems smaller than your last joint, though."

Rex Brunet struggled to keep his poker face and said, "Things have been tight lately."

"A fire and the loss of your investment with Augustus Investments…"

"You know about that?" Rex said, glaring at lawman in the dark gray pinstripe suit.

"Who doesn't? You crossed the Syrian and got burned. As for the investment scheme…well, Rich Allen and Cavanaugh saw you coming a mile off."

"Allen got his," Rex said. "I understand he's still eating through a tube."

"Guess you didn't hear about Sam, then?"

"No, what?"

“He’s gotten appointed as a judge to Municipal. He didn’t mention it to you?”

“No,” Rex said, “our relationship is professional.”

“Understandable. He shared his good fortune with just his friends.”

“Cut to the chase. What do you want here, Jones?”

“Just assessing the damage. You were the big dog in town until the Syrian came along. I’m a pragmatist by nature. If there’s going to be crime, it deserves competent management.

“I’m waiting for the smoke to clear from this donnybrook with you and the Syrian,” Jones said, looking directly at Rex. “I only back winners.”

“I’m still here and the Syrian’s gone.”

“True, but look at this place,” Jones said with a sweep of his arm. “A vacant grocery store? Your old place was a palace compared to this. Some believe you lost the muscle to stay on top.”

“Not a problem,” Rex said. “I move in and take his holdings.”

“Let me make a suggestion. Make your move now. Don’t use your regular guys. You know the kind I’m talking about?”

“I get your meaning, yeah.”

“You want them afraid, so when your guys come in to do business, they’ll have that incentive to play by your rules.”

“Jones, you’re one hell of a lawman.”

“Exactly,” Jones said and pulled several cut-glass vials from his coat pocket and laid them on the bar before Rex. “Party favors for the boys.”

At five in the afternoon, Lou never heard the shop’s steel front door open or close. He turned and faced the two long-haired young men in dark sunglasses.

“Sorry, boys,” Lou said, putting down the stack of boxes he’d been carrying, “I’m not hiring these days.”

"That'sss okay, Mr. Ssstahlman," one said with a thickened tongue. "That'ss not what were here for." Both young men removed their sunglasses, revealing their yellow eyes with slit pupils.

"Look," Lou said, "I don't want any trouble." He backed towards the rear loading dock door and cursed himself for moving the last of his private inventory offsite.

As the boys advanced, green scales emerged on their faces. The other young man said, "I'm assure you don't want trouble-" His words cut short as his jaws unhinged and a massive set of fangs flipped down from the roof of his mouth.

The last Lou heard was tinkle of breaking glass as the youths closed in.

"Vic," Jane's whisper echoed in the darkened atrium in the Crucible Club, "I really need some straight answers from you."

"Jane, I've told you. I have meetings during the day and trust me, you don't want to see my place. It's kind of a bachelor pad."

"You know, some of my girlfriends tell me that you are hiding something, but I trust you."

"Look, I'm not married and like I've told you before, the line of business I'm in—"

"Corporate security?" Jane countered. "Vic, we've been seeing each other for eight months. I just need to know if there is a future here."

Vic lowered his dark eyes and said, "I hope there is. Jane, there are things about me—"

"Vic!" Iggy said, emerging from the dark dining room archway. "I am so glad to see you. So much has gone wrong in the past few days."

Behind the wiry little restauranteur followed a very pale Rachel. Sheridan and Lamar, Iggy's bull-like bodyguards, lingered attentively in the background.

"Rachel," Jane said, moving to her withdrawn friend, "what's happened?"

"I got a call from Child Services today," Rachel said. "Sam filed a complaint. The social worker, Mrs. Sawney, just pulled him from class and put him in foster care pending investigation."

"Jane," Iggy said, "if you would be as so kind as to take Rachel back to the dining room. Considering the current situation, I do not believe we will open for service tonight."

Jane glared at Iggy.

"Please do not mistake my intentions, Jane. Rachel needs a friend in this time of crisis, one who is better equipped to comfort her than I am."

Although Jane's expression softened, she retained a faint air of hostile suspicion. Turning back to Rachel, she said, "Come on, Rachel," and guided her friend back through the shadowy archway.

"Jake was right," Rachel said, rocking back in forth in her chair, "never give Sam an opening."

"Rachel, you couldn't see this coming," Jane said, touching Rachel's hand.

"It doesn't matter what I do," Rachel continued, "he always wins."

"But, you broke away and you stood on your own for a year. You can't quit now. You got to fight for Bobby's sake."

Rachel sniffled and nodded. "For Bobby."

Back in the atrium the wild-haired little man took Vic aside and said, "I believe that this is symptom of the current state of affairs."

"You think, Iggy?" Vic growled. "This is why I never get involved in turf wars and why doing business with family is a bad idea. With the Syrian gone, nature abhors a vacuum."

"What about you? You operated under my cousin's aegis for a long time. Do you think that you've gone unnoticed by the locals?" Iggy said, glancing back through the archway. "You are a hot property and, like it or not, you have something to lose here."

"Damn it, for once, you're right,"

The massive doors of dark wood and wrought iron creaked open and four young men in loose jeans and black hoodies swaggered in.

"My pardon, gentlemen," Iggy announced aloud, "I'm afraid we will not be opening this evening—"

"It's okay," the leader said, "we're here on behalf of your new insurance manager, Mr. Brunet. He told us to give the place a good once over."

"You're a pretty bold one, sonny," Vic interjected, "dropping in unannounced without knowing who you're dropping in on. In fact, some call that stupid."

Iggy's bulging eyes shifted to Vic, who gave a reassuring wink back.

"Stupid? Fuck you, old man!" the leader spat. The exposed hands and faces of each of the boys writhed and twisted. Their convulsions rippled across their bodies in unison. The leader, who now bore the head of a great black wolf, bounded upon Vic and clamped its jaws on his throat.

One on the end in a scarlet hoodie waved its suckered tentacles and squawked. Sheridan pawed the ground and roared, "Red!" His running head butt slammed the creature against the rough stone wall.

Another sprouted black, spindly arms and flexed its split mandible, closing in on Lamar. Wrapping its arms around the bodyguard's massive girth, all eight of its beady obsidian eyes blinked in surprise as Lamar lifted the creature above his head and smashed it to the floor. Lamar raised his heavy black brogan and crushed its chitinous head like an eggshell, which burst with a gout of white pus. Smiling, he looked over to his brother, Sheridan, who studied the splattered red remains of the thing on the wall.

A greenish toad-like creature leapt past Iggy; before he could give chase, a scaly claw shoved him back into the corner. A grunting bellow issued out of a crocodile's gaping maw. Eye to eye with the monster, Iggy's grin grew to jack-o-lantern proportions. His pupils turned to vertical slits as he said, "Little poseur."

A stream of brilliant blue-white fire shot from Iggy's mouth.

Bypassing Iggy, the toad creature shambled towards Jane and Rachel. "Cav-aan-naw?" it croaked with webbed hands raised.

Jane grabbed a nearby pole that usually held their velvet ropes and thrust to keep the monster at bay. She felt a wriggling on her left foot. One of the silver-thread scorpions on her shoe detached itself and popped into three dimensions. After giving its tail a couple test stings, the little chromed beast scuttled over to the foot of the monster and jabbed. Turning around, it skittered back to Jane's shoe. The toad monster opened its mouth and collapsed.

The wolf ripped out Vic's throat with a powerful yank of its head. Vic's vision grew crimson in pain and rage; his fangs bared. He grasped the neck of the beast and wrenched. The sound of snapping vertebrae filled the air. Vic flipped the dead brute off him to drive his fangs deep in its throat; his bestial instinct promised the creature's rich, red sustenance would make him whole again.

"No, Son of Dragon!" commanded Iggy. His claw-like hand grabbed Vic's shoulder.

Vic snarled at the little entertainer who dare deny him his kill.

"Sheridan, get some of Vic's private stock, now!"

"Oh, my God," Jane said, covering her mouth in horror at the carnage of the atrium. Blood poured from his jagged throat as Vic crouched over the body of a dead man. His face had gone pale and his red predator eyes longed for her. She bolted to the open front door and into the city night.

"Ja-Ja," he managed to croak through his ruined vocal cords, reaching for her in futility.

Tears of blood joined the stains on his suit and shirt.

Underneath the hum of the mercury vapor streetlamps, the air filled with the crackle of police radios, concerned murmurs and idling engines as Prof made his way towards Lou's shop in the chill autumn evening air.

"Stay back, Prof," Nick advised, placing his palm on Prof's chest. "It's bad. Lou's gone."

"What happened?"

"Not sure yet. Looks like somebody got to him," Nick said. "The detectives are going to want to talk to you."

Nick watched Prof's expression change from bewilderment to grief. "Sure, I'll cooperate in any way. Lou was my friend."

"Serrano," a bespectacled young officer said, trotting up to Nick and Prof, "you said to keep an eye out for glass vials, right?"

"Yeah, Pennington, I've been seeing more of them around, lately. Not sure what they are exactly."

"I was first responder, tonight, Nick," Pennington said. "Just a call about a door being left wide-open. I found Stahlmann all cut up. I picked something up before Homicide kicked me out of the crime scene. Only…"

"Only what, Pennington?" Nick said.

"Well, I thought you meant vials like crack vials."

"Go on."

"I saw a couple shattered on the ground. Only, I don't think they were for drugs. They kind of reminded me of perfume bottles."

"You mean cut glass," Nick said.

"Yeah."

"Thanks, Pennington," Nick said. "You better go back to holding the perimeter."

"On it," Pennington said, hustling back to his post.

Prof listened to the footsteps of the men in dress shoes stop near Nick. He failed to make out the quiet murmurings between Nick and the men. Finally, Nick said, "Prof, I'm sorry…you're considered a Person of Interest. Combs and Taylor need to take you downtown."

Prof sat numbly through the entire interview. They took his prints and mouth swabs in the Municipal complex's bustling ward bay. The lead detectives, Combs and Taylor, demanded that he repeat his story and life details several times, with slight variations in the questioning. Prof replied to each question in a dull monotone; his practice in front of the doctors back at the hospital had served him well.

Sometime after midnight, Taylor slapped a file on his steel desk and said, "Your prints were all over the office, Mr. Clarke, but we agree there's no way you could have killed Stahlmann—"

"Lou," Prof replied quietly. "His name was Lou."

"Okay," Combs said, "I get it. Lou was your friend, but you must have known about his side business."

"Fishing?"

"No, smartass," Taylor snapped, "illegal guns. We've had Stahlmann on our radar for years, but couldn't pin him to anything. Hell, the Task Force has a whole file on him upstairs."

"Look," Prof said, "I just hung around his shop to listen to the ball games. I don't know anything about guns. He just let me come in out of the cold when I first got here and have a cup of coffee. All I know is that he was going to sell the place, retire, and go fishing."

"Funny thing is," Taylor said, "while going through the Task Force files, I happened to find one on you, Clarke."

"Interesting reading, I hope."

"Not really," Combs said. "Just a sad story about a divorced, drunk professor who went crazy and blind. Still, it makes me wonder why they have a file on you."

"Ask Jones or his lapdog, Sawney."

"Don't worry, smart boy, we will," Taylor chimed in. "The funny thing is, you're a Ward of the State. You know what that means?"

"My healthcare is funded by the state by federal mandate."

"No, asshole," Taylor said, "it means if you so much as litter, we can get you declared a danger to yourself and others and shuffle you back to the nut house. Good God, this is more leverage than we got on any parolee. We already have leads that you're connected to a couple of shady types other than Stahlmann. Gascon ring any bells? That little hustler has got warrants out the ass and some guy named Teppish. Bottom line, here, is we own you."

"Are you going to charge me with something?"

"No," Combs said, "but I'd be careful of what you do or say from now on, Mr. Clarke."

Much to his chagrin, Prof burned some of his winnings for cab fare back to the 'March. It was either that or take the offered ride from Detective Combs. As he walked through the lobby, J.J. at the desk said, "Hey, Prof. You got mail…two in a week."

"Who's it from?"

"Holden Forevict, 4545 Ustoreit Road. It's just a small manila envelope. It feels like someone mailed you a key. I don't know that street."

"Thanks, J.J," Prof said, taking the envelope.

"Prof, is everything all, right?"

"No, J.J.," Prof said, shuffling to the stairs.

Back in his room, Prof dropped into his chair at the table and cradled his head, too tired to ponder the consequences, yet too wired to sleep. He lost Stan, Lila, his job, his sight and her voice. Now, when he'd thought there was nothing left to lose, Lou was gone. His hands reached across the table and grasped the cardboard box. On its dusty top rested the pen he'd received as a gift so many months earlier. Taking up the pen, he opened the box for the first time in many days.

Four days later, Prof felt the chilly afternoon breeze on his face. The minister said something about Lou being both a busy worker bee in the hive of life and a pillar of the community. Prof's impassive countenance belied his distaste for the clergyman's artificial familiarity. He understood some needed it, but saccharine insincerity grated on his nerves. The Sunday church bells tolled in the background as he shifted uneasily in his seat next to the grave. He'd sworn never to enter Our Lady of the Nativity Cemetery after that dark winter night a year ago.

"Go in peace, Amen," the minister finished.

The wooden chairs rattled as the service attendees rose and shuffled away. Prof held his seat with his chin propped up on his white cane.

"Mr. Clarke?" Vivian Green said, taking a seat beside him. "There is someone who wants to talk to you."

"The name is Prof, Ms. Green," he said. "I am in no mood for small talk. Not here, and not with you. You could've saved him."

"I feel his loss, too," Vivian said, "but this is important."

"As important as knowing whom you gave my blood to?"

"I told you that is confidential and nothing's free. Please, go talk to him; this could benefit both of us."

From his vantage point, Jones watched the blind man poke and prod his way over with his white cane. This one appeared insignificant in the greater scheme of things, but Jones knew appearances weren't everything. It was time to secure the loose threads. He propped himself over the tall granite tombstone inscribed with:

Vincent Ritter
12/21/1977-12/21/2014

Prof stopped, sniffed the air and said, "Crocuses."

"Since I was here anyway, I thought I'd pay my respects," Jones said, grinning. "The three of us together again…"

"What do you want, Jones?"

"Me?" Jones said. "I'm just here to open the blind eyes, to bring out the prisoners from the prison, and those that sit in darkness out of the prison house."

"You don't strike me as the liberator of truth type."

"Who's to say, Professor? Oh, that's right. You haven't accepted the job, yet."

"How do you know about that?"

"Who do you think recommended you?"

Prof paused. "Why?"

"I've been puzzling over this myself," Jones said. "I understand Vince's part. He couldn't handle failure. That's why he called me in. But you're different, aren't you?"

"Not really, just trying to pull my life together."

"That's what it seems to me. Vince summoned me to straighten the city out. He didn't have the will or the stomach for it. It took me awhile to figure out who did what. I made some personnel changes as I saw fit," Jones said, "but you don't fit anywhere in this mess, Johnny. Yet, every time something doesn't go to plan, you're there."

"How do you figure that?"

"You were there," Jones said and slapped the top of the tombstone. "We all share the same birthday. You were there that auspicious night…"

Prof, stunned, said nothing.

"So, that leaves me with a problem. You're that last nut in the little plastic bag that doesn't show up on the assembly instructions. You don't fit anywhere, but I'll be damned if I'm going to toss you out," Jones said. "So, here's the options for you: One, take the job and mind your own business. It's the safe route. Two, I send you back to the hospital, where you can't cause any more trouble and your brain can just rot away. Three, you leave town, never come back and no more of your friends get hurt. Your choice, Johnny, but don't take too long or I'll choose for you."

Prof walked away.

"Oh, and Johnny?" Jones called out to the slump-shouldered man.

"What?" Prof said.

Jones tapped the top of the tombstone with a vial of blood.

The Serpent's Gambit

8:26 PM October 15th
Municipal Bus Terminal
2500 Reed Shore Drive

The darkened, near-empty bus ground to a halt and the doors opened with a hiss. Jake Cavanaugh's heart sank; the sound only confirmed his anxieties. He slung his duffel bag over his shoulder and dragged his feet for this homecoming. Under the bleak fluorescents of the bus terminal lobby, he paused to make the phone call he'd hoped to avoid.

"Hello?" the voice of his brother, Sam, replied.

"Sam," Jake said, his hands shaking, "I'm in town. Are you ready to finish this?"

The pause lasted forever. "Of course, Jake, I look forward it. Your key to the house still works. I'll be there in an hour or so." The phone clicked to silence.

Amidst the vending machines, the sole occupant of the waiting room, a man in a worn-out trench coat and dark sunglasses, hunched at one of the yellow plastic tables. Next to the man, a coil of thick black cable lay on the floor, a remnant of the ongoing renovation of the aging terminal. Jake considered the scene and exhaled; he found another marker on this strange trail he'd walked the last three days.

"Excuse me, sir," Jake said, approaching the man, "are you local?"

"About as local as anybody can be around here."

"Does the local bus still run out to Fisher?"

"You mean out past Wrightsway?"

“Yeah,” Jake said, “if that’s what they’re calling Union Square these days.”

“If it’s one and the same,” the man said, “then no, it’s gotten too tony to allow rabble like me easy access. The route terminates at the Hotel Mittelmarch these days, and it’s a good ten blocks to Walker Bridge. Your best bet is to get a cab.”

Jake looked out to the wet streets and said, “Damn. That’s out of my price range.”

“Sounds like you got to keep that appointment with Sam. Sorry, couldn’t help but overhear.”

“Yeah,” Jake said, taking a seat opposite the man. “Look, I’d appreciate it if you wouldn’t mention that you saw me here.”

“I don’t think that will be a problem,” the man said with a smile and touched his dark glasses.

“Uh, yeah…sorry, I guess you would be able to deny seeing me,” Jake said. “So, what are you doing here?”

“Getting up the nerve to leave.”

“Where you going? You don’t have any bags.”

“Just away,” the man said. “It’s kind of a spur of the moment decision.”

“You in trouble?”

“Not really,” the man said. “Just run into something I can’t fix.”

“Let me clue you in. If you’re determined to run, you got to be prepared. The buses don’t make many stops these days,” Jake said rummaging through the pockets of his army jacket. “Here, take ’em. I don’t need them anymore.” He dropped a couple of fried pies on the table before the blind man.

“Thanks.”

“And running is a bad habit to break,” Jake continued. “Trust me; I’ve got nine years of practice.” Jake pulled himself from the chair and hoisted his worn duffel bag over his shoulder.

“Wait a minute,” the blind man said, reaching into his breast pocket. “They say that good advice is worth what you pay for it. I believe yours is worth eighty.” He slid an envelope across the scarred top of the table.

"What's this?"

"Was my bus ticket," the man said. "Now, it's your cab fare."

Jake rubbed his unshaven jaw and said, "I made this for someone else, but I got a feeling that it was meant for you," Jake said and tossed a segmented wooden snake on the table and walked away, puzzled by the exchange. As with all the events of the last week, he sensed bigger things in play here.

The cold, misty breeze hit Jake in the face in the dank night streets. At the cab stand, Jake's suspicions stood validated; a lone, bone white taxi awaited him.

Prof considered his dilemma. Jones' threats at Lou's funeral had put the voodoo on him; Jones set up this game well. The slick lawman revealed his strategy in a way that Prof could not repeat to anyone. Breathing a word of this to any of his friends verified what they all suspected; he was insane. Jane, Nick and even Reyna would never believe him. Jones even held the blood vial from Vivian; he'd fought to hide his alarm while Jones tapped the vial atop of Ritter's tombstone. Hope remained, though; Jones failed to recognize the dearness of the contents of the vial.

In the cold weeks that followed, he'd stewed over this trap Jones had set for him and kept his distance from his friends. Tonight, he resigned himself to cut his losses and run. After stopping at a liquor store on Corral Street, he arrived at the bus terminal to buy a ticket, board a bus and drink himself into a stupor. In the morning, he would start over somewhere else.

He pondered his certain failure at facing Jones when the front doors of the terminal swept open with an icy gust of wind. A sole set of footsteps crossed the lobby with a sharp rap of a wooden cane upon the heavy tile floor. The footsteps paused at the table and the newcomer took the chair across from Prof.

"Pardon, *mon ami*," the newcomer said, "are you going to eat those fine confectionaries of yours?"

"No, please, help yourself."

"*Merci beaucoup*," the other said, ripping open the wrapping of one of the fried pies. "Mmm, apple…*très bon*," he continued between bites.

"You're welcome, glad they're going to some use."

"You know," the other said, "a fine repast such as this would go down much better with a libation and a good smoke."

Prof remembered a bleary Monday morning's Psychology elective class long ago. The instructor had pronounced Jung's axiom, "There were no such things as coincidences." He pulled the flask of rum from his coat pocket and plucked Lou's lucky cigar tube from his breast pocket. Setting these on the table, he said, "Just remember, they don't allow smoking, let alone drinking, on city property."

"I think this is not a problem. *Après tout*, no one cares what goes on down here amongst the dead men," the man said, taking a swig of rum and lighting the cigar. "Ahh, Cuban, not as good as the old days, but still good smoke."

"Dead men?"

"This depot is a place of transition, much like the crossroads. Death is just a transition. I think an educated man like you would know that."

"Might I ask your name?"

The man chuckled and said, "Like those *garçons Anglais* with long hair used to sing, 'I am me as you are he as we are all together.'"

Prof grinned and said, "So, you're the walrus…"

"No," the other said, "a traveler and a collector of stories, just like you."

"How do you figure you're just like me?"

"You carry a walking stick like I do and you listen to the stories of those around you," he said, rapping his gnarled cane once. "So, tell me your story, *mon frère*."

"I don't know," Prof said, shaking his head, "it's been a pretty strange journey."

The man laughed and said, "That's the best kind of story."

The buildings zipped past in the cold autumn drizzle as the cab meter ticked steadily. Jake wondered if his warrants were still outstanding. He would have preferred an anonymous bus ride, but that was out of the question.

"You sure you just want to be dropped at the Park?" the cabbie said. "It's kind of nasty out and there isn't much open now."

As a familiar building front passed on the left, Jake said, "Isn't that Cassidy's?"

"It's called the Night Café. I haven't gone there myself, but I've had a few fares that say it's real nice."

"My Dad used to drink there. I had my first legal drink there. Used to be a real dive."

"Things change," the cabby said. "Up to a couple years ago, Wrightsway was a dump. Now, it's money central. I can't even imagine what property is going for, now."

"I can. Dad's house is out here. It was a working-class neighborhood when I left…"

"I bet he made out like a bandit."

"No," Jake said, "he died a couple of years ago. It would've been nice for him…"

"Sorry to hear that," the cabby said, pulling the cab alongside the curb. "You going to be here long?"

"Don't know how long I've got… Why?"

"Can't say that I've haven't heard that before," the cabby chuckled. "I asked because I got another fare nearby later. I figure I'd kill two birds with one stone."

"Uh, look," Jake said, "I'd really appreciate it if you'd forget my face." He offered the cabby his entire wad of cash.

"Keep it; this ride is gratis. I'm doing this as a favor for an old friend," the cabby said. "As for your face, don't worry about it. I wouldn't know you from Paul, Lazarus or Clairvius Narcisse."

"Uh, thanks, I guess."

"See you around, chief," the cabby said, pulling up the hood to his sweatshirt.

The man listened to the last nine months of Prof's life in silence with only a grunt of agreement or a "hmm" of intrigue interspersed through the narrative.

"That's quite a story," the man said at the finish. "So, why do you think you're crazy?"

"Have you been listening?" Prof sputtered. "Things like this don't happen to normal people."

"Maybe or maybe not. Let me redirect my questioning. How do you feel now that you have told your story?"

Prof paused for a moment and sighed. "Better."

"So, unburdening your story lightens your soul, does it not?"

"Well, yes, but a voice in my head—"

"Real or not, *mon ami*," the man said, "her words changed you, yes?"

"Yes," he agreed, "but the rest—"

"Folks have been seeing these things for a long time," the man said. "Haunts, hoodoos and devils, I've heard all sorts of tales. In your case, does it matter? Their effects on you are real."

Prof remained silent.

"Real or not, I cannot say, but they sure make for an interesting listen."

As Sam promised, Jake's key still worked. Inside the foyer, the gold carpet had been removed and the wood floors exposed. Sam had replaced Dad's handmade furniture with bleached oak monstrosities. Glaring white sheet rock stood in place of the warm ivory plaster. From room to room, he roamed and noted the changes.

On his remodeling jobs, Jake indulged his curiosity by walking through the home before work began. Occasionally, Jake swore he experienced the lives of the inhabitants soaked into the wood. Here, Dad's house lacked memory, like a hotel room. He spied a purple bra draped over the brass footboard of the king-sized bed and remembered Sam declaring he was going to make his pile and move out to the Gates, away from this shabby, blue-collar neighborhood.

Back in the dining room, Jake opened his duffel bag. With reverence, he set up the battered chessboard on the white lace table cloth that covered the polished cherry dining table. He had done this a thousand times before; some took communion, others went to Temple, Jake and Sam played chess.

Dad instituted the ritual when they were eleven and thirteen. One night, Dad had come home late from Cassidy's and to find Jake and Sam beating the daylights out of each other. Jake forgot what had started the fight. With a tired shake of his head, Dad staggered up the stairs to bed. The next morning, Dad taught them to play chess with this same board and pieces he had whittled before he married Mom. After that, whenever Jake and Sam fought, Dad told them to take it to the chessboard.

Over the years, they played and played hard. Jake closed his eyes and pictured a rush of sly feints, harsh sacrifices and bold strategies; knights fell, pawns were trampled, and castle defenses shattered. As Jake won, he gained concessions, like the use of the pickup truck, and grudging respect from Sam. When he lost, he painted the house by himself and listened to Sam's jeers. Across this tired old chessboard, a battle of their wills played out; the stakes of the game grew steeper each time. He still felt the cold sweat from the last game as Sam tipped his white king over in defeat.

"Little brother," Sam said with a cold grin, "never bet what you can't afford to lose."

His hands shook as he scrubbed them under the cold stream of water at the kitchen sink; he needed a drink. Grabbing a tumbler from the cabinet, he reached for the dusty bottle of rum. Recently, he'd developed a taste for rum with lemon and sugar instead of the family recipe of neat bourbon. Jake sputtered into his rum when he caught sight of the grinning, skinny old black man behind him in the gilded mirror over the bar.

The man in the mirror said, "'Ey, Mr. Jake de Snake man, you remember your promise to Papa, you hear?"

Jake nodded. He didn't know what you were supposed to say to a ghost.

"So, you think if you endure for a year and a day, you'll get your sight back?" Prof's companion asked. "I heard that correctly?"

"That's what I have come to understand."

"So, tell me, *mon frère*, why were you planning on running?"

"I can't win," Prof said.

"Winning, *mon ami*? Oedipus never won, neither did that fellow, Jason. It seems to me the best you can ever hope for—"

"Is to face your fate, gracefully," Prof said. "Easier said than done."

"If it was easy, everybody would do it. Still, I remember some story about a big northern wolf man… What was it he said? Yes, I remember, 'Fate often saves undoomed the man…'"

"Whose courage is good," Prof completed the quote.

"If I heard correct," the stranger said, "you only need to cross the finish line; doesn't matter if she's with you or not."

"I can't leave her with him."

"This voice inside your head that you lost, is she worth fighting for?"

"I can't save her," Prof said. "He's too strong."

"I know, I know, it isn't much of a story without a romance, *mon frère*," the stranger addressed Prof from across the table. "Every story contains a message. Sometimes, you got to tailor the story in terms the audience understands." He picked up the toy snake in front of Prof and laughed. "You know, I think I have a story to share with you."

Sitting in front of the chessboard, Jake recounted the long trail that began so many months ago down south.

On the fifth of May, Jake kicked the new gravel of the parking lot in front of the freshly air-conditioned office trailer amid the dusty cotton field, the fifth one he visited today. The late spring air baked the humidity and dust into his clothes. Waiting, he always hated the waiting.

The door swung open and a heavy man with Elvis sideburns and slicked back hair clambered down the stairs. "You the carpenter, right?" he asked.

"That's me, Jake Cavanaugh."

"Ed Baston, foreman." He shook Jake's hand with a firm grip. "You ain't from around here, are you?"

"Nah, I'm from up north. I just follow the work."

"Jobber, huh?" Ed said. "Well, I'm kind of surprised. Most of you Yankee boys stay up north. Union jobs and all."

"Yeah, but with the union comes a lot of bullshit politics, you know. I just want to work."

"I can respect that, son," Ed said with a sigh, as he looked out on the fifty acres of dry brown earth. "But I won't be needing carpenters for few months." He pulled a pack of chewing tobacco out of his back pocket and loaded up his jowls.

"You sure? I don't have a line on another job around here and I don't have cash enough to move on."

"Shit, you jobbers are all the same. Never gonna stay put in one place and ain't gonna tough it out when things are rough."

"Look, I just need some work, if you don't—"

"Got plenty of work. Fact is, if you can prove your mettle, I just might see to hiring you on as a carpenter when we get to Phase Two."

"What have you got?"

"Well, we're tad bit behind on the land prep. Been getting laborers dirt cheap, mostly immigrants. I can pay you day laborer wages. Isn't much, but if you can hack it in a Georgia summer, we'll see about getting you on as a carpenter."

"I need the work and I haven't found anything else."

"Chances are good you won't find anything else around here. The Cragles kind of see to that."

"Pardon?"

"Local family; they're trouble, kind of a pack of dogs in a manger. Don't really want to work and damned if they'll let a bunch of illegals and jobbers take work they don't want to do," Ed said. "Hell, I hired one of them on as a team leader just to smooth things over."

"Smooth over?"

"Damn, son, just because there ain't any union around here doesn't mean there ain't any politics. Keeping a couple of them on the job site cuts down on the number of accidents and other sorts of mischief."

"Oh."

"Take my advice, Jake. You take this job just keep a low profile in town. Those boys go looking for trouble."

"I'll keep that in mind. When do I start?"

"Well, I recommend you get a good night's sleep and be here at seven cause you gonna earn that money. Here in Georgia, sunrise and summer come early."

"I appreciate the break, Mr. Baston."

"The name's Ed. Hell, it will just be nice to have another white man around here that speaks good English and ain't mean half the time and stoned the other half."

"I pretty much fill those requirements," Jake said, walking over to his truck.

"Jake, that your truck? The green one over there?"

"Yeah, kind of my home on the road."

Ed sidled over and inspected the metallic green paint job on the body. "Yes, sir, it's got more than a few miles on it, but you've taken good care of it. I really like that tool box on the back."

"Yeah, me and Old Green have been kicking around for a few years. I bought it used and been fixing him up here and there, when I have the money."

"Shoot!" Ed said. "What you got here is a genuine retirement wagon. A fellow with some spare time on his hands could put that long bed to all sorts of effective use. A younger man ought to have himself something fancier, like one of those SUVs. You ever interested in selling, let me know."

"What, and give up my sole possession?" Jake said, hopping into the cab.

"Just a thought, Jake, see you tomorrow."

Tomorrow, Jake thought. It was his answer to everything. He pulled away from the job site. Tomorrow, he'd be doing day laborer work. A tomorrow after that, he might be working as a carpenter and still another tomorrow farther out, he would be traveling on to another job. Jake recounted nine years of his tomorrows and they all ended in the same place. At the end of Main Street, he found his next tomorrow, a motel called the Mockingbird, an uncomplicated semi-circle of rooms with a grubby sign that proclaimed, "Weekly Rates Available."

After paying up for the first week and receiving the mandatory lecture by the doughy lady in the cheap dress about what she allowed and didn't allow in the motel, Jake dumped his duffle bag on the lifeless, queen-sized bed. Opening his wallet, he pulled just enough to get a meal from the archaic breakfast joint across the street. He paused at the studio picture of Rachel and Bobby, stuck in the plastic window of the wallet. She sent the picture last year while he was on a long job and felt safe enough to hold a post office box. They looked happy; of course, Sam wasn't in the picture, either.

As he did most nights after work, he retrieved the chessboard and the two plastic bags of pieces, one for black, one for white. After setting up the lines, he set his wallet, propped open to the picture, next to the battered old board.

At daybreak, Ed met him in front of the office trailer with an extra cup of coffee and a grin.

"So, you decided to give it a shot?" Ed said.

"Yeah, just decided I had to prove you wrong about jobbers."

"We'll see about that, it's still early. Where are you staying?"

"Down at the Mockingbird. It's cheap."

"You might have run into some of the crew down there. I understand that a bunch of them are staying there, five or six to a room."

"I didn't go out much yesterday. Just kind of stayed in and kept to myself."

"Well, they should be along any minute now. I usually get here early to read the paper and get a cup of coffee."

"Is that them?" Jake said, watching a group of twenty threadbare black men shuffle up the side of the road from town.

"Yeah, Haitians mostly. I ask to see social security cards and don't ask questions. Marilee, the little girl who does the bookkeeping, pays them at the end of the day. If they work, I got no problems with where they're from. Never saw so many fellas named Jean, though."

"I guess it is a pretty popular name from where they come from."

A gray Cadillac pulled into the gravel lot.

"Looks like Mr. Busby has come to drop off Marilee and make his rounds this morning," Ed commented as the front doors of the car swung open and a tall, fiftyish man with blow dried salt and pepper hair and a short sleeved white shirt climbed out.

"Good Morning, Ed," he said with a wave.

"Good Morning, Mr. Busby," Ed said. "Got a lot on the plate today; I figure we take down the tree line so we can get the heavy equipment in"

"Fine, fine. I have to make a few calls before I head on to a meeting this morning." He studied Jake for moment. "And you're?"

"Jake Cavanaugh," Ed cut in, "I hired him on yesterday. He'll be working with the rest of the crew until we need a carpenter. I figured we might as well try to line up the talent early."

"Always thinking ahead, Ed, I sure do appreciate that. Glad to have you aboard, Jack." He turned and hurried up the trailer stairs.

"Morning, Ed," Marilee said.

"Good morning, sunshine. How are you doing this morning?"

Jake smiled at the young blonde girl in tight jeans and pink sweater.

"Jake," Ed said, "this is Marilee, our bookkeeper. Marilee, this here is Jake. He's going to be working with the crew until we need a carpenter."

"Hi, Marilee," Jake said, "you handle payroll? I was wondering where I could get money orders around here."

"There's always the credit union," she offered.

"I was hoping for someplace I wouldn't have to show ID."

"You could try wiring from the convenience store," she said. "I believe they are more expensive, but they don't look too closely. Child support problems? I've heard it before."

"No," Jake said, going to join the morning huddle for assignments, "just trying to help out the family."

Doing the work legitimate tradesmen wouldn't touch in a million years, the crew got by on their off-the-books wages. By day, they sweated it out on the dusty job site with no complaints and eyes watching all newcomers. At night, they gathered in the motel courtyard for cards, booze, and music and hushed tones when a stranger passed their weather-beaten picnic table. They acknowledged Jake's presence when he passed them, but he puzzled them as much as they puzzled him. "Why would someone legit be doin' the shit work?" he heard one of them comment. They had their worries; he had his.

Wednesday after lunch, Ed told them to clear out the brush by the creek. Everyone groaned. Steep banks of thick red clay bordered the tepid, sluggish stream of brown water. The men's feet boots sank in deep with every step, and the soupy earth replied with "sluukk" as they trudged through the muck. Jake teamed up with a big, quiet guy named Henri who had honest muscles that came from work. They ended up on stump detail. Most of the pine stumps came up with a shovel, axe, and a little hard work, but the last one of the day was an old oak with deep roots. Jake should have hitched it up to Old Green to drag it out slow and easy, but at the time, that seemed like too much trouble.

He used the shovel like a lever while Henri hooked the pickaxe and pulled. Henri strained and leaned all his weight back on his pickaxe. The stubborn roots snapped with an explosive pop and he tumbled backwards down the bank with a yelp of surprise.

Jake leapt and slid down the embankment. Henri, lying half in the muddy water, wasn't moving. His eyes bulged in fear, as the large black snake with the familiar mahogany brown cross bands swam toward him. As second-nature, Jake jumped between Henri and the snake. The dark eyes of the snake stared and paused. The long moment hung between the man and the beast. With a hiss from its pristine white mouth, it whipped its powerful tail and swam away. "Lucky day," Jake exhaled. "Moccasins don't give second chances."

He proffered a hand to help Henri out of the mud. Hoots and claps broke the still air. The rest of the crew stood atop the bank.

After dinner, Jake studied the chessboard before him as the cool evening breeze wafted through the screen door of his room. The sharp rap of wood on wood roused him from his thoughts.

“Ey!” said the wiry black man with wooly gray hair. “Jake the Snake, you in there?”

“Yeah,” Jake said, pushing away from the table. “What do you want?”

“Drink, man!” the wiry visitor declared as he strolled into the room. “It isn’t good to be drinking alone, *mon frère*.”

"Sure, I got some bourbon—”

“Bourbon? That rots your guts right out. Here, try some rum. It’s good for what ails you.”

“Thanks, uh…”

“The boys call me Papa Pierre,” the old man said, glancing down at the table. “You play?” He pointed to the chessboard with his gnarled walking stick.

“Sure do.”

“Any good?”

“Good enough, if that’s a challenge.”

“That it is,” Papa said, easing down into the chair across from Jake.

The game went well enough; Papa was one of those subtle players who set up traps to catch you when you weren't paying attention. Midway through the game, Jake spoke up. "So, what's your story, Papa?"

“Stories now, is it, Snake Man?” Papa said and pushed away from the table. He lit a cigar and continued, “Me and the boys are from Florida. Too many immigration men want to send us back to Haiti. Nice up here, plenty of work, too cold in the winter though.” He finished with a rasping cough.

“So, why come here in the first place? America, I mean?”

“Mostly money, some of the boys send money home. Some of us had to leave, got pushed out.”

“Pushed out?” Jake pressed. “What do you mean, like political?”

“Isn’t that simple, Snake man,” Papa said with a wave of his hand. “Sometimes you win the big game, sometimes you lose, but you always got to finish it. You understand?”

“I guess so.”

“So, trade me your story, Jake. You’re not from here, and you got skills. Why are you living this way?”

“I lost couple too many big games. Couldn't afford to lose another one.”

“A wise man knows when to quit. You got any family?”

“Yeah,” Jake said, “I got a brother, Sam. He's a union lawyer.”

“That figures greatly, *mon frère*,’ Papa said with a slap on his knee. “You been losing to your brother?”

“Yeah, he’s the better chess player.”

“So, what'd you play, for money?”

“Yeah," said Jake, "and other stuff…”

"Lost both, eh? So, why'd you leave town?"

"Union blackballed me. No work and there were problems with the construction company Sam and I set up."

Papa spied the small wooden snake alongside the board. He picked up the wooden toy and examined it. "Your work, Snake Man?" he said.

"Yeah, it's for my nephew, Bobby. A replacement for his old one. It got broke."

"How'd it get broke?"

"The way I heard it, Sam lost his temper."

Papa put the toy down and focused on the chessboard. "Yeah, Jake, your game isn't over with, though you are playing the end game," Papa said. "Checkmate."

Jake blinked in surprise. "Uh, good game, Papa, I didn't see that coming."

"Yeah, Jake, you need to pay attention during the end game. The entire world changes in a couple of moves."

"Another game?

"No," Papa said coughing as he stood. "It's late, and we will talk later, *mon frère*." He patted Jake on the back and tottered out of Jake's room.

In the morning, the boys at the job site welcomed him with smiles and slaps on the back. When Jake gained Papa's trust, the rest of the crew accepted him without question. Work went easier; somebody always offered to lend a hand. During the day, he watched the crew fetch Papa water and offer part of their lunches to him. At the end of the day, Papa always stood at the front of the pay line. For a couple of months, Jake found a home amongst Papa and the crew.

One morning in late September, Jake popped his head into the office trailer.

"Good morning, Marilee," he said, "is Ed around?"

"No," Marilee said, shuffling timesheets at her desk, "he's down with a virus. You've been assigned to Sonny Cragle's team until he gets back."

"Great..."

“It won’t be so bad,” Marilee said. “You’re one of the five actual paychecks I cut. Sonny doesn’t care for the day laborers. Just don’t make waves.”

“Marilee,” Mr. Busby said, emerging from his back office, “I’m meeting the boys from Altus at the country club at eight tonight. You’re going to be there, right?”

“Cavanaugh,” Busby said, “Ed’s been telling me what an asset you’ve been. At this rate, I believe we’ll be able to start framing around mid-October. If you plan to stick around, I could always use another team player.”

“If you’ll have me,” Jake said. As he headed for the door, Busby and Marilee lowered their voices to quiet murmurs.

Out on the site, Jake found the scruffy, dirty blond man in cargo shorts and a hard hat surrounded by eight of the crew, including Papa and Henri.

“All right, Cavanaugh, glad you could make it!” Sonny said. “I was just telling the boys that we got trucks coming in with mix and sand. It’s going to be a busy day. You and Henri are going on spray duty. Got to keep the bloodsuckers down. Mr. Busby got investors coming in; don’t want them getting eaten alive.”

“Mr. Cragle, sir,” Henri said, “I’d be willing to switch out with Papa. I can unload a lot more than he can—”

“Thanks, Henri, but I want Papa on the trucks,” Cragle said. “I know how much you folks think of him and I think he’s a better fit unloading the trucks. Any other questions?”

The eight laborers cast sullen looks at each other, but none spoke up.

“Good!” the young team leader said. “If you need me, I'll be over here.” Sonny loped off to a lawn chair underneath a large oak.

Jake and Henri, dressed in bright yellow rain suits and masks, dragged spray rigs around the perimeter, squirting the noxious fluid on anything that stood still. Jake was sure they would be cooked in their own juices before noon.

"Okay, Jake man, time for the hose down,” Henri said as he turned the water hose on Jake.

"Wha—" Jake sputtered as a blast of sun-warmed water hit his face.

"You got to get the poison off you," Henri said as he maneuvered the hose. "Mixed with water, it just makes you sick. The powder will kill you dead."

"Thanks for saving my life. I guess we're even," Jake said, pulling a half-drenched pack of smokes from his shirt pocket. "Cigarette? I think you flushed most of the nicotine out of this pack."

"Thank you, I always believed in living healthy."

"Hey, Henri, what's with Papa? I mean, why does he get treated so well?"

"He's a *houngan.* He keeps spirits happy, so we keep him happy."

"So, why is he here?" Jake said. "I don't see much need for a houn-a-thing around here?"

"I am not privy to most of the details. He got crossways with some other *houngans*. They told him to get out or they'd kill his grandbabies. Best not to be talking about a man with the spirits; he'll always know what you're saying about him. I'd like to get over to the trucks and help out." Henri ground his cigarette out in the red dirt and walked off.

That night during their game, Papa slumped in his chair and assessed the board. His hands trembled every time he moved a piece or lifted his glass of rum.

"How do you keep the spirits happy?" Jake asked.

Papa looked up from the board with a cocked eyebrow. "Well now, Jake boy, you been listening to the boys. Yeah, I deal with the Loas. Most everybody does. I just know I'm doing it."

"How's it work?"

"You see," Papa said, "*les Invisibles* are all around. Here and over there. The thing is, they don't like to do things directly here. It's all done through proxies. You find a fellow with more juice, you make a deal him, and he goes and makes a deal on your behalf to one who favors him. Eventually, word goes up the chain and back down. If you're lucky, you might find a horse of one of the big ones."

"A horse?"

“Sometimes, one of the Loas takes a shine to one of us, not sure of the whys. I guess you say that they’re blessed. I remember one young lady who made a fine living as a matchmaker back home,” Papa said. “Some said Lady Ezuli rode her like a horse and it was Lady Ezuli who chose the pairs to be married off. The rest of us try to catch someone at the crossroads and make a deal. Sometimes it works; sometimes it doesn’t. Horses don’t have that problem.”

“So, you just make a deal and you get what you want, right?”

"Isn’t that simple,” Papa growled. "The Loas are a big family. Like most families, they bicker a lot and do things against each other. One of them may want a man to do this, but another may want the man to do that. In some ways, it’s like this chessboard. A bishop takes out a pawn on the other side, but gets taken by a knight."

"So, nothing ever really gets done, I mean, for real.”

"Ah, *mon frère*, they get done. First, you need to clear the pieces off the board. The endgame brings clarity; that’s why you got to keep your side of the deal simple."

"You mean like this?" Jake said, moving his rook into position. "Checkmate."

"Very good, Jake, you just about ready to finish your game.” Papa doubled over in a set of racking coughs.

"Papa,” Jake started, "are you—”

"Old, just old,” Papa said, rising unsteadily. “My game's almost over, Jake. I’ll be saying goodnight to you." Leaning hard on his cane, Papa tottered out the door.

Long before sunrise, Jake awoke to a pounding at his door. "Jake! You in there, man?" Henri called out.

"Yeah, I'm coming,” Jake said, pulling on yesterday's jeans and staggering to the door.

"They took Papa away,” Henri said, “early this morning, downtown. His coughing got bad. His consumption caught up with him. He was asking for you.”

Jake hated hospitals. The administrators tried to make these places feel clean, like spraying air freshener to cover the smell of rotting meat. Through the maze of hallways of chipped paint, an indifferent nurse with dark circles under her eyes led him to Papa, lying in a bed with tubes running into him.

"Hey, Snake Man," Papa said with a weak smile as he pulled the oxygen mask to the side. "You came, that be good."

"Papa, I didn't know…"

"Hush, mon frère. You weren't supposed to. The Loas got bigger things in store for you. I got words that might help you, but they come with a price. You willing to pay?"

"Sure."

"A free word of advice, *mon frère*. Never make a deal without knowing the price," Papa chuckled with a wet cough. "There's two brothers, some say father and son, but I always figured they're brothers. Baron Samedi, he's bold, brash and strong. Fire and graveyards be his strengths. You want a man dead or ruined, you deal with Samedi. Now, Samedi thinks he should be running things up here, but he got to contend with his brother. Samedi always plays strong, but he's careless sometimes. Damballah—"

"But, Papa, I don't—" Jake cut in.

"Hush, whelp! You got plenty time and I got very little," Papa said. "Now, Damballah, he's the rainbow serpent. He's strong, too, but he's also clever. He got a lot of juice, but don't flaunt it. He's a subtle one and his venom is death."

"I still don't see what this has got to do with me, Papa."

"It got everything to do with you. Samedi is a graveyard spider. Look at your life, Jake. You're stuck fast in his web. How long since you could make any gains? You're just going to repeat and repeat his game. You and everything you care about."

"Okay," Jake, chewing his words carefully. "If I'm caught up in this web, how do I break free?"

"My payment first, Jake. Samedi owns the graveyard and everyone in it. I got crossways with that skull-faced troublemaker one too many times up here. Samedi wants my shade to walk the earth for all times. I got to be buried above ground to rest," Papa exhaled. "Can you promise me that?"

"I promise, Papa."

"*C'est bon*," Papa said. "There's an old Greek fella who said, 'As above, so below.' You and your brother are playing out Damballah and Samedi's game. The only way out for you is to finish the game with him."

"I don't see how…"

"Jake, you got the juice. I saw that the day you faced down that snake. I've been waiting at the crossroads for someone like you to show up. Now that you know the truth, you'll see Damballah's mark on everything; you can't escape that. He won't let his horse fail…" Papa's words trailed off. No convulsions, no final gasp. Papa closed his eyes.

In a haze, Jake drove back to the jobsite. Even in early October, the heat still rippled up from the blacktop. Before leaving the hospital, he'd signed off as Papa's nearest relative in front of the perplexed admitting clerk and called the sole funeral home from the front seat of Old Green.

"There is a niche in the Catholic Brotherhood Mausoleum," the somber director remarked, "but that runs ten thousand. The deceased is listed as indigent. I can hold the body for no more than ten days before burial."

"Let me see what I can do," Jake replied and hung up.

Exhausted, he rested his forehead on the steering wheel. He never held on to more than five hundred dollars at one time, let alone ten thousand; he'd promised Papa something he could never deliver. A mid-morning flash of sunlight drew Jake's attention.

Across the street, he followed the reflection to its source—a display window in the used car lot across the street emblazoned with the logo:

Copperhead Auto Sales
"Buy, Sell, Cash Accepted

Jake blinked, remembering Papa's promise of seeing Damballah's signs everywhere from now on. Cranking Old Green, the starter rattled the engine to life.

Back on the jobsite, Jake pondered his options as he crossed the dusty gravel lot to the trailer. He could try taking up a collection from the crew. Certainly, they would chip in, but he knew that wouldn't be enough for the internment. He could walk away and let the state bury Papa. Across the side of the trailer, he spotted a writhing snake-like shadow and the hairs on the back of his neck prickled. He cast aside that idea immediately.

Inside the cool trailer, Marilee typed furiously on her keyboard.

"Morning, Marilee, I had to take care of some business down at the hospital."

"They're all talking about it," Marilee said. "It's sad he had to pass away so far from home." Her gaze never left the computer screen.

Jake noticed her long-sleeved silk blouse. "New? Seems kind of hot for this kind of weather."

"Mr. Busby is showing the Altus investors the property. He thought I should dress a bit more professional today."

On her left wrist, Jake spotted a fresh rope burn peeking out past the ruffled sleeve. Catching his puzzled look, she pulled her cuff to cover the raw mark. His concerned gaze locked onto her defensive one.

"You know," she said, "it's hard to get a job in a town like this. Let alone a good one."

A hiss of steam from the large percolator broke the moment. On the table covered by white paper sat the welcome treats for the big shot investors. Jake left the trailer, at a loss for what to say.

Outside, he stopped dead, as his phone rang. He made calls, not received them.

"Hello?" he answered.

"Jake," Rachel said, "Sam took Bobby." The hissing static masked the following moment of silence.

"Rachel," he said, "I told you to not to deal with Sam."

"What was I supposed to do? You're not here."

"I go back and I go to jail."

"Jake," she pleaded, "I don't know what to do."

"I can't help," Jake said and hung up.

"Everything ends up in his web," Papa's words rang in his ears. "You, me, all of us. You and everything you love. You're just going to repeat and repeat his game."

At his feet, he saw the twin tracks of a car that had sped into the gravel lot. The tracks ended at the back tires of Busby's pristine Cadillac. Off to the side, Mr. Busby and two men in white golf shirts talked business.

Busby waved Jake over to the trio.

"This is Jake Cavanaugh," Mr. Busby said to the two pale men. "He's going to be our lead carpenter on this project, and, I suspect, if he learns to play ball, he'll be with us a long time."

"Kind of like that secretary of yours last night," one of Busby's associates snickered.

"Enough of that, J.B. We don't want to give Jake the wrong impression," Busby snapped. He turned to Jake and said, "You might have a talk with Sonny about some staffing changes. I believe he's out by his tree."

Jake snaked through the maze of leveled excavations in the red clay, ready for the rows of houses to come, to the last oak next to the creek. Sonny Cragle slumped in his lawn chair next to his orange cooler, watching the crew dig.

"Cavanaugh!" Sonny said, pulling himself to his feet. "Heard you got lead carpenter, that's great."

"Thanks, Sonny," Jake said. Behind him, Henri worked a shovel, shaping a foundation. He felt Henri's stare burn into his back as he talked to the team leader.

"Why don't you come over here to the creek?" Sonny said, ambling over to the large oak, out of plain sight. He pulled a cigar and offered it to Jake. "Smoke?"

"Thanks, but I don't partake."

"Your loss," Sonny said, looking out over the sluggish creek below them. "You're gonna need carpenter assistants, right?"

"I got a couple in mind."

"Them? Fuck 'em, Jake. I guarantee you they'll scatter to the four winds cause Papa up and died on them. Now, I got a couple of cousins—"

"How do you figure they'll scatter?"

"Seen it lots of times with crews. There's always one who holds the rest of them together. Just like killing a snake, you lop off its head and the rest is useless," Sonny said, taking a long toke on his cigar. "If that old fucker couldn't take the heat, he should have stayed out of the kitchen or, in this case, the back of the semi."

Jake kept his temper down. He glared down at the dark, lethargic water five feet below them in the red clay. Just underneath the surface, a dark mass boiled and writhed. "You know what else they say, Sonny?" Jake said.

"What's that?"

"If you can't deal with the snakes," Jake said, striking the heel of his boot on the ground behind Sonny's feet, "stay out of the creek."

The crumbly earth gave way under the foreman's feet and Sonny tumbled headlong into the creek. He screamed when he broke to the surface, covered with a multitude of wriggling, newborn cottonmouths. Before he called for help, a grim smile crossed Jake's face.

Later, as the paramedics loaded the bloated body into the ambulance, Jake explained to the serious-eyed deputy, "He seemed like he'd been drinking a bit and I just didn't think about it when he got too close to the embankment like that."

The deputy weighed Jake's words before asking the gathering crew, "Any of the rest of you see what happened?"

"I did, sir," Henri said, raising his hand.

"What did you see? Speak up!" the deputy barked.

"Mr. Cragle been taking pulls off a bottle most of the day," Henri said. "You can check his cooler over there. The bottle is still in there."

The deputy opened the cooler and dug through the slushy ice and full water bottles. He pulled a half-empty whiskey flask out the cooler.

“I reckon this backs up y’alls story,” the deputy said, flipping his notepad closed. “Damn shame, though.”

As the crew dispersed, Henri looked back at Jake, once. Henri rejoined the crew to dig foundations and Jake stopped at the steel supply shed for a carton of insecticide. As he crossed the parking lot, he passed Mr. Busby and his investors in a heated discussion.

Marilee sat on the steps of the trailer, clutching her knees.

"Tell them to keep my last paycheck," he said to Marilee. "That should cover this."

He lifted the carton of insecticide.

Marilee nodded as she watched the carpenter climb into his green truck and drive off.

Weak and pale, Ed sat at the counter of the Breakfast Breakroom. With the money in hand, he waited for Cavanaugh to show up. The smell of frying bacon and brewing coffee did nothing for his queasy stomach; he yearned to crawl back into bed, but four thousand for Jake’s truck was too good to pass up.

“Afternoon, Ed,” Jake said. “You got the money?”

“Sure do,” Ed said and passed the roll of bills to Jake. “I get sick and everything falls apart on the site.”

“Here’s the title,” Jake said. “I already signed it over to you. If you would just do me two more favors, I’ll be out of your hair forever.”

“What’s that?”

“I need to stop at the funeral home before heading to the bus depot.”

In the cool, dark office of the funeral home, Jake cut the deal.

"It is a fine choice for the deceased," the balding director said. "How do I know you'll come back with six thousand more?"

"If I don't come back in five days with the money, you can bury him as an indigent and still make two thousand in profit." He left the cash on the antique desk in front of the director and left.

At the depot, Jake heaved his duffle bag out of the back of the pickup and pulled the old army fatigue jacket out of the top.

“A little hot for that,” Ed said, sitting in the driver’s seat of Old Green.

“Not for where I’m going.”

“You’re a bit young to have a jacket like that,” Ed said, observing the name patch on the Jake’s breast pocket that read, “Cavanaugh.”

“It was my Dad’s,” Jake said. “What’s on your mind, Ed?”

“I know you’re a jobber, Jake, but you can’t run forever. If you ever decide to settle down, well, it’s not so bad here. We’re not all Cragles and Busbys.”

“Thanks, Ed. I’ll take it under consideration. Get back to bed and take care of Old Green for me.”

“Watch yourself, Cavanaugh,” Ed said. He dropped the clutch and the truck rolled away.

“So, this Jones lawman fellow,” Prof’s companion said, stopping the narrative, “He’s *un méchant dangereux*? Is he not?”

“I can’t beat him.”

“You know the classic fault of such men?”

A flash of recognition crossed Prof’s face as he said, “Hubris…”

"Jake!" Sam said, as he lumbered into the dining room. "You look well for a dead man."

"A dead man who could screw up your inheritance claim, Sam. If I’m alive, you can’t sell the house."

"Trivial," Sam said, as he poured a tumbler of bourbon for himself. "You've been dead for two years on paper, anyway."

"If it were trivial, you'd have sold it already."

"And if you were to come back from the dead, you would be facing nine counts of fraud."

"You'd still have to split the inheritance and explain why your brother was still alive. Who knows? We might get to share a jail cell."

"So, we're at another impasse," Sam said. He looked at the chessboard on the dining room table. "And you want to settle this the old way? Name your stakes."

"Easy enough. I win, Rachel gets custody of Bobby and we split Dad's estate. I lose, you buy me out for ten thousand, you get the chessboard, and you'll never see me again."

"Hedging your bet already?" Sam said. "No matter, I think I can live with those stakes." He removed the flowery painting over the marble sideboard to get to the wall safe behind it and counted out ten crisp bills.

Jake took his seat at the table as Sam laid the money next to the chessboard and took his seat opposite Jake.

"One condition," Sam said. "I get to play black, as always."

"I wouldn't want it any other way. Are you ready to finish this?"

"Patience, Jake," Sam said, lighting his cigarette with a gold lighter. "I want to savor the moment. That's your problem. You never look before you leap."

Jake opened with his king's pawn and said, "Seems to me someone told me the water was deep enough to jump."

"Goes back to your lack of patience," Sam said, moving his king's pawn. "You wanted to get married and have enough money to do it right. I showed you the quick way and told you there would be risks."

"I took the fall and you took the money."

"Those were the stakes of the last game. I told you, never bet more than you can afford to lose." Sam maneuvered his king's knight and took Jake's pawn with a smile. "There's nothing sweeter than first blood. At this rate, it's going to be an awfully short game."

The first loss focused Jake's thoughts. Sixty-four moves were all he had; he hoped sixty-four moves was enough. "So," he said, "how'd you end up with that scar over your eye?"

Slowly, Sam ground out his cigarette in the crystal ashtray. "A good wife knows her place," Sam said. "Sometimes, I have to remind her of this."

Jake tried hard to suppress it, but the wince still crossed his face.

Sam's grin widened. "Don't worry, kid," Sam continued. "You couldn't have handled her, anyway." Sam took Jake's bishop.

"So, you kiss her?"

"Of course, she's my wife."

"Just curious…" Jake said, developing his queen.

"About what?"

"How's my dick taste? After all, you kissed her." Jake glanced up from the board; beads of sweat formed on Sam's reddening forehead.

"I walked into that one, but its human nature. A woman will always go for a lawyer with potential rather than an indigent carpenter," Sam said, grabbing Jake's queen. "I guess that's why it only took me six weeks to hook up with her."

The game ground out at an agonizing pace. Sam attacked; Jake defended. Piece after piece fell to Sam's offense, while Jake took none.

"You know," Sam said, as he grasped a pawn in his thick fingers, "when Bobby was born, I had a paternity test done."

Jake looked at the board. His king, his knight and a pawn stood alone in the center, surrounded by Sam's dark pieces. He bit his lower lip. He needed more time. "And?" he asked.

"Inconclusive, but then again…it's hard to tell paternity between brothers," Sam said, his breathing grew belabored. "You know, I'd accept a stalemate right now. You could walk away with the cash."

"No, we're in the endgame; the entire world changes in a few short moves." Jake moved his pawn to a safe square.

"That's the problem with you, Jake," Sam snarled, as he mopped his sweaty forehead, "You've never had a killer's instinct. You could have taken that bishop." Sam's hand trembled as he grasped his rook to take Jake's pawn.

"Just maybe I'm more of a killer than you know." He moved his knight back to the center of board and the faint church bells chimed to twelve.

"What the hell is this?" Sam gasped. Pain shot through his left arm, and Sam slumped forward.

"My last gambit, Sam, and checkmate," Jake said and pocketed the bills beside the chessboard. He dumped the black pieces back into the plastic bag; he'd clean them off later.

Looking at the safe, he considered the contents. In the end, he closed and locked the safe and replaced the painting. Rachel and Bobby needed a legacy from the two dead brothers. In the foyer, he took one last look at the remains of his old life and closed the front door behind him.

The bone white taxi sat at the curb with its engine purring. Jake walked up to the driver's window and asked, "Can you drop me at the train station?"

"Sorry, buddy," the cabby said from behind his dark glasses, "I already got one fare and I got to pick up another one down at the bus terminal. Trust me; you don't want to go where they're going."

Jake glanced back at the shadowy silent figure in the back seat. "Yeah, sure," he said. "It's clearing up and a walk would do me good."

"Hey, where'd you get that jacket?" the cabby called out. "They don't make them like that anymore."

Jake shed the army fatigue jacket and passed it through the window. "Get rid of the carton in the right pocket and be careful. It's some pretty nasty shit."

"Thanks," the cabby said. "Would it bother you if I took the name tag off?"

"No," Jake said, shouldering his duffel bag, "it's time for me to be someone else." He turned walked into the misty night.

"That's one heck of a story," Prof said.

"Isn't it, though?" his companion said. "The moral this fine tale is this: either you write your story or your story writes you, Professor John Clarke."

"How do you know my name?"

The whispery sound of car pulling up outside broke the conversation.

The old man's eyes lit up, spotting the bone white taxi at the curb. Rising to his feet, the old man said, "Sorry, *mon frère*, my ride's here."

The Jester's Gauntlet

8:26 AM November 7th
The Hotel Mittelmarch
1275 Reed Shore Drive

J.J., could you put this with this morning's outgoing mail?" Prof said, handing the letter to the balding desk clerk.

"Sure, Prof," J.J. said, taking the nondescript envelope. "The University? You take the job offer?"

"No, I don't think it's a good fit."

"Take it, Prof! Who cares if it's not your dream job?" J.J. said. "Do you think the 'March is my first choice for employment?"

"As much time as you spend reading the paper," Prof said, "I would say no."

"This is what happens when you have a Masters in Poli Sci and don't want to move to Washington. Any haven in the storm."

"Normally, I'd agree with you," Prof said, pulling on his gray wrinkled trench coat, "but not in this case."

"Just remember, Prof, any haven in a storm. It's a cold world out there."

Through the creaky revolving door, the frigid wind buffeted Prof. He'd spent half of the night composing the refusal letter and still considered dropping it in the trash can while crossing the shabby lobby. Reinvigorated by the bright autumn morning rush in the street, he steeled himself for what came next; Jones would consider the refusal a declaration of war.

After Lou's funeral, he considered his options. Take Jones' offer and live under his thumb; it looked like prison. The man at the bus depot nailed the second option; if he ran, he would never stop. Jones still held the blood vial and her; she may be a delusion, but she was his delusion. The slick law man built his trap well.

How long did he have until Jones pulled him off the street? He estimated two or three days until Jones got word. He raised his head and relished the strong sun on his face; he would miss this sensation.

Rounding the corner past the back of the hotel, he heard someone pull a coat zipper up and down from the alley. He recognized the tell from his flirtation with crime back in spring.

"Nate?" Prof whispered.

"Sorry, it's Neil Grazer," Nate said. "Mr. Gascon left town a while back."

"So, what can I do for you, Mr. Grazer?" Prof said. "Keep in mind that if I am seen anywhere near a known felon, they'll put me back in State Custody."

"The story sounds familiar," Nate said. "Perhaps we could meet where we last ran into each other. We can compare notes."

Prof nodded and moved on.

At the diner on Cedars Street, Prof took a meeting with his other contact, Nick.

"It all comes back to these vials, Prof," Nick said and put the small container of cut glass on the table, "and they all tie back to Jones...."

"What are they?" Prof said, picking up the vial and rolling it between his fingers.

"Don't know. It's some sort of drug, but from what I've seen, it's something a lot worse. You'd think I'm crazy if I told you."

"Consider who you are talking to. Everyone thinks I'm crazy. I have the paperwork to prove it."

"It changes people," Nick said, recalling the events in the warehouse months earlier. "I walked out of Jones' interview and found one planted on me."

"Seems that Jones said something about personnel changes."

"Well, Judge Adams is out and that dirtball, Cavanaugh, got appointed to the bench."

"The lawyer, Sam Cavanaugh?"

"Yeah, did you know him?"

"Ran into him a while back at the Night Café," Prof said. "He and his associates had a disagreement with the proprietors and got banned."

"Let me guess, Brunet and Reeve."

"I believe so; Reeve didn't care for my company."

"I wouldn't worry about Reeve," Nick said with a chuckle, "or Cavanaugh, either."

"Why's that?"

"Reeve, the mental giant that he is, got busted for trafficking in weapons and coke back in August. It was the highlight of my month. As for Cavanaugh, he died about three weeks ago, nicotine poisoning. They found him in a property he owned off Wrightsway Park three or four days after he passed."

"Sounds bizarre."

"At first, the detectives thought it was Rex. Word has it that there was a rift between the two of them about some investment scam gone bad, but poison wouldn't be Rex's style. They were looking at his widow, Rachel—"

"Rachel Cavanaugh?" Jane interrupted, refreshing Prof's and Nick's nearly-full coffee cups. "Sorry, I couldn't help but overhear."

"You know her?" Nick said.

"Yes," Jane said, "she's a friend."

"I responded to a domestic situation awhile back," Nick said. "It was her and her husband. Sam was a real piece of work."

"You don't think she was involved?"

"Not for me to say," Nick said. He peered at the small gold cross hanging around her neck. "That's new."

"It's...complicated," she said, tucking the cross back into her blouse and moving on to the next table. Nick noted the dark circles under her eyes.

"Curious," Prof remarked. "Everyone's acting strange these days."

"You see Nate, at all?"

"No," Prof lied, "not at all."

"They've issued a BOLO on him. He's going down for the long count. Prof, you're already on Jones' radar. With Stahlmann—"

"I didn't know anything about that," Prof shot back. "I only drank beer and watched sports with him." Prof shook his head and added, "In fact, the only person I can think he was close enough to…"

"Go on, Prof."

"Is Vivian Greene," the blind man said, startled by his own conclusion.

"Down at the clinic, right?"

"Yeah, but you're not a detective and this isn't your case, Nick."

"For what it's worth, I'm still a cop and this is still my beat, even if it's just Traffic. Just stay out of trouble, Prof."

Prof merely smiled at the remark.

Nick strode through the damp, leaf-strewn courtyard of the Ayrshire Clinic, past the smokers waiting for their number. Inside the double-doors, he removed his black service cap and walked up to the admitting desk.

"Can I help you, officer?" asked the young male nurse with black cropped hair.

"Good morning, sir," Nick said. "Is Ms. Greene here?"

"She's in consultations most of the morning. Is this urgent?" A murmur went through the line of patients.

"No," Nick said, "it's not urgent. I can check back later, thanks."

"Nick?" a soft, familiar voice called out through the sea of murmurs.

There stood Demetria, with wheat-blonde hair and a fresh-scrubbed tan face.

"I heard you left town," he said.

"I'm back," she said. Her bright eyes dampened and her smile grew wistful.

"Hey, Goldilocks?" the nurse said. "Is Exam Room 2 ready to go?"

"Taken care of, Terry," Demetria answered, adjusting the neck of her greenish gray scrubs.

Nick caught the glimmer of the delicate gold chain on which the vial of glass hung. His eyes met hers with searching curiosity.

"Can we talk later?" she said. "I have to go back to work."

"Sure, how about The Night Café at eight?"

"Thanks, Nick."

Nick watched her slowly push her mop bucket away and thought of a vibrant butterfly with a broken wing.

On the dusty second floor of the shuttered store on Bianchi Street, or as Prof now referred to it, Les Misérables Motel, Nate hurried about his tasks at hand.

"Should I start calling you Jean Valjean now?" Prof said.

"He got a record?" said Nate, picking through the fine suits on the makeshift clothing rack.

"Afraid so."

"Then I'll pass. I don't need an ID with baggage," Nate said, plucking a suit out of the lineup. "Here try this one."

"So, this is where you've been holing up all this time? Geez, Nate…"

"It's not so bad, Prof. I got a cot and a hotplate. Power's still on. If I want a shower, the YMCA is just up the street. I slide over to the library two blocks over and do my research."

"You realize that this stunt could get us both sent away for a long time," Prof said, pulling on the silk suit jacket.

"Sure, if we get caught."

"That doesn't bother you?"

"You know what bothers me, Prof?" Nate said, tossing a sheaf of printouts onto the cot. "All Jones has got to do is change his mind and we both get locked up. You want to lay odds on that one? It's not a matter of if; it's a matter of when. So, if we're cashing out, let's break the bank."

"Still, this is a big risk just to make a point."

"Risk is part of the game. You either own the game or the game owns you."

Jane huddled in her long, blue wool coat as she crossed the street to Wrightsway Park. The bright afternoon sun failed to comfort her as she approached Iggy, who perched upon the wrought iron bench in the middle of the park. Sheridan and Lamar loitered about in their ill-fitting suits a safe distance away.

"Jane!" Iggy said, hopping up from his seat. "Thank you so much for agreeing to meet with me."

"Good afternoon, Iggy," she said, keeping an arm's length away from the little man in the golden overcoat and white silk scarf.

"I guess your reaction should be expected," he said, looking down. "Revelations such as this, well, they are never easy."

"So why did you ask me here? Are you going to—"

"No, Jane, nothing of the sort," Iggy said, waving his slender hands in front of him. "First, I am not here on Vic's behalf. I am here because I was worried about you."

"Me?"

"It's obvious that you're not sleeping, and one can also assume you have been barricading yourself inside your apartment from sunset to sunrise."

"And you wouldn't have done the same? Considering what I know?"

"Considering what you know, yes," Iggy sighed, "but you know less than you think."

"For example…"

"If Vic wanted to cause you harm, would it not seem that he has had many opportunities already?"

"True, but now I know what he is—"

"You think he must do away with you? Am I correct?" He ran his fingers through his receding hairline of fiery red. "Jane, individuals of a, shall we say, certain persuasion, hide in plain sight. Occasionally, someone mundane realizes we do exist. What do you think happens?"

"I'm not sure."

"Nothing, Jane! We're legends and folktales; everybody knows we don't exist. To say otherwise makes you look like a lunatic. Jane, no one is going to come after you, especially not Vic."

"Vic…"

"He is planning to take his leave of the city. Frankly, I'm surprised he stayed this long. I venture to say, the only reason he stayed was you. You are the last person on the planet he would see come to harm." Iggy said. "Jane, forget about him, get some sun and get some sleep."

For the first time in many nights, Jane's drawn features relaxed, as she exhaled. She hugged Iggy and whispered, "Thank you."

"One more thing, Jane, dear," Iggy whispered into her ear on tiptoe. "A bit of interior decorating advice, hmmm?"

"What's that?"

"I'd do away with the garlic braids in your apartment windows. It's homey, but it looks like a bit like a delicatessen."

The haggard young man in the silver rental car clicked three more pictures of the couple—a short, red-haired man in a bright yellow overcoat and a tall brunette in a navy-blue coat. He tossed the camera into the passenger seat and made a call. "Dmitri?" he said. "I have confirmed the bait for the dragon."

How do I let him talk me into these things? Prof thought and shook his head. He shifted from foot to foot as Nate announced in a snooty lockjaw tone, "Raffles, party of five."

"Very good, sirs, if you will come this way," replied the maître d' of the Silver Oaks.

In the background, the chamber quartet spun its arrangement of Rossini's *Thieving Magpie* into the sedate atmosphere of the dining room. A waiter took Prof's arm and guided him through the sea of white tablecloths to the plush velvet chair waiting for him. Amidst the whispers of civil conversations, Prof relished the irony of the moment; he never imagined dining at the Silver Oaks, even when gainfully employed. Now, blind, broke, and under surveillance by the authorities, he sat amongst the city's movers and shakers, courtesy of a known felon.

"You ready to play, Mr. Lupin?" Nate said, setting up his laptop, a souvenir from his experiment with honest work.

Prof winced behind his glasses at Nate's exaggerated patrician tone. "Mr. Raffles," Prof said, "are you sure that a presentation such as this wouldn't be better suited in one of the private rooms?"

"Tried that," Nate whispered. "Fifty got us a center table. The maître d' wanted a cut of the proceeds for a private room. His name is Bob; I know him from high school. You play your part and we come out of this on top."

Nate's smile shined to life as his three marks filed in. His hours of sifting through the various vanity directories, corporate profiles, and credit reports yielded gold nuggets—three insulated trust-funded dupes who wanted to make a killing. Easy money always hooked the biggest fish.

"Ja, Mister Raffles," said a pale man with slicked back red hair, taking Nate's hand, "I am most excited to hear what you have to say."

"Thank you, Mr. Hästskit," Nate said. "I think you will be most impressed."

"I, too, Mr. Raffles," remarked a youthful man with long dark curls and poet's eyes, "have been looking forward to this presentation."

"Thank you, Mr. Zookléptis."

"Is this where I can make a pile of money?" a man with iron-gray braids, beaded headband and alligator cowboy boots said loudly, pumping Nate's hand. "Joe Coyote."

The other two marks' expressions soured at Mr. Coyote's brash introduction. Each took a seat around the table and Nate appraised the array of custom-made business suits and gold accoutrements. As he inhaled deeply to catch the scent of money, his pulse quickened. A fancier table and higher stakes, but he still owned this game.

Nate's internal rhythm synchronized to the task at hand, but his tempo tripped when he glanced to the host's desk. His best buddy, Bob, escorted Special Agent Jones, all smirk and strut, to the private dining room. Nate held his breath; with any luck, Bob would seat Jones facing away from the main dining room. Nick deflated as the big lawman took the seat facing Nate's tableau. Upon spotting Nate, Jones' light-hearted expression dropped to a hard scowl. With the stakes boosted to the stratosphere, Nate reeled from the rush. Leaning down, he whispered to Prof, "Play your part well, Mr. Lupin; we got a special member in the audience, tonight."

Jones arrived late for the dinner meeting, as planned. He wanted to give Mary and Tanya time to soften up the players before he made his pitches. He followed the maître d' past the mosaic frescoes of subdued pastoral scenes to the doorway of the reserved room. Peals of flirtatious laughter spilled from the doorway; he grinned. The girls and the wine already worked their magic.

He took his seat at the long table and surveyed his dinner companions. Of course, Mary Sawney's pregnancy only increased her radiance; she prattled with bright eyes to Phil Lyons, the local anchorman. Mrs. Collins, the pale, brittle wife of Reverend Collins, spoke in a low, desperate tone to Dr. Clayton, one of the board members of Sapienta Northwest, who nodded and leered. Meanwhile, Tanya, Mary's protégé, engaged in lively patter with Marv Teague, Rich Allen's replacement at Augustus Jones, followed Tanya's slim arm trailing underneath the table; he guessed it ended in the lap of smiling Reverend Collins. With a little patience, more cocktails and few more lapses in judgement, Jones expected his scenario to play out without a hitch with a few more mules in his stable before the night's end.

Looking past pudgy Marv at the end of the table, Jones assessed the main dining room; more opportunities sat out there. In time, he would seize them all. A broad sweep of an arm and a clear confident voice caught his attention; his jaw clenched. Dead center of the dining room, Gascon, the seedy con artist, addressed a table of men in sharp suits huddled about a laptop on the table. On closer inspection, he spotted that blind loser, Clarke, seated next to Gascon. Upon recognizing Jones, Gascon's quick gawk turned to a smirk. Bending down, he whispered to Clarke, who promptly smiled and pushed his dark sunglasses up the bridge of his nose with his middle finger.

"You see, gentlemen," Nate concluded, "The Merdescheisten Process is no longer a theory, but inevitability. Organic methane generation is a renewable, cost-effective procedure that will revolutionize the energy industry. With our fund, we can take advantage of not only directly investing in the industry, but using commodities such as pork, oil, cattle and fertilizer." He glanced over at Prof to drive the sale home.

"A.J.," Prof said, "that's a great presentation as always, but as a member of the steering committee, I have misgivings."

"Well, Arsène," Nate said, "voice your concerns. That's why you are here."

“The returns are to be great, sure, but just being an accredited investor by SEC standards is not enough. I just feel that given the nature of this kind of investing and the few remaining slots for charter investors…” Prof said, turning to address the other men seated. “Well, this may be a bad fit for you, gentlemen.”

“Well spoken, Mr. Lupin,” Nate conceded. “I will remind you that these men are considered super-accredited by our fund’s standards.”

“A.J., you’re a brilliant hedge fund manager, but you know just meeting the financial standards, no matter how admirably, does not show they have the acumen for this type of investment,” Prof said, standing up and giving a slight nod. “Gentlemen, I take your leave.” One of the hovering waiters took his arm and led him to the front door.

Nate scanned the spacious dining room, now abuzz with well-dressed diners pulling out their cellphones. He glanced up to the small dining room and gave a wink to Jones. “Now, gentlemen,” he addressed the three men, “you have heard my presentation and you have heard from Mr. Lupin. Take what he said very seriously.”

“I, for one,” Hästskit said, slamming his snifter of eighty-year-old armenagac next to the tall stack of plates, “am a bit insulted he dare imply I am a novice investor.”

” My friend, calm down,” the long-haired Mr. Zookléptis said. “All anyone knows about you is that you like to breed exotic animals and, well, that’s about it.”

“One should talk, flower boy,” Hästskit replied tersely, as his face reddened. “You’re just a messenger boy for daddy and your uncles.”

“If you two peckerwoods are finished,” Coyote said, pulling out his buckskin wallet, “I’m going to put my money where my mouth is.”

Nate’s eyes lit up as he watched Coyote swipe his glossy black credit card through the reader attached to Nate’s laptop. Mentally, he followed the money through the electronic labyrinth from the Cayman Islands, the Philippines, South Africa and finally, a bank wire from Ireland would zap a pile of clean cash to his account twenty-four hours from now. Hästskit and Zookléptis followed Coyote's lead. Nathan's exhilaration charged the air of the dining room.

"Look, Murray," Marv Teague spouted into his cellphone, "get me everything you can find on this Merdescheisten Process. If we can get in on the ground floor, we can make a killing here." He clicked the phone off and looked about the table at his silent dinner companions, staring at him. "What?" he said.

"Kind of rude to do that at the table," Dr. Clayton said, "and not sharing the opportunity with your friends…"

"You give me one tip to a pharmaceutical," Marv said, "and you think I owe you the world."

"Doctor," Mrs. Collins said, tugging on Dr. Clayton's sleeve, "I really need that prescription. My regular doctors won't refill it."

"Ladies, gentlemen," Schechter interjected, "I don't think this is the time or the place—"

"Oh, Aaron," Mary said with a smirk, "don't mind Mindy. She just needs her meds to stay disconnected."

"Disconnected?" Mrs. Collins said, glaring back at Mary. "You want to know why I need to stay disconnected?" The frail, demur lady rose to her feet and grasped the pristine linen tablecloth. With a solid yank, the tablecloth sailed off the glass-top table, sending the crystal wine glasses and candelabras tumbling, clattering and shattering. The crashing unveiling revealed Tanya's manicured hand wrapped around Reverend Collins engorged organ. "That's why," Mrs. Collins said, pointing. "That is why I need to stay disconnected."

"Maybe if you weren't such a drugged-out cow," Tanya countered, "Dickie might still be interested in you."

"Whore!" Mrs. Collins screamed, picking up a half-filled bowl of bouillabaisse and lobbing it at Tanya. In that moment, every peccadillo or half-imagined slight surfaced at the table and each member of the dinner party armed themselves with whatever was at hand, save for Jones, who sat at the head of the table.

"Gascon," he snarled through gritted teeth.

From the center of the dining room, Nate watched Jones' dinner party degenerate into chaos. The other diners turned to regard the spectacle of splattering food and wine with murmuring interest, and the chamber quartet ended their serenade with a sudden squawk.

"Ah, Mr. Raffles," Bob the harried maître d' said. "As I see that your party has left, there comes to the matter of the bill." He handed the small leather-bound folder to Nate.

"Very good," Nate said. He opened the folder and blinked. Looking up, he saw the three empty seats surrounded by stacks of finished dishes and empty wine bottles. He'd focused on his presentation so much that his marks had run up a tab for three thousand dollars. Calmly, he packed up his laptop and prayed that Prof would hold up his end of the bargain.

"Hello, 9-1-1?" Prof drawled into the disposable cellphone by the canal walkway. "I don't know if this is anything…I, mean, it could be a floor show for all I know. I just saw a couple of fellas walking into that Silver Oaks restaurant carrying rifles and wearing vests." Prof clicked the phone off and chucked it into the canal. He sighed; for better or worse, he'd declared which side he was on and Jones knew it now. He headed back to the 'March to pack a few things.

Nate ticked off the seconds, yet heard no sirens. He chided himself for this unseen wrinkle; the marks nailed him with a 'dine and dash.' Any minute, Bob would come back from the fracas in the private dining room and demand payment. High school friend or not, fast talk wasn't going to work this time. He always hated this final option. Reaching into his jacket pocket, he retrieved the small plastic cup. Faking a cough, he downed the syrupy contents. He braced himself as his stomach started to twist and rumble.

The thundering gout of vomit welled up from the pit of Nate's stomach as he doubled-over and spewed the noxious yellowish jet across the room. He pivoted on his heels to ensure wide-area coverage. Cries of disgust rose around him as diners bolted to their feet. Again, his stomach heaved. On the fourth spasm, he realized he no longer hurled food, but live, wriggling earthworms. He trembled as he felt the rippling in his lower intestines. A bolt of green gas shot from his rear end with a buzzer-like rip. Another followed it, only this time, Nate strategically aimed the blast toward a serving cart with a silver bowl of flaming Cherries Jubilee. The fireball ignited the front drapes, which set off the fire alarms and the sprinklers. Spent, Nate collapsed to the floor and watched a horde of drenched rats skitter out from their hiding places. The faint wail of sirens reminded Nate to crawl through the vomit, water, worms and rat droppings to the front door. The high heels and dress shoes of the patrons pounded and clipped around him.

Black smoke billowed out of the restaurant as the fire alarm lights strobed. Once through the glass front doors, Nate stood up amidst the panicked clambering of the fleeing customers. The bright red fire engines thundered up with their flashing lights. The metro police, of course, parked their cars crazily askew in the street with their weapons drawn. He buttoned his ruined jacket and proceeded towards the line of police with the rest of the throng, faintly hoping to save some vestige of his dignity. As he approached the column of grim-faced cops, he smiled; as the last of a protracted line of cons, this had truly been epic finale.

Expecting to be cuffed and stuffed, Nate blinked in surprise as he drifted through the skirmish line unapprehended. He clutched his stained laptop case tightly to his chest as he crossed the street. His three marks—Hästskit, Zookléptis and Coyote—sat on the bench, facing the debacle. Their stony expressions judged his every move. As he approached, all three stood and applauded.

"A brilliant understanding and application of bodily fluids," Mr. Zookléptis appraised.

"Runner," Mr. Hästskit addressed Mr. Zookléptis, "I was worried when your son submitted this candidate back in spring."

"I know, I know, Odinson," Zookléptis demurred. "The youth does have a tendency toward wine, women and song, but he does have an undeniable eye for talent."

"Can we get down to business?" Coyote cut in. "Okay, he passed the test. I don't see why we had to wear these ugly-assed skins, though." He looked down at his fine business suit and shook his head.

"We were undercover, Coyote," Zookléptis said. "At least you could have come up with an alias…"

"Couldn't be bothered," Coyote said with a wave of his hand. "Anyway, kid," Coyote said, turning to Nate, "you want the gig or not?"

"Doing what?"

"Making sure the world doesn't turn into that," Coyote said, pointing to the smoking Silver Oaks building. "We shake up the ant farm to keep things interesting."

"And make a little money on the side," Hästskit said, donning his sunglasses. "If you're really interested, I got this sweet Ponzi scheme using fire giants and a squirrel as shills—"

"Not now, Fire Keeper," Zookléptis said. "So, Nate, you in?"

"Know where I can get a new suit?" Nate said.

"I know this guy in Bangkok…"

The four of them faded from view.

Nick and Demetria sat in the flickering candlelight of the booth in the Night Café. Neither touched their meal or drank much beer. The jazz trio played a meandering, quiet tune, unusual for a Saturday night. Even the pool tables stood deathly quiet.

"You've changed, Demetria," Nick said.

"I thought I found what I wanted."

Nick nodded; in her eyes, where he once saw brightness, he saw a haunting sadness. "Did you find it?"

"No."

"Ms. Fox worried about you when you lit out like that. Have you gone to see her yet?"

"No, I couldn't face her after what I did. I don't want her or anyone to know."

"Demetria," Nick said, "I know about the vials. Like the one around your neck. I've seen what they do to people."

She locked on Nick's steady gaze; he'd changed, too. His solemn expression chased away her memory of the good-hearted cop, yet his clear-eyed compassion still shone through. "Nick," she said, "you don't know the half of it."

"I don't need to know all of it. Maybe someday. Right now, I need to know who gave you the vial."

"I don't know his name, but I met him right here in the café."

The trio's set ended with light applause. Out of the corner of his eye, Nick watched the sun-blond trumpet player saunter over to their table.

"Good evening, Nick," the man in the biker vest said.

"Evening, Gabe. Great music, as usual."

"Thanks, Nick. Who's your friend?"

"Demetria, meet Gabe," Nick said. "He's our resident bike mechanic, courier, jazz man, bouncer and all around good guy. Did I miss anything?"

"Nice to meet you, Gabe," Demetria said.

"A pleasure, Ma'am," Gabe said. His gazed dropped to the vial hung about Demetria's neck. "Didn't I see you in here a while back?" he asked.

"I used to come in here for lunch occasionally when I worked down on Wrightsway."

"You looked different, didn't you?" Gabe recalled. "Dark hair…I'd just started working here. I think you were having lunch with that cop."

"Jones?" Nick interrupted.

"That's the one," Gabe pronounced in a voice of thunder. "Gird yourself in righteousness, Nicholas, for soon, you will be called to battle."

Nick's fists curled.

Gabe looked Demetria in the eyes and said gently, "Little one, the way to the light is steep and hard; do not despair for thou art loved."

As his words echoed in her ears, Demetria's heart filled with hope and her burden of shame dropped from her shoulders.

"Anyway, that's just what I heard, kids," Gabe said.

Dazed by the weight of the Message, Nick and Demetria sat in silence. Gabe touched each of their shoulders and they snapped out of their trances. "Nice seeing the both of you," Gabe said. "I got to get ready for my next set." He walked back to the stage.

Nick gritted his teeth and a bright blue spark leapt from his clenched fist to the brass candleholder on the table.

Wide-eyed, Demetria's eyes met his.

"Don't worry about it," Nick said. "It happens these days when I get angry."

Jerry Sawney sat in his easy chair in the bright living room. "Sure, Bill," he said on the phone, "I'll get warrants for Gascon and Clarke. I'll walk them through myself."

He endured his boss's stream of curses with closed eyes.

"I know how important it is. I'll go downtown as soon as Mary and Tanya get back. I don't know, they said they were going to a charity auction. Right, I'm on it."

He hung up the phone and looked down at his lap. Enough was enough.

He spread the dark blue silk handkerchief over his left knee. He'd found it while rummaging through Mary's "mommy" purse looking for a pen. In the center of the handkerchief was a splotchy white stain. The gold thread of the initials "AS" glimmered in the corner of the cloth. Judge Schechter tucked one in his breast pocket every day. Schechter's smirking words, "Your wife was a remarkable woman," stung his ears.

He checked his watch one last time; the girls would be home soon. His service revolver was perched on his right thigh. Picking it up, he popped open the cylinder and loaded three bullets.

The Lady in the Scorpion Shoes

5:17 AM December 5th
Warehouse 17
775 Industrial Road

Underneath the weak incandescent lights of the dusty warehouse, Vic packed the last crate. Not much really—just a few suits and his stack of Bogart DVDs. He wondered how Bogie would have resolved this; picturing the shock and revulsion in Jane's eyes that night at the Crucible Club, he knew there would be no heartfelt moment at the foggy tarmac for them.

Realizing the futility of explanation, he'd kept his distance from her. With time, he hoped Jane would forgive and forget him. He sighed at his own hubris; he broke his rule of getting personal and Jane paid the price. Iggy, the idealist that he was, had approached Jane against his wishes and brought her some semblance of comfort. Vic took solace in Jane's relief.

In three hours, the air freight company would pick up the stack of shipping crates, including the long one filled with rich, dark Romanian earth, and he would be off to London. A prospect of a fresh start elsewhere provided hope that he would forget about Jane, too.

Sniffing the air, he paused; his taut senses confirmed what the security system failed to catch—several men lurking outside. He reached for his nylon flight bag, thankful he hadn't packed it yet. *Professionals*, he thought.

The steel garage door lifted with a deafening squeal of the power jacks. Eight men in black fatigues and ski masks scuttled under the mangled door. Crossbow bolts zinged and whizzed past Vic from seven of them.

The eighth, in heavy gloves and apron, test-flared his flamethrower and advanced. Vic charged the one brandishing the flamethrower and side-rolled past him. Bringing his forearms up, Vic slammed through the skirmish line and sprinted through the door. He allowed himself a quick grin. The yelps of the skirmishers caught in the arc of the flame stream reassured Vic he still retained his battle skills. One the bolts sank deep into Vic's back; shifting his form, he was met with wracking pain. "Dammit," he breathed, "either ash or hawthorn." Whoever these were, they knew their target.

He rounded the corner into another of the soldiers, this one carrying an AK-47 and wearing night vision goggles. Vic's right cross connected with the chin of the surprised youth, who spun to the ground. Vic spotted the blood-red Maltese cross on the shoulder of the black fatigues. An order he thought long extinct…

Outmatched, Vic bolted down an alley. Without blood or native earth, he could neither heal nor rest, let alone shift forms. The sky already slipped from black to a dark blue. Time ran tight; he needed shelter.

Across the empty streets, he sped out of the warehouse district. At Bianchi, he regarded a long row of empty storefronts. In the air, he caught a familiar but unexpected scent. He chose a debris-strewn alley and sprang up to the rusty second-story fire escape. The steel security bars came away with a two-handed tug and Vic slid through the window. The startled man sat up in the army cot and scanned the room with vacant eyes. "Who's there?" he asked.

"Professor Clarke," Vic said, "I need your help…"

"Mr. Teppish?" Prof said. "Jane's friend, correct?" He reached to switch on the small battery-powered lantern.

"No need, Professor," Vic said. "I see well enough in the dark."

"So, what can I help you with?" Prof said, wiping the sleep from his eyes.

"Well," Vic said, placing a knife in Prof's right hand and moving his left to the bolt imbedded in Vic's back, "could you remove this for me?"

"Vic," Prof said, "this is something for a surgeon. You need a hospital."

"No," Vic said, "not in the case. Please, professor."

Just before eight, Prof left Les Misérables Motel for the first time in daylight in five days. Since the Silver Oaks incident, Prof had moved into Nate's vacated digs in the old store. He hoped to stay free for just a bit longer. It wasn't much of a hope, but it was all he had. Living rough and greasy, he felt like he had slid back to last winter.

After digging the bolt out of Vic's back, Prof had helped him into a closet, which Vic sealed with the zips of duct tape. Crouching next to the door, Prof listened and nodded at Vic's instructions.

"This is insane, Vic."

"I am sorry I have gotten you involved in this, professor, but at this point, you are my only option."

"Okay," Prof said, "I guess I just go with the madness. It's been working for me so far."

"In my bag, there's an envelope. If you would take that to the Ayrshire Clinic and ask for Ms. Vivian Greene. She'll know what it's for."

"I know Ms. Greene."

"Next, I need you to go to Stahlmann's Mechanics on—"

"How did you know Lou?"

"I've done business with him time to time."

"You may not know this, Vic. Lou died six weeks ago."

"No, I hadn't talked to him in weeks. I've been planning to leave."

"Does Jane know?"

"Yes, Professor Clarke," Vic said. "She learned about my past. I thought it was best for both of us…to end it. How did Mr. Stahlmann die?"

"The cops aren't sure if it was a robbery or something else. I used to hang out and listen to the games with Lou. I didn't know about his business."

"He was very discreet; that's why I worked with him. You said this was six weeks ago?"

"The last day of September."

"That is troubling," Vic said. "He was keeping something for me."

"The shop is under lock until the public auction."

"I doubt he would have kept it on site," Vic said.

"You know," Prof said, digging through his battered suitcase, "I got this in the mail just after Lou died." He found the small manila envelope. "If you could undo some of that tape…" He slid the envelope under the door.

Vic laughed. "Holden Forevict," he said, "properly read is, 'Holding for Vic T.' Lou's faith was certainly well-placed, professor."

Well placed, Prof thought, as he pushed the door open and the chime sounded. *He trusted a blind, crazy, drunk before he trusted Vivian?*

Prof entered the U Store It Services on Corral Street.

"Good morning, sir," the young clerk said. "How I can I help you today?"

"Box 4545," Prof said, slapping the key upon the counter.

At 10 AM, Jane paused before the foreboding, iron-bound doors of the Crucible Club with Vic's words about confronting your troubles head-on ringing in her ears. She lifted and dropped the massive wrought iron knocker once. The doors groaned open and Sheridan or Lamar emerged from the darkness. She never figured how to tell the hulking bodyguards apart.

"Ms. Davis," the large man with the shaved head rumbled. "Good morning, good to see you."

"Good morning, Sheridan," Jane said, hoping she'd guessed correctly. "Is Iggy in?"

"Always in," Sheridan said, gesturing Jane to follow across the dark atrium. "Dining room."

Jane followed the plinking, bittersweet melody issuing from the archway. On the dais stage raised above the forest of upturned chairs on tables, Iggy sat in front of the glossy black concert piano under a harsh single spotlight from above.

"Good morning, Jane," he said, closing the piano keyboard. "You seem well-rested since the last time I saw you."

"Thank you, Iggy. It was your talk. Is Vic…?"

"No, Jane," the little restauranteur said, checking his watch. "By my estimation, he is already in the air to London and after that, who knows."

"I was hoping to—"

"I understand. I have had my share of unresolved partings. Trust me; he will always remember you kindly. I think you bought him some time."

"Time?"

"Vic is in a war of attrition; eventually, he'll become a monster. That's the way it works. For some, it takes more time, but eventually, they all become monsters.

"So, how did I help him?"

"It's a matter of staying connected with people and things you love. I once knew of a young man who left his wife and son to go seek something he thought was important at the time. After many years, he returned home to find only sand. He accomplished legendary feats, but lost the only thing that mattered," Iggy said and turned back to his piano. "Thank you for pulling my friend away from that fate."

"I had no idea. I thought vam—"

"Never use that word around him. He absolutely despises it. I assume you are here to check in on Rachel, no? She's in the office," Iggy said. "Now, if you'll excuse me, I do have to finish my rehearsal for tonight."

"Thank you, Iggy," she said, excusing herself from the entertainer.

She knocked on the doorway of the small dark office off the atrium.

"Jane!" Rachel said, looking up from her computer. "It's good to see you." In the corner, her little black dress hung on the coat rack and her patent leather pumps sat underneath, ready for this evening's service. The drawn lines on Rachel's face had disappeared and the bright twinkle in her brown eyes returned.

"I heard from friends about Sam, Rachel. I'm sorry."

"He dealt with shady people. I'm thankful it never led back to our home." She fiddled with a small, carved snake brooch attached to her green sweatshirt and said, "I think that karma caught up with Sam."

"Are you in trouble? In these cases—"

"No, Jane. They brought me in for questioning, but I was here that night. Iggy and the entire staff vouched for me. On top of that, Iggy unleashed Mr. Fafnir, his lawyer. I don't know what Mr. Fafnir said to the detectives, but I was out in forty-five minutes."

"So, you're going to keep working here?"

"I don't have to work. Sam left the entire estate in a trust fund for Bobby," Rachel said, "but I feel like we belong here. For the first time in a long time, Bobby and I have family."

"But, here? With these...people?"

"They've watched out for me far more than Sam ever did. It may not be the perfect solution, but it works."

"How's Bobby doing? I mean losing his father..."

"He's doing well now that Mr. Fafnir got him released from foster care. Instead of the afterschool programs, he's been coming here. Iggy wouldn't hear of leaving Bobby with strangers. Monday, Allen, the saucier, showed him how to julienne potatoes. Yesterday, I caught Bobby in the parking lot drawing little trumpets on the back wall with chalk. I was about to take away his television privileges, but Lamar came up and explained that he and Sheridan were teaching him cuneiform, and he learned quickly. Although they both agreed he was a bit young to learn Minoan Linear A."

"The Crucible Club has a new mascot?"

"It seems that way. It's been good for Bobby…and Iggy. He was showing Bobby chords on the piano just before you came in. I don't think I've ever seen Iggy happier."

"Rachel, I came here today about Vic."

"I can't help you. The only times he was here was with you. After that night a month ago, I don't think he wanted to come back here. Too many bad memories, I guess."

"I know," Jane said, lowering her eyes. "I got a call from Dr. Aksoy this morning to confirm my review next month. I would have expected an assistant to make that call, but he did ask about Vic."

"The only time he met Vic was back in May, when Iggy—"

"That's why I came in to check with Iggy. Something doesn't seem right."

"Well, I will let you know if I hear anything. By the way, Jane, I love your shoes."

Jane looked down at her scorpion-adorned shoes and said, "Reyna talked me into buying them back when I was having trouble. I think they've been good luck."

Rachel thought about the tiger opal earrings in the top drawer in her desk and said, "Reyna's got knack for those kinds of gifts."

Rex watched the young brunette exit through the massive doors of the Crucible Club from the seat of his Allente. He opened the disposable phone and said, "She's heading north on Bessemer, probably to the bus stop."

He pulled himself out of the Cadillac and strode across the street to the former foundry of crumbling red brick. He needed to mark his fresh territory. As promised, he passed some cash and Jones's vials out to some hungry kids who wanted to make their bones. Following the leads given, he'd targeted the machine shop down on Reed Shore; the old guy was running guns, but the kids hit a dry hole. At least he'd taken out one of the Syrian's as payback for the casino. The other tip led to this place; the boys he sent here disappeared. He never expected that. Insurance paid well, but he deserved cut a bigger piece of this pie. Whatever racket the little freak ran, he either had to deal Rex in or suffer the consequences.

That bent Fed, Jones, had left him hanging after Rex did all the heavy lifting. No visits or returning his calls. Over the months of the war, he'd taken a beating; first, the casino going up in flames, then Saul getting busted. Fuck Jones; he found contacts of his own. He heard the stories, but decided they were bullshit until the Saturday afternoon after he hit the machine shop and the club.

"Mr. Brunet?" a withered priest in a black cassock asked, standing in the middle of the storefront casino. "May I have a moment of your time?"

"Yeah, Father," Rex said, looking up from the meager receipts from Friday night. He looked forward to tearing Sonny a new one for letting the priest in.

"It has come to the attention of my order," the priest said, "that your ends match ours."

Rex placed a finger to his temple. Priest or not, no one walked in his place and demanded shit. Sonny made his move from behind. The priest spun and jammed his brittle palm into the solar plexus of Sonny's chest and the hulking tough dropped to the linoleum.

"Now, Mr. Brunet," the priest continued, turning back to Rex, "my sect is not one to be taken lightly."

Sanctioned by the Church, Rex thought, sauntering into the stone atrium, "*It was a license to steal. All for watching some waitress.*"

"Good Afternoon, Mr. Brunet," the short, goggled-eyed proprietor said. "How may I help you today?"

"Mr. Lanza, I'm glad to see you doing so well, even though our mutual friend has left town."

"We do what we must," Iggy said. "However, please remember that my friendship with the Syrian was based on mutual respect, not patronage."

"Of course, it's all about respect. I trust you will show me the same, as well."

"You sent negotiators last time, Mr. Brunet; did they not deliver my message?'

"No," Rex said, "seems they never came back; however, I have other friends. You like your liquor licenses? Or how about health inspections?"

"I have lawyers for that sort of nonsense," Iggy said with a dismissive wave. "Frankly, Mr. Brunet, I am beginning to find you tedious."

"Tedious?" Rex growled, advancing upon Iggy.

From the dining room, Lamar and Sheridan rumbled in behind Iggy.

"My associates," Iggy said, "are quite skilled at removing unwanted rubbish."

"Iggy," Rachel said, emerging from her office, "I need this signed—"

"Rachel!" Rex said. "I've been so worried about you since Sam passed away."

"Thank you for the wreath, Mr. Brunet," Rachel said. "I'm sure that Sam would have appreciated it."

"Has the estate been settled yet?"

"In one hundred eighty days, or that's what Mr. Fafnir told me. There's really not much there."

"I know, "Rex said. "It's all in a trust for Bobby. I was with him when he set it up. The thing is, Sam passed away owing me a sizeable amount."

"I can give you Mr. Fafnir's number and you can declare a lien if you have the paperwork."

"There's the thing, Rachel. It was a verbal agreement. You don't want little Bobby going through life thinking his dad was a deadbeat, do you?"

"Bobby's smart, Rex," Rachel shot back, "and he's a good judge of character, not just his father's."

"Mr. Brunet," Iggy said, stepping between Rex and Rachel, "say what you want about me, but my employees are sacrosanct. You have overstayed your welcome on my premises. Good day, sir."

Rex returned the stern gaze of the wispy little restauranteur. He glanced up at the two behemoths towering behind Iggy, waiting for one word from their boss. "All right, Lanza," he said, "this is the last time you get in my way." He left the atrium.

"Why, Mr. Brunet," Iggy called out, "for once I am in total agreement with you."

As the massive front door closed, Iggy turned to his stocky bodyguard and said, "Sheridan?"

Sheridan cocked his eyebrows and snorted in acknowledgement.

As Jane waited at the bus stop, she considered Iggy's words and attempted to reconcile her heartache with her fear. From the night back in February when Prof told her "to take a chance," she'd cherished her moments with Vic—the late-night jazz club haunts, the moonlit walks alongside Gulf Canal, and the whispered exchanges in her brass bed. Each sweet memory was now tainted by the sight of Vic crouching on that cold stone floor, red-eyed and snarling. The gentle man she loved was a monster. She'd seen the signs, but ignored them, much like she had with Rich. But unlike with Rich, she dared to hope for something more with Vic.

For many nights after she fled the Crucible Club, she'd cowered in her apartment, waiting for him to come for her. At any time in the last year, he could have taken her, yet he let her live. Seeing Rachel smiling again after the months of her own ordeals gave her pause. Rachel had taken a chance and found shelter and acceptance for her and Bobby among monsters. Jane had rejected hers, and the world looked empty and gray for her decision.

"Ms. Davis," a young man with a thick Italian accent said, "if you care for your friend, Mr. Teppish, you will come with us."

Roused from her thoughts, Jane said, "Pardon?" She sensed someone else standing behind her.

"Please come with us," the man in the black wool coat reiterated, gesturing to the open door of the dark blue Mercedes. In his other hand, he trained a small automatic pistol on her.

"It is in your—and his—best interest to comply," the one behind her urged with an eastern European accent.

She noted the blood-red Maltese cross on the man's lapel.

Carl slumped against the cinderblock alley away from the morning sun; coming down from Blue Flower sucked ass. While riding the high, he owned the world, but the crash left him wrecked and twisted. He got his first taste in September while hanging out with Topper and his Hoodie Crew. They'd passed around a vial of cut glass with the "party honey."

"You see what I mean?" Topper said.

"Yeah," Carl breathed, "fuck…yeah." His synapses exploded with the hit of Blue Flower. "Where'd you get this shit?"

"The Big Man at the old grocery store."

Carl looked over at his buddy, Rico, and nodded. They knew what their next stop was.

"Sure, boys," the suited man at front door said, "if you pay a visit to that metal shop just off Reed Shore, you know, Stahlmann's?"

Carl and Rico nodded eagerly.

"Good," the man concluded, "a vial each now and a vial afterwards."

The nights blurred together as he and Rico hit the ground running, awakening every morning to a half-remembered impression of a splatter of blood or a woman's scream. Every afternoon, they trudged back to the casino in the grocery store for more. The hours between hits dragged; the tips of Carl's fingers blackened and smelled of rotten copper. His veins turned angry red and stung their way up his arms and legs. None of it seemed to matter; he barely noticed that Topper and his crew were nowhere on the streets these days. Even laid-back Rico changed; he glanced about nervously and muttered, "Either you eat the Flower or the Flower eats you," endlessly.

Rico always tapped the Flower as soon as he got it; Carl always held a little for the bad mornings. This had been a bad morning. After waking up, he'd looked over at Rico's grimy mattress. Rico, his life-long buddy, had skipped out.

But he left his shoes, clothes and belt laid out on mattress, covered with a greenish pus.

"Sorry, kid," the man said in front of the storefront, "no candy this morning, but there is someone the boss is looking for."

Carl downed his last drop of the sweet honey and dropped the vial. The man with the dark sunglasses and white cane eased off the bus from Corral. Now, he'd get all the Blue Flower he'd want.

"Johnnn Clarke?" Carl slurred.

A scaly, clawed hand grasped Prof's throat and slammed him against the cinderblock wall. His cane and the package clattered to the ground.

"Thought ssso," the man hissed. "Lotss of people looking for you…good bounty." Carl let the Blue Flower work its magic.

From behind, the clawfoot of the iron crowbar bit deep into Carl's shoulder. With a fierce yank, Carl spun about like a top to face his assailant. The man with short-cropped hair and storm cloud eyes stood with grim determination.

"Serpent," the man commanded, "you are rebuked."

"He'sss mine." Carl's fangs flipped down as his jaw unhinged.

"As you were, serpent," the man in the pressed jeans and spit-shined boots countered, "so shall you be, crawling on your belly with your brethren." He raised the crowbar.

Prof heard whisper of the swing slice the air yet connect with nothing. He detected the furtive rustlings near the overturned trash can.

"On your feet, soldier," the man said to Prof as two hands grabbed Prof's lapels and hoisted him to his feet.

"You don't look any worse for wear," the biker inspected.

"Thank you," Prof said,

"My pleasure. Never liked snakes."

"I'm guessing you're one of the owners of the bike shop across the street."

"Yeah, the name's Mike. You're the one they call Prof?"

"Used to be a professor. These days, I'm just John Clarke."

"Well, here you go, John," Mike said, handing Prof his cane and package. "Time for you to finish your mission."

"Mission?"

"You got a better word for what you're doing?"

"No," Prof said, "I guess not, although if I have to deal with stuff like that…"

"I wouldn't worry about the opposition forces," Mike replied. "I'd say your way is pretty clear. I'd go with you except me and my brothers are authorized as cadre in this op."

"Cadre?"

"You know…training and organizing partisan forces behind enemy lines. Intel dissemination. Which reminds me, Stahlmann was your friend, wasn't he?"

"Yeah," Prof said.

"It always hurts when you lose cohorts, Prof. There's no way around it, though," Mike continued. "You realize that his entire estate was bequeathed to that free clinic a few blocks over?"

"You mean Ayrshire? Vivian's?"

"Draw your own conclusions," Mike said. "That woman doesn't give anything away for free. It's not in her nature."

"I'm going there," Prof said.

He placed an envelope in Prof's hands and said, "When you're finished with your dealings, hand this to her."

"What is it?"

"Just tell her its payment for services rendered."

In Vivian Greene's office, Prof waited for the nurse. As the mad activity of the clinic rattled beyond the thick wooden office door, he readied himself for the exchange.

"Mr. Clarke, good afternoon," Vivian said, closing the door behind her. "You look like hell."

"Been busy," Prof said. "I'm actually here on a friend's behalf." He offered the roll of cash. "I believe you know him, Vic Teppish."

"How do you know Mr. Teppish?" Vivian said, a note of surprise creeping into her tone. "Why didn't he come here himself?"

"He's a friend of a friend. He asked me to pick up his order. Obviously, he could not do this himself."

Vivian opened the small refrigerator and retrieved the small Styrofoam cooler. "So, where is Mr. Teppish?"

"Couldn't say for sure," Prof lied. "He told me to meet him at Wrightsway Park at eight tonight."

He took the small container and rose from the chair. "Thanks, Vivian, for all that you've done. How are you, with Lou's passing and all?"

"It's difficult," Vivian said, lowering her eyes.

"Funny thing," Prof mused. "In all the time I spent over there, I never knew about his side-business. But I guess you deal in shady business, and you meet a shady end."

"That is obvious."

"You know he was selling the shop."

"We talked about that, Mr. Clarke. He wanted out."

"Didn't realize it myself," Prof added. "Vic and Lou were business associates. Small world, I guess."

"Very true," Vivian said.

"Even though I'm educated, I still miss a lot. For example, how did Jones end up with my blood vial? How did he end up at Lou's graveside service? Another thing, I understand the clinic is going to get the proceeds from Lou's estate."

"All right, I set it up, Mr. Clarke," Vivian snapped. "Is that what you wanted to hear? You think this clinic pays for itself? No! I do what I have to do to keep it afloat."

"Was Lou part of the deal, too?"

"No," Vivian said. "I was told he wouldn't be harmed. What do you want out of this?"

"Nothing," Prof said, walking out the door, "you already got the best of me." He paused. "By the way, another friend told me to give you this for services rendered." He tossed the heavy envelope on the desk and left.

With shaking hands, Vivian picked up the phone and made the call.

"Yes, he was here, and no, he didn't say where he was going or staying," she reported. "I expect payment as usual."

After hanging up, Vivian's attention turned to the envelope on the desk. It was too heavy for a letter and something round made an imprint on its white surface. She ripped it open and a polished copper bracelet of intertwined wires dropped into her hand.

Her tears flowed.

Under the dark autumn sky, Prof climbed the steps to the Hotel Mittelmarch one last time.

He left the parcels with Vic in the upstairs of the abandoned store an hour earlier; he didn't want to experience what would come next. While Vic made his manic preparations for his next move, Prof sat in the corner and considered his circumstances. Mike was right; he couldn't live like this anymore. If anything, it proved to everyone that he was a sad wreck of a man.

"Mr. Clarke?" Vic said. "I am finished. Thank you for your help. I believe that this will be the last time we meet." He grasped Prof's hand and shook once.

"Happy to be of service. In your own way, you have helped me come to a decision."

"How's that?"

"Sometimes, the only way to deal with a problem," Prof said, picking up the battered cardboard stationery box, "is to meet it head on. It's my time to do this."

"I have often told Jane that," Vic said and clambered out the window.

Now, Prof stood in front of the lobby desk with the box in his hands.

"Prof!" J.J. said. "Where've you been? Your rent's due."

"J.J., I need you to do a favor for me," Prof said. "If you would just put this box up, I believe I will be going away for a while."

"What's going on?" J.J. said. "You disappear for almost three weeks and you come back looking like shit. I've had cops and social workers looking for you and wanting to see your room. Then there's that other guy that just left."

"What guy is that?"

"I don't know, he's been in here a couple of times looking for you; a little on the fat side, has a goatee, looks like one of those hipster-types. He said he'd be over at the Night Café if you decided to show up."

"Thanks, J.J.," Prof said and turned back to the creaking revolving door. "If you could keep that box safe for me, I will reclaim it eventually."

"Sure," J.J called after him. "Where are you going?"

"To meet my fate," Prof said, "with as much grace as I can muster." He pushed his way through the door and across the busy Reed Shore Drive.

The Night Café was sedate, even for a Sunday night. The jazz trio played a low, meandering instrumental piece just above the din of the patrons.

"Prof!" Theo said. "It's been awhile since we've seen you. Everything okay?"

"Hi, Theo, it's been complicated."

"There's a man who's been asking about you. He says he's a friend of yours. I seated him at a one of the tables, his choice," Theo said. "Something's off about this."

"Thanks, I guess it's best not to keep the man waiting," Prof said. He needed no help winding through the maze of small tables.

"John!" Stan said, rising from his seat. "You're not the easiest man to get in touch with."

"Hello, Stan," Prof said, recognizing his former roommate's voice, "I've been keeping busy. How are things?"

"Things are going great," Stan said. "Lila made partner last month and *City Music Panorama* has been a success."

"Good to hear. So, how's Lila?"

"She's doing great. We got a lovely place north of the city."

"You gave up your apartment downtown?"

"Yes," Stan said, "Lila and I thought it would be better for our professional lives. She said you were planning to move when you two were together."

"Really," Prof smirked. "Did you get to cover the AltFest out in Denver?"

"No," Stan said with a sigh. "We needed to go to Donna's high school graduation, you know, her cousin. Again, Lila said you would have done it."

"Sorry to hear about that," Prof said. "I knew you were looking forward to it. So why are you here, Stan?"

"Lila and I were worried about you, John."

"Worried?" Prof said. "It's been more than a year since I heard from either of you."

"I know. The way things played out... Well, we didn't want anyone to get hurt, especially you. We were waiting for the right time to tell you."

"What, Stan?" Prof snapped loudly. "That you were banging my wife on the side? I don't think there's a right time for that."

The conversation at the nearby tables died off.

"John, this isn't the right time or place for this. Anyway, Lila wasn't happy and your career, well—"

"You came all the way into town to tell me this? You waited a year for this?"

I got a call from Human Services, or Lila did. They said you've been acting erratically and that someone needed to talk to you. Lila is really worried, so I thought I'd check in."

"I'm fine. It's not perfect, but I am fine."

"Are you?" Stan said. "From what I understand, you haven't been back to your room in that flophouse in a couple of weeks, and you look like you've been sleeping in your clothes."

"And?" Prof said. "Do you think I need help?"

Stan gazed his friend in the dark glasses and wrinkled long coat. Lines of stress crossed John's face, waiting for Stan's reply. The two plainclothes detectives moved to either side of John.

"Mr. Clarke," one of the detectives said, "will you come with us? We would like to take you someplace safe."

"Yes, John," Stan said, "I think you do need help."

Prof stood and offered no resistance as the policemen led him out of the café.

Under the cloudy night sky, Vic stood atop the tar roof of the abandoned store on Bianchi Street. His side still throbbed from the bolt wound packed with earth, but the pint of fresh blood invigorated him enough for what came next. He closed his eyes, now crimson and glowing, and drew in the scents of the dark city around him. Sifting the through the sensations, he focused on one sweet familiar one, laced with fear.

"Jane…" he hissed. As he raised his arms, he disregarded the consequences and cast aside the last shreds of his humanity. Fiery rage coursed through his veins as his leathern wings spiraled him up past the fog-shrouded rooftops.

The handcuffs cut into Jane's wrists as she sat in the metal office chair in the center of the control room. To her left, two men in black fatigues watched a bank of monitor screens in the low light, scanning the outside of the solid, squat building. Each spoke swift, guttural commands into their headsets.

During the ride, the driver, dressed in a double-breasted black suit like his associates, piloted the car and never looked back at the three passengers in the backseat. The austere one, called Dmitri, reassured her that she would come to no harm, while the other young man kept his pistol pressed against her ribs. The Mercedes purred through the busy streets as Dmitri frowned, checked his watch, and watched the sun sink behind the skyscrapers. Jane recognized the vacated bank branch because she rode past it on the bus everyday as she commuted from the University to the diner. The Mercedes pulled into the small lot with three black utility vans, and her captors hustled her through the dusty entrance, past the teller desks where men in black fatigues unloaded aluminum cases, and through the vault doorway.

"Sit!" Dmitri commanded, pointing to the lone, steel office chair.

Jane complied, looking straight ahead. She wasn't going to give them the satisfaction of seeing her afraid.

From behind the long table laden with sharpened wooden stakes, black automatic rifles and glittering swords, a wizened priest shuffled to her and flicked holy water at her from his silvered aspergillum. He watched with watery cataract eyes as she flinched.

"*Toccare il mio bambino*," the priest demanded, thrusting the ancient crucifix of olive wood at her.

Bewildered, she stared back at the bent little holy man.

"*Toccare!*" the priest implored and shook the holy icon.

Understanding, Jane reached out and touched the cross.

The priest's expression relaxed and he trundled off to Dmitri, satisfied with the result.

"She is clean," Fra Geppi stated to Dmitri.

"Good," Dmitri said. "Thank you, Father." He silently gave thanks for the elderly priest's assignment as chaplain to the unit. Fra Geppi was a familiar constant; modern ecumenical politics complicated operations unbelievably. Already, Dmitri promised concessions to the Turkish academic that he would have never made thirty years earlier. A local sect even refused to aid their operation. At one time, these things would have been unthinkable; now, he had to deal with this.

"Mr. Brunet," Dmitri said, "you do not understand. This man is very dangerous. I understand that you wish to acquire his businesses, but I think it would be best if you were to vacate the premises."

"I've held up my end of the deal," the craggy-faced criminal said. "You got his woman. I want to get everything that's coming to me—the goods, the connections and the cash."

"He is a hardened individual. I doubt you would be able to make him give you such things."

"Really?" Rex said and looked towards Jane. "Seems to me we have a bargaining chip right here."

"She complied with us and Fra Geppi agrees she is untainted. I will not allow her to come to harm, even though she has consorted with something unholy. Mr. Brunet, you have been duly compensated, as has the doctor. Do not let your greed dictate your actions."

"For a man who's called Dmitri the Blade," Rex snorted, "you seem a bit soft."

"Make no mistake. I have thirty men surrounding the premises should you decide to do something foolish."

Jane kept her head down and listened to the conversation. She knew they spoke of Vic and they planned to use her as bait. She hoped Vic had left for London; she was willing to face the consequences. In her heart, she knew Vic would have done the same for her.

"Sentry one, report!" one of the men at the monitors commanded.

The monitor in the upper left went blank.

"Security three, are you there?" the other said into his microphone headset.

Another monitor on the far end of the bank went black.

Paulo rubbed his hands and refocused the black spotter scope on the front doors of the former bank two stories below them. Just before sunset, he, his watch partner Santi, and the rest of the platoon had celebrated a somber Mass with Fra Geppi in preparation of this duty. It did little settle his nerves.

"Wish we were still in Rome," he whispered. "It's too cold here...and the damn Russian won't let us smoke."

"Quiet, Paulo," Santi said as he readjusted the bipod of the heavy-barreled rifle. "Dmitri knows better than you or me."

Neither soldier heard the deadly whisper of wings descend upon them.

"No reply from Sentry six," the soldier at the monitor bank said, and another of the screens flickered to blackness.

Alessandro peered at the darkening floor to ceiling windows as he and the five recruits braced behind the tellers' counters. The chaos outside buzzed through his earpiece. In the vault behind his skirmish line, the two coordinators at the surveillance station barked for reports outside, but only received static in reply.

"Ready, men," he said and two lifted their loaded crossbows while two others ignited their flamethrowers.

"Marco, lower the lights."

The youth spun the dial of the lighting array and the bank lobby darkened, yet the windows remained pitch black. Around the edges of the glass entrance, black smoke seeped into the lobby.

Before Alessandro could shout a command, the tendrils of smoke shot across the room and engulfed the six men in billowing darkness. Alessandro saw the red-eyes and fangs form from the smoke and heard to the abrupt screams of his men cut short.

Inside the vault, the last screen went black and the lights died. Immediately, the emergency generator kicked on and filled the room with a hellish red light. Rex edged closer to the door with his pistol drawn, wide-eyed, sweat pouring down his face.

Dmitri lifted the ancient sword from the row of long stakes of ash wood on the table. He ran his hand up the length of the heavy blade and murmured a quiet prayer to the blood red Maltese cross upon the hilt. He turned to the two at the consoles and said, "It is time; let him in."

Without question, one of the soldiers yanked down the heavy switch and rushed with his cohort behind Jane. The vault door creaked outward and revealed the inky blackness beyond. The air whispered with the high arc of an object tossed into the vault. It landed with a hollow, pulpy clatter and rolled to Dmitri's feet. Alessandro's horror-stricken eyes stared up at him.

"A bank," a voice said from the darkness. "After all these years, you'd think you clowns would find a new gimmick." The slow, steady footsteps echoed and the assailant stepped into the dim red light of the vault.

Shaking, Rex aimed his pistol at the back of the dark-haired stranger's head and fired. With a wince, the man turned to Rex and touched the back of his head. "If this is your best, little bandit-chief," the man said, disdain flaring in his eyes, "you're in over your head again."

Dropping his smoking pistol, Rex slid out the vault doorway and broke into a clumsy sprint.

Eyeing the table of holy weapons, Fra Geppi crept forward, trembling. Vic spotted the old man in the dusty black cassock, looked him in the eye, and slowly shook his head. The priest crawled back to his corner.

"Demon!" Dmitri roared and charged with the sword. "It is time you were sent to hell!" The gleaming blade drove home through the small of the creature's back.

Vic looked down at the point of the sword protruding from the front of his light blue dress shirt. A blackish stain spread across his stomach. Grabbing the blade of the sword hilt, he yanked it free. Pivoting on the balls of his feet, he hurled the blade to the far side of the room and faced Dmitri. One lightning-fast kick, then another shattered Dmitri's knee caps and sent him sprawling forward. "After seven hundred years," Vic glowered down at the crippled soldier, "you geniuses ought to get a clue."

"Come no closer, creature!" one of the youths in black fatigues threatened. He held a combat knife at Jane's throat.

Vic paused.

As the sound of popping filled the air, the silvery scorpions scuttled off Jane's shoes and up the legs of her captors. Both screamed; the knife holder's muscles seized with wracking convulsions and the knife sliced deep into Jane's exposed neck.

"No!" Vic said, as he leapt to Jane. With one hand, he pressed against her wound, and snapped the chain on the handcuffs like spider webs with the other. Her pulse weakened; he watched the color drain from her face. He bit into his own wrist and dribbled his life blood into her mouth. He placed his ear on her breast and listened to her heart quicken as his vision dimmed and darkened. At least he would leave this world a man instead of a beast.

In the hazy last moments, Vic felt two gentle hands lift his head and draw them to Jane's supple neck. He nipped and drank of her warm sweet blood. He caught images of sunlight reflecting off the diner counter, the smell of coffee brewing, and the clear blue sky peeking between the skyscrapers.

In her own miasma, Jane crossed the moonlit plains with her pack on the hunt, flapped over a gas-lighted city and found peace on the turret of a crumbling castle, high in the mountains. Her eyes fluttered open and looked down to see Vic nuzzling her.

"Hey," she said, gazing into his dark eyes.

"Hey, you," he said back.

Standing up, Vic's cool gaze met Dmitri's slack-jawed stare. Walking over to the table, Vic picked up one of the three-foot long stakes and said, "Dmitri the Blade, am I right?"

Dmitri nodded.

"You know, I used to have a nickname, too," Vic said, studying the spear in his hand. "At one time, you would have learned the hard way how I earned that moniker."

Dmitri opened his mouth to reply.

"However," Vic said, tossing the stick aside, "I'm trying something new. You get a pass this time. You tell the boys back at the Chateau, if they try something like this again, it will not be...pleasant. Do you understand?"

Dmitri nodded.

Vic helped Jane to her feet and wrapped an arm around her waist. At the door, he paused and said, "You know that is one heck of a pair of shoes."

Shoeless and beltless, Prof sat on the thin mattress in the holding cell. Tomorrow, they would transfer him to the hospital, but tonight, he still smiled at what he had accomplished today.

Rex looked over his shoulder. No man with blazing red eyes followed him and now, he waited for the cab to take him to the airport. Low on funds, but he had enough to get him to Miami and lay low for a few weeks. Screw Jones and those crazy Catholic freaks. When things calmed down, he'd come back and rebuild. He checked his watch again. His flight left at eight. He had a little more than an hour.

Although Monday morning, the street seemed quiet. It was early, anyway. Rex heard a faint squeaking and churning coming up the street. He looked and saw nothing out of the ordinary.

"Reach for the sky, mister!" a boy yelled. The freckle-faced blond youngster sat astride a brilliant gold BMX bike. Atop his head, he wore a fiery red cowboy hat, and in his hand, he held a chrome-plated cap pistol.

"Get out here, kid," Rex growled, "I'm not in the mood for games."

The hammer of the pistol slammed and the shot rang throughout the street. Rex fell into the gutter, staring at the lightening sky.

The kid blew the smoke from the revolver and holstered it. He yanked a phone out and said, "Sheridan? Yup, it's Freddie. I'm going home. I'm tired of dealing with these greenhorns."

He clapped the phone closed and pedaled away from the oncoming sunrise.

Reality Bleeds In; Fiction Bleeds Out

10:00 AM December 17th
Courtroom C
1 Justice Plaza

All rise," the bailiff intoned, "the State versus John Clarke. The Honorable Judge Aaron Schechter presiding."

Prof listened to the solemn rustle of the rise and fall of the attendees complying with the bailiff's command. One last time, Miriam Armstrong, the serious young advocate at his side, inspected her row of files and documents on the defense table before them. Satisfied with her preparations, she readied herself for the final assault. This fourth and final hearing, the first Prof appeared at, determined his fate. In the lull before this battle, he reviewed the last twelve days of his life.

In the morning, they transferred him from Municipal to the hospital. After a long morning of processing while handcuffed to a chair in the busy hallway, the intake staff allowed him to shower and shave under supervision. An orderly handed him a pair of sweats without the waistband cord and escorted him to this small room with no sharp corners and a stainless-steel mirror.

"You need anything, Mr. Clarke," the orderly, Wallace, said, "just knock on the door and let me know." The reinforced door with the small, safety glass window eased shut with a locking click.

Smooth surfaces surrounded him as he sat on the thin, vinyl-covered mattress of his cot. The metal door felt tacky with multiple coats of what Prof imagined was institutional green paint and the air carried a sterile emptiness devoid of scents. With a dripping sink providing the only stimulation, he waited for Jones to make good on his threats.

After five bland meals served with plastic utensils, the door swung open and admitted a man in penny-loafers. He took a seat across from Prof and said, "Good Afternoon, Mr. Clarke, I'm Tom Durbin, the unit manager."

"Good Afternoon, Mr. Durbin," Prof said, noting the clue to the time of day the man gave him.

"Do you understand why you are here?"

"I have an idea, but please, elaborate."

"A petition has been filed for your welfare," Tom said. "It is believed that you are unable to take care of yourself."

"I've been on my own for a year. I have a residence and I haven't starved to death."

"True, but Human Services tells me you hadn't been back to your apartment in weeks."

"Interesting, I kept all of my appointments with Ms. Sawney."

"Your case has been reassigned," Tom said. "However, on review of Ms. Sawney's file, it was noted that you associated with people with criminal backgrounds. This is a direct violation of your conditional release."

"So, no charges?"

"Not now," Tom said. "However, if you sign a voluntary commitment, I believe it will not be pursued."

"And if I don't?"

"Right now, you are under a seventy-two-hour observation," Tom stated. "I can order another one after that. Mr. Clarke, surely you understand that you are not a well man. I am concerned that you can't function in an outpatient setting."

"I was doing well enough for the last year. I believe I will refuse."

"I'm sorry you see things this way, Mr. Clarke," Tom said, knocking on the door. "I hope you will reconsider." As Tom left, the door closed behind him.

After eight more meals, Prof paced out the dimensions of the ten by twelve room one hundred fifteen times. Beyond the door, he heard the electronic crackle and hiss of the television in the commons room and the familiar whispers of the patients. Between the periods of quiet and the faint echoes of socialization, he made a game at guessing the time of day.

"Sorry, John," Wallace, the orderly, apologized each time he brought Prof a meal. "Only patients under treatment get rec room privileges."

A day later, Tom popped his head into Prof's room to inform him that he'd authorized a new seventy-two-hour observation. Prof shook his head and said, "Whatever."

The next day, the parade started. One after another, the doctors, nurses and social workers stopped by for their visits in the mornings and afternoons. Prof affably greeted each visitor and recounted a sanitized version of his life. Each asked if he missed his sight. "Of course," Prof said, "but what can I do about it?" They countered with asking if he felt lost and isolated. He replied with, "No more than anyone else in this world."

Sunday afternoon, the door swung open. He recognized her warm, cinnamon perfume; he'd bought her first bottle when they were two struggling grad students.

"Lila, I hope you are well."

"You can drop the gentleman prisoner front, John," she snapped, plopping in the interview chair. "You're not Dumas, de Sade or Kafka."

"I'm sorry," Prof said.

"Quit apologizing. God! I never could stand that about you."

"Point taken. Why are you here?"

"Isn't it obvious? You're in here for treatment, but you don't seem to realize that."

"So, this is a tough love session, is it?"

"I get a call while I'm in conference with a client and they said you were in trouble," she said. "After all this time, you still have me as your emergency contact. How pathetic is that?"

"I didn't think—"

"You never think, John. That's always been your problem. Your head has always been in the clouds. I hoped you would grow up."

"You mean like Stan?"

"At least he knows how to play the game," Lila said. "You had it all, but you couldn't be bothered to learn politics. Everyone compromises, but not you; you jumped out of the ivory tower and ended up in the gutter. What did you expect? A band of angels would save you?"

"No, but I am making out okay."

"You call this okay?"

"It's not perfect, but I am surviving. Lila, I am sorry that you and Stan got pulled into this."

"John," she said, softening her voice, "we still care about you."

"I know… Look, I was hurt, but I understand now. We were on separate trajectories for a long time before things fell apart. I didn't see it or I didn't want to see it. You weren't happy with the way things were going and I wasn't either. It wasn't the best ending, but I can live with that." He sighed and added, "I wish nothing but the best for you and Stan."

"John, just accept the help."

"No, Lila. There is nothing wrong with me. You may not think so, but I know otherwise and, really, that's all that matters. Thanks for stopping by."

"Then I'll leave you to your own little world," she said, getting up and knocking on the door. "Let's see how far those voices in your head get you."

After the door closed, Prof slumped in his chair. Lila's last jib stung. During the stiff client dinners Lila hosted, one of the other couples inevitably asked, "So, John, what do you do for fun?" He always mentioned writing stories and he relaxed and described his latest project. Most acknowledged it and moved on, but occasionally, one of the well-dressed business-types leaned in to hear more. Lila, steering the conversation back to business at hand, teased aloud how only her husband heard voices in his head and shot him a withering glance, letting him know he would pay for this latest faux pas later.

In the stillness between meals, the walls closed in upon Prof as he reflected upon the last year. Perhaps, they were right; he was crazy. What if the touchstone he relied upon, her voice, was just a pipedream? In his desperation, he'd pinned his hope, his sight, and regaining his life on a delusion. He longed to hear her silvery voice and to sense her saffron presence, but even in this fairy tale he may have created, she was beyond his reach.

In the maze of these dismal conclusions, Prof discovered a bright thread of logic to follow as he dredged up that night he lay on the floor of his home office, blind and naked.

"To create something new," she said, as her cool hands stroked his chest, "you have to destroy something old. It's the way it works."

Prof considered his time alone over the last year and what he lost prior. Looking back, his old life and where it led resembled one of the crumbling houses he passed every day—something in need of demolition.

"Make it from one winter morn to the next, three hundred sixty-six days…and you get your sight back, if you survive."

He remembered the rainy night at the bus station when the ragged stranger observed he only needed to make it to the first day of winter. A delusion or not, he'd wished she were by his side on that morning, yet he questioned everything he lived through in the last year. Again, the stranger's words rang in his ears—real or imagined, his experiences had changed him and the transformed man remained.

Holding his head up, Prof resolved to greet the winter solstice a free man.

Monday morning, Prof received a new visitor.

"Mr. Clarke," the young woman said, "I am Miriam Armstrong, your patient advocate."

"A pleasure to make your acquaintance, Ms. Armstrong," Prof said. "I am baffled with this process."

"Miriam, please,"

"Certainly, Miriam," Prof said. "They keep extending my stay here. I don't think that I've shown myself to be a danger to myself or others. In fact, they make these decisions without my input."

"It is irregular, but within the law," Miriam said. "I think they are trying to get you to consent to a voluntary commitment. It would be at least ninety days."

"And if I consent, they pump me full of meds until I'm a basket case. I won't allow it; I want out."

"They will just keep you here and renew the seventy-two-hour observations."

"Until I break down and agree, correct?"

"Unless we were to file a writ of habeas corpus—"

"Let's do it," Prof stated.

"Mr. Clarke," the young woman cautioned, "if we do this and we fail, you get an involuntary commitment of at least one hundred eighty days."

Prof considered her words. Finally, he said, "If we do this, there's one thing we need to do."

"What's that?"

"Win."

Wednesday night, Prof sat in his chair listening to the dripping faucet. Miriam had left a fresh suit at the nurse station. Tomorrow morning, Wallace would watch him shower and shave to prepare for his court appearance. Although he was too agitated to sleep, he enjoyed a quiet peace for the first time in over a year. His sight and circumstances no longer mattered. He almost missed the door to the room opening behind him.

"Good evening, Jones," he said without looking back. "It's after visiting hours."

"It's never too late for me, John. I just wanted to drop by and say goodbye."

"I'm not going anywhere."

"I beg to differ. By filing that writ, you just sealed your fate and signed up for one hundred eighty days of Thorazine, electroshock and who knows? Maybe neurosurgery. By the time, they're done with you, you're going to be a zombie."

"A bit early to gloat, isn't it?"

"John, you got it all wrong. I'm not here to end you; I'm here to help you out."

"I suppose having Lila visit was your doing."

"I thought she would talk some sense into you. Although, I was disappointed in your reaction."

"I thought about ripping into her, but it just wasn't worth it. A violent outburst would just be another black mark against my name."

"You mean like hearing voices?" Jones said.

Prof heard the clink of glass. Jones set a blood collection vial on the stainless-steel sink.

Calmly, Prof said, "I don't know what you're talking about."

"Of course, you don't. All those lonely nights that you mumbled to yourself."

"Lots of people talk to themselves."

"Are you sure? How many have voices that answer back?"

"I do not hear voices," Prof said.

"Thrice denied," Jones said and tucked the vial back in his breast pocket. "I guess I was mistaken. Still, you should have taken the offer I made you."

Prof laughed.

"What do you find so amusing? You realize everyone sees you as a crazy blind man with no future?"

"You know, Jones," Prof said, "I just realized something. You're blinder than I am."

"How do you figure that?"

"You see something; you take it. You never stop to ascertain the value of what you grab. You think I'm important, but you have no idea why."

"You're going to tell me why you are important?"

"No, the thing about grasping for shadows is they are usually everything you despise about yourself. It took me a while to figure that out. Good night, Jones."

Prof never heard the door open to let Jones out, as if his presence evaporated like a wisp of steam. Minutes later, the door opened and Wallace asked, "You talking to yourself again, Mr. Clarke?"

"Just saying my prayers," Prof said and climbed into bed for a restful night's sleep.

At nine-thirty a.m., Nick fidgeted in his navy-blue blazer and slacks. He hated wearing the clip-on tie, too. The spry old man clipped up the granite front steps to meet Nick at the top. Judge Adams' bright blue eyes sparked amidst the grayness of the morning.

"Good morning, Nicholas," the judge said. The quick trot up the stairs supercharged his enthusiasm. "Are you ready to finish this?"

"Sure, judge; I don't see what this will accomplish, though."

"We're fighting the good fight, Nicholas; the fight in itself is the accomplishment." Judge Adams looked at Nick's worn out red gym bag and said, "That is hardly acceptable for court."

Nick shrugged and said, "Never had much use for a briefcase."

"Or a professional wardrobe, either," the judge said. "We'll see to that later." He handed Nick his venerated brief bag. "You are my paralegal-in-training, after all."

The judge took the lead and they swept through the lobby of the Municipal building.

A brief stop at the Registrar's desk confirmed Courtroom C was their destination.

"Most unusual," Judge Adams said. "The Superior Court hearings are held on the ground floor."

"I'll get the elevator."

"A waste of time, Nicholas," the judge said, rounding the corner from the elevator bay. "I've always preferred the stairs to the elevator. Expedience over convenience."

Up the six flights of stairs, their frantic footsteps echoed. At the dusty top landing, the judge pulled at the safety door and said, "It's locked with one of those magnet devices. It seems someone does not want us to attend this hearing."

Nick opened his gym bag and retrieved the steel mallet. Currents of blue electricity flowed along the length of the hammer as Nick reared hammer back to strike.

"No!" the judge said, grabbing Nick's arm. He took the hammer from Nick's grasp. Shaking his head, the judge said, "I see I am going to have my work cut out for me, Nicholas. You have a few rough edges."

The judge ran his hands over the hammer, reshaping it into a small, silver gavel. He handed it back to Nick and said, "Lesson one, force must be applied judiciously."

Nick tapped the door's magnetic lock. Sparks flew, the door clicked open and the lights flickered off.

In the darkness, Judge Adams said with a sigh, "So much work…"

A confused murmur filled the court.

"What's happening?" Prof whispered to Miriam on his right.

"Power outage," she said. "The lights…never mind, they just came back on."

Judge Adams and Nick walked down the center aisle, through the rail gate and took seats to Prof's left at the defendant's table.

"Please, Mr. Clarke," Judge Adams whispered, "look straight ahead. You need legal counsel and I am offering my services, free of charge. If you accept my help, please nod your head."

Prof nodded.

"Hey Prof," Nick whispered.

Prof turned his head toward Nick.

"Mr. Clarke?" Miriam whispered to the distracted blind man.

"Nicholas," Judge Adams said with an upraised finger, "you're here to observe."

"Sorry."

"Look straight ahead, Mr. Clarke," Judge Adams said, "and listen carefully to what I have to say."

Nick surveyed the court. From his high perch, Judge Schechter stared at the former holder of his seat on the bench, whispering in Prof's ear. Clarke nodded agreement with each whisper. In the back row of the gallery, Jones glowered at him. Nick grinned and winked back.

Although in court many times before, Nick forced himself to pay attention this time. Prof's advocate, Miriam, a young, mousy brunette in granny glasses asked for motions and called out objections. Quickly, Nick understood she was more of tiger than a mouse. When the doctor and the psychologist both took the stand, the quiet lady reduced their official-sounding opinions to a rubble pile of "errs" and "uhhhs."

Stan, a friend of Prof's, sort of a hipster-type with a goatee and a pencil-thin moustache, took the stand. He mentioned how distant John had become, almost reclusive. With lowered eyes, he stated John's professional failures measured against his recent promotions had broken John's confidence.

"So, in your opinion," Miriam asked in cross-examination, "your illicit affair had nothing to do with Mr. Clarke's emotional well-being?"

"Objection! Your Honor!"

"Sustained," Judge Schechter said.

"I withdraw the question," Miriam replied sweetly. "No further questions."

His testimony completed, Stan slunk out of the witness box with a hang-dog expression.

Lila, Prof's ex-wife, testified next. Nick watched the thin woman in the beige pantsuit squirm in the chair as she answered the questions, all the while checking her watch. Lila nipped back with short replies which informed the court that her ex-husband was an unmotivated dreamer who drank too much. Nick thought about life with this woman and decided drinking would have been an option for him, too. Not a bad woman, but wound way too tight.

Ms. Armstrong listened in silence through her testimony. Upon cross-reference, she wielded the same question as a switchblade. "Do you think your illicit affair could have been a catalyst for John's emotional trauma?"

"Objection!"

"Sustained!" Schechter said. "Ms. Armstrong, I warn you…"

"I'm so sorry, Your Honor," Miriam demurred, "I withdraw the question. No further questions."

Lila left the witness stand with a taut face.

As Lila and Stan exited the court room, red-faced, Nick grinned at his new appreciation for court work; it was kick-boxing without the bruises.

Finally, the bailiff took Prof's arm and led him to the witness stand. After the swearing in, Schechter looked over his steel-rimmed glasses and said to Prof, "So, Mr. Clarke, we have heard testimony from experts and character witnesses. I would like to hear from you."

Prof paused for a moment to collect his thoughts and the judge's advice. "Your Honor," he began, "I've had a tough year. I lost my job, my marriage and my sight, but I never wished harm to myself or anyone else. All I can do is to keep going. Jobs come and go. Love happens or it doesn't. As for my sight, the doctors told me this is temporary, but if it's not, I can make do without out it. All I can do is hope and I still do."

"What do you have to say about the implication that you cannot care for yourself?" Schechter asked.

"My life's not perfect, but I have survived on my own for the last year," Prof said with a faint smile. "If not, I get by with a little help from my friends."

Schechter considered Clarke's words. He looked to the gallery and saw Jones' burning gaze. Down at the defendant's table, Judge Adams' piercing blue eyes informed Schechter who judged him.

"Petition denied," Schechter announced and the knock of the gavel resounded through the court. "Mr. Clarke is released under his own recognizance. Court dismissed." Schechter arose from the bench and fled to the refuge of his chambers.

Outside of the courthouse, Justice Plaza thrummed with lunch-time life.

"Remember, Stan," Lila said, "we're meeting Colin and Laura at the Silver Oaks at eight."

"What about the Crucible Club? I thought—"

"No," Lila said, "their account is way too important to gamble on one of your…'finds.'" She checked her watch again and continued, "God, I lost half a day on that."

"At least it helped John out."

Lila's hazel eyes stormed for a second and she said, "He's beyond help. He'll always be a dreamer. Remember, eight." With that, she spun away to retrieve her Lexus from the garage.

Stan watched her clip away with her portfolio swinging and entertained the notion that John had gotten the better end of the deal. Turning in the opposite direction, he ambled back to his office at the magazine. Underneath the bronze fountain of Lady Justice, a loud staccato of a lone trumpet solo split the air and trailed off.

Leaning on a massive, curbed Harley, the tall, blond biker dropped his trumpet to his side and the small crowd applauded. He nodded appreciatively as coins jingled into the open case at his feet.

"Hey, guy!" Stan said. "You play at that place, the Night Café, right?"

"Sure do," the biker replied.

“I’m Stan Winslow. Editor of *City Music Panorama*, maybe you’ve heard of me or read my blog.”

“I’ve heard of you and the magazine,” the biker said, gathering up the loose change and tucking his trumpet away. “Not a fan of either. Rock and roll lacks challenge. A four-four beat isn’t brain surgery.”

“Yeah, well,” Stan countered, “I was wondering why you play at that dump down on Reed Shore.”

“I like the place. Good people who watch out for their friends.”

“Didn’t seem too friendly to me,” Stan said. “The waiter gave me the cold shoulder. I stiffed him on the tip, though.”

“Well, Stan, you screw over a man’s friend, what do you expect?” Gabe said. “By the way, speaking of tips, hold out your hands.”

Gabe opened his large fist and thirty dimes dropped into Stan’s cupped hands.

In the alcove, Prof sat and waited for his release papers.

“Thank you, judge,” Prof said.

“I should be thanking you, Mr. Clarke,” Judge Adams said. “I had forgotten what it was like to work the other side of the bench. Nicholas, I believe there are offices to be had down on Wrightsway Park, would you check into that for me?”

“Noted, judge,” Nick said, scrawling in his notepad. “Everyone calls him Prof.”

“So, Your Honor,” Prof said, “you are going to continue to practice?”

“Yes, Prof, and please, do not refer to me as ‘Your Honor.’ I am no longer on the bench. I am Ray Adams, Attorney. Curious they have an age limit for judges but none for practicing law.”

Heavy footstep stormed up to the trio. “This is where the victory party is being held,” Jones snarled.

Nick’s hands curled into fists and his jaw clenched.

"Special Agent Jones," Judge Adams said. "What a lovely surprise."

"So, you're practicing law again?" Jones said.

"Yes," Adams said, "I plan to take on a role of a defense attorney. Law without compassion is just another form of tyranny, wouldn't you agree? Now young Nicholas here, in a few years, will be an assistant DA. I am sure you will enjoy working with him."

Nick broke into a cold smile.

Prof chuckled.

"You find this funny, you blind freak?" Jones reached into his coat and smashed the blood vial upon the white tile floor.

Prof caught the briefest hint of saffron and his heart sank.

"I am so sorry you will be leaving us soon, Special Agent Jones," Judge Adams said. "I did stipulate in our first meeting that no innocent blood would be spilled. I am sure your superiors in Washington will be most disappointed."

"John?" Miriam said. "I have your release paperwork."

"What?"

"And," Miriam said, handing Prof his cane, "you should get the rest of your personal belongings from the hospital. Who were you talking to?"

Prof listened for Judge Adams, Nick or Jones and heard nothing. "Just to myself, I guess."

He spent the afternoon going from bus to bus to get his bundle of clothing from the hospital. Exhausted, he leaned his head against the cold window as the city rumbled by. Had the three men he had known for the last year just blinked out of existence before him? Or had they just wandered off before Miriam arrived?

Prof shuffled through the revolving door of the 'March, too tired to contemplate whether he had won the battle but lost the war.

"He's back!" J.J. said. "I guess they declared you not crazy?"

"Yes, J.J., but I have my own doubts. Is my stuff in storage?'

"No, Prof, your stuff is still in your room. I just couldn't do it, but you still owe three weeks back rent."

"Thanks, J.J."

"Oh, and Prof," J.J. said, reaching under the counter, "you'll probably want this."

He handed Prof his stationery box. "And you got a piece of mail."

Prof took the rich, textured envelope and said, "Any idea who sent this?"

"Can't say, it wasn't addressed or stamped. Someone must have hand-delivered it."

From the envelope, Prof caught the fragrance of saffron.

Valentine's Balm

10:30 AM December 20th
Ayrshire Avenue Free Clinic
2050 Ayrshire Avenue

As bright sun flooded through the windows of the empty clinic, Terry wished to be somewhere else on this Sunday morning. He slouched in his chair at the admitting station and re-read the letter:

Dear Terry:

I am sorry to do this, but I cannot go on working at the clinic. Over the last few months, I have come to question my effectiveness as administrator for the clinic. I tendered my resignation downtown. I recommended you as my replacement. The clinic needs new blood.

Vivian

An hour earlier, he'd rolled out of bed and planned to spend the day doing laundry and watching the ball games, a brief respite from the clinic. His only mistake was checking his phone messages; Vivian had called early this morning and asked him to meet her down at the clinic. "Damn," he said under his breath. Vivian never called him on Sunday unless it was an emergency. He pulled on his jeans and a semi-clean sweatshirt, grabbed his pea coat and trotted out of his apartment.

Now, he sat his admitting desk. Vivian nowhere in sight and this note had been attached to a potted plant wrapped in gold foil. For weeks,

Vivian had performed her duties in the halls of the clinic, her brilliant green eyes dulled. Terry noted she'd quit her private consultations and he no longer waited for her after-hours customers. Due to the frantic daily pace, he'd shrugged off the changes as circumstantial. The knocking at the front door derailed his train of thought.

"Goldilocks!" he said, opening the door, "what are you doing out here today?"

Demetria frowned for a second.

"Sorry, Demetria," Terry said, "you know I'm just kidding."

"I know, Terry. I was going to meet someone for lunch at Wrightsway. I forgot my heavy jacket on Friday. It was a long shot anybody would be here, but it's turned cold out there. What are you doing here?"

"Vivian called me down here this morning."

"Is there something I can help with?" Demetria said. "I mean, I'm just the cleaning crew."

"Unless you know something about health administration," Terry said to young pixie with short blond hair, "I don't think there's a whole lot."

"What's going on?"

"Vivian resigned."

"When?"

"This morning, I guess," Terry said, running his hand through his short black hair. "It looks like I will oversee this train wreck for a while."

"I might not be able to help right away, but I just got accepted into the LPN program," Demetria said. "It's a long way off, but it's a start. I'd like to put my name in when I start trials. It's the least I can do since you and Ms. Greene gave me a second chance."

Terry remembered the quiet woman who'd filled out the employment application in the corner of the waiting room a couple months back. She had half-heartedly handed the clipboard to him and left; he noted she had checked off the box for criminal convictions. On her background check, he noted she had been a local girl who moved south for six months, gotten married and carried six counts of shoplifting. Vivian made the call on hiring her.

"It's a minimum wage job, we need house-keeping," Vivian said. "As for the convictions, well, and we all do things to survive."

"Demetria," he said, "you've shown up and done excellent work. You never let us down. As for the legal problem, by the time you're ready to take boards, you should be in the clear."

"That's what my boyfriend and his boss tell me."

"Anyway, welcome to the butcher shop. It's just me and this plant," Terry said, pointing to Vivian's gift on the counter.

Demetria looked at the plant with the clump of leaves at the base with the long stem that sprouted a ladder-like array of smaller shoots. "It's an asphodel," she said. "We could plant it next spring next to the rosebush when it flowers."

"I think Vivian would like that. I'll go grab your coat."

With Terry's departure, she drew closer to the dormant asphodel. Among the base leaves, a bracelet of copper wire encircled the stem.

"Here you go," Terry said, tossing her coat to her. "Sorry I can't let you back there, yet. Clinic policies."

"I understand," Demetria said, donning her blue nylon jacket. "I've got a long way to go."

"I was just wondering, Demetria. Why do you go by your middle name?"

"It was my mom's name; I don't like my first name."

"Really?" Terry said. "Persephone sounds so pretty."

"You're leaving, Jane?" Reyna said.

"I'm afraid so," Jane said. "I have a Fellowship at Oxford. It happened so fast. Dr. Ruthven and Dr. Varney were impressed with my work. They felt it dovetailed with their own line of research."

"So, no more troubles at school?"

"I met with Dr. Aksoy this morning. He seemed surprised, but I don't think he's too upset to see me leave. We never agreed on anything."

"To say the least," Reyna said, "I'm so happy for you, but I will miss you."

"It's time to move on. Reyna, thanks for being there when I needed help," Jane said, handing Reyna the shoe box.

"Jane, you paid for these. They're yours."

"Reyna, I don't need them anymore. I don't know what I would have done without them, but I don't need them now."

"If you're sure," Reyna said, putting the box on the counter. "What about Vic?"

"It wasn't going to work out, I can see that now," Jane said. "But our time together…it made me, and him, better. I have no regrets." She reflected on their pre-dawn parting at the misty air cargo field. Her smile waxed bittersweet.

Reyna said, "You look like you're ready to take on the world."

"I think so, I've got to get packed."

"Jane," Reyna called after her, "you're still wearing that ugly coat."

The chimes on the door jangled merrily on her exit.

Reyna watched Jane merge into the throng of bustling Christmas shoppers and disappear. She turned her attention to the shoe box on the counter when the chimes jingled and a cold gust of air entered the shop.

"Hello, Reyna," the blonde said.

"Demetria?" Reyna said, hardly recognizing her former shop clerk.

"Yes."

"How long have you been back?"

"A couple of months," Demetria said.

"Why didn't you drop by, sooner?"

"I didn't want anybody to know I was back," Demetria said. "I was ashamed. I had to do things…" Tears welled in her eyes.

As Reyna stepped from behind the counter, she spotted the vial with a brass stopper, hanging around Demetria's neck. Reyna ran her manicured finger down the length of vial and a string of impressions bombarded her:

a darkened, gravel parking lot, fear, trading cash for plastic bags from shadowy men, desperation, a slovenly, ill-lit trailer, despair. Finally, she sensed a white light and a long bus trip back to the city. Reyna embraced Demetria and rocked her gently.

"Sometimes, little one," Reyna said, "the only way we can grow is to go through those dark places and times."

"I made it through," Demetria said. "I'm not sure how, though."

"The how doesn't matter at this point; you pulled yourself out of it," Reyna said. "The only advice I can give you is to learn from what you've been through. You know you will always have a place here."

"Reyna, I appreciate that, but I belong at the clinic. I think that's the place for me."

"I guess it was it time for you to find your place. You will come back to see me, won't you?"

"Sure, Nick is working over at the Harris Building," Demetria said, pointing to the stately building across the park. "He's resigned from the force and gone back to school."

Reyna stepped back to her counter and said, "Looks like I'm going to be short-handed for a while." She opened Jane's shoebox and inspected the pair of black sling-backs.

"What are those?"

"A customer return," Reyna said, "I guess they're no worse for wear. Back to the shoe loft, unless…" She shot Demetria a sly look.

"At one time, maybe," Demetria said with a laugh. "I don't think they're my style, anymore."

"Just checking."

"Anyway," Demetria said, "I promised I'd meet Nick for lunch. He's busy setting up the new office." She left the shop and moved onto the busy street.

Reyna watched Demetria flutter across the park to meet her love. The dark little caterpillar had become a butterfly. She turned back to the shoes and wrinkled her nose. She counted the embroidered scorpions on each. One shoe had eight; the other only had seven.

Doctor Aksoy despised making his own tea as much as he despised being at school on Sunday. He took comfort in the fact that that Davis woman was no longer his concern. Whatever the Christians planned had not blown back upon him and his hands remained clean. He took his cup and settled into his plush chair and surveyed the paperwork before him.

He almost missed the four-inch-long silver scorpion perched on his answering machine.

After stepping off the Gulf Canal Bridge, Prof stopped at the edge of Wrightsway Park and lifted his head to the sky. The cold, dry wind cut through him, but he felt the bright afternoon sunlight on his face. As the crowd of shoppers surged around him, he smiled; it was good to be out.

He'd spent the last day and a half cloistered in his room at the Middlemarch. For hours, the invitation envelope of rich linen paper had lay untouched. Over the last year, he mastered the ability to avoid the obvious, harsh truths; this envelope was the sum of his delusions. Through the long night, he added and subtracted people, places and events from his memories. He examined each piece of his experiences in the last year, looking for proof that the memory was real. In the end, all his tests remained inconclusive. He knew Lila and Stan were real, but beyond that, who knew?

"If your only hope is an illusion," he reasoned, "to what lengths would you go to make it real?"

At dawn, with shaking hands, he'd opened the invitation and ran his fingers over the heavily-embossed lettering and sighed. Tonight, for better or worse, he would know the truth.

After showering and shaving, Prof lit out of his room and through the lobby. If it all ended tonight, he was determined to make peace with it in his own way. The smells of cedar, cinnamon, and roasting chestnuts filled the air as he made his way through the crowd to the boutique with the red awning rustling in the wind.

"Prof!" Reyna said. "I haven't seen you in weeks."

"Hi Reyna," Prof said. "Sorry I haven't been around. I've had a lot on my mind."

"Seems like everyone's been busy. Jane was in earlier. She's gotten an opportunity over in London."

"Oh…"

"And even Demetria is back in town. She's changed and she's dating Nick, you know, Officer Serrano."

Prof stood erect, alert and aware in his neat and pressed heavy wool jacket; the sad, broken man she'd saved from Nick a year ago was a distant memory. "What's wrong, Prof?" she said.

"I'm afraid I will be leaving tonight and I wanted to say good-bye."

"Where are you are going?"

"I can't say for sure, but I'll know it when I get there. I just wanted to say thank you for all the help you've given me."

"Jane said the same thing, earlier. In some ways, you're a lot alike."

"I've always admired her. She's worked through a lot of things that would've beaten others down."

"As I said, you're a lot alike."

"I have to be going," Prof said, extending his cane. "You're busy with Christmas and all."

"Prof," Reyna said, "I just got a new vendor and he sent over a few samples. I guess there was an error in shipping." Reyna went to the back of the store and emerged with a garment bag and a shoe box. "I don't know if I'm going to keep doing business with this Gascon Enterprises."

"I'd keep them. I got a feeling it will keep things interesting."

"It's a tux, not name brand, but it's pretty well made. I don't know if you have any use for it, but I'd like you to have it to remember me by."

Prof took Reyna in his arms and whispered, "Ms. Fox, there is no way anyone would ever forget you."

Late in the afternoon, Reyna reflected a moment on her visitors. In a way, she felt like her cubs were leaving the warren. She was busy with receipts during the dinnertime lull when the shop chimes rang out.

"Are you Ms. Fox?" asked the young lady in a pink sweater.

"Yes, I am. What can I do for you?"

"I was wondering if you sold my Uncle Al this," she said, pointing to the gold charm bracelet around her wrist.

"Yes, I did," Reyna said. "You must be Cindy. Al talked about you all the time. What brings you, here?"

"I'm going home for Christmas," she said. "I thought I'd stop back and see Uncle Al's shop, but…"

"He's gone home. He's happier there."

"I know, but I still miss him."

"Cindy," Reyna said, "he was always happiest when he spoke of you, and he was so proud of you for going to school. How did your first quarter go?"

"4.0 across the boards," Cindy said. "Only, I just don't feel it."

"What do you mean?"

"When I was in high school, I liked making Mom, Dad, and Uncle Al proud by doing well," Cindy said, "but now, I don't know what I want."

"That's what being young is all about," Reyna said. "Figuring out what to do with your life."

"I met a man this summer who said the same thing," Cindy said. "Everybody called him Prof."

"I know him, he's a smart man," Reyna said. "If you are not ready for the world of academics, how about a career in high fashion? I'm looking for a new assistant."

"I'll think about it," Cindy said, turning to leave. "I'll let you know when I get back after the first of the year."

As the door closed, Reyna considered staying open another hour, but she remembered Perry and Shannon invited her for dinner. It wouldn't do to show up empty-handed. Cheesecake opened so many doors.

At eleven, Prof adjusted his bow tie. Dressed in the tuxedo that Reyna had gifted him, he stood ready to finish this. He grabbed his cane and tucked the stationery box under his arm.

In the lobby, J.J. looked up from his paper and said, "Looking good, Prof!"

"Thanks, J.J.," Prof said, pausing before the desk. "Is my tie straight? I have a date."

"Looks good to me. Who's the lucky lady?"

"You wouldn't believe me, J.J. Don't wait up." He went through the creaky brass revolving door.

With his cane extended, he strode across the empty street, as he had done so many times in the last year. His pulse raced, as he approached the doors of the Night Café at a quarter 'til midnight, as the invitation specified.

"About time you got here," Uri said, jingling a ring of keys.

"Uri?" Prof said. "What are you doing here?"

"I've been locking up the place for Theo and Joey. Gabe got me this gig."

"Is Gabe around?"

"Nah, he and the bros already lit out. Time to move on. I just stuck around to let you know I appreciate that someone actually took my advice."

"You mean to think about what you're doing."

"You got it," the biker said. He clapped Prof on the back and handed him the key ring. "Now, buddy, go in there and do us all proud. Romance the living shit out of her."

Uri moved past Prof and Prof continued to the door. Up the street, he heard the biker mount his ride and rip the ignition. The roar of the engine reminded Prof of the flapping of mighty wings.

Inside the silent café, he inhaled the scent of saffron. She had taken the center table for two.

His way cleared; he padded over to the seat opposite her.

"On time," he said, "as instructed."

"You made it, Prof."

"Please, I prefer John. I am no longer a professor. I'm something else."

"John," she said, "you've more than earned that. How do you feel?"

"Feel?" he said, rising to his feet. "I've staked the rest of my life on a mirage. The only way back for me is to follow this to the end. But…"

"But what?"

"If this is nothing more than a series of hallucinations, it means none of my friends are real. All the people I cared about are figments of my imagination, including you."

She rose and placed a finger on his lips. Her arms circled his waist and she rested her head upon her chest. "It all comes down to one thing," she whispered. "Does it really matter in the end?"

A moment passed. "No," John breathed, "in the end, it doesn't matter."

Her lips closed on his.

The black silhouettes of the buildings of the skyline stood against a purple background.

The purple changed to dark navy followed by streaks of pinks, reds and yellows. John replaced his dark sunglasses to shield his weak eyes from the sunrise. He sat on the crumbling red brick doorstep with his bowtie undone. In his hands, he fumbled with a sunny yellow crocus bloom. At his feet was the stationery box.

"Must have been one heck of a party, sir" the young police officer said, towering over him. "What's your business here?"

"Good morning, officer," John said. "You're right, it was a party. I just wanted to stop and watch the sunrise."

"Well, all right," the officer said, "you don't seem like you're up to trouble." He turned away to continue his rounds.

"Excuse me, officer," John called after the cop. "You wouldn't know an Officer Serrano?"

"No," the cop said, "but then again, I was only assigned this beat a couple days ago."

John looked behind him at the boarded front of the building of solid brick. Standing up, he peeped through a crevice of the battered green front door. The inside was a shadowy, dusty shamble of chair and tables. John's hopes sank; no, the café had never existed.

Some paint, maybe a few hanging brass lamps, he thought. *Definitely an old-school snooker table.* He stopped himself. In the end, it wouldn't bring his friends back.

"Just another compromise," he sighed. He spotted his stationery box at his feet. Sitting down, he examined its jumbled contents: microcassettes, index cards, notepads and loose-leaf paper.

The label of one of the microcassettes read, "My Friend, Lou."

He picked up one bent index card and read the scrawl:

"Welcome to Fox Fashions," a female voice droned. "A bold choice for bold women."

A coffee-stained paper napkin read:

"Nathan barreled down the damp brick alleyway clutching the brown paper parcel. His blood pounded. They were closing in. A wild careen around the corner almost landed him on his ass."

He tucked the box under one arm and the white cane under the other. Smiling, he needed to get to a computer; he wanted to visit his friends again.

In the bright sunlight, he was off.

A small, red, angular face popped out of alley to watch the man in the tuxedo stride away. She wiggled her nose out of curiosity and then scurried back down the alley.

THE END

Last call at the night café

You're still here? Great! Thank you for your time. A mentor told me long ago that of all the things that someone can give you, time was the one thing they could never recover. With regards to that piece of advice, I will make this brief.

I picture Herman Melville sitting at his desk and listing out his three greatest ambitions:

1. Write a rollicking adventure on the high seas
2. Write the definitive history of the whaling industry
3. Write an allegorical story of man and his boundless ambition

Mr. Melville looked at the list, checked his pocket watch and shook his head. "I don't have time for three books," he thought. He pulled out a fresh sheaf of paper and started writing *Moby Dick.*

One hundred seventy years later (give or take), I sat down and decided on what book I wanted to write. My choices were:

1. A series of wild stories with a wide range of characters in a surreal hard-boiled landscape
2. A story of a man digging himself out of hole of his own making
3. A metaphorical story of Jungian archetypes of one person to make changes in his life, using Camus' Actor example as found in The Myth of Sisyphus.

I studied my options, checked my computer clock and shook my head. "I don't have time for three books," I thought. I opened a fresh new document file and started writing *Remanded to The Night Café*.

Yes, it is a frivolous comparison, but it does illustrate why this book came to be. If the Melville scholar, who insists on mailing me whale-shaped letter bombs, would cease and desist, I would be most grateful.

The first two goals seemed within my grasp. I imagined sitting with Rod Serling, Thorton Wilder and Raymond Chandler sitting in a smoky bar and hashing out a new collaborative project. Just a few city blocks populated by everyday people and a lot of weird happenings. The only problem was they couldn't come up with a way to tie the whole mess together.

Coincidentally, Albert Camus and Carl Jung overheard their conversation and added their suggestions. Of course, Carl would have mentioned, "there are no such things as coincidences."

Well-dressed Albert thought that this protagonist, faced with insurmountable obstacles, might find a way to face his own death by re-enacting it over and over. After all, he had success with this concept in an essay awhile back.

Serling, Wilder and Chandler, being from the tough, "can do" generation of Americans, protested the idea of an inevitable failure. The steady hard stares across the table portended the bar fight that was to follow.

Carl disarmed the situation by offering the idea that the characters in the story were also archetypes of the protagonists consciousness. As their plots resolved, the protagonist's own worldview evolved and he found his own path.

After a tense moment of consideration, they all retook their seats at the table. Raymond looked over at me and said, "Are you getting this down, Kid?"

This was the quickest way to explain the how and why of *Remanded to The Night Café*. I apologize for the dramatic license.

Last bit of business and I'm out.

In the last few years, the publishing industry changed. The oligopoly morphed into a free market model. For minimal expense, you can write and publish your work for world-wide exposure. This may change in the future, but right now, it's yours for the taking. No excuses.

I'll be waiting to see what your efforts bring.

Best Wishes
M.E. Smith
8/21/2017

mesmithwriter0@gmail.com
mswpublishing.com

(somewhere in Georgia)

Made in the USA
Lexington, KY
10 November 2017